PORTRAIT IN SMOKE

Danny April is obsessed. He buys out a little collection agency in Chicago, and that's how he first meets Krassy. He'd never seen anyone so beautiful. She was Krassy Almauniski then, when he first runs across her picture in his files. She's gone through several identities since then. As Danny tries to track her down, each new name presents him with a portrait of a woman on the move. Krassy is climbing up the social ladder, one sucker at a time. There's the photographer who signs off on a charge account for her, later arrested for larceny. And the ad executive... he gets off lightly. He gets to walk away with his pride. Not all the men who Krassy meet are so lucky. But Danny knows he'll be different. So he keeps looking... until at last he finds her.

THE LONGEST SECOND

When I awakened, I stared straight above me at the ceiling... I attempted to turn my head. It was then I realized that my throat had been cut. The pain ran down both sides of my neck... I gasped, choking for air. The next day I regained consciousness again... Suddenly it struck me that I didn't know my own name!... They check his fingerprints and find out that his name is Victor Pacific. He has no memories of who he is, what he is, or why someone tried to kill him. He remembers the name Horstman. But he has no idea of how to find him. All he can do is to begin a search for the clues to his former life. Then he meets Bianca—but will she be able to help him before they strike again?

Portrait in Smoke

The Longest Second

Bill S. Ballinger

Introduction by Nicholas Litchfield

Stark House Press • Eureka California

PORTRAIT IN SMOKE / THE LONGEST SECOND

Published by Stark House Press
1315 H Street
Eureka, CA 95501, USA
griffinskye3@sbcglobal.net
www.starkhousepress.com

ISBN: 978-1-944520-48-9

Book design by Mark Shepard, SHEPGRAPHICS.COM
Proofreading by Bill Kelly
Cover art by James Heimer

First Stark House Press Edition: June 2018

FIRST EDITION

Contents

Two Tales in Tandem

by Nicholas Litchfield

Bill S. (William Sanborn) Ballinger, who sometimes used the pen names B.X. Sanborn and Frederic Fryer, was a prolific American author and screenwriter responsible for over two hundred television scripts, twelve motion pictures, and thirty books. He contributed scripts for popular TV shows like *Cannon*, *M Squad*, *Ironside*, *I Spy*, *Bonanza* and *The Outer Limits*, as well as multiple episodes of Mickey Spillane's *Mike Hammer* and *Kolchak: The Night Stalker*, both starring the inimitable actor Darren McGavin. In 1961, he won an Edgar Award for one of his teleplays for *Alfred Hitchcock Presents*. He also wrote for the big screen, providing the screenplays for *The Strangler*, a low-budget movie based on the Boston Strangler files, and *Operation C.I.A.*, a spy movie featuring Burt Reynolds in his first lead role in a feature film. Incidentally, Reynolds, who had a torrid time making the movie, contracted schistosomiasis during a fight scene in a contaminated river and, later, described the picture as the worst film he ever made, remarking: "If it played on a plane, people would be killed trying to jump out."

Of all Ballinger's achievements, it is his fiction that brought him his best success. His novels, several of which have been made into movies, have sold more than ten million copies in the U.S., have been reprinted in thirty countries and translated into more than thirteen languages. Newspapers like *The New York Times* and the *San Francisco Chronicle*, and renowned authors like Lawrence Block and John D. MacDonald, have praised him for his inventive ideas and plot structures and his suspenseful writing, and noted book critic Anthony Boucher once described him as "a major virtuoso of the mystery technique." Nevertheless, Ballinger remains an under-appreciated writer, his books long out of print and his name unfamiliar to many.

It is not always clear why some authors have lasting appeal and others tumble into obscurity. Ballinger was one of those writers whose books sold well domestically and overseas, and at least three of them received great critical acclaim when they first came out. Once out of print, they tended to remain that way and, rather surprisingly, it has been twenty-five years since one of his novels appeared in print in the U.S. Many have yet to be reprinted.

Thankfully, this fine, two-in-one volume from Stark House Press, which comprises *Portrait in Smoke* and his Edgar nominated *The Longest Second*, marks the long-overdue reissue of a couple of Ballinger's most prized mysteries. In fact, *The Longest Second* is back in print for the first time in nearly fifty years.

These stories, personal favorites of the author, were also favorites of legendary mystery author Brett Halliday, a friend of Ballinger's. In his foreword to *Triptych*, a three-book collection published in 1972 that includes these novels and the tremendous *The Tooth and the Nail*, considered by many critics one of the finest suspense novels of American writing in the twentieth century, and certainly one of the most riveting mysteries I've read, he writes of *Portrait in Smoke*: "After twenty years I have never forgotten the thrill of reading it for the first time, and my mounting excitement as chapter followed chapter to an ending that I defy the reader to guess beforehand.... Anyone who reads the story of Danny April and Krassy seldom forgets them."

Ballinger began work on this, his third novel, in 1949, while living in Chicago. Prior to this, he had experienced some small success with his hardboiled debut, *The Body in the Bed*, which was a Hammett-style private-detective novel featuring tough, Chicago PI Barr Breed, which Boucher described in the *New York Times* as "faster, brighter and fresher than recent bosoms-and-brandy sweepstakes." He had high hopes for Ballinger early in the author's career, considering him "the most experimental of all established professionals" in the mystery genre. Unfortunately, the Barr Breed sequel, *The Body Beautiful*, published the following year, proved something of a disappointment. Boucher called it "a pitiful let-down," branding it "a museum of every cliché of plot, style and action." It would be the last Barr Breed mystery Ballinger penned.

He didn't disappoint with his subsequent novel, though, which was published in 1950 by Harper, now the flagship imprint of HarperCollins. From plot, theme, and style, to characters and point of view, there was little clichéd about *Portrait in Smoke*.

Told from two different perspectives, it is the story of callous, ambitious beauty Krassy Almauniski and her unscrupulous journey from the Chicago slums to wealth and respectability in the affluent Gold Coast district. Her darkly absorbing tale is pieced together by the main protagonist, Danny April, the new owner of a minuscule Chicago collection agency, who first learns about Krassy while examining past files of closed accounts. Attached to her file is a faded newspaper clipping from ten years earlier announcing her the winner of a regional beauty contest. Danny, believing her to be one of the most beautiful girls he has ever seen, becomes hopelessly infatuated with her and determined to track her down. As he investigates her movements across Chicago, delving into her irregular life through his conversations with those who met her, he writes:

"...I found myself thinking of her as my gal. She became just as real to me as if I was going to meet her for a date every night. I'd looked at her picture so many times, I could trace each feature with my eyes closed."

This strange fixation is in keeping with the character's obsessive nature. The photograph reminds him of a girl he was enamored with when he first came to Chicago, at age fifteen, and trailed around the city. In the case of Krassy, he goes that one step further. Consumed with desire, he is intent on trying to forge a romance with her. His obsession draws him down a dark and unsavory path that leads to danger and downfall.

What makes this novel unusual is the way Ballinger divides the story between first and third person perspectives, alternating between Danny and Krassy's point of view, which has the effect of revealing the delusional nature of Danny investigation. The more he learns about Krassy, the more inaccurate his understanding of her, to the point that the fully fleshed character in his mind bears little resemblance to the real woman.

> "That was enough for my mind to work on, and when I mixed it with all the things I thought of, and made up, and how crazy I was just for the sight of her, it all became confused and the lines blurred, and changed, and overlapped. Just like I said, it was like trying to paint her picture in smoke. One minute she was real, and right there; and the next minute she was fading, and I couldn't stop her from disappearing completely."

With Krassy, Ballinger paints a very convincing and intriguing independent woman who, having escaped a life of hopelessness, poverty and despair, wishes to better herself and improve her chances of a prosperous life. Her bleak childhood in the stockyard district "developed within her a shrewdness and cunning" and an understanding that in order to attain the life she desires she must capitalize on her physical appeal, exploiting her looks "as other woman used an education, or a trained talent, or social connections...or hard work." But she is incapable of love and happiness, and her unwholesome pursuit of a comfortable life in the company of a polished gentleman with a fine job and plenty of money will surprise, appall and fascinate the reader.

We are presented with another morally corrupt central character in *The*

Longest Second, which first appeared in 1957. Although here, Ballinger offers an interesting twist: what would happen if a bad guy had a go at being a good guy? Again, the author uses first and third person narratives and employs alternating chapter plot structures, with two storylines working in tandem, then coming together for a powerful, startling climax.

Set in New York City, Ballinger's residence at the time, the story is structured most similarly to *The Tooth and The Nail*, penned two years earlier. Where that story jumped back and forth in time between a court trial and related events in a magician's life, *The Longest Second* switches between a police investigation and an amnesiac's search for his true identity. Unlike in the previous novel, the main protagonist, Victor Pacific, is deliberately stripped of personality and emotion. Recently, his throat was slashed and he was dumped on the steps of an apartment building, and when he wakes, in hospital, he is suffering from total amnesia and unable to speak. His unknown past is at the center of the mystery. Even the police are dubious about his true identity, as there is an unaccountable gap in his army record, as well as erroneous information.

Upon his discharge from the hospital, still without memory or voice, he goes in search of answers using tidbits of information gleaned from the police. A notepad and pencil is his chief method of communication.

He begins by interviewing Bianca Hill, the woman who found him bleeding to death on her doorstep. Out of sympathy and kindness, she provides him with a temporary place to live and employment as a silversmith, assisting her with her small jewelry business.

Alas, he isn't content to simply enjoy his new situation. Adages by Nietzsche, such as "blessed are the forgetful: for they get better even after their blunders," are the few things that have stuck in his mind, but he doesn't heed the advice. Plagued by recurring nightmares and confusing flashes of obscured memory, he is compelled to delve into his murky past and learn the truth about himself until he becomes "caught up in wrappings of the unknown" and trapped by his own ignorance of past danger.

Part of the brilliance of *The Longest Second* is in observing Vic's emotional development as the story unfolds. At first, fragile and detached from emotion, he steadily grows into the wily, resourceful man of old, lacking compassion and guilt. He has never been one to "assume any personal obligations" or "ties of sentimentality," and so now he works at erasing all "emotional indebtedness" to Bianca and other new acquaintances. But it is not as straightforward as he would hope.

"Within you there is an unbreakable will which protects you, a hardness which shields you from everything...and everybody...except yourself," Bianca remarks. With the layers of his personality peeled away, he is no longer the case-hardened person he was before. He is softer and more vulnerable, and finds he is bound, against his wishes, to the "attractive, affectionate, amusing" Bianca, who has penetrated that hard veneer and, ultimately, exposed a weakness in him for others to exploit.

Innovative and cleverly told, *The Longest Second*, like *Portrait in Smoke,* is a thrillingly unique, affecting tale that deliberately defies mystery genre conventions with its original dual plot format and ambiguous, unpredictable narrator. Neither gimmicky nor contrived, it is a cunningly deceptive work that is full of twists and shocks, and has a storyline intended to continually keep you guessing about the past and the present.

Halliday said of Ballinger's three greatest novels: "I wish I had written just one of them." I am sure a great many other famous authors of that era felt the same way. Available again, at last, for the first time in decades, these two powerful, provocative tales from the fifties are as fresh and impressive today as when they first startled and enthralled the world and earned their place as mystery classics.

—January 2018
Rochester, NY

Nicholas Litchfield is the founding editor of the literary magazine *Lowestoft Chronicle*, author of the suspense novel *Swampjack Virus*, and editor of seven literary anthologies. He has worked in various countries as a tabloid journalist, librarian, and media researcher. He writes regularly for the *Colorado Review* and his book reviews for the *Lancashire Post* are syndicated to twenty-five newspapers across the UK.

Portrait in Smoke

Bill S. Ballinger

To LAURA Who is Everything
That Many Women Are Not

CHAPTER ONE
Danny

If I shoot off my mouth to the wrong guy, I'm a goner. And besides, who'd believe me?

But the whole thing doesn't make sense. It doesn't make any sense at all. I been thinking about it and talking it over with myself. And then on top of that I get dreams. And it still doesn't add up. I can't understand why it happened. I go over the whole thing, step by step, and then after a while it gets hazy. It's like trying to paint a picture with a bucketful of smoke.

At first the picture of Krassy starts out clear and distinct. Then the edges move a little and it starts to get fuzzy. Then all the lines overlap and the edges curl up and start forming crazy whirls and swirls ... and you don't have a picture any more. I try to take my mind and grab the lines and pull them back straight, but the lines are really smoke and they slip away. And then all I have is hazy blue smoke which stretches all over the picture.

That's the way it is, and maybe I'm making it up in my mind. About the smoke part, I mean, because the day it started was a smoky, hazy Chicago day. Smoke from the factories sifts in and mixes with the damp lake air, and it lies in soggy, gray felt blankets all over the city. Then the damp air turns into a fog, and the smoke mixes with it, and then the mixture hangs suspended and motionless and everybody goes around saying, "Christ, what a day!"

The smoke and fog cuts off the tops of the great big beautiful buildings down in the loop ... but it doesn't touch the real Chicago. Not the dirty, little two- and three-story buildings which straggle along as far as you can see. And the smoke doesn't make any difference to the stinking little shops with hand-drawn cardboard signs in their windows advertising bicycles repaired, men's clothing slightly used—50 per cent off, dresses cleaned while-U-wait, swap your old furniture here. Or all the neon signs advertising billiards, taverns with beer on tap, girl shows ... the most beautiful girls in town, hotel rooms walk up two flights to the lobby.

Sometimes the smoke hangs from rusty iron fire escapes which stick out from the second stories over the street. Their end steps balance in the air, and when the signs are turned on, they throw crazy patterns and shadows on the patched sidewalks. The smoke covers a lot of things, but it doesn't cover it all.

Anyway, it was that kind of a day when I got a message that my grandfather, old Charlie April, had died and left me twenty-five hundred bucks.

I went into a little bar down the street and put a couple drinks inside me and thought about the old man and tried to feel sad. But I couldn't feel too bad. I'd always sort of hated his guts because he was a mean old bastard.

He was the only living relative I had, and when I was a kid I'd lived with him. He'd worked as a fireman on the Erie Railroad and every so often he'd get liquored up and get into a fight at the end of his run. Sometimes he'd still be mad when he came home. Maybe just pounding things with his fists made him feel better. I don't know. Anyway, one night he came home, drunker than hell, and knocked my brains half out. I left home.

I was fifteen.

I came to Chicago and started working around. Finally, I landed a job with the International Collection Agency; it wasn't much of a place to work but I stayed on. Mostly I wrote threatening letters to deadbeats who wouldn't pay their bills and traced skippers and dunned suckers.

It didn't add up to more than forty or fifty bucks a week, which meant a room on the third floor of a walk-up. There was a cheap dresser and a brass bed with a faded, old linoleum rug on the floor. In one corner there was a beat-up bridge lamp, and a sagging overstuffed chair. In another corner, I had me a washbowl, bolted to the wall. It had only one tap that worked and petered out a weak stream of water. Down at the end of the hall was a can which ten people all tried to use at the same time.

I used to lie on my bed and trace pictures in the designs caused by the tears in the rotten old green shade at the window. The dusty sunlight coming through the holes made all kinds of different patterns which you could change by shutting one eye and then the other. Sometimes you could do it by moving your head just a little bit. The walls to all the rooms were so thin that the only privacy you had was sitting around with your own thoughts. But I didn't have much choice, so I kept on living there and working with International Collections.

Then I got word about Grandpa April's insurance, and for the first time I felt maybe I had a chance to make a break.

The union buried the old man, and I went over to Indiana for his funeral. I didn't feel sad or unhappy because it'd been ten years or longer since I'd seen him. Nobody was at the funeral except the undertaker and me. He was there because he'd been paid, and I was there because I was the only one left.

All the way back on the train I kept thinking about that twenty-five hundred bucks and what the hell I could do with it. I knew damned good and well I'd shoot all the dough if I kept it around where I could get my hands on it.

So I decided I'd try to buy some kind of business with it.

But for twenty-five hundred bucks you don't buy much. When I got back to Chicago, I started nosing around and heard of an old guy by the name of Clarence Moon who wanted to sell his collection agency. I figured it was better than a hamburger stand, or a leased gas station, because it was at least the kind of a business I knew something about. I went to see him.

Clarence Moon was a big, fat slob of a man about seventy years old. He was completely bald except for a fringe of long white hair which hung just in front and in back of his ears. The top of his head was dirty enough you could see white streaks on the skin where he'd scratched with his fingernails. He had a little two-room office located in an old loft building down by the Civic Opera building.

There wasn't anything in the front office except a decrepit old desk, covered on top by a cracked piece of glass; a swivel-backed desk chair, and one straight wooden chair for clients. An aged 1929 Underwood typewriter stood on a small table by the side of his desk. In the back room were a dozen green filing cabinets, each with three drawers. Stacked on top of the cabinets and in the corners were old clippings, magazines, and correspondence. I sat down on the straight-backed chair while the old man sized me up. I sized him up back. He was a rummy ... if I ever saw, or smelled, one.

"My name is Dan April," I finally said. "I understand you want to sell out."

The old man pawed at his vest and tried to button it. There were only three buttons on it, and beneath, his belly bubbled and rolled. "I've considered the possibility," he said. "That is, if I find the right party."

"Nuts," I said, "you'll be lucky to sell out to anybody. How much you asking?"

"I want thirty-six hundred dollars," he replied. He shot a quick glance at me, then dropped his eyes and started fiddling with his vest buttons again.

I thought it over. A collection business is a funny thing. You get paid just for the bills you collect. But even so, if no one gives you overdue bills, you don't have a business. Once you get a company sending you their bills to collect, if you do a pretty good job, you keep getting their business year after year. There's nothing to buy like machinery or merchandise; you don't have to worry about dealers, or outlets, or any other damn thing. You just get the chance of doing business for the same old accounts.

"How long you been in business?" I asked Moon.

"I've been here for thirty-five years," he said proudly. Again he started fumbling with his vest and I could see he had the shakes bad.

"Go ahead and have a drink," I told him.

"I don't drink during office hours," he said with pride. Then his pride punctured and ran out of him like dirty water. "However, my arthritis has been bothering me lately, and I think I'd better have a short one." He made a grab for his desk drawer and hauled out a bottle of Old Culpepper. He twisted the cork out and dropped it to the floor and took a long haul. Then he reached down, picked up the cork and handed the bottle to me.

"No, thanks," I said and watched him put the bottle away. "How many accounts you got?" I asked.

He started to answer me a couple of times and stopped before a word got out. He wanted to lie to me, but he didn't have enough nerve left to try it. Finally he said, "Six. Six steady ones that is. I used to have thirty-six. But since I've been ... ill, I've only been able to handle six."

I knew what that meant. Moon had lost thirty accounts because he'd been too damned drunk to handle them. But if six accounts still stuck around with him, that meant they'd probably stick with me, too.

"How about letting me see your books?" I asked him. He pulled out the middle drawer and handed me an old, dog-eared ledger. All it contained was a column of figures with dates of collection. At the end of each month was a gross total. I looked in the back of the book and for the year before he'd done enough to gross himself three thousand dollars. Leafing back through, I saw he'd made fairly regular entries for half a dozen small firms, which made up the bulk of his business.

We sat around and I asked him some more questions. His business wasn't worth very much and he knew it. Finally, I got up and started to leave. "Look," I said, "I'll give you two thousand bucks for what you got left."

He started to protest.

"Skip it," I told him. "I'll call you tomorrow and you tell me then. Take it or leave it." I went out the door just as he made a dive for the drawer with the bottle of liquor.

I knew then ... he'd take it.

That night I went to bed and did some figuring. I figured that with plenty of work, I could build the business back up to making a few bucks. Even if I didn't do any better than the old man, I'd still break even. When I finally went to sleep, I dreamed most of the night and got my dreams all mixed up between old Charlie April and Clarence Moon. In the morning I'd quit hating old Charlie and I felt sorry for Moon the rummy.

I had breakfast and went to a phone and called Moon's office. I knew I was a sucker, but I felt sorry for the old guy, and I couldn't help myself. "Look, Moon," I said, "I been thinking it over and this is my last offer. I'll pay you two thousand cash now ... and another thousand in one year."

The old man swallowed on the other end of the line. "All right, my boy," he said, "the Clarence Moon Collection Agency is yours."

CHAPTER TWO
part 1 Danny

I walked down to State and Van Buren where International Collections is located. I got in the office an hour and a half late. The girl at the switchboard said, "Jeez, Danny, you're going to catch it! Crenshaw's been looking all over for you." I took off my coat and hat and left them in the reception room.

Sitting down at my desk in the main office where five other collectors were all busy, I started cleaning the desk out. It didn't have much in it, but I wanted to clear out of the place completely. Crenshaw, the office manager, saw me and came barreling up.

"Where the hell you been, April?" he shouted.

"Around," I told him.

"Around!" and he laughed through his nose. "You better be around here more, if you expect to be around here!" He waited for a laugh. It didn't come.

"Very funny, Crenshaw," I told him. "But personally you give me the creeps."

He stopped like he'd been shot and turned red. He opened his big, ugly mouth to bellow.

"Shut up!" I said. "For five years I've wanted to kick you in the middle of your big, fat ... lard. And now's a good time to do it."

The office was still. Crenshaw backed away with his butt up against a desk. I pushed my personal belongings into my pockets and walked out to the reception desk. In the doorway, I turned around and looked back. No one had moved. I waved to Bud Glasgow, whose desk had been next to mine, and went out.

When I got to the Clarence Moon Collection Agency, the old man was gone. He hadn't taken anything out of his desk except the bottle. On top of the desk were the door key and a note typed on the Underwood:

> DEAR MR. APRIL:
> I'll be in for my money tomorrow. Good luck.
> Sincerely,
> CLARENCE MOON

In one off the side drawers of the desk, I found a stack of correspondence going back maybe three months. I sat down at the old typewriter and started answering it.

That night, after dinner, I went back to the office and began going through the old green file cabinets in the back room. They were jammed with years-old correspondence and data cards. For each collection that comes up, a card is filled out containing as much information as is known about the person you're trying to collect the dough from. Where he lives, if he's married, his age, where he works, how much salary he makes, what his reputation is, credit rating if any, the kind of merchandise he usually owes money for, and stuff like that. If a guy is constantly back in paying his bills, the cards are kept up to date for each collection.

From the data cards, a collector can usually tell how rough it's going to be to collect his dough. Also they save a hell of a lot of time digging up information.

Old man Moon had saved every damned data card since he'd been in business. Most of them were out of date, and in the last few years his information had been skimpy and his writing more shaky. The cards weren't filed in any particular order, but they were roughly grouped together by years. It was a long, tough job going through those files, trying to pull them together and throwing out all the trash. Every night for a month I went back and worked for hours on the files.

One evening I started working on a file which was ten years old. A couple hours later, I pulled out a data card which had the name "Krassy Almauniski" on it. Clipped to the card was a faded newspaper story, with the picture of a young gal in it.

She looked out from the picture with a special, proud smile on her lips. I laid the picture to one side, then picked it up again and studied it closely. Her eyes were light, either gray or blue, but heavily lashed and her blond hair was in thick braids around her head. There was a certain dignity to her I can't explain. She was very young and without a doubt one of the most beautiful girls I've ever seen.

Under the picture was the story. It read:

> Miss Krassy Almauniski, 4120½ South Hempstead, today was announced the winner of the *Stockyard Weekly News* beauty contest. Miss Almauniski, who was selected from over thirty entries, will receive one hundred dollars from the *Stockyard Weekly News*, a beautiful, fitted leather traveling case from Browser's Trunk and Leather Company, a new suit from Solomon's Dress Shoppe, a stunning hat and coat from Edna Mae's Thrifty Shoppers Mart, a permanent wave and manicure from the Glamour Beauty Salon, a five-dollar book of taxi coupons from the Red-Top Taxi Company, and a case of beer from the Deep Well Brewing Company.

Something about that picture started a memory clawing and scratching around in the back of my mind. There was something sad about it ... something unhappy ... and I couldn't place it at first. And then in a rush I had it! The memory, that is. It went back to the first summer I'd arrived in Chicago and I was still just a kid, plenty broke and plenty lonesome in the big city, but I was growing up fast. For the first time I was becoming conscious there were girls in this world, and it would be nice to know some of them. But I didn't know anybody yet who could introduce me to them, and I was still too shy of them to try to pick one up on my own.

But a guy can dream.

Well, it was in the summer ... a blistering, hot Illinois night. There wasn't the stirring of a breeze, a breath of wind except along the lake front. The beaches were jammed with families, and kids, and couples just sitting in the sand. Waiting for a cool breath of air to come in across the lake, or waiting for the night to end, or just waiting to fall asleep. A lot of the older women had taken off their dresses and were waiting, quietly, in their slips and thinking about going back to their walk-up, oven flats and the washings and things they had to do the next day. Their husbands were stripped to the waist, and maybe they were thinking about their factories and benches. I don't know.

But I couldn't sleep, either, that night in my two-by-four room. So I'd walked up to the North Avenue beach, and along the concrete breakwater which sticks out like a crooked arm. I sat down, and swung my feet over the side and sat there hot and uncomfortable and lonesome. I looked out across the lake, and occasionally the lights of an excursion steamer would show far out. And dotted as if they were fireflies, would be the lights of the small, private boats and occasionally I'd hear some music from a radio coming across the water from a boat, and once in a while voices and laughter.

And as I sat there, I began to hate the boats, and the guys who could afford to have them, and the beautiful dames riding on them. And I thought about shagging errands for two bits, and delivering telegrams for a dime, and unloading vegetables for trucks at thirty-five cents, and all the things I'd been doing to try to keep alive.

Little by little, my eyes got accustomed to the darkness, and I noticed a girl sitting on the breakwater ... maybe ten feet away from me. She had her legs drawn up in front of her, with her arms clasped around them, and her chin resting on her knees. She was staring off across the water, too, as if she were waiting for something ... or seeing something. She was absolutely motionless. I don't know if she'd been there when I walked by; maybe she had, and in the darkness I hadn't seen her. Or perhaps, she'd come along afterward, and had been so quiet I hadn't heard her. But when I first saw her, it gave me a start.

I couldn't see her features distinctly, but even in the darkness, I knew she was young and pretty, and probably about my age. I kept glancing over at her and I wanted to say something, but she didn't even seem to know I was sitting there, and she kept staring out over the lake. I tried to think of something clever to say ... of introducing myself ... of striking up a conversation. But not only could I think of nothing to say, I was embarrassed by the prospect of her scorning my clumsy advances, and perhaps calling the park police.

So I sat there, more conscious of her by the minute, and wondering what to do about it. Then silently, and in one swift, easy motion, she swung to her feet and started slowly to walk down the breakwater to the beach. Without hesitation, I was on my feet and following her ... at a respectable distance. She walked down the breakwater to the beach, and followed the winding, crowded walk to the underpass across the Outer Drive. As I followed her, crazy thoughts ran through my mind ... like walking up beside her, taking her arm without saying a word. Or asking her if I could drive her home ... but I didn't have a car. I could see her naked back, white in the darkness ahead of me, and even then I was conscious of the swing in her walk as she went down the hollow, vibrating underpass. She came up on North Avenue, and continued west toward Clark Street. Two blocks away, on the corner of Clark and North Avenue is a big, cheap drugstore, and she turned into it. I stopped outside the door, while she climbed on a stool at the soda fountain and ordered a coke. In the light of the store, I really saw her for the first time. Around sixteen, and beautiful as hell, with long, braided golden hair. She was wearing a cheap, faded blue cotton dress, with no back; the dress had been washed so many times, it had reached a light delicate blue color ... lovely with her hair. I knew that color of blue, all poor families know it too well. And I could tell that she didn't live near the beach, either, because her arms and back wore only a soft tan, the kind of a tan you pick up just going outdoors, and not living on the beach.

As I stood there watching her, I could see the soda jerk talking with her, and she smiled back at him. I was jealous of the guy, and would have given anything to be able to talk to her and receive a smile. He didn't ring up the sale of the coke, and when the girl offered him the money, he grinned and waved it away. She got down off the stool, and headed toward the door. Quickly I turned my back, and stared into a window while she passed behind me. Then I heard her feet break into a quick, little run and as I swung around, I saw her scrambling aboard a streetcar headed for the Loop. For just a second, the possibility of catching the car, too, flashed through my mind. And then I let it die. I couldn't afford to waste the carfare. Tomorrow, I still had to find a job.

Well, that was the one and only time I ever saw her. But for a long time afterward, I thought of her many times. Who was she? Where did she live? How could I meet her? I never found out. I never saw her at the beach again. Lots of times, I built up ideas in my mind, and I worked out what I'd do if I ever saw her. And sometimes I'd make up the fact that I had a lot of dough, and I'd see myself dancing with her, and I was dressed in a pair of white flannel pants, with a double-breasted blue coat, and was wearing black-and-white shoes ... and she had on a long evening gown, and we were somewhere very fancy ... and stuff like that.

Dreams die hard when you're just a young punk, and I kept remembering that girl for a long time afterward. Even after I'd met other gals and found that lots of things can just rub off. After a while, I maybe thought back on me, and my actions and what a jerk I'd been about being afraid to meet her. And finally I forgot about it completely. I hadn't thought of her in years.

Until I saw that newspaper clipping!

Even then, I couldn't be sure it was the same gal. I'd only seen her once, and the details and memory had faded. But there was something about Krassy Almauniski, and the girl at the beach, which brought back the old memory. And then suddenly, I found that I hadn't forgotten it at all. I picked up the clipping again.

The story was dated March 31, 1940. I picked up the data card attached to the clipping and read the date the card had been filled out; it was September, 1940, nearly six months after the story. On the data card was a list of merchandise which she had bought, including irons, radios, traveling bags, watches, jewelry ... not expensive ... and clothes. The total was over $1,200, which is a good pile of bucks. I whistled to myself when I saw the amount, but I whistled more when I saw the card had been marked "paid in full." Maybe it was a hunch, or maybe it was just damned curiosity, but something made me look for the old 1940 ledger.

I finally found it jammed away in the bottom of the lower drawer in a file cabinet. I turned to September and looked down the list of payments received in that month. There was no payment listed for Krassy Almauniski, and she wasn't listed in October, November, or December. But the card said she'd paid in full.

I shrugged. What the hell. The bills were outlawed now, and I set her card to one side, but I put her picture in my pocket. The rest of the evening I spent on other cards, but I couldn't get Krassy Almauniski out of my mind. I decided the next day I'd call Moon and find out what he knew about it.

When I opened my eyes the next morning, she leaped immediately into my mind. Old man Moon had been in a month before to pick up his dough, and had left a phone number at his rooming house to call in case I wanted to reach him. I called his number, and a surly, bitchy voice told me the old man hadn't been home in weeks. I hung up the phone and went down to the office. Several times during the day I pulled the clipping out of my pocket and looked at her picture. Always, her calm eyes smiled back at me, and I found myself trying to read thoughts into them. I cussed my curiosity up and down and then decided I'd go out to 4120½ and see her. I could always pretend I was on some kind of business.

Forty-one twenty and a half South Hempstead was a stinking, narrow little house sandwiched in between two larger but equally crummy houses. Ramshackle wooden steps ran from the sidewalk to a little porch high up on the face of the house. A rusty pipe railing followed the stairs. The windows facing the street, under the steps, had been boarded up and stared blankly. The entrance to the house was through a battered doorway on the perching porch. Once the house had been painted, but years of smoke and soot had rotted its complexion like smallpox. A red brick chimney poked weakly through the middle of the roof, and rusty, corroded troughs clung scab-like under the eaves.

I climbed the stairs and knocked at the door. The windows, on each side of it, were smeared and greasy. Then I saw a curtain twitch for a moment. Finally the door opened and a woman with tremendous bulging hips and thickly knotted ankles looked at me suspiciously. She had an old Mother Hubbard wrapped loosely around her, and you could see her huge, deflated balloon busts bounce against her belly.

"I no want," she said and started to close the door.

"Hold it," I told her. "I want to talk to you."

"I no want. I no buy," she replied and shoved the door against my hand.

I kept it open. "I want to talk to Krassy Almauniski," I told her. Her tiny, suspicious pig eyes regarded me sullenly. She raised a red, chapped hand, with big purple veins on the back of it, and pushed her dirty gray hairs over her ears.

"No Almauniski here," she said.

I reached in my pocket and pulled out a dollar bill. Five bucks would've made her suspicious. I handed her the dollar and said, "I want to talk to Krassy Almauniski. I want to give her a job."

The old hag took the buck and shook her head.

"Is her father and mother here?"

"No Almauniski here," she repeated. "Almauniski die back ago."

"Her father died?" I asked.

She nodded her head.

"Where's her mother?"

"No mother," flatly.

"What happened to Krassy?"

The woman shook her head, and shrugged. "No Almauniski here," she repeated.

I gave up and walked down the stairs to the street. I hauled out Krassy's picture and looked at it again. It seemed impossible that anything as beautiful could have come out of a cesspool like the house above me. My next move was obvious. I walked down Hempstead and stopped at the first dive I came to; going up to the bar, I ordered a beer and took the glass back to the phone booth with me. There I looked through the classified telephone directory under "Publishers—Newspapers." I found the *Stockyard Weekly News* listed and tucked the address away in my mind. Finishing the beer, I hiked over to the newspaper office. It was about five blocks away.

The *Stockyard Weekly News* was located in a small, two-story brick building. The building was split into two parts by a concrete dividing wall straight through the middle. On the ground floor, the right side of the building was occupied by a barbershop, with a take-out liquor store in back of it. Separated by the concrete partition, the newspaper was located in the left side of the building. Upstairs, on the second floor, it looked like there might be a few ratty rooms and apartments.

I walked in the door of the paper, and about six feet inside it there was a dirty, scarred counter running the width of the narrow office. Hanging on one end of the counter was a swinging gate on sagging hinges. Back of it was a roll-top desk, a long battered office table piled high with bound copies of the paper. A shoulder-high partition of clapboard partly concealed an ancient flatbed press, and several type cabinets.

A young guy maybe twenty-seven or -eight was seated at the desk clipping stories from exchange papers. I walked up to the counter and he looked up at me.

"Is the editor in?" I asked.

"I'm the editor," he said. Slowly he got to his feet and slouched over toward me. When he got up next to me I could see he was tough. Plenty tough. He had a swarthy skin and a nose that had been broken and never set. His hair was slicked back and heavily oiled and I could smell lilac water in it. He placed his hands, palms down, on the counter and hunched his shoulders over it. "Anything you want?" he asked.

"Yeah," I said, "I want some information. The best place to get information is from an editor. That's why I'm asking you."

I could see him relax a little under the blarney. "What you want to know?"

"I'm trying to locate a girl named Krassy Almauniski," I told him. "Do you know her?"

"What you want to find her for?" he asked.

"She took out an insurance policy about ten years ago," I said, "and dropped it after a couple years. Anyway, she's got a small refund coming and we'd like to get it off our books. So far we've been unable to find her."

Finally he said, "I haven't seen her in ten years."

"Did you know her?" I asked.

"Yeah," he said, "I knew her."

"She won some kind of a beauty contest with this paper, didn't she?"

He laughed shortly. "Sure," he agreed, "she won a beauty contest. My old man was editor of the paper then. Me? I worked around the shop here after school. I knew her." He picked his hands up from off the counter and shoved them in his pockets. "What's your name?" he asked.

"April," I told him. "Danny April. What's yours?"

"Mike Manola," he told me.

"Does she have any relatives living?"

"No. Her old man was a crazy Pole who was living with some dago bag. He got killed out in the Gary mills a couple years after she disappeared. The old bag is still living at the same place, but there's no other family I know about."

"When was the last time you saw Krassy?"

"The day she won the beauty contest, here. She came to the office, collected her ... prizes and left. I haven't heard of her since."

"She win some good prizes?" I asked.

He dropped his eyes to the counter and studied it a moment before replying. "Yeah," he said flatly, "she won some good prizes." He turned around and walked back to his desk.

He was through talking. I left the office. Down the street, I resisted the temptation to take another look at Krassy's picture. By now, I could see her face each time I closed my eyes.

CHAPTER TWO

part 2 Krassy

Krassy Almauniski opened her eyes and stretched in her bed. She stiffened motionless for a moment before slowly relaxing again. "March seventeenth ... St. Patrick's Day," she told herself with satisfaction, "my birthday!" She jumped from bed and walked across the bare floor to a small mirror which hung by a wire from a hook in the wall. She unbuttoned the faded man's silk shirt, which hung nearly to her knees, and pulled it over her head.

"Starting today," she told herself, "things are going to be different."

At seventeen she had the figure of a mature woman. She had been that way since she was fourteen. Leaving the man's shirt on the floor, she slipped into her overcoat and tiptoed quietly into the hall. She heard the heavy turning of bodies in the next bedroom and then the rhythmic rattle of the bed. She stood motionless for a moment. "Oh, God!" she said softly, "they're at it again."

She hurried into the tiny, dirty toilet. Turning on a thin stream of water, to keep it quiet, she quickly washed her face and hands, hoping her father wouldn't hear her.

"He's busy," she told herself, "busy with Maria." She gathered her coat around her and sneaked silently back into her room. Her father and Maria were still rustling in the other bedroom.

Quickly she started dressing. As she shrugged into her cheap, pink rayon brassiere, she winced with pain from a large, red bruise on her breast. "Damn Mike Manola," she cursed, "goddamn him." But as she swore, she realized she must be careful with Mike, not make him sore, not make him angry enough to withdraw his support. She needed Mike Manola, even if it meant standing in dark doorways while he kissed and pawed her.

"You don't like me," Mike had accused her.

"Sure I like you, Mike," she replied.

"Then why don't you break down?" he asked.

"I like to kiss you...."

"Kissing is kid stuff," Mike said and pulled her to him in the darkness. She had felt his hand working its way up the outside of her thigh, then across her stomach. In strained terror, mingled with a wild anticipation, she'd waited for his hand to continue moving ... until it had cupped itself around her breast. In the blackness of the doorway, she'd felt Mike's body probing against her. Suddenly he bit down on her lip, and his hand tightened around her breast.

"Don't Mike ... don't ... please." She tore her mouth away from his and tried to separate their bodies. Mike had pulled away in the darkness, but his hand still grasped her breast.

"Why not, Krassy ... why not?" Mike whispered breathlessly.

Suddenly the words spat from her mouth. "I can't stand it! I hate it ... your hands make me sick!" Mike's fingers had clenched together, with a terrible anger, and she had screamed in pain. Then Mike had dropped his hand and turned out of the doorway. All the rest of the way home, her breast had throbbed with the fire of Mike's bruise.

Now completely dressed, Krassy slipped back into her coat and hurried toward the stairs. A creaking board shattered the stillness, and her father's voice stopped her.

"That you, Krassy?"

"Yes, Paw," she said.

"What you doing up so early?"

"I got to get to school early today," she said. "Besides this is my birthday and Mike Manola wanted me to meet him at the drugstore."

"You stay home for breakfast!"

"Mike wants to buy my breakfast, Paw," Krassy replied. "It's for my birthday!" Without waiting for his reply, she hurried down the stairs and into the street.

At Miller's Drugstore she found Mike sitting at the counter waiting for her, his face still sulky from the disappointment of the night before. Krassy climbed on the stool beside him and patted his arm. "It's swell of you to buy me a birthday breakfast," she told him.

"Yeah," he agreed, "I must be nuts. There's plenty gals who'll give a guy a little break for being nice to 'em. Jesus! I must be outa my head."

"You help me win the beauty contest, and you won't be sorry, Mike," Krassy whispered with a promise heavy in her voice.

Mike was doubtful. "Is that a promise?" he asked surlily.

"Sure, it's a promise, Mike."

"Oh, sure ... sure, just another come-on," said Mike. "The minute I start trying to love you up a little, I get all the thanks in the world!" His voice mimicked her. "'I can't stand you ... yatty, yap!'"

"Not this time, Mike," she said. "And you'll be the very first boy who's ever touched me."

Mike heartened visibly. "Christ!" he said. "Well, how about breakfast ... anything you want."

Krassy looked at his dark skin, with his arrogant nose, and white smile. "It won't be so bad," she told herself. "Anything will be better than what I got!"

"Come on, Krassy, order up," urged Mike.

Krassy ordered the Number One Breakfast, with tomato juice, two eggs, two strips of bacon, toast, marmalade, and coffee. It cost forty cents. Mike doubled the order.

After breakfast they caught the streetcar to the high school. On the way, Mike explained his strategy.

"This whole beauty contest is just an advertising promotion my old man dreamed up," he said. "It's just to help him sell more ads. He gets stores to give away prizes to the winner. For a couple of weeks he builds it up in his paper. He furnishes the stores with ballots and every customer gets one vote for every ten-cents worth of merchandise they buy. The customers vote for whoever they want as beauty queen. Then when it's all over, the stores buy more ads to congratulate the winner."

"I don't care," said Krassy, "I want to win it."

"Don't worry," said Mike, "you can't lose. My old man will make me count the ballots, because he's too damned busy to do it himself. I'll have all the extra ballots I need right at the office, so if you don't win when I count the votes ... I'll fill out extra ballots until you do." Mike threw back his head and laughed. "It's a pushover!" And then more soberly, "But don't let my old man catch on. He'd murder me!"

"I think you're wonderful," said Krassy. She tucked her hand through his arm and pressed her hip slightly against him. She could see him start on the seat. Krassy smiled secretly. "Soon," she said, "soon. ..."

After school, Krassy hurried home. Dunc Tingle walked part of the way from the car line with her.

"How about going to a show Saturday night?" he asked. Tingle was a tall, skinny boy with pinkish red hair, and tight, coal-black eyes.

"I can't, Dunc," said Krassy, "I got to see Mike."

"You going steady with Mike?"

"Sort of," admitted Krassy.

"You're going to end up back of the old eight ball with a guy like that," said Dunc.

"If I do it's none of your business," said Krassy and turned quickly away. But deep inside her, she was smiling. "I won't end up back of the eight ball with Mike ... or any other man," she thought. "They're easy to handle if you know how. Why, look at Paw and Maria. Ever since Maria moved in, big and fat and sloppy, all Paw does is sit around that stinking kitchen drinking wine and getting charged up. Then he takes Maria to bed and makes love to her all night. Sex must be awful damned important to a man. That's all any man thinks about!

"With Mike helping me, I'm bound to win. Then I'll get out of here. I'll go away where nobody knows me or knows Paw ... and I'm going to live right and dress right. Someday I won't have to take anything from anybody!"

Her mind skipped to her immediate problem on hand. "If I win this contest, I'll get a new dress and some new clothes. And I can get my hair done. Then I'll run away. But I'll need money." She considered it carefully. "I could get Mike to give me some dough," she thought, "but Mike won't have very much. I guess I'll have to figure out another way to get it...."

She climbed the stairs to the high, little porch and let herself in the door. She could hear Maria moving around in the kitchen.

"Hello, Paw," she said, "aren't you working today?"

A tremendous figure of a man was hulked down over a sagging davenport. He lifted his head and regarded her bleakly. "Why in hell don't you stay home oncet in a while?" he asked. "Go on and help Maria."

"All right, Paw," she agreed meekly.

"All right!" he shouted in sudden anger. "Isa that what you tell alla boys chasing you ... All right, Richard, all right Victor, all right, Mr. Godalmighty!"

"You know I don't!"

"I don't know any sucha goddamned thing. All I know is you runa round ... day and night ... like any little bitch in heat. Now geta out and help Maria before I get sore!"

Krassy dropped her coat over a chair and walked out into the kitchen where an old black iron range ... stuffed with coal ... was blazing angrily away. Maria in a sleazy kimono, and greasy felt bedroom slippers, was waiting patiently at a chipped and battered gray enamel sink. Water trickled slowly out of a tap into a large kettle she was holding.

"What're we having for supper?" asked Krassy.

"Spaghett," said Maria.

"Can't you cook anything besides spaghetti?" asked Krassy.

"Is good enough for peoples," said Maria.

"I'll be a son-of-a-bitch!" yelled her father from the couch, "ifa you're getting so damned fine for spaghetti you no have to eat!"

"I know it," said Krassy, "and I won't eat it much longer."

A week later, Krassy stopped at the *Stockyard Weekly News* to see Mike. Mike wasn't in, but Caesar Manola, Mike's father, was there. Caesar Manola was a worried man in his early forties. With an invalid wife, slowly dying of tuberculosis, he struggled to earn a living with his small weekly paper. The bloody stench of the stockyards district spelled poverty to Caesar Manola and most of the men living under its stinking mantle.

In one of the world's squalid districts, Manola wrote his pathetic news items concerning the nonentities of his neighborhood, sold advertisements to merchants with one foot constantly in bankruptcy, set type for his paper, and ran the rattling flatbed press in which it was printed. On Saturdays when the paper was distributed, small boys of black, coffee and cream, yellow, and white delivered it house to house for ten cents an hour.

Manola had seen little beauty in his life, less pleasure, and no hope. He sat in his office typing bills to his advertisers. Krassy Almauniski walked up to the counter and asked for Mike.

"Mike isn't here," Caesar told her.

"Will he be back soon?"

"Fifteen or twenty minutes ... want to wait for him?"

Krassy smiled at Caesar. "Not particularly. I just wondered how the votes are coming?"

"Are you entered in the contest?" he asked.

"Yes," she replied. "I'm Krassy Almauniski."

Caesar nodded. "I've seen your name. I think you are right up there.

Come on in and sit down. Ask Mike when he gets back, he's counting the votes."

Krassy walked through the little swinging gate toward Caesar's desk. The big table was littered with galley proofs, library copies, and general debris. Krassy perched on the corner of Caesar's desk and smiled down at him. "I've heard a lot of nice things about you," she told him.

He smiled back. "Who from ... Mike?"

"Oh no," she said, "I hardly know Mike. I've seen him around once or twice, that's all. I'm lots older than Mike...." She paused, then continued, "I know I look young, but I'm really twenty-one." She gracefully swung her weight from one hip to the other.

Manola was suddenly conscious of the way her thigh swelled against his desk. He tried to push the thought away. "It's hard to tell a woman's age. The old ones try to look young, and the young ones try to look old ... You know, it's funny, though, I haven't seen you around."

"I graduated from high school four years ago," said Krassy, "and I've been working in Michigan City until a couple weeks ago. I just came back."

"Ohhh," said Manola. He glanced up quickly, and in her vantage point above him he could see the soft sweep of the underpart of her leg.

"I'm surprised, though...." Krassy continued.

"Surprised?" echoed Manola, forcibly moving his eyes away.

"Yes," said Krassy, "I'm surprised that the paper isn't offering a prize, too."

"The paper only sponsors the contest," Manola explained. "The different merchants give the prizes."

"I know that," replied Krassy, "but I think it would be swell if the paper gave a cash prize, too. It would make the whole contest seem so much more ... important."

Manola shook his head. "No chance," he said. Krassy looking down on him thought he looked old and tired.

"Well," she said, "I must be running along...."

"I'll tell Mike you were in," said Caesar.

"Don't bother," said Krassy, "he probably wouldn't know who you meant."

Caesar hesitated for a moment, then he asked, "Are you going to be around tonight?"

"I guess so, why?"

"If you want to stop back here around nine, I'll buy you a drink."

Krassy shook her head. "I don't think it looks good, me being in the contest and everything, stopping in your office so much."

"You could meet me someplace else," said Manola.

"Where?"

"How about Dixie's?"

Krassy had heard of Dixie's ... a neighborhood bistro of local repute, but she had never been there. She turned his suggestion over in her mind, considering it carefully. As a rendezvous, she thought it might indicate that Manola didn't want to be seen with her publicly, because he was married. And as far as she was concerned, the suggestion of Dixie's pleased her because she had little fear of running into her own contemporaries.

"All right," she said, "I'll meet you at Dixie's at nine." She stretched herself down from the desk and walked to the door, feeling Manola's eyes following her. "See you now," she said and left the office.

After dinner, that night, she hurried to her room and changed into her good dress. Slipping on her overcoat, she stuffed a cheap costume necklace, rouge, and lipstick in her pocket. Beneath the coat, she hid a pair of high-heeled shoes. Then walking calmly downstairs, she made her way serenely to the living room door.

"Where you going?" asked Anton Almauniski.

"To a movie with some of the kids," she replied.

Almauniski eyed her suspiciously but could see nothing wrong. She was without make-up and wearing saddle shoes.

"All time you run around ... going ... going ... going," he said. "Someday you be sorry."

"She go out with man," said Maria suddenly and with decision.

"You keep out of this," cried Krassy and turned on her in fury. "You don't talk enough English to know what the hell we're talking about!"

Almauniski rose from his chair and raised his fist. Krassy dodged around him and opened the door. "I'm going to a movie with some kids," she repeated. "I don't care whether you believe it or not!" She slammed the door and ran down the steps. On the sidewalk she continued running for a block, gradually slowing her pace as the distance lengthened from her home.

Three blocks farther on she stopped in an oil station and went into the women's toilet. She carefully washed her face and hands with warm water and dried them on paper towels. Taking out her rouge and lipstick, she did an expert job of make-up before the mirror bolted above the washbowl. She kicked off her saddle shoes and slipped into her high heels. Finally, she clasped the cheap brass necklace around her throat. "Nobody who didn't know me wouldn't guess I wasn't twenty-one," she told herself with pride.

Picking up her saddle shoes, she went to the front of the station. "Can I leave these shoes here tonight?" she asked the attendant. "I'll pick them up in the morning."

"Sure," said the attendant, "you can park your shoes with me any time you feel like it." He grinned broadly.

Krassy smiled back at him. "Thanks," she told him, "you're nice." She walked down to the corner and caught a streetcar. Ten blocks later, she got off in front of Dixie's. She was nearly half an hour early, so she started walking slowly up the block looking in the tired shop windows.

"Someday," she thought, "I'll walk into Saks and buy anything I want without even asking the price. I'll buy anything I want and nobody will have to give me the money. I'll have all the money I need!" She stopped in front of a secondhand dress shop and considered the clothes on wire hangers in the window. "And I'll know what to buy ... and how to buy it," she added.

At nine o'clock Caesar Manola drove up to Dixie's in a 1932 Pontiac. Originally a sedan, it had worked its way down in the automobile world until only the front half of the body remained. The rear of the body had been sawed off, and reconverted into a small truck. Manola used it to haul papers, and as a pickup truck for supplies in his business. He saw Krassy waiting for him under the muddy red neon sign which alternately spelled DIXIE'S and BEER.

"Waiting long?" he asked as he got out.

"No," lied Krassy, "I just got here." They entered the tavern and stepped into a dimly lit room rank with the sour smell of beer. A long bar ran down one entire side of the room, and it was crowded with men and women perching on stools. Back of the bar was a narrow, frosted mirror, with bottles arranged in military rows on glass shelves in front of it. An occasional orange-colored bulb gave enough light for the bartenders to work by, but kept the customers from easily reading the labels on the bottles.

Manola led Krassy past the tiny tables which jammed the center of the room, and worked his way toward the back where booths, upholstered in imitation red leather, hugged the walls. Finding a vacant one, he guided Krassy into the booth, and sat down beside her. A weary waitress slogged a wet cloth across the table tops and waited impatiently for their order. "What'll yuh have?" he asked.

"I'll have a whisky coke," said Krassy. On several notable occasions, she had sipped a few swallows from bottles of coke spiked with whisky. She didn't like it, but it was the only drink she was familiar with. She ordered it now.

"You mean a Cuba Libre?" asked the waitress.

Krassy didn't know if she meant a Cubra Libre or not. "Yes," she said with dignity, "that'll do."

Caesar Manola ordered a double bourbon with plain water. When Krassy's drink arrived, she tasted it. "This is just a whisky coke after all," she exclaimed, "with some lime in it!" Manola looked at her in surprise.

"Don't you drink?" he asked.

"Oh, sure," said Krassy. She didn't explain further.

By eleven o'clock, Manola was getting drunk. Krassy had finished two Cuba Libres and had managed to spill two others, but she, too, was feeling the liquor. "I can think all right," she told herself, "but it's getting hard to talk." Then she became conscious of Manola's hand on her knee. He wasn't squeezing; he wasn't exploring; his hand was resting there ... waiting. Krassy snuggled her leg against his for a brief moment, then withdrew it. Under the table, his hand moved quickly up her leg and around her waist.

"I like you, Krassy," he said.

"I like you, too, Caesar," she said, "but ..." Her voice trailed off.

"But what?" he wanted to know.

"You'll get sore if I tell you."

"I won't get sore," Manola promised solemnly.

"Well, I still don't know why you won't give a nice cash prize to the contest winner," Krassy said defiantly.

"If you win, maybe I will give a prize," said Manola.

"Oh, Caesar!" cried Krassy. "You will?"

"Maybe," he said. "Maybe I'd give a prize if you'd be nice to me."

Krassy caught her breath. "Don't say that, Caesar," she said, "it sounds like ... well, you're trying to buy me."

"Perhaps I am," said Manola soberly. "I'm not kidding myself, Krassy. That's the only way I'd ever get you. I don't have any money. I'm nearly broke." He stopped and finished his drink before continuing. "But if you'd be my girl friend ... I'd do damned near anything for you." His left arm tightened around her waist. Krassy held her breath and sat perfectly still. "How much of a cash prize do you think I should offer ... just in case you won?" he asked. His fingers brushed lightly over her breast.

"One hundred dollars!" Krassy said with quick decision. Manola withdrew his hand. Wearily he ordered another drink.

When they left Dixie's, Manola drove Krassy straight home; letting her off near the corner by her house. As Krassy climbed out of the ancient truck, Manola looked down at her and said, "I'll see what I can do about that prize." Krassy stood straight and beautiful in the light of the street lamp. She turned a serene face up toward Manola.

"You're sweet, Caesar," she said, "I'm sure you'll never regret it."

The following day Manola drove the old Pontiac into Luke's Honest Used-Car Lot. Luke, a dapper, sleek man, with prominent front teeth, walked out of a small wooden shack which was located on the lot and served as his office. A number of sagging, motorized vehicles variously identifiable as 1928 Oaklands, Model A Fords, and assorted Chevies up to 1935 stood like tired, worn, worked-out nags at invisible hitching posts.

The pride of the lot, a 1940 Buick stood glistening in glory, on a small, plank platform near the street. Luke tried to sell it during the day, and drove it for his personal use at night. Luke walked up to Caesar Manola and picked up the end of former conversations.

"Christ, Manola," he said, "I been thinking it over and I still can't do no better."

"Okay, Luke," said Manola, "I'll take the seventy-five bucks."

Luke ignored this sudden acceptance of his terms. "Hell, there ain't no calls for cars today. They're a drug on the market. You think 1938 was bad ... let me tell you, Manola, this is a hell of a lot worse. I can't sell the ones I got...."

Fear that Luke might not buy the car grabbed Manola in the stomach. "You offered seventy-five for it last week," he said.

"Sure," said Luke. "I know you and the Missus need the dough."

"Okay, okay," said Manola in relief.

"So I'll take it anyway ... mostly to help you out." Luke looked piously at his dirty fingernails. "How is your old lady anyway?"

"About the same," said Manola.

"Hell, guy, with this dough you can have her lung collapsed and maybe that'll help her, huh?"

"Yes," said Manola.

"Those fat doctors are all sons-of-bitches," said Luke, "you'd think they was all little Jesus Christs in white coats. But they won't do nothing if you don't have some of that old dough to pass around regular.... believe me!"

"Some of them are all right," said Manola.

"They told you cutting that lung out would help, huh?" asked Luke.

"They thought it'd help," hedged Manola carefully.

"Okay, so come in the office and I'll give you the dough," said Luke as he headed back toward the wooden shack. "Don't forget to bring your transfer paper and title with you," he called over his shoulder.

Caesar Manola climbed out of the old Pontiac and without a word followed Luke into his office. There, Luke paid him seventy-five dollars in fives and tens. Manola walked all the way back to his newspaper office.

On March 29, two days before the contest winner was to be announced in the paper, Mike arranged with Krassy to appear at the *Stockyard Weekly News* office for her official notification of winning the event. When Krassy entered the office, Mike met her at the door. Caesar Manola was seated at his desk.

"You're Mike Manola?" Krassy asked.

"Yeah," said Mike, "your face looks familiar." He winked at her and rolled his eyes toward his father seated behind him.

"I'm Krassy Almauniski," she replied. "I received a card that you wanted to see me."

"Oh, sure!" said Mike. "I want to be the first to congratulate you. You've been elected the winner of the *Weekly News* Beauty Contest." He kept a very straight face as he turned toward his father. "This is Krassy Almauniski, the winner of our contest," he said.

"How do you do, Miss Almauniski," said Caesar Manola. "Congratulations. I also got additional good news for you ... the paper is offering a cash prize of a hundred dollars."

Mike Manola's mouth dropped open. He stared at his father in amazement. "A hundred bucks?" he asked.

"Yes," said the older Manola, "it's a good promotion for the Paper!" He didn't look at Mike.

"Thank you, Mr. Manola," said Krassy, her heart singing with excitement, "I really don't know what to say...."

Mike recovered sufficiently to turn to Krassy and resume business. "Miss Almauniski, we want to take a picture of you tomorrow, so this afternoon if you'll see the merchants who sponsored this contest, they'll give you your prizes. We got to take your picture tomorrow in time for our next edition."

Krassy left the *Weekly News* office triumphantly. "A hundred dollars," she told herself, "a hundred dollars ... and new clothes. Soon I'll be out ... I'll get away and never see the yards again!" She hurried to Solomon's Dress Shoppe, featuring dresses from $2.98 to $14.98, and lady's suits from $12.50 to $27.50. David Solomon regarded her sourly as she announced the reason for her visit.

"Maybe you should like a nice little house dress, yes?"

"No," said Krassy, "I want a suit."

"And I suppose for nothing you want I should give you my best $27.50 fitted suit which is an actual bargain if I was asking twice that much?"

"Yes," said Krassy.

Solomon was not impressed with such directness. Among his customers he was used to it. But half an hour later, Krassy walked from his shop with a new, black suit. Her only concession to Solomon's ranting was that she would make such alterations as were necessary.

At Edna Mae's Thrifty Shoppers Mart, she finally selected a plain little hat, with a half-veil. It cost $2.65 and she selected it with the idea of adding as many years to her appearance as possible. Edna Mae, a large friendly woman, entered into Krassy's selections with warmth and as much good advice as it was possible for her to give concerning her shoddy merchandise. Krassy finally selected a $17.50 (the highest price range) beige coat, with black trimming around the pockets.

Quickly, Krassy picked out an imitation leather suitcase fitted with imitation ivory comb and brush, three cosmetic hot ties, and a small round celluloid box for powder from Browser's Trunk and Leather Company. Wearing her new hat and coat, with her new suit packed in the suitcase, she stopped at the office of the Red-Top Taxi Company and received $5.00 worth of cab coupons. Using the phone in the Red-Top office, she arranged with the Deep Well Brewing Company to deliver the case of beer to her home.

Then she went to the Glamour Beauty Salon for her permanent and manicure. It was after six when she left the beauty shop, her hair stiff from the treatment, and hurried home.

Slowly she climbed the stairs and opened the door. Anton roared across the room at her, "It's time you got home, goddamnit!"

He and Maria were sitting in the living room, the case of beer in the middle of the floor. The case was nearly empty and the discarded bottles were littered around the room. Anton had stripped off his shirt, and his great chest and arms glistened under the light of the solitary bulb which hung on a wire from the center of the ceiling. He had loosened his belt and unbuttoned the front of his trousers.

Maria sat upright in the middle of the sagging davenport, her eyes flat and black behind half-closed lids. She was half out of the thin cotton dress which covered her widening body.

"I won the contest," said Krassy, "I've been collecting my prizes."

"You ain't good enough to win no prizes," said Anton. "You're lying!"

"She sleep with man," said Maria.

"You dirty dago," said Krassy. "What about you? You're not married to Paw!"

Maria made a high, whining sound and leaped from the davenport, with her hands outstretched before her. Krassy grasped an empty beer bottle at her feet and stood her ground. As Maria rushed by Anton he swung his huge fist, catching her in the side, and knocked her across the room. Maria smashed against the wall and crumbled slowly to the floor. Anton arose to his feet and shuffled toward Krassy.

"If you been out whoring, I kill you," he said.

Krassy fled upstairs to her room. Anton sank unsteadily at the round oak table in the living room and rested his forehead against the edge. "Goddamn everything," he said in a choking voice.

The next afternoon Krassy didn't go to school. She returned home at noon, while Anton and Maria were both away, put on her new clothes and packed her few belongings in her new leather bag. Then in her high heels, she walked to the closest store and ordered a cab. On the way to the *Weekly News* office, she stopped at the beauty salon and asked permission to leave her suitcase. From the beauty salon she went to the newspaper office.

Caesar Manola was seated at his desk when she entered; no one else was in the office. "God, Krassy, you look beautiful!" he told her.

Krassy slowly pivoted around so he could admire her. "Do I look all right?" she asked.

"You look wonderful," Manola assured her.

"Where's Mike?" asked Krassy. "He said he wanted to take my picture for the paper."

Manola laughed. "I sent Mike down to the Loop on an errand," he said. "I told him I'd take your picture in case he didn't get back." Manola chuckled. "Today, where I sent him, I don't plan for him to get back," he added.

"No?"

"No," said Manola. "Today I plan to give you that hundred bucks!" He rose from his desk and picked up a small camera, "Come on outside. I'll take your picture now."

Krassy followed Manola out to the sidewalk. Squinting toward the sun, Manola posed her against the front of the building and took several shots. Then he took her arm and led her into the office again. He placed the camera on his desk, and picked up an envelope lying there.

"Here's your hundred dollars," he said.

Krassy took the envelope, avoiding his eyes, and put it in her purse. "Thanks, Caesar," she said, "thanks ... a lot."

"Let's go upstairs," said Caesar.

"What's upstairs?" asked Krassy.

"I keep a room upstairs," he explained. "Sometimes I work here most of the night, so I sleep up there once in a while. Come on, Krassy ..." he took her hand and gently urged her toward the back of the shop.

Krassy permitted herself to be led in silence. She followed him back of the thin partition where the small flatbed press was standing. A narrow door opened to a steep flight of unfinished wooden steps ascending to a dark hall on the floor above. Following Manola up the stairs, she thought, "this can't be happening to me ... this isn't true. I never really believed he'd give me a hundred dollars ... I don't want him to touch me." She paused in the grimy hall while Caesar Manola opened the door to a room.

In the backwash of her panic, a cold voice of reason whispered softly, "Don't kid yourself ... this is what you've been waiting for ... you planned this ... you *knew* it would happen. You've taken his money, now pay him off! Then you're free, Krassy! You'll be free of Maria and the old man, you'll be free of Caesar and Mike, and the Yards ... and Hempstead ... and...."

"Here we are," said Manola and stood aside to let her enter. Krassy stepped into a narrow little room containing an army cot covered with a khaki blanket. By the cot was an old kitchen chair ... once painted red. A mirror, with distorting streaks, in a heavy wood frame, hung on the wall. Caesar walked across the bare floor and half lowered the shredded, rotting brown shade at the window. Then he turned to Krassy and put his arms around her.

"Sit here on the bed beside me," he told her and she followed his order mechanically. Quietly she lifted her hands to her head and removed the new hat. Caesar leaned over her and kissed her on the lips, the weight of his body gently forcing her down on the cot. Stretching on the cot, beside her, he placed his lips on her neck just beneath her ear.

"Listen to me, Krassy," he whispered, "listen to me for just a moment. Stay with me ... be with me ... never leave me. I love you, Krassy. I'd do anything to make you happy. I feel young again. For the first time in years ... I have hope and ambition and dreams. The Yards aren't important any more. We'll go away ... someplace together. I can get a job...." He paused for a second. "You do love me a little, don't you, Krassy?" he asked softly.

Krassy turned her head on the pillow and nodded silently. "Mother of God," she prayed to herself, "make him stop ... make him keep quiet. Make him get it over with...."

"Kiss me, Krassy," Manola urged. She felt his hands working at her blouse, gentle hands that didn't hurt. "You'd better take off your new suit," he whispered, "if you don't it'll get mussed." She was half conscious of his hands helping her to slide the jacket from around her shoulders, and she arched her back while he slipped her skirt down over her hips. The walls of the room pulsed and throbbed, moving in slowly around her, while the low ceiling moved higher and higher ... pulling away ... until it looked like something viewed through the small end of a telescope. Then the ceiling was blotted out by the shoulders and head of Manola.

She steeled her mind into a blankness, unfeeling and unseeing. She existed in an empty space for an eon of tortured time.

Then feeling Manola's body flung away from her, she was jerked back into consciousness, with a far screaming in her ears. In terror she raised her shoulders from the cot and saw Mike Manola standing over Caesar lying on the floor. Mike was kicking his father in the head.

"You bastard! You dirty, no-good-son-of-a-bitching-bastard!" Mike was screaming in a high, thin voice and tears were streaming down his face. "My girl ... she's my girl..." He choked on his sobs.

Caesar Manola grasped Mike's foot, and twisting it suddenly flung him against the cot where he half sprawled over Krassy. Caesar pulled himself to his feet as Mike charged at him, showering him wildly with blows. Caesar Manola swung a tremendous blow, in a wide looping arc, that landed solidly on his son's nose.

Krassy heard the bones crack ... a sound like someone stepping on a matchbox.

Mike fell to the floor, blood pouring from his nose and mouth in a spurting, crimson stream. His screaming was stilled. While Caesar dropped to his knees by his son's side and tried to stop the red, gushing torrent, Krassy gathered together her clothes, and unnoticed, quietly slipped away.

Downstairs, she dressed hurriedly in the pressroom, her mind cold, numb, and detached. When she finished dressing, she picked up her purse and walked to the Glamour Beauty Salon. There she recovered her suitcase. Then calling a Red-Top cab, she drove away. Krassy never returned to the Yards again.

A month later, Mrs. Manola died.

Two hours after she died, Caesar Manola committed suicide. Because of the Church, they weren't buried together.

A week after that, Mike Manola returned to Chicago and took possession of the *Stockyard Weekly News*.

CHAPTER THREE

part 1 Danny

I went back down to the Loop, after talking to Manola, determined to forget all about Krassy Almauniski. After all, nobody had seen her for ten years. She'd probably left town, gotten married, or died.

And furthermore, what the hell difference did it make to me?

At least that's what I kept telling myself. I wrote letters at the office, called on a few habitual deadbeats, and pried out a few collections here and there. With the rest of my time, I called on some new accounts and tried to sell them the idea of letting the Clarence Moon Collection Agency handle their business. I lined up some new business that way, and things were looking up a little bit. During the day I was busier than the devil.

But at night it was different. I'd go to bed, and in an hour or two I'd wake up and then I couldn't go back to sleep. I'd try to squeeze all thoughts out of my mind ... with a sort of mental rubber squeegee ... but I could never quite do it. Little by little, I'd get around to thinking about Krassy. First her face would start to form, all indistinct and hazy, then it'd become clear and beautiful and the next minute she'd be sitting in the room with me.

I'd think up all the smart cracks I could think of, and feed them into the conversation like a radio comedian. I'd hear her laugh chime out ... and I was a hell of a big guy, all right.

But it wasn't good enough. Because always in the back of my mind was the question: "Where is she now?" She could be anywhere in this world, or this continent, or this country, or this state, or this county, or this town. And if she was in Chicago? Well, there're over five million persons in this area; somewhere in that milling mess might be Krassy. After ten years, she'd be around twenty-seven years old. That was all I knew.

But I've done a lot of skip-tracing. Enough to know that most people follow a pretty definite pattern all their life ... even if they're taking a powder. So, I'd hunch the pillow up high under my head, light a cigarette and lie there in the dark trying to figure out the next move Krassy made when she left the Yards. At that time she was around seventeen, had a new suitcase, a suit, coat, and hat ... and one hundred bucks. With that much dope, it might just be possible to pick up the end of the string ... someplace. But where?

That hundred bucks Krassy had was probably more dough than she'd ever known existed in the world. But being broke all her life could do one of two things to her. She'd either blow the dough plenty fast ... or ... she'd hang on to it like a terrier. There was something about Krassy's picture that made me think maybe she'd hang on to it. So, if she was trying to hang on to it, she probably wouldn't have busted off for New York or Los Angeles or someplace in between. She'd probably stay here in Chicago ... at least for a while.

But she couldn't live on a hundred bucks forever; so she'd have to get a job. What kind of a job? She hadn't any experience I knew of, so she'd have to end up clerking or waiting on tables. But then I remembered how beautiful she was, and I knew that she certainly must know it herself. At least to some extent. So why shouldn't she try to cash in on her good looks? Show business? Show business was obvious.

I felt pretty good that I'd followed the string that far. But the more I thought about it, the less satisfied I was to let it stand at that. Chicago isn't a good show-business town. Damn few shows ever originate in Chicago. Most of them start in New York. She might have made the grade in one of the big night clubs or hotels, but she'd have to know how to sing or dance even for that. I didn't know if Krassy could do either, but remembering that old termite trap where she'd lived ... I doubted there was enough dough for dancing lessons. Before dropping the idea, entirely, I decided I'd talk to Abe Blossom, a guy I knew. In the collection business, you don't make much dough, but you sure make plenty of contacts. Abe had been a theatrical booker for twenty-five years, and once I'd tried to collect some dough from him. It had been impossible. While I was trying to twist his arm, we'd sort of become friendly. I figured Abe might recognize her picture.

Abe's got an office in the Woods Building, and I went in to see him. He's a square, stocky little guy who always dresses in gray. He wears light gray suits, with a gray, hand-painted tie, and gray suede shoes. He has a bright red face, tucked under a stiff mat of gray hair, and his cigars are big, long and black.

"Greetings, Danny," he said. "Draw up a stump and let your muscles sag."

"Hi, Abe," I said, "how's business?"

Abe shrugged his shoulders. "All the joints where they got gambling, business is good and I can sell acts. All the joints where they ain't got gambling, I can't sell nothing. So they put the heat on the casinos, and nobody makes nothing including my acts of which I get ten per cent ... of nothing."

"That's tough," I said.

"Don't let it bother you, man," said Abe, "it's been going on for years."

"Look," I said, "maybe you can do me a favor. Have you ever seen this gal?" I pulled out the clipping with Krassy's picture and handed it to him.

Abe looked at it carefully and slowly whistled. "She's quite a dish," he said.

"Yeah," I agreed, "she is."

"What's her name?"

"Krassy Almauniski," I said, "but maybe she changed it."

"Jesus! With a handle like that she'd have to change it," Abe told me. "Is she in show business?"

"I don't know," I said. "I got a hunch maybe she was."

Abe handed the clipping back to me. "I don't know nobody by that name," he said, "and I don't ever remember seeing her around." That don't mean she wasn't around, but if Abe don't remember her ... it means she sure as hell didn't make the grade around here.

I put the clipping back in my pocket. "Abe," I said, "if you were a babe with looks like that and didn't have any training in anything ... and had to make a living ... what'd you do?"

"I'd get in show business," Abe said promptly.

"We just got through hashing that over," I said. "What else would you do?"

Abe spit the soggy end of his cigar into a bright, brass spittoon by the side of his desk. "Maybe I'd go into modeling," he said. "A lot of dames with no talent but plenty of looks make a good living out of having their pictures taken. Maybe I'd try that."

I hadn't thought about Krassy being a model, but the more I kicked the idea around, the better I liked it. I thanked Abe and left.

First, I had some basic stuff that had to be done. I went to the main office of the telephone company, and went through all the old Chicago and suburban directories for the last ten years. Krassy had never been listed in any of them. Next I tried the gas and light companies. A clerk told me, in both places, she'd never been a subscriber to either service. The address on Clarence Moon's old data card had been her original home address, but it was obvious that Moon had contacted her someplace else. Where? I didn't know.

The merchandise which she'd originally charged was listed by items, but didn't give the merchant who'd sold it. I cussed old Moon for his sloppiness.

Finally, I went to the Retail Credit Bureau, and being in the collection business, they gave me all the help they could, which was nothing. They had no record of a Krassy Almauniski.

Then suddenly it made sense. What Abe said about her having to change her name was true. Krassy had changed her name. But, now, what the hell was it?

I didn't know her new name, but I'd give anybody eight, five, and even that her initials remained the same "K.A." For some damned reason, most people keep their same initials when they change their names. Maybe it's easier to remember, or maybe it's like the small boy who got a new boomerang for Christmas. He had a hell of a time throwing the old one away.

Looking for a gal with the initials "K.A." wasn't too much of a help, but it did help a little. At least I'd made up my mind I'd never find a girl by the name of Krassy Almauniski.

This much I had to go on: she was around 17, in 1940; she was blond and beautiful; her initials were K.A. and I had a picture of her. So with that dope, and my clipping, I started making the rounds of the model bureaus in Chicago. By comparing the present lists to the ones doing business ten years ago, I narrowed my calls down to around twenty-five.

The first seventeen were disappointing. I walked the pavements, climbed stairs, and rode in elevators. Most of the office girls in the bureaus had only been in their jobs a year or two. Checking the records of their models ten years back, with initials of "K.A.," didn't dig up anything.

But one other thing popped out of all this poking around. Krassy had never worked as a photographic model either in Chicago or any other major city. No one recognized her picture, which wouldn't be true if she'd appeared very much nationally in magazines and papers.

On my eighteenth call, though, I struck pay dirt. It was at Monica Morton's Model Bureau and School. Monica Morton was a distinguished looking dame in her middle forties, with solid-silver hair and a well-preserved figure. She went to some lengths to inform me once, *some* years back, she'd been a Conover model. I stood around the desk in her reception room, and polished up a couple nice apples for her. She ended up by calling me Danny and digging into her files.

She came back with a couple glossy print photographs and a small index file card. "You're sure I'm not going to get this girl in trouble giving you this information?" she asked me.

"Naw, Miss Morton," I assured her, "you'll be doing her a favor." I repeated the old gag about the refund on the insurance policy.

She handed the photos and card to me. It was Krassy all right. But the card was made out for "Katherine Andrews." It gave her age as 20, height 5 feet 7 inches, bust 35, waist 24, hips 34; hair blond, eyes gray, home address Hannibal, Missouri; Chicago address on East Banks Street. Krassy had already started to hide herself in the city.

I looked at the photographs and caught my breath. That same lovely face, with the calm, serene eyes, looked back at me. The heavily braided hair had been replaced with a long, glistening page-boy that hung, gilded, to her shoulders. Her lips had that same quiet, proud smile that I'd learned by heart from the newspaper clipping.

"I'll be glad to pay you for one of these photos," I told Miss Morton.

"That's all right, Danny," she said, "we have an extra copy, so you can take one. We always take shots of our graduates and keep them in our reference files."

"When did you see Kras—I mean Katherine Andrews last?" I asked.

"Years, simply years ago," Monica Morton replied. "I don't think she's been back since she finished her course."

"She took a course from you, huh?"

"Oh, yes," said Miss Morton and glanced at a series of small symbols which had been written on the side of the card. "She took our most expensive modeling course. In those days it cost $250; today it costs twice that much."

"What do you teach?" I asked. "How to walk around?"

Monica Morton gave me a sympathetic smile. "Modeling as a successful career requires much more than that," and she took off into a well-rehearsed sales talk. I listened. And when she was through, I understood that Krassy had studied professional make-up, hair styling, voice modulation, diction, how to dress, social and professional etiquette, conversational English; how to use her hands and feet, how to walk and how to sit, and ... as far as I could make out ... even a little dramatic acting.

"Was she good at all this stuff?" I asked Monica Morton.

"As I remember her, she was an excellent student," she told me. "She was one of the most beautiful girls I've ever seen, and she photographed marvelously ... simply marvelously. She was very serious and studied hard. We were all surprised when she graduated and then never followed through on her training."

"You mean she never worked as a model?"

"Exactly," replied Miss Morton. "After graduation, she simply never came back. She took the six-month course which requires ten hours a week. After she completed it, she simply disappeared. We wrote her several times when jobs came up, at her address at East Banks Street, but the letters were returned to us. I guess perhaps she left town."

When I left Miss Morton, I took Krassy's picture with me and grabbed a bus up Michigan Boulevard to East Banks Street. East Banks is a short, narrow little street on Chicago's Near North Side. It only runs a few short blocks in from the lake. Mostly it is filled with rooming houses which've been converted over from the old, original mansions which lined the street.

The house where Krassy had lived was on a corner. It was an old, brownstone house, four stories tall, with a high tower climbing up the front and sticking out a full story above the roof. The top of the tower had battlements like an old castle turret. Whoever had originally built the house spent a hell of a lot of dough on it. I've seen a lot of post office buildings which weren't as big as that house was.

I climbed the stairs and pushed a button by the side of the double front door. The doors were twice as high as I am, and the upper part of them was etched in frosted glass. The design whirled around into shocks of wheat, flying doves, and intertwining ribbons. One thing, though, you couldn't see through them.

The door was opened by a tall, horse-faced woman with artificial blond hair which needed a retouch job plenty bad. She was wearing a plain brown suit, and had heavy, horn-rimmed glasses. The frames had red brilliants set in deep. I asked for the landlady, and she told me I was talking to her.

Introducing myself, I pulled out a picture of Krassy and said I was trying to locate a Miss Katherine Andrews who'd lived there in 1940. The landlady said her name was Miss Dukes and would I please come in.

I walked into a tremendous hall which was practically bare. There was a clothes tree, umbrella rack and old hand-carved table with a phone on it. The floor had all kinds of curlicue patterns made from blocks of different colored wood inlaid in it. In the middle of the floor was a small, round, nondescript rug. Miss Dukes led the way into the parlor which was another cozy room, slightly smaller than the Notre Dame gymnasium, with tall bay windows stretching from the floor to the ceiling. The room was furnished with creaking davenports, golden oak tables, and overstuffed chairs from the 1920s, and sported a fireplace. The fireplace was finished with little, pink, glazed tiles ... about the same color as a ready-made birthday cake. Over the fireplace was a big, blown-up photograph of Miss Dukes. It was good. Miss Dukes looked fifteen years younger, and those fifteen years made a lot of difference.

I gave Miss Dukes the old story about the insurance policy and she said yes, she'd known Katherine Andrews, who'd lived there for six or seven months in 1940.

"Did Miss Andrews leave a forwarding address when she left?" I asked.

"No," said Miss Dukes, "she didn't."

"You mean she just packed up and left?" I asked.

"Yes," replied the landlady, "she left one day with her suitcase."

"Did she owe you any dough?"

"No," said Miss Dukes, "she didn't."

"Do you have any idea why she might've left?"

"Yes, I do!" she said. Suddenly the bars were down and with fury in her voice she continued, "She probably knew her fiancé was going to be arrested. She didn't have the guts to stand by him!"

Her answer stopped me for a minute. So Krassy had been engaged! But if Krassy was engaged and in love with a guy, I couldn't believe she'd ever desert him. Particularly when the chips were down.

"Who was she engaged to?" I asked.

"A young man who lived here," Miss Dukes answered. "A fine young man. His name was Larry Buckham. He was a newspaper photographer and worked for the *Daily Register*. He took that picture of me ... up there," she nodded at the huge blow-up above the mantel.

"Where did Miss Andrews work while she was here?" I asked.

"She didn't," answered Miss Dukes sourly. "Her folks lived in Minneapolis and sent her money."

Again the old cover-up. Krassy was filling in all her tracks. Why? "What happened to Buckham?"

"After he was arrested, the police held him for a day or two, and then let him go. He was fired from the paper."

"Didn't he come back for his stuff?"

"What stuff? The police took everything."

"Why'd they arrest him?"

"I'm sure I don't know," said Miss Dukes. I could tell from the sudden tightening of her mouth that she was through talking. Maybe she didn't want to talk any more, maybe she didn't know any more. Anyway, I got up and thanked her. She didn't walk to the door with me. She just sat on the faded old davenport and looked at her picture over the mantel. I let myself out.

The next day I went over to the *Daily Register* office. It was a lousy day, too. It was raining and the wet streets in the Loop splashed muddy water, all mixed with oil, every time a car went by. I felt depressed as hell and was just about ready to give up trying to trace Krassy. There didn't seem to be any percentage for me even if I did find her. But something, inside, kept urging me to find out about Larry Buckham and what happened to him. "Just find out about Buckham," I told myself, "then wipe your nose and keep it clean. Krassy doesn't mean a thing to you. She doesn't even know you're alive."

The picture editor, at the *Register*, was a guy named Bob Berry. He'd lost most of his hair, but what remained he carefully parted in the middle and brushed it out, fanlike, to cover the biggest possible area. The day I saw him, he'd been to a dentist. He had a little trouble talking because he was having two front teeth put in with a bridge. The dentist hadn't finished and all I could think of was that song about "all I want for Christmas is my two front teeth." So Berry whistled on his "w's" and nearly spit in my eye on his "p's." It turned out Berry had been working on the *Register* when Buckham was canned, although he hadn't been the picture editor then.

"Christ, fellow," he said, "that's a long time back. I remember Buckham all right, but I don't remember too much about the details. He was picked up by the larceny detail for something or other, and he made some kind of a settlement with them. They let him go, but the paper canned him. There weren't any stories on it, that I remember."

"How's that?" I asked.

"I don't think he was booked, in the first place; and in the second place, it wasn't important. Hell, a hundred mugs a day get picked up for larceny around town. Buckham wasn't anybody important, so the papers probably played it down. They don't like to give publicity to a crooked newspaperman, anyway."

"What happened to Buckham after he left the paper?"

"I don't know. He left town. I know damned good and well he couldn't get a job on any other paper around here."

"Did you happen to ever meet Buckham's girl friend ... a Katherine Andrews?"

"No." He paused for a moment and thought back. "He probably had a girl friend all right. I remember be was a good-looking son-of-a-bitch." Berry stopped. "Say, come to think of it ... I think he did have a gal who was a stenographer or secretary or something."

All I said was, "Huh?"

"Yeah," said Berry dredging up the old memories, "come to think of it, I remember he did. It's like this: When the cops let him go, Larry beat it ... wherever he went. All the photographers here have a desk." He pointed at two rows of them, with three desks in each row. "Buckham had a desk up near the window, while mine was in the back. He'd been on the staff when I was hired. Not that we were ever at our desks much, but I decided I'd move over to his old one. I cleaned it out and threw away the collection of crap in it. But there was one of those stiff-backed pads, with wide lines in it, ruled down the middle, like secretaries use to take dictation. It was filled with shorthand, and in the back of it were some diagrams ... squares, and stuff. I was an eager beaver in those days and thought maybe I'd stumbled on something important. So I took it down to the business office and had one of the secretaries down there decipher it."

"What was in it?"

"Not a goddamned thing! It was full of quotations like 'One precious hour, set with sixty golden minutes' ... a lot of stuff like that. The secretary said it looked like beginners' exercises."

"Did Buckham write it?"

"No," said Berry, "it was in a girl's writing, all right."

"What about the diagrams?"

"What about them? Nothing to 'em as far as I know. Just squares, and scribbles, and so forth...."

"Was her name in it?"

"Christ! I don't remember," said Berry impatiently. His phone rang and he picked it up and started talking rapidly. I waited until he hung up and said, "Thanks. I'll be glad to buy you a drink."

"Never use the stuff except on holidays and holy days," he said.

"Incidentally," I said, putting on my hat, "was that all that was in the book ... just shorthand exercises?"

"That's all. Except some scribbles in the back ... diagrams ticktacktoe, maybe ... or something."

I left the *Register* and walked down Randolph Street in the rain. It was late afternoon and the drizzle had turned into a steady rain. It was getting dark, and the gray sky seemed so close overhead that you could reach up and poke a hole in the sprinkling system with your finger. Randolph glowed in a neon haze. I stopped in a bar, bought a drink and tried to put some facts together.

At midnight, I was home, lying on my bed, smoking a cigarette and still trying to figure it out. Krassy had been going to school studying to be a model. She'd been engaged to Buckham. Yet Buckham was running around with a secretary. I couldn't imagine any guy being engaged to Krassy, and going around with another babe on the side. Maybe he'd gone with the secretary before he met Krassy? Maybe that's where he got the shorthand book?

But why, for Christ's sake, keep an old shorthand book knocking around in your desk for six or seven months, which was about the length of time he knew Krassy before he was arrested?

But on the other hand, suppose the book belonged to Krassy? If it did, it was important enough for Buckham to keep in his desk. Sentimental reasons, perhaps, but reasons good enough for him to do it.

That brought up another question: where did Krassy learn her shorthand? She might have picked it up in commercial classes in high school. Or maybe she was going to a secretarial school. It didn't sound logical ... the secretarial school, I mean. Because that would mean she'd been going to two schools at the same time.

But my insides were pounding with excitement. Just the thought of picking up her trail, again, excited me. The idea of all the work involved in trailing her to the school wasn't so good. It would take time. A hell of a long time.

And I could be wrong so damned easily. I had no way of knowing that notebook really belonged to Krassy. But I knew I wouldn't rest until I found out.

So the whole routine started all over again. I checked telephone directories, credit references, utility records, and even police records for Katherine Andrews. But this time it was tougher. I ran across a number of Katherine Andrews and it took a lot of sweat eliminating them and proving to myself they weren't Krassy. Finally, I ended up facing the prospect of making the rounds of the secretarial schools. There were literally hundreds of them. However, by checking back in the old directories, I eliminated about fifty per cent of them to start with.

That still left too many so I had to do some more figuring. If Krassy was living on East Banks Street, and going to Monica Morton's in the Loop, it stood to reason that she'd try to go to a school located either on the Near North Side, or the downtown Loop area. She didn't have to, of course, but it'd be more convenient if she did.

By checking addresses, I again eliminated over half of the remaining schools. I still had plenty left; it would take me months to cover them. That meant I'd have to eliminate some more before I could get started; it wasn't too risky, eliminating them, because if I guessed wrong, I'd end up covering the ones I tossed out, anyway.

But if I guessed right, I'd save a hell of a lot of work. I knew that Krassy had left home with $100; she'd paid Monica Morton $250 for her modeling course, so Krassy would probably select as inexpensive a secretarial course as she could. Where she got the dough to pay Monica, or where she could dig up the dough for the secretarial school, I didn't know. But I thought I could gamble on the fact that Krassy was short of money and would buy pretty close on price.

By using the telephone, and pretending I was interested in taking a course, I picked out the schools which offered typing and shorthand at the cheapest prices. If they were the cheapest in the field today, they had also probably been the cheapest back in 1940.

Now while you can use the telephone to get general information, you sure as hell can't use it to start digging up information that's buried deep back in the years. I started hitting out on interviews with the different schools whenever I had time. It wasn't too easy, because in the meantime I tried to keep the Clarence Moon Collection Agency in business and continue to make some new business calls. But other than that, day and night I thought of Krassy and kept picking away at the ball of string trying to find its loose end.

About five or six weeks later, I was walking down East Ohio Street and I pulled out the list of secretarial schools I always carried. I'd make my regular business calls, then if I was near a school on my list, I'd stop in there, too. That way I kept cutting the list down all the time. There was a school called the Goodbody Business Institute, on my list, which was located on Ohio. I stopped in.

To reach Goodbody, you climbed two flights of stairs in a narrow building which was flanked by a stationery store on one side, and a small flower shop on the other. The first floor had a hardware store; the second floor was evidently converted apartments because I could smell soup cooking somewhere. Goodbody was located on the third floor, in the front of the building, at the top of the stairs. It was a large, dusty room, with a dozen desks in it, each desk supporting an old typewriter. Three or four girls were pounding away on typewriters, while an ancient phonograph played a military march. The girls were typing in time to the music. Just inside the door, I was stopped by a low railing which formed a small square cut off from the main room. Right on the other side of the railing, a grizzled veteran of the keys, with too much make-up, tired lines in her face, and brilliantly hennaed hair, was filing her nails. I asked for Mr. Goodbody, and she informed me she was Miss Goodbody. There wasn't, there hadn't been, and there never would be a Mr. Goodbody, she added.

She laid down her nail file and grinned at me. "That's good news," I said, "maybe I'll have a chance, then."

"Son," she said, "you're just thirty years too late! But come on in."

I went in and sat down at the desk beside her. I gave her the old story about paying the insurance premium and asked if she knew Katherine Andrews. By that time, I'd made so many calls and told the story so many times, I'd become careless. I damn near slipped up.

"No," she said, "I don't recall any Katherine Andrews. Wait a minute, though." She pulled out a big, black entry book, marked 1940 and looked in it. "Nope," she said finally, "we never had a Katherine Andrews. We did have a Karen Allison, but that's not what you want."

"Okay and thanks," I said. I got up and started toward the door. Then it hit me what she'd said. Katherine Andrews ... Karen Allison! The old psychological switch on initials! I turned back to Goodbody and pulled out the picture of Krassy. She took it and looked just once.

"Sure," she said, "that's the girl. Karen Allison."

I came back in and sat down. I could feel my hands shaking, so I didn't say anything for a minute. I lit a cigarette and offered her one which she took.

"Where'd she go when she left here?" I asked finally.

"She got a job someplace and that's the last I know." Goodbody took a drag on the cigarette and rolled her eyes at the ceiling. "Let me think ... you know she was a good kid. I never got to know her very well. She paid her tuition, worked hard, and minded her own business. And a gal like that, with her looks! Brother, she usually has a swarm of wolves hanging around a mile long." She seemed pleased with the description. "But I never saw any hanging around her."

"Where'd she go to work?"

"That's what I'm trying to remember. Don't get your water hot. Now let me see.... oh, hell, I can't remember, but it was some advertising agency on Michigan Boulevard."

"Tell me what you do remember about it," I urged, "maybe I can locate her anyway...."

"She'd done pretty well ... developed into a good secretary. Not too slow, and not too fast either. She was a good steady hundred words a minute, as I remember. She'd made up her mind she was going to work in some ritzy advertising office. And I'll be darned if she didn't."

Miss Goodbody puffed on her cigarette and thought back. "One day she came in with a heavy piece of engraved stationery," she continued more slowly, "with a phony name at the top and a fancy Gold Coast address. But it had *my* telephone number on it. She wanted me to write her a personal recommendation that she'd been my private social secretary for five years."

"Did you write it?" I asked.

"Sure," she replied. "Then some man called and asked for 'Mrs. Gottrocks' and I said that was me. He wanted to know about Karen and I said she'd been with me for five years, was perfectly honest, and a good girl. He wanted to know why she'd left my employment and I told him I was leaving on a honeymoon with my third husband and didn't want a good-looking young girl around. He laughed and said he knew what I meant. I guess she got the job, because I never heard from her again."

"Can't you remember the name of the advertising agency?" I asked. I had visions of covering about four hundred agencies in Chicago.

"No," said Goodbody, "but I do remember it had a real long name."

"How long?"

"Plenty! It was something like ... well like Pard, Lard, Suffiled and

Burp...." She waved her hand.

"Are you kidding?"

"Sure, I'm kidding," she said, "but it was a long name and sort of ran together. It had four or five names in it."

"Will you help me look through the directory, now, and see if you can recognize it?"

"Sure," said Goodbody, and she got up and returned with a classified telephone directory. I turned to the section listing advertising agencies.

"You sure there weren't two or three names?" I asked.

"Nope," she replied, "there were at least four or five."

There were only a few with that many names in a firm, listed. Miss Goodbody quickly identified the company she meant. It was Jackson, Johnston, Fuller & Greene.

CHAPTER THREE

part 2 Krassy

Krassy rode the Red-Top cab downtown to the Loop. Each block carried her farther away from the Yards ... from Anton, Maria, Caesar and Mike. It took her farther away than the mere physical space involved; it took her away from a complete life, a way of hopelessness, poverty, and despair. It took Krassy Almauniski away from the Yards forever, but it did not take her away from herself.

Relaxing in the seat of the cab, Krassy dug a clipping of rooms-for-rent from her purse. Several of them she had marked with a pencil. Again scanning the list, she asked the driver to continue through the Loop and let her off on the corner of Division Street and Lake Shore Drive. Krassy tore the coupons from her book, and handed them to the driver, and then, in a sudden gesture, handed him a quarter tip. The cabby eyed her speculatively. "Thanks," he said and hesitated. Finally he added the word "Miss."

Krassy stood with her suitcase and looked around. From the Drake Hotel, on Oak Street, to the south, Lake Shore Drive swung in a tremendous and beautiful curve to North Avenue on the north. Majestic apartment buildings faced east to Lake Michigan, and their thousands of gleaming windows, like golden eyes in the sun, followed the streams of traffic surging past on the Inner Drive to where they merged and were engulfed in the roar of the mighty Outer Drive. This was the whitewashed face of Chicago. This was the Chicago Gold Coast. The street of fine broadcloths, silks and furs. Nestling to its backside, nudging and nosing, is the Near North Side of Chicago ... the heart and the strength of much that has brought past fame to the sprawling city.

Here, in a twilight fringe, are the countless small rooms, the studios, and tiny apartments in which have lived the painters, the musicians and the writers who have alternately loved and hated their city. Here, too, at some time in their wanderings have lived the actors, the photographers, the radio people, the dancers, the singers, and the night club entertainers, the young college graduates, the newly-arrived-in-Chicago secretaries and stenographers. And here, mixing side by side, have been kept the mistresses of the mighty businessmen, the dice girls, the amateur whores, and the professional prostitutes.

Blocked by Lake Shore Drive and Lake Michigan to the east, the Near North Side extends only a few blocks west to Clark Street ... where pretense ends. Once again the city becomes dirty, filthy and vicious and tiny grubby stores elbow and squirm their way forward on small frontages in their constant search for customers. Bounded on the north by North Avenue, the Near North Side turns, trickles, and twists its way down to Chicago Avenue, and somewhere in a few blocks south loses its way in the maze of office buildings, stores, night clubs, and cafés.

But safely within its boundaries no one asks questions, because no one really cares.

To Krassy it meant escape and safety. Picking up her suitcase, she slowly walked north on Lake Shore Drive to Banks Street, then she turned west looking for an address. It was a large, old brownstone house with a great tower in the front. She climbed the front steps and rang the bell by the side of the high, frosted-glass doors. In a moment the door was opened and a tall, slender woman with light brown hair, and a thin face, stood facing her.

"You advertised you have a room for rent?" asked Krassy.

"Yes," replied the woman, "do you want to look at it?" Her eyes searched Krassy.

Krassy stepped inside and set her suitcase down in the reception hall. Motioning her to follow, the landlady led the way through the hall to a great, sweeping staircase which was carpeted with a narrow strip down its exact center. On the second floor the great stairway became a series of smaller steps to the third floor. From the third to the fourth floors, it was narrow and steep and wore no carpeting at all. Walking down the corridor, the landlady opened a door at the end of the dark hall. Outside the door was another tiny stairway.

"Where does that lead to?" asked Krassy pointing to the stairs.

"That goes up to the tower room," replied the woman.

"Does somebody live there?" asked Krassy.

"Yes," said the landlady. "It's been rented for five years."

Krassy followed her into a small room. It contained a large double bed, a dresser with mirror, one straight-backed chair with a faded tapestry seat. One corner of the room had been curtained off with elderly cretonne drapes. Back of the drapes a metal rod had been hung across the angle of the corner to serve as a clothes rack. A single window, long and narrow, faced on Banks Street. Heavy maroon, plush drapes, remnants of another room's past glory, fell straight and stiff with grime from the top of the window to the floor.

But it was still the loveliest bedroom Krassy had ever seen. "Your ad says six dollars a week," said Krassy.

"Yes," said the woman. "I allow no cooking in the room," she added, "and there's a bathroom at the end of the hall."

"I'll take it," said Krassy. She opened her purse and took out a ten-dollar bill and two ones. "This is for two weeks."

"Who do I make out the receipt to?" asked the landlady.

"To Katherine ... Andrews," said Krassy.

"Is your home in Chicago?"

"No," replied Krassy, "I'm from Minneapolis."

"Are you working here?"

"I'm going to work as soon as I find a job."

"My name is Miss Dukes," said the landlady. "I'll give you two keys ... one for the front door which is locked after eleven o'clock, and the other for your room. You don't drink?" she asked suddenly.

"No," said Krassy, "I don't drink."

"That's good," said Miss Dukes. "I run a nice place here and I don't permit any drinking in the rooms." She turned and went out, returning in a few minutes with Krassy's luggage. Krassy opened her suitcase and removed her two dresses. She hung them back of the cretonne curtain.

Her long, silk, man's-shirt-nightgown and a single change of lingerie she tucked into one corner of the big dresser drawer. The brush and combs, and cosmetic bottles from her fitted bag she placed neatly on top of the dresser. Then she stretched out on the big bed. For a moment she was conscious of a peculiar, burning sensation within her loins. Momentarily she thought of Caesar Manola, then she flicked her mind to darkness and went to sleep.

For several weeks, Krassy kept carefully to herself, avoiding the other roomers and making her plans. Each morning she drank a cup of coffee and ate two doughnuts; each evening she ate a hamburger and drank a glass of milk. Carefully she watched her money, and walked from her boarding house to the Loop and back, on her trips looking for work. She had no intention of taking a job clerking or working in a restaurant. She wanted a job where she could meet "the right kind of a man." The "right kind" was nebulous in Krassy's mind other than he had a fine job, plenty of money, and he was polished and a gentleman. To meet this man, Krassy knew her only chance was through business, by working in an office and making a good impression. Krassy's life in the Yards had developed within her a shrewdness and cunning.

She had no illusions about a woman's place in a man's world. She was used to the idea of men drinking, lusting, squandering pay checks, mistreating their children, and beating their wives. Krassy knew that what she would get, she must get through a man.

"I'll get a million dollars," she told herself fiercely. "I'll get it and I'll keep it. But first I got to meet the guy who's got it." She knew that she didn't dress right, her English was incorrect, she was uncertain of "what was etiquette." But she also knew that she had that mysterious power of attracting men ... of looking at a man and making him want her. In that power was her weapon ... and her fortune.

But first she must get a job. Krassy scoured the secretarial schools until she found the Goodbody Business Institute which offered a course in typing and shorthand for one hundred dollars.

"That includes the use of the typewriters, paper, and music," explained Miss Goodbody. "It also includes me dictating to you for shorthand exercises." It was the cheapest course that Krassy could find, so she took it.

"Do I have to pay for it in advance?" asked Krassy.

"I never had a student that could yet," said Miss Goodbody. "But you can pay me twenty-five dollars a month; as a matter of fact, you *better* pay me twenty-five bucks a month ... or no course."

Krassy enrolled with Miss Goodbody, under the name of Karen Allison. She was sorry she'd told Miss Dukes her name was Katherine Andrews, but she hadn't had time to give much thought to a name when the landlady had asked her. She had realized Krassy Almauniski would never do; she must have a name that sounded good ... *refined* like. In her room at night, she'd thought about it. Finally, she decided on Karen Allison. She kept the same initials, because it would be easier to remember until she became accustomed to it.

Krassy started going to Miss Goodbody four hours a day, to practice typing and shorthand. Grimly she sat hour after hour typing to the rhythm of a phonograph record, or sat taking dictation while Miss Goodbody read ancient letters aloud, or quoted from small volumes of adages, proverbs, and jingle poetry. At night she studied her shorthand book at home, trying to burn the symbols in her memory.

Then she met Larry Buckham.

As she was entering her room, a tall, slender young man was descending the narrow stairs from the tower room. He stopped and stared at her for a long moment. In his hand was a small camera with a flash attachment. Krassy stood, hand on her door, her face upturned toward Buckham on the stairs. Suddenly he raised his camera and the flash bulb exploded in light before her eyes.

"Good Lord," he said, "do you live here?" He lowered his camera and started to remove the burned bulb from it.

"Yes," replied Krassy, "do you?"

"Right upstairs there ... in the tower," he said. "Come on up ... let me take some more shots of you."

"Some other time," said Krassy unlocking her door, "you were going out."

Buckham followed her into her room and sat down on the straight-backed chair, holding his camera on his lap. "It wasn't anything important," he said. "Each Thursday night I go down to a Camera Club meeting. I'd rather stay here and take your picture."

"Is photography your hobby?" asked Krassy.

"No," said Buckham, "it's my job. I work for the *Daily Register*. But I want to get out of the news business and get into commercial photography. There's more money ... and more fun ... in doing covers, advertisements, portraits, and things like that."

Krassy removed her coat and hat and hung them back of the cretonne curtains. "When are you going to start all this?" she asked.

"Just as soon as I get enough dough saved up. It takes a hell of a lot of money to open a studio. Cameras and equipment cost like the devil.... I've got some money now, but not enough. Say," he exclaimed, "have you ever done any professional modeling?"

"No," said Krassy.

"I know some photographers that could probably use you. I'll be glad to introduce you to them. You can pick up a lot of dough that way if you're any good."

"I'm not good," replied Krassy. "I don't know anything about it."

"It's easy," said Buckham. "Of course, you could go to a modeling school, but I wouldn't advise it. It costs too much money and they give you a lot of stuff you'd never use. You know...." he waved his hand disparagingly.

"What do you mean?" asked Krassy.

"Oh, stuff like this," and Buckham unfolded a paper he had in his pocket and started turning the pages until he came to an advertisement. "Here's one from Monica Morton's Modeling School: Be Charming ... Be Beautiful ... Be Lovely ... Be A Cover Girl! Yattata, yattata, yattata. Get this: Feminine Charm Program! Figure Control, Posture and Walking, Voice and Diction, Style Co-ordination, Individual Make-up, Individual Hair Styling, Personality Development, Social Graces and Etiquette ... and so forth and so on! That's a lot of malarky! All a photographer wants is something that photographs well."

Krassy had stopped in the middle of the room. Her head was tilted slightly to one side; her gray eyes were looking straight at Buckham, but she didn't see him. She was seeing something, perhaps, in a world where Larry Buckham and photographers didn't exist. "Maybe you're right," she said softly.

"Sure, I'm right," said Buckham. "Why waste all that dough? You know, I could teach you enough about modeling and posing for you to get by."

"All right," said Krassy suddenly, "I'll pose for you, but I won't pose for anybody else. I don't want to be a model."

Buckham was surprised by the intenseness of her answer, but he didn't argue with his good fortune. "Swell," he agreed, "come on up to the tower with me and I'll take a couple shots tonight." Krassy accompanied him up the stairs to the tower room.

It was a room about fifteen feet square, with windows on all four sides. Cream-colored drapes, operating on small tracks like a stage curtain, covered the walls as well as the windows. A large studio bed, which made up into a couch during the day, several easy chairs, a chest of drawers in black Chinese lacquer completed the room. Stacks of photographs, proofs, prints, and mats stood in all the corners.

"I've lived here about five years," Buckham explained, "and I sort of fixed this place up myself. I got in good with Dukes by taking her picture when I first moved in. I soft-soap her once in a while, and she's let me keep this room ever since." He pulled the drapes away from the windows on all sides of the room.

"It's like floating in your own private balloon up in the air," said Krassy.

"That's why I like it," he replied. "Incidentally, my name is Larry Buckham ... I've been so busy talking I don't even know your name."

"My name is Katherine Andrews," said Krassy.

Buckham began setting up his reflectors and equipment. That night he took fourteen portrait shots of Krassy.

By the end of the week, Krassy was eating breakfast and having dinner with Larry Buckham each day. He'd tap on her door in the morning and they'd walk to State and Division. In a little restaurant there, they would eat and talk until Buckham was late starting for his office. In the evening, they'd meet for dinner at one of the many small cafés on the Near North Side. Krassy was careful to eat well and solidly, but never expensively. With Buckham paying the checks, she had cut her food bill to exactly nothing.

Buckham was a tall, sensitive man in his late twenties, highly emotional. He was filled with great enthusiasm which was countered by periods of bleak despair. A good craftsman, he had buried himself deeply in a world with no horizon other than photography. This love and devotion to his work, he transferred to Krassy. Within a month after meeting her, he proposed.

"Let's get married, Kathy," he said. "I've got a good job ... I'm making ninety bucks a week. That's plenty to live on. You can give up that secretarial school and we'll find an apartment to live in."

"But what about your studio?" she asked. "If you married me it might be years before you could break away from your job."

"To hell with the studio!" said Larry. "I've saved up over three hundred dollars, and I've got about two thousand bucks already tied up in cameras and equipment. If we get married, it'll just take a little longer, that's all."

"All right," said Krassy, "we'll get married. Not right away, but we'll plan on it." Buckham took her in his arms and kissed her hungrily.

That night, after the rooming house was asleep, Buckham came to Krassy's room and stayed with her for the first time. He slipped silently down the stairs and gently scratched his fingers over her door, and when Krassy opened it for him, he tiptoed quietly in.

In the darkness of the room, and the privacy of her bed, Buckham buried his face in her breasts. "I love you, Kathy," he said. "You are everything in the world to me ... you're good, and desirable, and my entire life. You *are* my entire life ... I don't know what I'd do...."

Krassy held him closely to her and gently ran her small tongue around the outline of his ear working his passion to a frenzy. Then she gave herself to him. "I don't like it ... I don't like it," she told herself, "but maybe someday I will...."

Nightly, Buckham slipped quietly down the narrow tower stairs to Krassy's room. During the day, he lived only to see her at night. And each night, he helplessly watched for the gray dawn outside her window which would send him back upstairs to his own room.

"Marry me now, Kathy," he'd plead.

And Krassy would reply to him firmly, "Not yet, Larry, I've paid for my secretarial course and I want to finish it...."

"But why, Kathy? Why?"

"I know I'll never use it, but if we're married ... I wouldn't ever finish it. And I hate to ever leave anything unfinished."

One night as he was lying with his head on her arm, his face against her throat half buried in the long, golden hair which fell to her waist, Krassy told him, "Larry, I'm not going to let you make love to me any more ... until we're married."

"What?" exclaimed Buckham sitting up in the bed.

"It isn't right," said Krassy. "I don't feel right about it. After we're married ... then it will be all right."

"Don't you love me?"

"Yes, I love you, Larry. But I don't feel right about this ... I'm not that kind of a girl ... I've never done this before...."

"Good God!" he said, "I'll marry you tomorrow. I want to! How about it?"

"I don't think we should," said Krassy patiently. "I don't think we should get married until we are all ready. We should have a cute little apartment where we can live, and we should have the furniture all paid for, and everything nice."

"How long will that be?" asked Larry slowly.

"About six months, if we save our money and try hard."

"You mean I can't make love to you ... for six months?"

"Oh ... maybe once in a while, Larry. But not every night."

The next day Larry gave Krassy three hundred dollars with which to buy furniture. Krassy found a small furniture store which offered a "complete living room suite for only $298." Carefully she memorized all the details in the window ... an overstuffed davenport, overstuffed chair, two imitation walnut-finished end tables, a coffee table, a nine-by-twelve flowered rug, and a floor lamp. The furniture was cheap and shoddy, and Krassy knew it.

But Krassy didn't buy it.

Instead, she enrolled at Monica Morton's Model Bureau and School. She paid Monica Morton two hundred and fifty dollars, in cash, for the most expensive course she had. The remaining fifty dollars Krassy kept for her own needs. Her original hundred dollars had dwindled to less than fifteen.

That night, Krassy let Buckham into her room again. She described the living room set she had purchased in vivid, glowing terms, and drew little sketches of furniture arrangement and rooms for him, in the back of her secretarial notebook.

"They're keeping it for us," she said. "It's all paid for, and whenever we want it, they'll deliver it. I have the receipt and I'll put it away until we need it."

Larry kissed her. He was too happy to care what she did. But in the cold gray of the dawn, when he left her bed, he stopped for a moment and slipped the notebook, tenderly, in his pocket.

By September, Larry was impatient to be married. All summer Krassy had received ten or fifteen dollars a week from him. "We need a lot of little things ... mostly for the kitchen," she explained. "Dishes ... and silver ... and pots and pans. It all adds up, darling, but we must have them." Then receiving the money, she would stretch it out to cover her own expenses. She bought two inexpensive dresses at clearance sales, in conservative good taste, as Monica Morton had advised her. During the day, she worked increasingly hard at Goodbody's and she developed a careful competence in typing and shorthand. She owed Miss Goodbody fifty dollars on her tuition, but she had made careful plans to pay it.

Listening to Buckham's talk in the evening about commercial photography which invariably ended with fabulous stories about advertising agencies, Krassy soon decided it was a world where she belonged. A world where art directors received $25,000 a year salary and copy chiefs $40,000; where account executives and vice-presidents had incomes ranging up to $100,000 a year on the big accounts. Some of the stories were true, some were false, some were hearsay, others were wishful thinking which had become part of the advertising legend.

At Monica Morton's, Krassy heard much the same stories. Legendary stories of girls who made their fortunes posing for national campaigns, and whose pictures were recognized in every home in the nation. If Krassy did not want to become a model, she at least wanted to become a part of the world of this Aladdin's Lamp and meet the men who rubbed it. She began to canvass the big Michigan Avenue agencies ... looking them over, evaluating the stories about them, making up her mind.

Among the biggest, the most gaudy, and the most incredible was the firm of Jackson, Johnston, Fuller & Greene. This was the company, Krassy decided, she would work for.

By fall, Krassy had purchased all the theoretical living room furniture and kitchen equipment possible. Larry, in a sudden spurt of independence, had decided that his own bedroom furniture, in the tower room, was good enough for them to start. He was urging Krassy to set a definite date for their marriage.

"In a month, Larry," she promised. "We'll get married then and be together for always. But I do need some new clothes, and I've been trying to find some material to make them. I want to be married in a new dress...."

"I'll buy you a new dress," said Buckham. "I'll buy you anything you want."

Krassy shook her head demurely. "That wouldn't be right, darling. After all we're not married yet ... and it would be bad luck for you to buy my wedding dress...."

"What difference does that make?" he demanded.

Krassy shrugged her shoulders. "None, probably," she admitted, "perhaps I'm just superstitious." Then suddenly her face brightened. "I know what we could do," she said, then she pursed her mouth sadly, "noooo ... that wouldn't be right, either."

"What are you talking about?" asked Buckham.

"Well," said Krassy, "we could open a charge account at one of the big department stores. We could say I was your wife, and then when the bill for my dress comes next month, we'd already be married and it would be all right for you to pay it."

"That's a swell idea," he agreed. "I'll meet you tomorrow at noon and we'll open an account."

A few days later, Buckham received two charge-a-plates in the mail. One for Mr. L. A. Buckham, and one for Mrs. L. A. Buckham. He proudly gave the plate to Krassy. "Okay, honey," he said, "here's that wedding dress of yours."

Krassy was very busy. First, she bought a plain white smartly tailored dress and a dramatic hat to go with it. They weren't expensive and she showed them to Larry. He was enthusiastic.

Then she rented a small, one-room apartment on East Delaware Street, registering as Karen Allison. The rent was $80 monthly, in a respectable building, and she paid a week's rent in advance when she took the apartment. "I'll pay you the balance by the end of the week," she told the manager, "when I move in."

Day by day, Krassy had made purchases at the department store; a set of matched, white leather luggage; a small gold wrist watch; a gold cigarette lighter; a portable radio; a traveling iron; an onyx and seed pearl dinner ring; a pair of fox furs. She was careful to select nothing too expensive, but the total came to nearly twelve hundred dollars. By pawning them, she received three hundred dollars in cash.

"But I need something for myself," she thought. She bought and charged two new suits, two matching pairs of shoes, a cocktail dress, and a smartly styled black coat. The clothing she carefully stored in her new apartment on East Delaware.

At Miss Dukes, mail was delivered twice each day. The postman left it in a heavy iron box on the front steps, and Miss Dukes would carry it in to the wobbly, round table in the hall. As the roomers returned home at night, they'd stop at the table and sort through the mail. On the first of the month, Krassy made a special effort to be the first person to go through the mail, both morning and afternoon. On the third of October, a bill from the department store arrived; it was addressed to Mr. L. A. Buckham. Krassy quickly snatched it from the rest of the mail and concealed it under her coat. Reaching the safety of her own room, she tore open the envelope. It was a statement for over twelve hundred dollars. She carefully shredded it into small pieces and flushed them down the bathroom stool. She kept flushing it until the last small piece of soggy paper had disappeared.

That same day she called on a small printer located on Grand Avenue, just east of the lower level off Michigan. She arranged with him to print her a dozen letterheads and envelopes on a heavy, expensive bond paper, social correspondence size. The letterheads read:

GERALDINE K. VAN DOREN
1444 LAKE SHORE DRIVE
CHICAGO, ILLINOIS

After additional consideration, she added the Whitehall exchange of Miss Goodbody. It was her home telephone number which Krassy had found listed in the telephone directory.

The printer wanted to set the letterheads in type, but Krassy insisted that a copper engraving be used. The engraving, Krassy discovered, cost a great deal more than type, but she was willing to pay for it.

The printer shook his head at her extravagance. "It won't cost you a couple dollars extra to print up a hundred letterheads," he said.

"But I only need a dozen," replied Krassy.

"You already got the cost of the copper plate," the printer argued, "and it don't cost hardly anything to run off the extra paper."

"A dozen will be more than I need," said Krassy.

The printer finally gave up in exasperation. Krassy only smiled to herself.

The morning of October fifteenth, Krassy failed to meet Larry for breakfast, and she left the rooming house considerably later than usual. It was a beautiful day with a light fall haze in the air. Two blocks away, the lake was rolling in long, slow swells, picking thoughtfully at the concrete breakwater. As Krassy stood for a moment on the steps of Miss Dukes, she saw an elderly man, obese, with straggling white hair hanging beneath a pinched brown hat set squarely on the top of his head. He was turning up the walk, looking at the number of the house.

Something in his manner, or perhaps it was her own instinct, sounded a small note of warning to Krassy. The day was no longer beautiful, the haze in the sky turned the color of smoke from back of the Yards. She shivered and it wasn't from cold. As he passed her on the walk, she suddenly touched his arm and stopped him.

"If you're looking for someone in the house," she said, "I'm afraid there's no one home." She added, "I'm the last one to leave this morning...."

The old man turned impersonal eyes on her. They were rimmed in red and bloodshot. She could smell the raw, rank fumes of whisky ... fresh on his breath this morning. Politely he lifted his hat, in a brief tilt, and replaced it securely on his head.

"I'm looking for Mr. or Mrs. Buckham," he said.

So soon! Krassy thought. She hesitated for only a moment. "I'm Mrs. Buckham," she said. "Can I help you?"

"I'm a credit investigator," the old man replied, "I just wanted to stop by and pick up a check for your account at the store."

"My husband isn't home," Krassy told him, "and I can't sign a check. He'll send you one tonight."

He shook his head. "I'm sorry then," he said, "because I must see your husband. I'll have to go down to the paper to see him."

Krassy thought quickly. Then tears welled in her eyes, and choking back a sob she said, "I know I can trust you ... let's go someplace where we can talk." Fumbling for her handkerchief, she turned her face away. "I'm going crazy," she moaned softly. "When I tell you ... you'll understand."

The old man regarded her thoughtfully "All right," he said finally, "where do you want to go?"

"Not in the house. If anyone should hear, I'd die of shame. Let's go down the street and get a cup of coffee. I'm so upset, I haven't been able to eat...."

Silently, side by side, they walked down State Parkway to Division. Going into a chain drugstore, they seated themselves in a booth. Krassy ordered a cup of coffee, and the old man ordered nothing. "Well?" he asked.

"I don't know where to start...." Krassy said helplessly.

"You know it's pretty serious," said the old man, "ordering things deliberately if you know you can't pay for them. Mr. Buckham, unfortunately, opened a new account in the middle of the month. If the store had realized how high the charges were, in proportion to his reported income, it'd never permitted that large a bill to run up."

"He's a beast!" cried Krassy. "Oh, I hope you get him!"

The old man looked surprised. "That's no way for a wife to talk about her husband."

"I'm not his wife!" Krassy dropped her eyes in shame. "I'm not and I never will be." She put both hands to her mouth to repress her sobs.

The old man shifted in his seat uneasily. "Maybe you better tell me what you're talking about...." he suggested uncertainly.

Krassy opened her purse and removed a newspaper clipping. It was the story, with her picture, which had appeared in the *Stockyard Weekly News* concerning the beauty contest. Krassy had secured a copy of the paper and had kept the clipping. Now, in her hands, it became a deadly weapon. She handed the clipping to the old man and he slowly looked at the picture and read the story.

"That's me," said Krassy, "that was me just six months ago. After that picture appeared, Larry saw it. He came out to my house and asked me to pose for him. He's a newspaper photographer, too, you know?"

"Yes," said the old man, "at the *Daily Register*."

Krassy nodded. "He promised me that he could get me a lot of publicity ... and I'd make a lot of money. I believed him." Krassy stopped and wiped her eyes. "I even came downtown to live."

"Next he told me he loved me ... and I believed that, too. He said we'd get married. Then ... then ... after he'd gotten me all involved ... and made me live with him ... he said he'd never marry me until he had enough money to quit his newspaper job...."

Krassy's slender hands quivered on the table top, and the old man reached out and gently patted them. Krassy drew a deep, sobbing breath.

"I didn't dare go home. My father would kill me for being a ... bad woman. I had no place to go ... no one to take care of me except Larry. I loved him, Mr.... Mr.?" she stopped her story in a question.

"Moon," the old man replied, "Clarence Moon."

"God, how I loved him, Mr. Moon!" she cried softly. "Until he started to drink ... then he became a beast. One night he came home drunk. He told me he had an idea how to get enough money to start his own studio. If I helped, him, he promised to marry me."

The words were tumbling out easily now, one after another in a strong, damning thread. She rocked gently from side to side. "He said he'd open a charge account and get me a charge-a-plate. I was to go down and charge things, then take them out and pawn them for what I could get." Once again Krassy fumbled with her purse and placed a thick roll of pawn tickets on the table. Moon silently picked them up.

"I didn't want to, Mr. Moon ... I pleaded with him ... I begged him not to. He just laughed ... and then, he struck me!" She lifted her fingers and gently felt her lip. "He made out a list of things for me to buy, and every day he was at me to get them. The days I didn't go to the store, he'd get drunk and treat me filthy!"

"What about the women's clothes you bought?" asked Moon.

Krassy caught her breath. "He has another woman ... he gave them to her ... I know he gave them to her!" She spit the words. "But he made *me* buy them...."

Moon nodded gravely. "How much money does Buckham have?" he asked.

"I don't know," replied Krassy wearily, "but he has two or three thousand dollars worth of cameras and photographic equipment."

"That will help," Moon said. He searched her beautiful tearstained face. The anguish and despair he saw there convinced him. Slowly he stood up from the table. "Maybe I shouldn't do this," he said. "Perhaps I'm just a sentimental old fool. I never married, so I never had a daughter. If I had, I hope that she might have looked like you ... only have better sense. I'm going to have Buckham arrested on a larceny charge," he paused. "If I can't find you, I can't have you arrested, can I?" he added.

"No," said Krassy, "you can't.... "

"Well, suppose we just forget this talk we had and you disappear someplace where I can't find you. Like going back home to your dad."

Krassy smiled with sudden hope. "Oh, yes ... yes!" She, too, stood and standing on her toes kissed the old man on his forehead. "Thank you, Mr. Moon," she whispered, then turning she walked swiftly out the door.

For a moment Clarence Moon stood by the table. Reaching inside his coat pocket, he pulled out a small medicine bottle marked "cough syrup." He took a long drink from it. The smell indicated a high alcohol content. It might even have been straight alcohol.

Krassy hurried back to Miss Dukes and packed her suitcase. When she left, no one saw her go. She caught a cab and rode directly to her new apartment on East Delaware.

That afternoon the police arrested Larry Buckham. They didn't believe very much of what he tried to tell them. If it hadn't been for Miss Dukes, Buckham might have been sent up. Between the *Daily Register* and Miss Dukes, the police withdrew charges when Buckham sold all his photographic equipment and paid the store in full. The store was happy to drop proceedings, even if old man Moon did want the book thrown at Buckham.

Buckham was canned from the paper.

When he left town, he didn't have even a Brownie No. 2 Kodak to take with him.

CHAPTER FOUR

part 1 Danny

I didn't waste any time getting over to Jackson, Johnston, Fuller & Greene. I didn't go that same afternoon I talked to Goodbody, but I did go the next day. I was following Krassy now into places where it was going to be tougher to get people to talk. I knew I had to look better, and have a better story than the one I'd been using if I was ever going to get past the reception desk at the advertising agency.

After I left the business school, I went home and got out my blue suit and took it down to the corner and had it pressed. Then I went to see a young guy I knew who was working for an insurance company. I'd first met him a couple years before when I was taking some courses in night school; I was trying to make up for leaving school so early and lamming it away from home. And this guy, Cage, was in a couple of the classes, too. I liked him, and we used to go out and have a couple beers once in a while.

We talked about this and that for a couple minutes, then I said, "Look, pal, you got to give me some kind of an identification card ... something that shows I'm working for your company."

"I can't do it, Danny," he said, "the company's strict as hell about that."

"You got to," I told him, "it's plenty important and I promise you won't get any kickbacks on it." I explained about just starting my own business. "I got a big collection to make," I lied, "and I been trying to trace a deadbeat. I lost him but I know where I can pick up the string again. I got to have some identification or I won't be able to get anybody to talk."

"There's nothing phony about this?" he asked.

"Naw," I said, "all I want is just some identification so I can ask some questions." We talked about it, back and forth, and finally this friend of mine agreed to get me a card. He was a nice guy and worked as a file clerk in the Northern Transcontinental Insurance Company office. He sneaked an employee's identification card out of the supply room and gave it to me to fill out. When I got through with it, it read:

THE NORTHERN TRANSCONTINENTAL
INSURANCE COMPANY
Chicago, Illinois

Name of employee:	Daniel April
Position:	Claims adjuster
Years employed:	Nine
Height:	5'-11"
Weight:	175
Hair:	Black
Eyes:	Blue
Distinguishing marks:	None

Signed by: *George M. Cage*
Executive Vice-President

Naturally, George M. Cage was the name of my pal. When he saw I'd signed his name, he got sore. "For Christ's sake, Danny," he said, "I'll get kicked the hell out of here if anybody sees that!"

"Nobody's going to see it," I told him. "Besides if any guy should call and check up on that card, he'll ask for whoever signed it. Right?"

Cage wasn't sure about that.

"This way, he'll talk to you and you can vouch for it," I added.

Cage still didn't like it. He didn't like it at all, but he agreed to let it ride, and back up my story if I needed him. We shook hands and I promised I'd meet him later and pop for drinks and something to eat.

That night, at my rooming house, I polished up my story a little, and thought about Krassy. I wondered what I'd do if I ran into her at the advertising agency. But after thinking it over I decided she probably wasn't there. Ten years in one job is a long time. She was probably married by now, had six kids, and was big and broad across the beam. It made me sick to think about it.

I took out the old newspaper clipping and the glossy print I'd gotten from Monica Morton and looked at them. She was lovely; and I'd lived with her in my mind so long that I felt I'd known her all those ten years. I got thinking what it'd be like to have a gal like that. Maybe she wouldn't want to live on what I could make. But that wasn't being fair to Krassy! Look at what she'd lived in at the Yards. She'd been engaged to some newspaper punk until he got himself in a jam. I didn't blame Krassy for busting her engagement. If a guy gets in trouble with the law once, he'll probably do it again. Krassy was too nice a gal to be married to a potential con. If she loved a man, what he had didn't make any difference; I knew she was that kind of a girl.

All night long I rolled and tossed, and in the morning I didn't bother to go to my office. I made myself wait over three cups of coffee until it was ten o'clock, then I went over to Jackson, Johnston, Fuller & Greene. The offices covered the twenty-ninth, thirtieth, and thirty-first floors in a big, plushy building on Michigan. The reception room was located on the twenty-ninth floor, and when I got off the elevator, I walked down the marble hall and through an Old English doorway. Inside, seated behind a neat little desk, was a burnished redhead. My newly pressed blue serge suit didn't fool her for a minute. She gave me the old one-two with her eyes and looked bored.

Her desk had six or eight telephones on it. Nothing else. Every couple of seconds, a phone would ring and she'd say, "Yes, Mr. Blunt.... You'll be back at eleven-thirty. Thank you." Or, "Yes, Mr. Harris.... No. No one called while you were out. I'll check you back in." She kept this up with hardly a pause, and then she'd scribble figures on a couple typewritten sheets that had long lists of names on them.

"How do you keep 'em all straight?" I asked her.

"I don't," she said briefly.

"I'll bet you do a pretty good job of it," I said and grinned.

She began to thaw a little. "I don't make many mistakes," she admitted.

"Do they all have to report to you?" I asked.

"Sort of," she said. "Everyone is required to report when they're out of their offices, or leave the building. That way, if something important comes up, we know where they are, or when they'll be back."

I agreed solemnly. "By the way," I said, "my name is Danny April. I thought I'd have to see the office manager, but you'll be able to help me even better."

"What do you want?" she asked.

"I'm trying to locate a Miss Karen Allison."

"Does she work here?"

My belly dropped. "She did work here," I said.

The redhead came right back. "I've been here three years, and there hasn't been a girl by that name since I started."

"Maybe I'll have to see the office manager after all," I said.

"Mr. Bard has charge of the office force," she said. "Did she work in the office ... or was she on the creative staff?"

"What do you mean by creative staff?"

"Was she a copywriter, a radio writer, an artist? Did she work in production ... printing, engraving?"

"Hell, I don't know," I said. "But I think maybe she worked in the office."

She started to get suspicious. "Are you a personal friend of hers or something?"

"No," I said, "but I want to do her a favor. I want to pay her some dough, and I can't find her." I handed her my Northern Transcontinental Insurance card. She glanced at it briefly. "Her aunt, Mrs. Joan Harmon Allison, from Minneapolis, died and left her as beneficiary ... a small insurance policy. But we've been unable to locate Karen Allison. This was the last address we had for her."

The redhead relaxed. "They're pretty strict around here about giving out information," she said. "I'll see if Mr. Bard will talk to you." She picked up a phone, jiggled a couple times and got the switchboard. In a moment she was talking to Mr. Bard and she explained what I wanted. Then she turned back to me. "He'll see you," she said. "His secretary will be out in just a moment." I sat down on a long, leather davenport, and by the time I'd reached the middle of an old copy of *Time*, Bard's secretary came out of a little side door and motioned to me.

"This way please, Mr. April." I followed her down a series of halls, with doors opening off like rabbit hutches. Occasionally harassed-looking guys, with bunches of paper in their hands, would bound out of the doors and down the halls like their pants were on fire.

"Busy, huh?" I said to the secretary who was padding along with a sure homing instinct.

"Not particularly," she replied. "They do that all the time." Eventually we reached an office door, marked in gold letters H. R. BARD. She opened the door and waved me in. I walked into a fairly small office, containing a double-sized desk, settee, two lounge chairs, a small drum table with a brass lamp on it. All around the base of the lamp, ivy and small cactus had been planted. On the walls, in groups of six and eight, pictures in matching frames were hung. The whole effect was to give you enough room to take a breath ... if you stood sideways in the middle of the room.

Back of the desk, old man Bard was making a big show of reading some correspondence. I could hear his stomach rumbling halfway across the office ... as if someone was blowing through straws in the bottom of a glass. After counting maybe to forty, he slowly raised his eyes and said, "Yes?"

I showed him my card and went through my explanations all over again. "What's the number of your office?" he asked. I gave him the Insurance Company's number which I'd memorized. "Then ask for Mr. Cage, he's the executive vice-president," I told him. Bard kept his eyes on me and started to reach for his phone. When he saw I didn't care if he called, he dropped his hand and said, "Well, I guess we don't need to bother about that. However, here at Jackson, Johnston, Fuller & Greene we're very careful about talking. You understand, don't you, that we serve some of the greatest corporations in America. We know their innermost thoughts and secrets; we have information which is strictly confidential. Besides, it has never been our policy...."

"I'll give you eight, five, and even we got more dough at the Northern Transcontinental Insurance Company than you've got at Jackson, Johnston, Fuller & Greene," I cut in.

He sat and looked at me for a moment, his mouth still open for his next words.

"Besides," I continued, "all I want to know is if you got a girl working here named Karen Allison. It's got nothing to do with the color of next year's lawn mowers."

Bard started to laugh. "All right, April," he said, and then laughed some more. I thought the guy was a little touched. "We don't have Miss Allison with us anymore."

"She did work here?" I asked.

"Yes."

"How long?"

Bard thought it over. "I think she was with us for about three years," he said. "She started sometime in 1940 and it was late in the fall of 1943 ... somewhere around there ... that she left."

"Where did she go?"

"I don't know."

"What'd she do? I mean what kind of a job did she have?"

"She started out as our receptionist," he said. "Then she was promoted to personal secretary to Mr. Collins."

"Who's Mr. Collins?"

"Mr. Collins is vice-president of Jackson, Johnston, Fuller & Greene," he explained seriously and with some awe in his voice. "He's the account executive on the Joy Drug account ... one of the largest advertisers in the world."

"Those the guys who make Joy Toothpaste and cold tablets ... and that stuff?"

Mr. Bard winced slightly. "Yes," he said, "that *stuff* ... and a lot more."

"Could you give me the last address you had for Miss Allison?" I asked him.

Bard pressed a buzzer, and in a moment the secretary who'd guided me to his inner sanctum popped back through the door. He told her what he wanted. She popped out. Bard and I sat and looked at each other without anything to say. Finally, his phone rang and he picked it up. Reaching for a pencil he scribbled an address on a memo pad. He hung up the phone, tore the sheet off the pad, and handed it to me. "That's the last address we had for Miss Allison," he said. "I'm afraid it won't do much good," he added, "it's seven years old."

I thanked him and stood up. Just as I reached the door, I turned and said, "Do you think it would be possible for me to see Mr. Collins? Maybe Miss Allison might've dropped a hint where she was going?"

"I'm sorry, April, but I think you're wasting your time trying to see Mr. Collins," Bard replied. "He's a very busy man ... he hasn't time to see anyone ... he hardly has time to see himself."

"Look, Mr. Bard," I said, "sure, Mr. Collins is busy. But suppose Miss Allison needs this money? Suppose she's sick ... or out of a job? Even a big man like Mr. Collins wouldn't object to taking just one minute to help a young gal get a break."

"Perhaps not," said Bard and shrugged. "I don't think Collins ever took time to be human to anyone. Anyhow, I'll call and try to get you an appointment." He called the switchboard and asked for Collins' office; he successfully got past a secretary and was talking to Collins. He was no longer as impressive, nor as glib, as when he was talking to me. Bard talked to Collins with a hell of a lot more respect to his face, than he'd talked about Collins to me. He told Collins about me, and then said, "He wants to see you at your convenience, Mr. Collins, when you're not busy. I told him you probably wouldn't be able to see him." Collins said something and Bard hung up with a surprised look. "Collins said for you to go on up to his office," he told me. "Do you know where it is?"

"No," I said.

"It's on the thirty-first floor," he explained. "I'll have Miss Pierson show you up." He buzzed, and his secretary popped back in his office again. I followed her through the maze of corridors to the elevators. We caught one to the thirty-first floor. Here there was another, smaller reception room presided over by a blonde. She, too, was seated at a small desk, but it only had three telephones on it. Miss Pierson handed me over to her and gave her instructions concerning my delivery. As she left, she waved her hand at me. "If you can't find your way out, chum, just call Peerless Pierson, girl pathfinder." She caught a passing elevator and disappeared.

The blonde walked out from behind her desk and pointed down the long, broad hallway. "Mr. Collins' office is at the very end, to your right."

"Thanks," I said and walked in the direction she pointed. At the end of the hall was a heavy, walnut-paneled door with the name "Stacy H. Collins" lettered on it in a signature ... a copy of Collins' own writing. I knocked on the door and entered a small office, knee-deep in carpeting, with an efficient-looking secretary seated at a desk. She was middle-aged, wore glasses, and was pounding hell out of a typewriter. She looked up from her work, and I told her who I was and that Collins was expecting me. She checked with Collins and said, "Mr. Collins will see you now." She got up from her desk and opened another door for me.

It opened into Collins' office. A huge, corner job with windows on two sides. Venetian blinds hung at the windows, and over the blinds were drapes. There was a big fireplace in the office, with a long settee in front of it flanked by end tables and lamps. Several groups of chairs, with cocktail tables, stood around in it, and in one corner was a big, walnut carved desk.

From this desk, you could look up the Outer Drive nearly as far north as the Edgewater Beach Hotel, and trace the shore line of Lake Michigan as far as you could see. Off to one side of the desk, with the door slightly ajar, was a private shower and dressing room. Directly behind the desk was a small, cabinet bar with a freezing unit and ice cubes. It was one hell of a fine layout.

Collins was a fairly good-looking guy, somewhere in his middle forties. He was short, stocky, and his square face wore a smooth, emotionless expression. He had a good tan, which looked fine with his thick, black hair which was growing white around the temples. Nothing moved in his face ... no emotion, no expression. Except for his eyes. He had bright, black eyes which looked hot and tired ... and wary. They didn't go with his empty face at all.

I introduced myself, which he acknowledged with a nod, but he made no effort to get up and shake hands. I explained to him about the insurance payment for Karen Allison. Halfway through my spiel, he cut me off. "Bard told me all about it," he said. "What do you want to know from me?"

"I understand Miss Allison was your secretary for a while?"

"About two years," he replied.

"Well, Mr. Bard didn't know where she might have gone ... and I thought maybe at some time she might have said something about her future plans to you."

"Not that I remember."

"Did she ever mention any place she'd like to live ... or go for a vacation? Anything like that?"

Collins leaned back in his chair. He opened a box of cigarettes, selected one and lit it with an expensive silver desk lighter. "It's been so long since she left that it's hard to remember," he said exhaling a deep breath of smoke.

"Did she write you after she left?"

"No," he said, "there was no reason she should."

"Did she say why she was leaving?"

His eyes burned at me hotly, but his face didn't change. The phone rang and he picked it up. He gave several short answers and hung up. He paused for a moment, "She said she was leaving town and that was all," he said finally.

That stopped me. Was this the end of the line? I tried to keep my face and voice steady. "She didn't say where?"

"No." He stopped for a moment and seemed to be listening. "Come to think of it," he went on slowly, "I have a feeling it might have been New York."

"Was she a good secretary?"

"Excellent."

"Didn't she ever use you for references?"

"Never."

I turned toward the door. "Thanks for your time, Mr. Collins," I said.

His voice didn't change; his face was expressionless. "I'm afraid I wasn't much help," he replied indifferently. His voice hung in the air for a few seconds and he reached for his pen on the desk and started signing some letters. Deliberately he laid his pen to one side and turned back toward me. "You know, April," he said, "I've often wondered what happened to Miss Allison. I hope you find her. If you do, I'd like to know."

"You would?" I asked.

"It isn't important," he shrugged, "but I'd be glad to make it worth your time ... just for my own curiosity."

Leaving the building, I walked out to Michigan Boulevard feeling lower than hell. There was only one chance left. I pulled out the old address Bard had given me. It was in Oak Park. I caught a bus going down Michigan and transferred to an el. All the way out to Oak Park, I thought about

Krassy. I thought about that bill Clarence Moon had marked paid; I thought about Katherine Andrews studying with Monica Morton and living at Miss Dukes'; I thought about Karen Allison studying with Miss Goodbody and working at Jackson, Johnston, Fuller & Greene, and living in Oak Park. Oak Park is a good Chicago suburb ... and a long, long way from the Yards, in more ways than distance.

When I got off the el in Oak Park, I caught a cab; I didn't know my way around the suburb and I had no idea where Krassy's old address was. The cab pulled up in front of a good apartment building; it wasn't big, but it was good. It was four stories high, with three apartments to each floor ... two in the front of the building, one in the rear. By the mailboxes were listed the names of the tenants, but there wasn't any "Karen Allison." In the basement there was a buzzer marked "Phillip Fromm, Supt."

I rang the button and waited.

In a few minutes there was a clicking at the heavy plate-glass door leading into the building from the lobby. Opening the door, I went down a short flight of stairs. At the foot of them, a door was open and an elderly woman poked her head, nearsightedly, out of it.

"Is Mr. Fromm in?" I asked.

"No," she said. "He went downtown and won't be back for a while, and if you're looking for an apartment there ain't no vacancies."

"I'm not looking for an apartment," I told her, "I'm trying to locate a former tenant who lived here by the name of Allison."

"Nobody here by that name," she said.

"I know that," I said, "but maybe she left a forwarding address."

"How long ago was she here?" the woman asked.

"About seven years ago."

"We only been here a little over four years ourselves," she said.

"Who was superintendent before your husband?"

"I don't know," she said.

"Does your husband?"

"No."

It seemed hopeless. I was getting very tired, but I made one final effort. "Who's the rental agent for this building?"

"Bromberg & Spitz," she said, "downtown in the Loop. They got offices downtown in the Loop," she repeated and closed the door.

That night I had dinner with Cage. We ate in a cafeteria "Why so sad, junior?" he asked me. "Haven't you located that guy you're after yet?"

"No," I said.

"Which reminds me," said Cage, "I want that card back."

"I got to keep it," I said, "I'll give it back to you in a couple days. It looks like I'm washed up on this deal, but I got one more try to make tomorrow.

I got to call on a real estate outfit by the name of Bromberg & Spitz."

Cage nearly choked on his coffee. "Jesus Christ," he said, "don't flash that card around that office! We do a lot of business with them."

"You do?" I asked.

"You're goddamned right we do," Cage replied. "I see letters from them every week in the files. We insure a lot of their stuff. It runs into big dough!"

"Who writes the letters from Bromberg & Spitz that you see?"

"Some big shot name of Keeley."

"Do you know him?"

"Hell, no. I don't know anybody over there. I just file letters they write to the insurance company." He slapped his cup down on the table. "Listen, Danny," he was alarmed, "don't go getting me in trouble."

"I won't, pal," I told him. We finished eating and I paid the check. Afterward we bowled, and I beat Cage three games, but I still paid for the games. Then I popped for a couple beers, and called it an evening. I went home and went to bed.

The next morning I called Bromberg & Spitz and asked to talk to Mr. Keeley. He answered the phone in a deep, booming voice.

"This is Parks at the Northern Transcontinental," I said.

"Yes, indeed," boomed Keeley, "and how are you, Mr. Parks?" He didn't know me from nothing, but the way he sounded I was an old Boola-Boola chum of his.

"I'm wondering if you could give us the name of the superintendent who had charge of your Oak Park Building in 1943?"

"Which building?" asked Keeley.

I gave him the address. "If he is still employed by you, could you please give us his present address, too?"

"Is anything wrong?"

"Not a thing," I told him cordially. "Just a routine matter regarding a lapsed policy. I hate to put you to any bother, but you can probably clear it up for us in a few minutes ... otherwise, it might take us a long time."

"I understand. No bother at all, I assure you," said Keeley. I'll have my secretary call you back."

"That'll be fine. Many thanks!" I said. I took a beat, but not too slow, because I didn't want him to hang up. "On second thought," I continued, "maybe I better call her back in half an hour or so. I'm just leaving the office ... and I might be gone the rest of the day. Thanks just the same." I hung up. Fast. Because I didn't want him to suggest she could leave the information for me.

I fidgeted around my office for forty minutes, wrote a couple routine letters, made some other phone calls, and then called back to Bromberg & Spitz. I asked for Mr. Keeley's secretary and she got on the phone.

"Oh, yes, Mr. Parks," she said. "Mr. Keeley asked me to get some information for you. I have it right here. The superintendent you're referring to is Frank Royster. He was moved to another building in 1946."

"Is he still there?"

"Yes," the girl replied. "He has charge of the Lake Plaza Apartments, 6103 Sheridan Road."

"Thanks," I said and hung up.

I managed to keep busy the rest of the morning. At noon I swallowed a sandwich and gulped a cup of coffee. Then I caught a Sheridan Road bus to 6100 north. The Lake Plaza Apartments was another small, four-story building, jammed in between a big building on the corner and a large mansion to the north. I found Royster's name and punched his buzzer. A tall, lean guy with an overhanging nose, and a long, sharp jaw looked at me from the other side of the locked lobby door. His eyes were plenty unfriendly. I motioned for him to open the door. Grudgingly, he did so.

"Are you Royster?" I asked him.

"Yes," he said.

"Mr. Keeley, at Bromberg & Spitz, sent me out to talk with you personally," I said. I could see the name Keeley meant plenty to him. He forced a smile on his ugly face and opened the door wide.

"Come on down to my apartment," he invited. I followed him to the basement where he opened an apartment door. It was small, neat and clean, but there was a "feel" around it of a bachelor's apartment. You can't put your finger on it, but you can feel it.

"You're not married?" I asked.

"No," he said, "I never got around to it." He sat down on the neat, overstuffed davenport and waved me to a matching overstuffed chair. I offered him a cigarette; he took it, and I struck a light for both of us.

"It's important I get in touch with a Miss Karen Allison," I told him. "She's a beneficiary to a policy issued by my company ... the Northern Transcontinental. She lived in the building at Oak Park while you were there, I believe." I was watching him carefully.

"Yes," he said. He looked uncomfortable.

"Do you remember her?"

"Pretty well," he admitted. "She was a good-looking dame." He swallowed and his big Adam's apple jumped up and down.

"She moved in 1943, didn't she?"

Royster stared at the end of his cigarette and was obviously thinking back. "Yes," he said slowly, "it was in 1943 ... sometime in the fall. I think she had an October lease."

"Did she say where she was going, or did she leave a forwarding address for her mail?"

"No," he said. "She didn't leave any word of any kind."

"Did she have a furnished apartment?"

"All those apartments were unfurnished," he said. "She didn't have no worries ... she had plenty of furniture."

"Did she sell her furniture when she moved?"

"I don't think so."

"Then she must have moved it," I told him. "Do you remember the company that hauled it away?"

For a long time he was silent. He started to say something, then changed his mind. "No," he said finally, but he didn't look at me when he said it. "I don't remember the company."

I had a strong hunch he was lying. I jumped to my feet and jammed my hat on my head. "Goddamn it, Royster," I shouted, "you're lying! Just as sure as God made little green apples, for some reason you're lying ... and I'm going to report it to Keeley. You're holding up a court process, and I hope Keeley kicks your ass out of this job!"

"Now ... wait a minute, wait a minute!" said Royster. His face was mad, but he didn't let himself go. "I can't help it if I can't remember...."

"I'll be a stuffed son-of-a-bitch if you can't remember," I told him. "You remember something all right!"

"Sit down," he said, "and let me think." I sat down and waited while he went through a routine of thinking ... to save his face. Finally he said, "I don't remember the name of the company that sent the truck...."

"So you *do* remember something," I said. "At least, now, you remember there was a truck!"

"Why, yes ..." he said, "I remember a truck coming for it, now. But it wasn't any of the companies I was familiar with."

"What do you mean?" I asked.

"Well, when most people move they usually use a moving company that's pretty close to them. Or from the same general area, at least. It's cheaper ..."

"Then you didn't recognize it, huh? It wasn't from Oak Park?"

"No," he said, "it wasn't from Oak Park."

"If you remember well enough to know it wasn't from Oak Park, you got some idea what it looked like."

"I don't remember," he said.

"The hell you don't," I said. "I want you to tell me what that truck looked like. What color was it?" He didn't know.

"Listen, Royster," I told him, "I'll find that truck. I'll find it whether you tell me or not!"

"It was green," he said.

"If I find it and it isn't green ... I'll not only have you fired ... I'll work you over, myself ... personally!"

"Hey, wait a minute," he said, "maybe it was blue!"

"So now it's blue? You sure it was blue?"

"Yes," he said.

"What was the name on it?"

"I don't remember that. If I did I'd tell you."

"What else do you remember about it?"

"Well, there was a wide white stripe, maybe a foot wide, painted all around the top of the truck ... just under the roof."

"Anything else?"

"No."

"You sure?"

"Yeah...."

"Okay," I said. "I'm not going to bother to thank you. But, brother, if you been lying to me ... you'll see me again." I walked out. He was still seated when I left.

The next day I started in on that old telephone. I got a list of all the moving companies from the 1943 classified telephone directory. There were between five and six hundred of them. I didn't know where to start, so I just started at the top of my list and worked my way down. I'd call a number and ask for the manager. When he got on the line, I'd say, "I'm with the Chicago Safety and Traffic Council. We're making a survey regarding the color of trucks and night driving. What colors are your trucks painted?" Right away the guy would tell me. My next question would be, "Have they always been painted that color?"

I found out that usually a company kept the same color year after year ... sort of like a trade-mark. Most of them used red, orange, or yellow. I'd thank 'em and hang up. If they said their trucks were blue, I'd ask if they used any stripes of white on them. Some of them did, but none painted a stripe of white right under the roof.

Some of the companies had gone out of business, but most of them were still kicking. When I called the Lima Trucking Company, three weeks later, with my three-hundred-and-sixty-seventh nickel, I found they painted their trucks blue, with a white stripe under the roof. They always had painted them that way as long as they'd been in business.

The next day I went out to see them. They were located on the West Side and were an average-sized outfit. The Lima Trucking Company offices were in a big storage warehouse with the same name painted all along one side. In the office, a thin anemic-looking guy in shirt sleeves and vest came up to the counter to see what I wanted. I showed him the card from Northern Transcontinental, and gave him the usual story of the insurance policy.

"Of course," I said, "I know it'll take a little work to look up your records, but I'll be glad to pay you for your time."

"Sure," he said, "what do you want to know?"

"See if you moved furniture for a girl named Karen Allison from Oak Park, around the first of October in 1943?"

"It'll take a little time," the guy said.

"How long?"

"Maybe an hour. What was the Oak Park address?"

I gave it to him. "I'll walk up the street and get something to eat," I said. "I'll be back in an hour."

Fifteen pinball games later, I returned and he tossed one in my face. "Nope," he said, "as far I can find out, we didn't move any Karen Allison."

"You're sure?"

"Yes," he repeated.

"Did you move *any* dame from that address?"

"Sure. One named Candice Austin."

I fumbled the cigarette I was lighting. "In October, 1943?"

He cleared his throat. "Yes," he replied.

That was it! It couldn't be a coincidence. Krassy had changed her name again; this time she'd dropped the "K" initial but she'd retained the same sound with a "C." Using "Austin" instead of "Allison" was running true to form. She'd probably taken it from Austin Boulevard in Oak Park.

"Where'd you move this Austin woman?" I asked.

"Some stuff we moved to Evanston, but most of it we brought down here and sold, from the warehouse," he said.

"Do you have the address in Evanston?"

"Sure," he said. He went back and picked up a big, canvas-bound ledger with pink sheets of flimsy paper; he started leafing through it. In a couple minutes he raised his head. "It was the Lake Towers Hotel in Evanston," he told me.

"Thanks," I said. I gave him five bucks.

CHAPTER FOUR
part 2 Krassy

Krassy moved into the apartment on East Delaware. It was small, with a living room that held a hideaway bed, and a small sliding door which opened to a tiny Pullman kitchen. But there was a large bathroom with a shower, and a large closet which was more than sufficient to hold her limited supply of clothing. But her wardrobe was growing. Including the dress and hat with which she had left the Yards the spring before, she had bought two new dresses during the summer, and the white dress and two suits which she had charged to Larry Buckham. She was so happy with her new clothes, her apartment, and her new freedom that she forgot Larry Buckham, Miss Dukes, and Clarence Moon.

She promptly called on Miss Goodbody, taking with her several sheets of the engraved stationery she had ordered made up. Miss Goodbody amiably agreed to write her a letter of recommendation.

"What do you want me to say?" she asked Krassy.

"Write to whom it may concern," said Krassy. "Just say I've been your social secretary for five years and I'm honest and trustworthy ... and if anybody wants additional information to call you."

Miss Goodbody sat down at her desk, and dipped a blunt, stub-nosed pen in black ink. In a cramped, slightly illegible hand she wrote:

> To Whom It May Concern:
>
> Miss Karen Allison has been employed by me in the position of social secretary for the last five years. In that period of time, she has proved a fine employee in every way ... capable, conscientious and dependable. It is with deep regret that I find it impossible to continue with her services. If any prospective employer should care to call me for additional information, I'll gladly give my complete recommendation concerning Miss Allison.
>
> Sincerely,

"You want me to sign that Van Doren name?" she asked Krassy.

"Yes," Krassy told her. So Miss Goodbody added the signature of "Geraldine K. Van Doren."

"You won't forget that name if anyone calls you at home and asks for it?" Krassy was anxious.

"Of course not," said Miss Goodbody. "In the first place, no one hardly ever calls me, and then I'm not used to being called Missus," she laughed.

"And you'll give me a good send-off?"

"Don't worry, dear," Miss Goodbody replied. "When I get through, they'll think you're Katherine Gibbs, herself."

With absolute composure, Krassy presented herself at the office of Jackson, Johnston, Fuller & Greene. With assurance in each step, she marched down the marble hall on the twenty-ninth floor. Dressed in a smart black suit, her blond hair burnished and shining, she matched the girl at the reception desk stare for stare.

"I'd like to see the office manager," Krassy told her.

The girl was the first to drop her eyes. "Do you have an appointment?"

"No," said Krassy, "I don't. But I'm looking for a job and I'd like to make an application."

"What kind of work do you do?" the girl asked.

"I'm a secretary," Krassy replied.

The girl looked surprised. "Oh," she said, "I mean you'll have to see Mr. Bard. He's in charge of hiring all the office help, with the exception of the people in the creative end."

"May I see Mr. Bard?" Krassy asked.

"Just a minute," the receptionist told her. She picked up one of the many phones on her desk, and asked the switchboard for Mr. Bard's office. "Hello, Mr. Bard," she said, "this is the twenty-ninth floor reception desk. There's a girl here looking for a secretarial job. Do you want to see her?" There was a slight, disapproving tone in her voice which Krassy resented. After a slight pause, the receptionist added, "Yes, Mr. Bard ... I'll tell her."

Krassy knew that Mr. Bard was not going to see her. She reached out suddenly and picked the phone from the receptionist's hand. "Pardon me, Mr. Bard," she said, "I'm Karen Allison ... Mrs. Van Doren's secretary."

"Mrs. Van Doren?" asked a man's voice on the other end of the wire. She could feel him struggling to attach significance to the name.

"Yes," said Krassy, "Mrs. Geraldine ... K.... Van Doren." She managed to put just enough importance in her inflection. Immediately, she felt the reaction from the other end.

"Oh, yes ... certainly. Mrs. Van Doren," replied the man's voice in artificial recognition.

"I've been her social secretary for five years," said Krassy, "but she's leaving for Mexico and isn't taking me with her. She said that even if you couldn't give me a job, you knew so many people ... that you might tell me who to see ..." Her voice trailed off helplessly.

"Why, certainly ... certainly," said the man's voice. It sounded pleased and important ... and now that no job was to be requested, it sounded relaxed.

"I'm very busy today, but if you'll wait a few minutes I'll be glad to talk to you."

"Thank you," said Krassy. "I'll wait." She replaced the phone and met the receptionist's angry stare. "Thank you, too," said Krassy politely.

She crossed the reception room and seated herself on a long, modern divan with a red lacquered coffee table in front of it. Idly she leafed through a magazine. In a short time, a secretary appeared and escorted her through the numberless corridors to Mr. Bard's office.

"How do you do, Mr. Bard," she murmured. "I'm Karen Allison."

"Yes indeed, Miss Allison ... won't you be seated?"

Krassy seated herself sedately and with her ankles neatly touching each other. She leaned forward in her chair and placed Geraldine K. Van Doren's letter on the desk. While Mr. Bard read it, Krassy made up her mind about him. She read him as easily as he read the letter.

"Hmmmm," he cleared his throat, "very nice, very nice. I'm trying to remember when I saw Mrs. Van Doren last...." he said.

"I don't know, Mr. Bard," she replied. "Mrs. Van Doren has so many interests ... it might have been either business or social."

Mr. Bard nodded his head in agreement, but his face remained slightly puzzled.

"The only job I've really had," said Krassy, "was with Mrs. Van Doren ... and I hardly know where to start to look for another." She lowered her head and looked up at Mr. Bard from under her delicate brows.

"You do type, don't you?" asked Bard.

"Oh, yes! And I take dictation, too. I handled all of Mrs. Van Doren's correspondence ... both social and business. It was very heavy, you know...."

"Can you do a hundred words a minute?" asked Bard.

"Easily," replied Krassy with complete honesty.

"Really, Miss Allison, I wish I could help you...." said Bard beginning to slide into his turndown. But Krassy headed him off.

"That's wonderful, Mr. Bard," she said with enthusiasm and smiled at him brightly. "I knew you'd help me. Already I feel at home in this beautiful office...." Bard attempted to regain control of the conversation while Krassy continued breathlessly. "Everyone here seems so nice ... it will be wonderful to work here ... and I know you'll be the swell—the finest boss in the world!"

"We have no bosses here at Jackson, Johnston, Fuller & Greene," Bard pronounced sententiously, "we all work together. I always pride myself on not being a boss...." He stopped suddenly and caught his tongue. He was trapped.

"You'll always be my boss," said Krassy in deep admiration, "and I'll always love it."

Mr. Bard was uncomfortable, but it was with difficulty he repressed the desire to throw out his chest and strut like a turkey around his desk. "We have a very large office force now," he said slowly, "I don't know just where we'll be able to work you in...."

"Any place, Mr. Bard," Krassy assured him. "I'll be happy to do anything you want."

"Well," said Bard lamely, "see me tomorrow at nine o'clock."

"Thank you," said Krassy. For a moment she stood in his doorway and looked at him fondly. She smiled. Bard smiled back. "I'll see you tomorrow," she said.

"Yes," agreed Bard. After she was gone, Bard sat in his chair and wondered what he was going to do with her. "God!" he told himself in surprise, "I didn't *mean* to hire her." He decided to call Mrs. Van Doren ... maybe there was still an out. After he had finished the call, Krassy was still hired.

Krassy became the receptionist on the twenty-ninth floor reception desk. Miss Brandywine, the receptionist of the previous day, was given two weeks' pay and ... with deep regrets from Jackson, Johnston, Fuller & Greene ... was informed her services were no longer needed. Krassy took over her desk and duties which consisted of checking all personnel, including executives, in and out of the office; maintaining contact with the thirtieth and thirty-first floors; and holding an impregnable line of defense against all salesmen who wanted to make appointments.

Krassy was viewed with suspicion and distrust by the other women employees. Miss Brandywine had been popular with her women co-workers and the story of Krassy "getting her job" soon became common office knowledge. Krassy ignored her current unpopularity and concentrated on her work. She was always pleasant ... especially to Mr. Bard, who hurried past her desk each morning and seemed slightly embarrassed. After that first interview with Krassy, he never again saw her privately.

As Krassy became increasingly familiar with the office procedure of the advertising agency, she heard daily the magic name of Stacey H. Collins. Collins was vice-president of Jackson, Johnston, Fuller & Greene, and controlled the business and billing of the great Joy Drug empire. Collins had married the daughter of Hugh Stanton, president and chairman of the board of the drug company. The day he married Virginia Stanton he received the Joy Drug account. One week later, he became vice-president of Jackson, Johnston, Fuller & Greene. Collins, however, was not a remittance man; he had the background of fifteen years' experience in the advertising business. He was energetic, aggressive, and capable.

Collins was also ambitious.

Krassy was ambitious, too. She decided that Stacey Collins was a man worth knowing. To that end she made her plans, but she had patiently to await their maturing. Collins' office was on the thirty-first floor; he was seldom seen on the twenty-ninth. The first time Krassy saw him hurrying down the marble corridor, he swept past her without a glance. He was trailed by two harried copywriters and an art director. All were talking and arguing.

"He doesn't know I'm around," Krassy thought. "But he will!" she added to herself. Collins was a man with a square build and powerful body which controlled a tremendous driving power. He wasn't a tall man, but he wasn't short, either. Around five feet, nine inches tall, he walked with a thrusting stride of assurance. Krassy quickly evaluated his black, fierce eyes; the stiff, dark hair; and his intense face. "I must think about this," Krassy told herself. And she did.

Four months later she stopped Mr. Bard as he passed her desk in the reception room. "May I see you for a moment, Mr. Bard?" she asked the office manager.

"Certainly, certainly...." he replied. Bard stood for a second visibly hesitating about asking her to his office. Finally he asked, "What can I do for you, Miss Allison?"

"I understand Miss Moore, the receptionist up on thirty-one, is leaving," Krassy replied.

"Yes," said Bard, "she's getting married."

"If you haven't already arranged for a girl to take her place, I'd like to be transferred up to her desk," Krassy told him.

"Why?" asked Bard. "It doesn't pay any more salary than you're making down here." Krassy was earning $42.50 per week.

"That's all right," Krassy replied, "it isn't the money. The agency ... and all the work that goes on ... well, it fascinates me. I'd just like to know more about it. And then, maybe, someday I'll be more valuable to the company."

Bard beamed his approval. "I like to hear young people say that!" he said. "It proves they're thinking right. They have the right spirit. I'm sure you have a great future ahead of you, Miss Allison."

"Thank you," said Krassy demurely. "I ... I hope you're right."

When Miss Moore left, the girls in the office all chipped in and bought her an automatic toaster which sat on a large, stained-walnut tray. The tray had a wonderful little device that neatly trimmed the crusts off the bread.

The coolness which had surrounded Krassy on the main reception desk did not follow her to the thirty-first floor. Here were half a dozen typists together with the personal secretaries of the officers, and account executives, of Jackson, Johnston, Fuller & Greene. Sandwiched between the twenty-ninth and thirty-first floors was the busy, rushing, hectic, bubbling, grouching, half-mad thirtieth floor which housed the "creative departments."

In neat little stalls, like blooded stallions, row upon row of copywriters pounded typewriters and squeezed dry their brains in an eternal search for new ideas to be used in their newspaper and magazine copy. In equally neat stalls, soured radio writers wrote repetitious commercials and grouched about "this whole goddamned business." Carefully protected from the public by glass partitions, a row of artists and layout men daily turned out artwork with the wonderful, mechanical precision of machines ... only occasionally exploding into a heated uproar.

A mastermind, from the executive department, had conceived the brilliant idea of subscribing to a wired music service to relieve the dread monotony. He had read an article stating where such a music service had also increased the efficiency of the workers in an iron pipe manufacturing plant eighteen per cent.

The service was installed in Jackson, Johnston, Fuller & Greene, and from 10:00 A.M. to 11:00 A.M. each morning, and from 2:00 P.M. until 4:00 P.M. each afternoon, the artists were fed a steady diet of phonograph records.

During the daily concerts, the artists made up new lyrics containing the largest selection of pornographic words possible. These they sang to the wired music accompaniment at the top of their voices.

At first, the copy chief, the radio director, and the art director had all protested ... not only to each other, but to their individual staffs. When the art director called down one of his artists about it, the others left their boards and gathered around to listen.

"Look," explained the artist who had just succeeded in setting a new lyric about a revolutionary type whorehouse to the music of 'Ah, Sweet Mystery of Life,' "I'm drawing this dame here. Who am I drawing it for?"

"For Re-Newal Form Brassieres," replied the art director.

"Sure," agreed the artist, "and she's got to have a big set of knockers, right?"

"Well ... right."

"Okay," said the artist, "a couple more songs like that and she'll have the biggest set of knockers you ever saw ... and the client will be so hot he won't go home for a week!"

Gradually the copy and radio departments formed the habit of joining the art department on good rousing choruses, and the sound of the singing drifted up to the sanctimonious thirty-first floor. After a month, the wired music service was discontinued.

Krassy seldom ventured into the wilds of the thirtieth floor. The appraising eyes of the artists made her uncomfortable. The writers with practiced ease coined words, phrases, and double talk that made her feel unschooled, uneducated. She felt the great holes gaping in her unfinished education, but she carefully preserved a serene, untroubled face. A sense of security would follow her return to her desk in the quiet dignity of the thirty-first floor, after one of her few trips to the creative departments.

From the first day, at her new desk, Krassy had made it a point to greet Collins by name when he appeared in the morning. Coolly, efficiently she would say, "Good morning, Mr. Collins," then await a reply. The first morning Collins stopped in his stride and looked at her. "Good morning," he replied briefly and then hurried on. Krassy never varied the routine. Eventually, Collins asked her name, and after that he would reply, "Good morning, Miss Allison."

One afternoon, Mrs. Collins stopped in the office and asked Krassy to announce her. Virginia Collins was a tall, slender woman with an easy grace. She wasn't beautiful. Krassy thought she was hardly even attractive. She had a long, thin face, rather full lips, and brown eyes. Her eyebrows were natural and full, plucked only across her nose. Her light brown hair was cut short and waved casually around her face. She was wearing a cream-colored mink coat thrown carelessly over her shoulders, with the sleeves hanging empty at the sides. Under it, Krassy could see a knitted, sea-green suit.

"So that's the Mrs. Collins?" Krassy watched her walk down the corridor and turn into her husband's office. "I don't think she's so much...."

Krassy had been at Jackson, Johnston, Fuller & Greene a little over six months when she first saw Virginia Collins. In that time, she'd never gone out with any of the men that worked for the agency. All the executives were married; only in the creative departments were there single, unmarried men. At the Christmas party, which Krassy attended shortly after she'd started working at J. J. F. & G., she had met many of them. One by one they'd asked her to dinner in the months that followed. But Krassy was not interested. She wanted no entangling alliances; she desired complete freedom to work out her plans concerning Collins.

But as the months went by, Collins remained as unapproachable as the first morning Krassy had spoken to him. She became restless and worried ... financially. The money she'd received from Buckham was nearly gone. She had stretched her small salary endlessly to pay her rent and keep her clothes together. Her meals, usually sandwiches and coffee, she ate in her apartment; at the office she missed lunch entirely. After some consideration, Krassy decided there was one copywriter with whom she might have an occasional dinner.

Tim O'Bannion was one of J. J. F. & G.'s senior copy men. His writing sparked many of their top campaigns. O'Bannion was an easy, insolent

Irishman, cynical of each product and service of which he wrote. He wore mismatched slacks and jackets, usually with moccasin-type shoes sporting heavy rubber soles. He consumed four packs of cigarettes a day, but drank only in moderation. At thirty years of age, O'Bannion made a salary of $18,000 a year, which he promptly spent on one woman after another. Meeting a new woman, he would stay with her just long enough to thoroughly explore her body, and pick her mind clean of ideas, thoughts, and inhibitions. As soon as he felt he completely knew her, he promptly lost interest.

O'Bannion and the girl always parted on the best of terms; sometimes he would call her up after a year, and she was usually glad to hear from him. O'Bannion had met Krassy at the Christmas party and been attracted by her. His invitations had been politely refused. He then started to drift by her desk on the twenty-ninth floor, from day to day, stopping to talk to her. When she moved to the thirty-first floor, Tim moved his calls with her.

"Ah, Karen," he would say,

> ... Thy beauty is to me,
> Like those Nicaean barks of yore,
> That gently o'er a perfumed sea....

He would stop, stare at her, and suddenly ask: "Then what the hell did all those little boats do?"

Krassy, embarrassed and ill at ease with the poetry, would attempt to ignore the question, but O'Bannion would pin her down and delight in her squirming. "Now ... now, Karen ... or may I call you Miss Allison? This is the jack-pot question. What did all those stinking little boats do? Go out and sink themselves?"

Krassy would be forced to admit she didn't know the quotation.

"Why, Karen," O'Bannion would rejoice, "I think you're illiterate, I'm disappointed ... I'm disillusioned ... and for your information all those little boats

> The weary, way-worn wanderer bore,
> To his own native shore.

Krassy, angry at the closeness of O'Bannion's barbs, would busy herself with her phones. O'Bannion would wait patiently until she was finished.

"How about having dinner with me tonight, Karen?" He'd throw a leg over the edge of her desk and blow great clouds of smoke in the air, while waving aside her refusal. "Just think, Karen," he would say, "along with your dinner, I'll give you a free lecture on American poetry."

Or O'Bannion would suddenly appear at her desk and reach in his bulging jacket pocket. Carefully he would remove sheets of scrawled notes, short stubby ends of copy pencils, a cigarette lighter, a package of cigarettes, and a large bunch of keys. Finally, he'd present her with a bunch of slightly withered violets.

"I know they're not much, Karen," he would say seriously, "but after all it's the sentiment that counts. What does it matter that I removed them from the cemetery this morning?"

Krassy would watch him warily, not knowing if he was serious. Leaving the violets, O'Bannion would return to the thirtieth floor.

The night Krassy first had dinner with O'Bannion, he called for her at her apartment. She made him wait in the lobby. When she appeared, he made no mention of his long wait and suggested the Continental House, a restaurant famous for its food. O'Bannion appeared to be well known and the headwaiter welcomed him cordially. Throughout dinner Krassy found herself listening to O'Bannion in rapt attention as he talked well on many subjects. When he took her home, he dropped her outside her building door and made no effort to kiss her good night.

But the next day, he sent her a dozen roses. They were awaiting her when she returned from work.

O'Bannion continued, thereafter, to take her out to dinner several times each week. Seemingly oblivious to her charm, he made no physical advances and contented himself with talking. Holding forth on books, the world, politics, the theater, art, science, ballet, and philosophy, he held her curiosity. Gradually Krassy relaxed with him and found herself looking forward to his dinners. She was interested in the new world which he opened up for her in his conversations. She began to read some of the books he mentioned. Several times on Sunday, he took her to the art museum and pointed out masterpieces and artists' techniques, giving her résumés of their lives. Krassy absorbed it all.

One evening O'Bannion appeared at her apartment carrying a small, portable phonograph and several albums of records. In his coat pocket was a wrapped bottle of Grand Marnier. He gave the phonograph to Krassy and presented her with the albums. "I thought you'd like this," he told her, "I didn't think you had one." It was the first time he had been in her apartment and he glanced around.

Krassy piled records on the phonograph, and O'Bannion opened up the tiny kitchenette. Taking four glasses from the metal cupboard, he filled two of them with the liqueur and two with ice water. Then seating himself on the couch, he handed a set of the glasses to Krassy.

"Try it," he said.

"What is it?"

"Grand Marnier," he replied. "You'll like it."

Krassy cautiously sipped the liqueur, and she felt the sudden, sweet warmth of it slip quickly over her. "It's good," she agreed, "I've never tasted it before."

"There're a lot of things you missed," he told her, "and the chances are you'll go right on missing most of them. Oh, you'll probably get what you *think* you want...." He stopped and shrugged. "Basically I'm just a sensualist. I like things I can feel, and taste and hear and enjoy. Nothing else is really important." He looked at her and picked up an album. "Maybe that's worse than being the way you are."

Krassy sipped her drink and stretched contentedly. "What albums did you bring?" she asked.

"Bach and Brahms," he said, "and a couple others ... Sibelius, Monteverdi and Couperin."

"Tell me about them," Krassy urged.

O'Bannion launched into a sweeping description. Sitting listening to the music, feeling the warmth of the liqueur within her, Krassy studied his face, his gestures, the play and rhythm of his words. She felt a restlessness building within her which was both new and strange. Occasionally his hands brushed her arms lightly and she found herself anticipating the next touch of his hands. "Why, I want him," Krassy told herself in surprise, "I want O'Bannion."

As he arose from the lounge to change the stack of records and pour more liqueur, she watched him move across the room to the tiny kitchenette. "All he does is talk," she thought. "He talks to me, and all he does is seduce me, rape me with words ... he's drugging me with restlessness, and creating a desire that doesn't exist. It never will exist except in my own mind, and it's turning everything wrong and upside down. He wants me. I know he wants me ... and all he has to do is reach out to me, but he never has. And now I want him. I want him worse than he wants me!"

O'Bannion returned to the lounge and sat down. His eyes touched hers briefly, and what he saw in them convinced him that he should reach out. With practiced ease he built her desire to a burning flame, then quenched it.

With her head on his shoulder, Krassy drew great sighing breaths. O'Bannion lit a cigarette. "Someday, Karen," he said, "you're going to be quite a woman." Krassy regarded his detachment with anger. But the restlessness and desire which had drained from her body, leaving only a drugged satiety in their place, were too strong to battle. She turned lazily on her side and put her arms around his neck.

"Do you love me?" she asked.

"I hope not," said O'Bannion.

"Why?" asked Krassy.

O'Bannion's sleepy blue eyes, wise in the loving of a score of mistresses, regarded her thoughtfully. "Probably I'm afraid of you, Karen," he replied. "Any man who gives himself up to your love is placing himself in a strange world. I don't know what you're looking for, my sweet ... and I'm not sure that I want to be the guy who helps you find it."

Krassy slowly flexed her fingers, curled and uncurled her toes. Luxuriously she strained her body tense, then relaxed it as a spring would uncoil. "Am I so strange as all that?" she asked.

O'Bannion suddenly arose. "Yes," he said, "you're as strange as all that.... You are the most beautiful woman I've ever known. You're too beautiful to be real." He regarded her intently. "Ah, perhaps that's the rub," he continued. "You're not real."

Krassy leaned on one arm and looked up at him. "What do you mean by that?" she demanded sulkily.

O'Bannion hunched his shoulders, then slowly dropped them. "I can't tell you, Karen ... I don't know myself. You look like a woman but you feel like a savage; you walk like a mannequin equipped with all the defense mechanisms of Freud. You listen ... you seldom talk. What kind of a woman is that? And I keep wondering ... why don't you talk? To hide your ignorance? I wish I knew. I don't know, Karen, really," he spread his hands gently from his sides, "but there's one thing I do know."

"What?"

"I want to see you again tomorrow night."

Krassy smiled to herself.

But Krassy smiled too quickly.

She took O'Bannion for her lover but she never succeeded in dominating him. O'Bannion spent several nights each week with her ... taking her to the theater, opera, and ballet; he bought her books, and music albums, and presents ... many of them expensive. But never once did he give her money, and never once did she find out with whom he spent the other nights of the week.

Krassy looked forward to the nights which he would spend with her, and she found herself building an emotional ebb and flow around their life together. Within her, however, there were certain demands which O'Bannion never completely filled. Physically, he lighted fires which burned and left her breathless, but emotionally he escaped her hunger for domination. And it was this domination, this feeling of power ... in the moments of love when a man is subjugated to a woman's own desire and is helpless to find release without her consent ... that Krassy wanted. She wanted to see O'Bannion squirm in his need and desire for her, but she never did.

"I don't love O'Bannion," she told herself repeatedly. "I need him, but I don't love him." What was more important, however, Krassy respected him. Through O'Bannion she found her way into the worlds of music and literature and art ... all the things real and superficial ... which she knew so little about. She learned to use his phrases, and lifted in part and in full his ideas, likes, and prejudices. She took them for her own, and the fact that they represented an ultimate and sophisticated appreciation, based on education, income and opportunity, which she had never possessed bothered her not at all. Krassy, without knowing it, was adding a penthouse to a basement excavation without bothering to construct twenty solid floors in between.

O'Bannion's relationship with Krassy continued uninterrupted into the fall of 1941 ... and then Krassy made her first contact with Stacey Collins.

The offices of Jackson, Johnston, Fuller & Greene closed promptly at 5:00 P.M. for the office force. The executive and creative departments continued until their work was finished. One late fall evening Krassy had lingered at her desk until 5:30. The phone rang from the main switchboard. The operator was trying desperately to locate Anne Russell, Stacey Collins' secretary. Collins was calling from Cleveland and Miss Russell had left the office for the day. Finally, Collins asked to talk to the receptionist on the thirty-first floor if she was in.

"Miss Allison," asked Collins, "are you sure that Miss Russell has left?"

"Yes, Mr. Collins," Krassy replied, "she left about half an hour ago. Is there anything I can do?"

Collins thought a minute. "This is very important," he said, "and I'd appreciate it if you'd follow through for me. I have a meeting with the Joy people first thing in the morning. It's damned important and concerns our entire budget and schedule for next year. Somewhere I've misplaced part of my papers ... and I must have them. In my desk is a carbon copy of all the material bound in a dark blue cover. The book says (Proposals for Joy Drug, 1942). Please arrange to get that material to me by morning!"

"Yes, Mr. Collins," said Krassy, "I'll put it in the mail immediately...."

"To hell with the mail!" snapped Collins. "It may not be delivered in time. The board meeting is at ten o'clock in the morning. I'll have to leave my hotel by nine o'clock. That material has to be here by then. Get in touch with Miss Russell when she gets home and have her bring it. Tell her to fly over! Do you understand?"

"Yes, sir," she replied. "What hotel are you staying at?"

He told her and hung up.

Krassy caught her breath. "This is it!" she thought. She went to Collins' office and found the blue notebook in his desk. Placing it carefully in front of her, she sat down in his leather chair and called the airline reservation office. She made a reservation for the late night flight to Cleveland.

Krassy never called Miss Anne Russell.

She hurried to the twenty-ninth floor and explained to Mr. Bard that Mr. Collins had requested her to bring the material to Cleveland. Waving Collins' authority in Bard's face, she quickly obtained money for tickets and expenses. Then with the notebook and the money, Krassy returned to her apartment. Quickly she packed her suitcase, and left before O'Bannion appeared. She had a date with him that night. Catching a cab to the Palmer House, she checked her bag and had dinner. After dinner she went to a show until it was time to meet the airport limousine.

Shortly after midnight, Krassy knocked on the door of Collins' room in Cleveland. Collins, who had spent the evening drinking at a club with clients, was getting ready for bed. Half drunk, he wrapped a robe around him and opened the door. Swaying, he stared stupidly for a moment. "Miss Allison," he finally said.

Apologetically Krassy stepped within his room. "I'm sorry, Mr. Collins," she explained, "but I couldn't locate Miss Russell, so I brought the material myself. I knew how important it was...." She let the words trail away.

"Why ... thank you," said Collins. He stood inside the door looking at Krassy, confused by both the liquor and circumstances. Krassy brushed past him, to the center of the room, and unwrapped the package she was carrying.

Handing the notebook to Collins she said, "I hope this is the right material."

Collins looked at it and nodded his head. "Yes, that's it."

With a smile of relief Krassy said, "I wonder if I could get something to eat? The dining room is closed downstairs, and I didn't have a chance to eat anything in Chicago before I caught the plane...."

"Certainly," agreed Collins. "Where are you staying? Did you check in here?"

"I haven't yet," said Krassy. "I just arrived and came right over with your material."

"All right. I'll call room service and order you something," said Collins walking over to the phone. Beside the phone was a half-finished highball. He picked up the drink and downed it quickly. "It was nice of you to come," he said, "and after you've eaten, we'll get you a room here." He jiggled the telephone impatiently. "Hello? Room Service," he said, and proceeded to order Krassy a club sandwich and a pot of coffee. "Anything else?" he asked her. "They only have sandwiches and things like that this time of night."

"A sandwich will be fine," Krassy told him.

"If you don't mind, I'll have another drink while you eat," Collins said. He ordered up another bottle of soda. In a few minutes a waiter appeared with Krassy's food. After he had gone, Collins opened his suitcase and removed another bottle of Scotch.

"Here, let me do that for you," said Krassy taking the bottle from his hands. She poured a tremendous shot of Scotch in a glass, dropped in an ice cube, and splashed soda on top. She passed the glass to Collins who immediately took a drink. Krassy seated herself in a chair, and placed the sandwich and coffee on an end table by her side. She started eating her sandwich.

Collins sipped at his drink and watched her. "You are quite a person, Miss Allison," he finally said. "Tell me about yourself."

Krassy glanced up at him and smiled shyly. "I think you are a very amazing man, too, Mr. Collins," she replied, "I'd lots rather hear about you." She put her coffee cup down on the end table. "You know," she continued, "I've always admired you ... so very much. Suppose you tell me about yourself. I know it would be a great deal more interesting."

Collins finished his drink, and walked unsteadily to the dresser to pour himself another. "What do you want to know?" he asked.

"For one thing," replied Krassy, "I've watched you day after day in the office. You're always busy ... always rushing. Don't you ever get tired?"

"Yes," said Collins, "I get plenty tired. I get so goddamned tired I feel my brains turn to jelly. I get so fed up ... with the rush and the push ... and the details, I want to jump out the window. But I don't," he added.

"When you feel that way, then what do you do?"

"I go out and get drunk ... like now," Collins told her. "I get rip-roaring, deadly, rotten drunk until I can't think any more. Then it takes a day or two to get over my hangover, and by that time I feel better."

"Maybe you'd better have another drink now," Krassy told him. "You're tired and disgusted about something, aren't you?"

"Yes," said Collins, "I'm plenty disgusted. Clients expect you to be a witch doctor. You always have to have a magic remedy, a magic idea to settle their ills. It's all their own goddamn fault most of the time ... no foresight, no imagination. They fuss and fumble around and get one foot in the bucket, and can't get it out. Then they expect you to have some brilliant idea to pull them off the spot..." He finished his drink and handed the glass to Krassy, unconscious of his action. She took the glass, arose from her chair and mixed him another.

"They're always looking for a quick, easy way out," Collins continued. "They expect their advertising to make up for lousy sales co-ordination, expensive and wasteful manufacturing, stinking marketing and merchandising. Oh, what the hell!" He took another drink.

"Why do you do it?" asked Krassy.

He thought a moment. "Because I need the dough," he replied frankly. "It's the only way I can make all the money I want to make. Sure I beat my brains out, but they pay me for it ... they pay me plenty!" Collins was getting very drunk now, but he continued to speak clearly. Only his eyes were blurred and unfocusing.

"I'll have a drink now, if I may," said Krassy. "If you'll finish yours, I'll mix us both a round. Then I must be going."

Collins finished his drink and handed his glass to Krassy. Once again, she poured it half full of Scotch and added a little ice and soda. For herself, she poured a few drops to cover the bottom of her glass, and filled it with water.

Collins took his drink without question and slumped down on the side of the bed. Krassy, primly, took her seat once again in the chair.

"What do you want out of life, Miss Allison?" Collins asked suddenly.

"Oh, I don't know," replied Krassy. "I've never thought about it too much. A home and someone to love me ... just like any other woman, I guess."

Collins nodded solemnly. "You'll get it," he told her heavily. "You're a very beautiful woman. A beautiful woman can get anything she wants out of life...."

"Hurry and finish your drink, Mr. Collins," urged Krassy. "Then I must be going." Collins finished the whisky in his glass. Slowly, deliberately holding a steel control over each small motion, he placed the glass on the floor by the side of his bed. Straightening up, he held control for a moment longer, then with his feet over the side, he sank back until his head touched the covers. "Good night, Miss Allison..." he said, and passed out.

Krassy sat quietly in her chair and waited for fifteen minutes. Then cautiously she arose and walked over to the bed by Collins. She placed her hand on the side of his face and shook it gently at first, then with increasing force. Collins remained unconscious. Easily, quietly, Krassy removed his shoes and socks, unwrapped the robe he was wearing and slipped it off. Then pulling down the covers, she rolled the snoring Collins between the sheets. Darkening the lights in the room, leaving only the light in the bath which peeped through a nearly closed door, Krassy undressed. She hung her clothes deliberately around the room. Wiping the lipstick from her mouth with her fingers, she smeared the crimson in streaks across Collins' face.

Naked, she climbed in bed beside him, and promptly went to sleep.

At 7:30 in the morning the phone rang, and Collins rolled from the bed, staggering in his sleep to answer it. The polite telephone voice informed him it was seven-thirty and he was being called as he had requested. Hanging up the phone, he dropped wearily in a chair, and for the first time saw Krassy. A cigarette in his mouth, a burning match in midair, he exclaimed, "I'll be goddamned!"

"Good morning, darling," sang Krassy and stretched her rounded arms above her head.

"I'll be goddamned!" he repeated and shook his head to clear it. "Did you stay here last night?" he asked foolishly.

"Don't you remember?" asked Krassy.

"I don't remember much of anything," Collins said and ran a limp hand through his hair. "After you ate ... things are pretty hazy ... I, uh, thought I went to sleep. Say! Didn't I pass out?" he asked anxiously.

"Not for a while you didn't," replied Krassy with only a touch of insinuation in her voice. Collins stared at her. "You know, Stacey," she continued, "this isn't a very pleasant 'morning after' welcome you're giving me...."

"I'm sorry ... I mean, I ... oh, hell ... what is your first name?" he asked.

"Karen."

"Honestly, Karen, I don't remember a thing...." He took a deep drag on his cigarette. Krassy deliberately stretched again, carefully arranging that the sheet should casually pull away. The bleak morning light shimmered in silver along her body and turned to gold when it touched her hair. Collins stirred uneasily. "Did I ... I mean, we did ... uh, last night?" he asked.

Krassy laughed. "Maybe you've forgotten," she told him, "but I haven't!" She stood beside the bed and clutched her slip tightly to her body. "Order up some breakfast, darling, while I take a shower." She disappeared.

Sitting at a small, immaculately set table, heavy with linen and silver, Collins awaited her reappearance. When she returned, he drew up a bedroom chair for her and then reseated himself. Sipping a glass of tomato juice he regarded her seriously. "You know, Karen," he said, "I've laid myself open to a lot of trouble ... if you want to make it."

"I don't know what you mean," Krassy replied.

"Well," he hesitated, "I've never ... ever mixed business and pleasure before. It isn't good policy. Women at the office ... or in my clients' business, I've left strictly alone. It always causes trouble...."

Krassy bit deeply into a piece of toast, and sipped her coffee. "Really, Stacey," she said, "I'm free, white, and twenty-one ... I wanted to stay last night, just as badly as you wanted me to stay. I haven't asked for anything ... and I don't expect anything from you ... or anyone else!" Her voice became low and husky. "I knew what I was doing ... even if you didn't, evidently. I'm not sorry. I've always admired you ... and last night I felt I was a very lucky girl." Her voice picked up determination. "But last night is all over ... it's gone and past. Forget it completely if you like ... and I'll forget it, too." She paused for a moment and glanced up at him. Then lowering her eyes she continued, "I'll catch the first train back to Chicago."

Collins' thoughts and emotions were confused. The thought of her, as he had seen her this morning standing beside the bed ... he tried to shrug it away. And last night? He wished he could remember. Perhaps he was doing her an injustice; it made him uncomfortable. "She's a gorgeous thing," be told himself, "and maybe she isn't playing me for a chump. Maybe she *really* does like me for myself...."

Krassy didn't return to Chicago that day, or the next ... or the next. Collins called Chicago and explained to Bard that he was keeping Miss Allison over to do some urgent secretarial work in connection with the board meeting. Krassy did, however, return to Jackson, Johnston, Fuller & Greene two days before Collins.

A week after Collins' return, Miss Anne Russell, Mr. Collins' secretary, was transferred to other duties on the twenty-ninth floor. Collins explained it to Bard. "Miss Allison is on her toes," he said. "She bailed me out of a tough spot in Cleveland. I need people like that around me."

"Very true, very true," agreed Mr. Bard, "but I understand that Miss Russell went directly home from the office. She was home all evening and never received your message." He shifted uneasily under Collins' deliberate stare. "Well ..." he concluded, "I admit, she might be alibiing ..."

"It's not a question of alibis," returned Collins. "Miss Russell didn't deliver my material. Miss Allison did."

"Oh, yes," Bard agreed and cleared his throat. Damn my stomach, he thought, I wish it didn't rumble when I get nervous. "Miss Allison is a very fine employee."

After Krassy installed herself in her new office, one of her first callers was O'Bannion. He deliberately sniffed the air. "It's getting goddamned rarefied up here, isn't it, baby?"

Krassy shifted uneasily. "It's a wonderful break for me," she told him.

O'Bannion sunk his hands deep in his jacket pockets. "You're not the only one who's getting a wonderful break," he observed.

"Stop it!" she told him angrily. "It's a fine position. I earned it ... and I'm proud of it!"

"Look who's trying to kid O'Bannion," he told her quietly and walked out of the office.

Krassy saw Collins only one evening a week. Between his duties at the office, his trips out of town, and his appearances at home, Collins had little time for a mistress. O'Bannion continued to see Krassy several nights each week, drifting into her life and out of it in a quiet, thoughtful way. O'Bannion was still able to arouse her to heights of passion that Collins never touched. Krassy still wanted O'Bannion, still needed him. Occasionally she demanded his attentions in a peremptory manner. O'Bannion responded deliberately and detachedly.

Only once was the subject of Collins mentioned between them. Krassy, herself, brought it up. O'Bannion, who had failed to keep two consecutive dates with her, aroused her wrath and desire in equal parts. "You're still angry because I took that job with Mr. Collins," she accused him.

"I am?" he asked in surprise.

"Yes, you are!" stormed Krassy. "You hate Collins for being nice to me. You're jealous of him! But there isn't anything between us, darling ... honestly." She slipped her arms around his neck and looked serenely in his eyes.

"I'm not jealous of Collins," he replied, "and I don't care whether you sleep with him or not."

"How can you say that! Tim, you know I couldn't sleep with two men ... not at the same time! What do you think I am?"

"I don't know," O'Bannion replied.

Krassy drew back as if he'd struck her. "You don't?" she whispered.

"Look, Karen," O'Bannion told her, "I'm not criticizing you, I'm not judging you ... and I'm not in love with you. There are probably two billion persons in the world right now. Each one wants something out of life, and I suppose each one has certain ideas on how to get it. If, for instance, you want to sleep ... with an automatic water pump, like Collins, that's your business."

Krassy dropped the subject and never brought it up again. But she remembered O'Bannion's description of Collins and cursed him for it. Collins was like an automaton, she thought. Efficient, emotionless, pulsating with driving power and ambition, but incapable of lifting her to any heights of emotional response. Krassy by this time, however, had discovered an age-old, feminine secret. She hid her discontent with Collins, and forced herself into a display of emotion to please and satisfy him, and placate his masculine ego. The response she found natural to O'Bannion, she imitated and played back to Collins. Sometimes she thought O'Bannion knew this.

"Once I told you, you'd grow into quite a woman," he said with a cynical smile. "Baby, you're getting to the point where you can even fool yourself. That's quite a feat."

After several months, Collins became cautious about visiting Krassy in her apartment on East Delaware. "I'm too well known," he told her, "to get by much longer without getting myself in trouble ... and you talked about. I think you'd better plan to move, where I won't be running into people I might know."

"Yes, dear," Krassy agreed. "Where would you suggest I move?"

Collins, who lived with his wife in Winnetka ... north of Chicago on the lake, thought it over. "How about Oak Park?" he suggested. "I don't know many people out there."

"I can't afford to pay much for an apartment," Krassy told him, "and I don't have any furniture."

"Don't worry about that," Collins assured her, "find a nice, quiet place. If you need furniture, I'll take care of it." Krassy did find a nice, quiet place in Oak Park. It was a small, dignified building on a tree-lined, residential street. She was pleased with herself ... and pleased with Oak Park, a stolid, well-behaved, and stuffily respectable community.

Her apartment had a large living room, with a fireplace and a great picture window; a small, cozy dining room with French doors on two sides; two bedrooms and two baths; and a large, gleaming kitchen. One of the bedrooms she planned to remodel into a library and music room. The rent was $200 per month. Unfurnished.

When she told Collins about it, he gave her a check for a year's rent in advance. "Pay it yourself," he told her, "and keep the lease in your name. See about getting furniture for it." Krassy called on a smart decorator who had a small shop on Michigan Boulevard. His name was Cecil, and she told him what she wanted. Gently flapping his hands in the air, he ridiculed her conventional tastes. Krassy, who was impressed by his talk of moods, textures, fabrics, and balance, hastened to withdraw her own suggestions and left the matter of decorating and furnishing entirely in his hands.

Cecil finished with the apartment and Krassy was entranced with it. She had seen similar apartments only in the four-color reproductions of slick, home-furnishing magazines. When she received his bill, Krassy caught her breath, but Collins raised no objections. He gave her another check. "You know, Karen," he said casually, "you better plan how much you'll need to run your apartment each month. You can't do it on your salary."

Krassy admitted that she couldn't.

"Besides, you'll need new clothes occasionally," he added. "But I don't think we'll be going out very much," he concluded thoughtfully.

"I understand," said Krassy.

"I'm glad you do," Collins told her. "When I have the time to be with you, I want to relax ... to unwind, and take it easy. I don't want night clubbing, or entertaining ... or anything else."

"But you want me?" asked Krassy.

"Yes, Karen, I want you," Collins told her and put his arms around her. The discussion ended with Krassy receiving $500 a month extra to run the apartment and buy her clothes.

"He'll just take it off his personal expense account," Krassy told herself. She rather liked the idea.

The night O'Bannion first saw the apartment, he whistled. "I admire your taste," he told her seriously. "I imagine it took a great deal of work."

"Yes," Krassy said, "I'm very proud of it." She wasn't sure if O'Bannion was being satirical.

"I couldn't have done better myself," he admitted, "but frankly it's a little too feminine for me." He dangled his wrists and smiled. Then Krassy knew he didn't believe her.

"When are you leaving dear old J. J. F. & G.?" he asked after a pause.

"I'm not leaving. Why?"

"Oh, I just thought you might be...." O'Bannion was vague.

"I'm not leaving," Krassy repeated virtuously. "Why, with all this expense ... I'll need every penny I can make to pay my rent and get the furniture paid for." Collins had suggested, once, that she might leave the agency, but Krassy vetoed the idea. She wanted to maintain at least a reasonable front of being respectably employed. And she didn't want to be pushed completely into the background of Collins' life. At the office, she could keep in touch with him and his activities.

O'Bannion cheerfully accepted her explanation, and said, "Christ, Karen, I'll swap jobs with you." But his trips to Oak Park became fewer. On the evenings they were together, he made no effort to establish their old intimacy. Stretching out in a chair, he would talk for an evening on any subject that crossed his mind. At midnight he would leave, pausing only to kiss Krassy briefly on her lips.

After he was gone, Krassy would roll and toss in her bed wanting O'Bannion, her body burning. But she knew, too, that the days of the old relationship were gone. For her own good, and for the protection of herself with Collins, O'Bannion must leave her life. No longer her lover, no longer sharing a secret from Collins, Krassy considered O'Bannion a potential source of danger to her security.

One evening she asked Collins: "Do you know Tim O'Bannion at the agency?"

"The copywriter?"

"Yes," said Krassy, "he's the one."

"What about him?"

"Well," said Krassy, "I met him last year at the Christmas party. Before I met you, he took me to the opera several times. I never particularly cared for him, but he ... well, he kept pestering me, and I finally went out with him once or twice."

"Seriously?" asked Collins.

"Oh, no!" said Krassy, "but I guess he thought he was in love with me ... or something. I haven't seen him for a long time but lately he's started coming up to your office ... and bothering me again."

"What do you want me to do about it?" asked Collins.

"Well ... couldn't you transfer him?"

"You mean, fire him? Don't you, Karen? I'll see what I can do about it," Collins promised.

Collins never had the opportunity to follow through on his promise. That was the night of December 6, 1941. On December 7, there was trouble in Hawaii. On December 8, Timothy O'Bannion enlisted with the United States Marines.

Krassy never heard of him again.

By December 14, 1943, two years later, much had happened in the world, but little had happened to Krassy. She was waiting in her apartment in Oak Park for Collins to appear for dinner. Her life with Collins had become static. With increased responsibilities, Collins was working later hours at the office; he was staying away from his home longer; and he now spent most of his leisure time with Krassy in Oak Park. But the life was a secret and quiet one and Krassy was becoming bored. Collins was her only lover, and since O'Bannion had left, Krassy had never wanted another man. Through careful saving of her allowance and her own salary from the office, Krassy had managed to build a small, but creditable savings account. That had been her only accomplishment.

That ... and getting herself pregnant.

Krassy was pleased with the idea. Not that she intended to have the baby, but she was pleased with the weapon it gave her against Collins. That the weapon might be a two-edged knife which could cut both ways, she realized. However, it did steel her resolve to make a break with Collins.

She was waiting now to tell him. There was a knock at the door and Krassy opened it. The building superintendent, a man named Royster, was waiting there. "Good evening," he said, "I just wanted to tell you the wood for the fireplace finally came."

"That's nice," Krassy replied, "deliver it to me tomorrow."

"I can bring it up now," said Royster.

"No. Don't bother tonight."

"It wouldn't be any bother at all," he persisted.

Krassy looked at him with distaste. He was a tall, thin man with a sourly inquisitive face. She felt that Royster was too curious, too familiar with her. Deliberately she had kept apart from the other tenants in the building to prevent forming friendships which might lead to questions. Royster she had tried to keep at a distance, but she was uncomfortably aware of his probing. She felt that he knew about Stacey Collins, and although he treated her with an offhand respect, Royster never addressed her by name ... never Miss Allison. And she resented his air of confederation.

"No," Krassy repeated, "deliver it tomorrow. I'm expecting guests now."

Royster slowly appraised her, making no effort to end the conversation. "What time tomorrow?"

Krassy started to close the door. "I'll let you know when I get home from the office...."

Royster placed his hand on the door, stopping it short. Then he dropped his hand and turned at the footsteps in the hall. Collins was approaching. "All right," Royster said to Krassy, "I want to get it out of the basement." He walked away.

Krassy turned to Collins. "I can't stand that man!" she said.

"Who? The janitor?"

"Yes, Royster," she replied. "He gives me the shudders."

Collins walked in the apartment and removed his coat and hat. Krassy hung them neatly in the small hall closet. "Are you tired tonight?" she asked him.

"Christ! I'm always tired," Collins replied. He rubbed his hand over the back of his neck, and gently kneaded the muscles. "I've got a hell of a headache."

"Sit down, darling," Krassy told him, "I'll get you a drink before we eat" Collins half sprawled on a long, low modern divan. Krassy went to the kitchen and poured two martinis from a shaker which she kept in the refrigerator. To one she added an olive, to the other a small onion. Returning to the living room, she handed the martini with the onion to Collins. "You'll feel better," she assured him.

Collins smiled and lifted the glass in her direction. "Well, here's cheers anyway," he replied. Krassy seated herself across from Collins, watching him warily. She waited for a few minutes, until he had finished his second drink and started his third, before she began to lead the conversation in the direction she wanted.

"I wonder where this will all end, Stacey?" she mused.

Collins paid little attention. "The war, you mean? Oh, it'll end pretty much like all wars ... nothing accomplished, really ... and nothing gained...."

"No, I don't mean that," said Krassy. "I mean about us."

"I don't know," he replied. "Why, aren't you happy?"

"I feel like I'm living in a vacuum," said Krassy. "You and the apartment are my entire life. What life I have ... I have to live secretly. It isn't good, Stacey."

Collins sensed an urgency in Krassy's conversation. It made him uncomfortable. "Well," he conceded slowly, "we don't go out much ... maybe we should."

"No, it isn't that," replied Krassy. "It's a lot deeper than that ... it's hard to explain." Krassy stopped a moment marshaling her thoughts. She couldn't explain to Collins that she didn't care what people thought, because in her own devious way she did care. She cared a lot. She wanted a name, and security against ever returning to the Yards. She wanted independence from Collins whose word could turn her out of Jackson, Johnston, Fuller & Greene ... and who could close the door of her apartment in her face.

As far as morals were concerned, Krassy believed it was a matter of opinion ... her opinion. She believed in using her sex as other women used an education, or a trained talent, or social connections ... or hard work. These things, too, she couldn't explain to Collins.

Krassy realized she was facing herself, and Collins, in showdown. She hadn't planned it this way, but suddenly the situation was there. She couldn't keep the vacuum airtight forever. Already, little cracks and breaks were letting enough oxygen in to start her breathing again. Collins must face her problem, too. He must decide. But already, Krassy sensed, Collins' decision had been made. He had made his decision years ago, but it was necessary that it be brought out and discussed

"Well?" asked Collins.

Krassy, startled, looked up. "Oh," she said, "I was thinking. I've been thinking about it for several days ... how to tell you. How to be diplomatic ... if being diplomatic is important. And I guess maybe it is...."

"What are you trying to tell me?"

"Bluntly ... I'm going to have a baby."

Collins' face didn't change. He leaned slightly over the couch and set his martini glass on the cocktail table. "Are you sure?" he asked.

"Entirely," replied Krassy. "I've been to the doctor and I've passed all my tests with flying colors." She smiled briefly.

Collins was silent. The silence hung between them as an invisible glass partition. Krassy could see through it to Collins. For a moment, she wasn't sure that her voice could reach him, and she felt she was sitting in a perfectly insulated soundproofed room. "Say something," she said and her voice sounded heavy in her ears.

"There isn't much to say," he replied.

"There's plenty you could say."

Collins evaded her eyes. "What?"

"You could say you were happy ... and you'd marry me."

"I want another drink," he told Krassy. Rising from the divan he took his empty glass to the kitchen and poured a martini from the shaker. When he returned to the living room, Krassy hadn't moved. "I can't marry you, Karen," he told her. "You know that."

"I don't know it," Krassy said.

"But I'm already married...."

"Men have been divorced before."

"If I divorced Virginia, old man Stanton would cut my throat."

"You don't love her," Krassy told him.

"Perhaps I don't, but she's good for me."

"Good for you!" snapped Krassy. "She's good only for the Joy account."

"That's what I mean," Collins said flatly.

Krassy turned cold eyes upon him. In them, Collins thought he could read her contempt, but he was in error. Krassy's instinct had told her she could never break Collins away from his wife and her connections. Now she was trying to decide how far she could go ... how far to goad him ... before forcing the inevitable showdown. She was eying him intently, cautiously measuring him as a wary adversary.

"There's more in life than money," Krassy said. "I'd hate to think you didn't have enough ability to get another job. After all, is Virginia just a meal ticket?"

"You know better than that," Collins' voice assumed a patient, reasoning tone. "Sure, I could get another job, but never one like I have now ... and you like money and luxury just as much as I do. There are only a few advertising accounts which have the appropriation of Joy Drugs. It takes all kind of politics to get those accounts ... years of making contacts and pulling strings...."

"Even marrying," said Krassy shortly.

Collins assumed a different tack. "Look, Karen, why get all steamed up about this? We've had two good years together ... let's keep what we have. You can see a doctor, there're plenty of them. Have something done...." he shrugged the sentence off, unfinished.

"I don't intend to have anything done," Krassy told him.

"Good God! Why not? Women have operations ... like that ... every day!"

"Because I want the baby!" Krassy told him.

Collins argued her decision, but Krassy remained firm in her defensible position. Finally Collins told her, "If you have the baby, you can't stay in Chicago."

"I know it," Krassy said, "I think I'll go to New York. No one knows me there, and I'll simply say I've been married and divorced."

"How will you live?"

"You'll give me enough to live on," Krassy told him flatly.

Collins' face instantly became still and watchful. His black eyes searched her face intently. "Are you trying to blackmail me, Karen?" he asked softly.

"No," Krassy told him, "I won't do anything sneaky or undercover. I'll sue you right out in the open court!"

"That wouldn't be very smart," he replied.

"I know it," said Krassy, "but I'll do it, if there is no other way. You want to keep the Joy account, you don't want to keep the baby. All right! You keep your wife and your business, I'll take my freedom and my baby. But you, Stacey, are going to pay for it!"

They talked until late in the night. Collins wanted Krassy to remain, to continue their life together. But the break had been made, and the breach was complete as far as Krassy was concerned. This was her opportunity to make a break on her own terms. She made the most of it. Finally, reluctantly, Collins agreed to give her forty thousand dollars in treasury bonds, five thousand dollars in cash, and all the clothes and furniture in the apartment.

Collins didn't stay in the apartment that night ... or ever again. The next morning, at Jackson, Johnston, Fuller & Greene, Krassy handed in her resignation with two weeks' notice. The girls on the twenty-ninth and thirty-first floors bought her half a dozen pairs of black market nylons for a going-away present.

Krassy found a small apartment in Evanston at the Lake Towers. She rented it under the name of Candice Austin. Her own apartment, in Oak Park, she sublet with the approval of the rental agents. She decided to keep only enough of her furniture to use at the Lake Towers. The rest she sold.

The evening before she moved, she spent packing her clothes. Tired, she climbed into a steaming bath and stretched luxuriously in the soothing water. The tub filled with bubbles glistening in white and lavender and rose. Submerged to her chin, she scooped the water in long sweeps over her body. Suddenly she was conscious of a man's figure standing silently in the door.

It was Royster watching her with hungry eyes.

"How did you get in here?" she demanded, her voice cracking suddenly in fright.

"I got a passkey," he answered, never moving his eyes.

The fright was quickly overtaken by a wave of shaking anger. Stepping from the tub, Krassy walked past Royster who stepped aside as she passed. He followed her to the living room. Krassy walked to her small, walnut writing desk and picked up a pair of long, wicked scissors.

She turned on him quickly. "Get out!" she said. "Get out!" She held the scissors chest high and pointing out ... as the boys in the Yards fight with spring knives.

"Now ... don't be like that," Royster said. He took a step toward her.

"Get out!" she commanded, her voice high and intense with hate. "Get out ... you goddamn, dirty, lousy, no good, son-of-a-bitching bastard! Get out ... get out! Or I'll rip out your guts!"

Royster stepped back, his eyes wide and frightened. Krassy followed him, step by step across the living room, to the hallway, and to the door leading into the corridor the scissors gleaming evilly in the subdued light. She slammed the door behind him, and put the night chain on the door. Outside, in the corridor, she could hear Royster. A deep breath whistled slowly from his throat. "You dirty slut," he said.

The next day, Royster watched a blue moving van, with a broad white stripe, haul Krassy's furniture away. He stayed in his apartment, watching from behind the curtains.

"The dirty slut!" he muttered to himself.

CHAPTER FIVE

part 1 Danny

Now in telling about this, I hope I can make you see it the way I saw it. I know it's screwy for a guy to see a picture and start chasing a gal he's never met, particularly when he doesn't know what the percentage will be ... even if he finds her. But something kept pushing and prodding me, and all I knew was that if Krassy Almauniski was still alive, I had to find her.

All those days and weeks and months when I was running down leads, I found myself thinking of her as my gal. She became just as real to me as if I was going to meet her for a date every night. I'd looked at her picture so many times, I could trace each feature with my eyes closed. But by this time, I could hardly tell what was real and what I was making up in my own mind. I'd find myself talking to her and holding conversations, and then I'd realize I was walking on my heels and I'd try to stop it. Then later on, I'd remember some of the things she'd said to me, or what I thought she had said, and I'd have a hell of a time convincing myself it wasn't real. The things I'd found out about Krassy ... where she was born, and going to Mrs. Dukes' to live, and getting engaged to Buckham, and going to school at Goodbody ... all made me respect her. A gal like that didn't have many breaks, and so she'd tried to make some for herself. Then she goes and gets herself a job with Jackson, Johnston, Fuller & Greene, and works her way up to being a big shot's secretary and having a nice apartment in Oak Park. It proved to me she had plenty on the ball.

That was enough for my mind to work on, and when I mixed it with all the things I thought of, and made up, and how crazy I was just for a sight of her, it all became confused and the lines blurred, and changed, and overlapped. Just like I said, it was like trying to paint her picture in smoke. One minute she was real, and right here; and the next minute she was fading, and I couldn't stop her from disappearing completely.

Believe me, it was a hell of a situation.

I still had a living to make, so I had to do some work at the Clarence Moon Collection Agency, but I begrudged every moment I wasn't working at finding her. Even with the little work and time I put in the office, my business was growing and I was starting to make a little money. So one day when Bud Glasgow, who used to work with me at the old International Collections, got canned he came over to see me. Bud was a nice little guy who wore rimless glasses, and had worked for old man Crenshaw at International ten or twelve years. He didn't have too much ambition, but he could write bloodthirsty collection letters, and he was steady and dependable. So I told him he could come in with me on a percentage basis. I'd only be able to pay him twenty-five bucks a week, but I'd give him twenty per cent of everything he collected. That would work out to a better deal than he'd had at International anyway, so he was glad to take it.

I left Bud in charge of the office, and writing letters, and covering the telephone, and I did the outside collections where it was necessary to get a little tough. I also kept on making a few calls to get new business. The rest of the time I spent trying to find Krassy.

After I got the address of the Lake Towers from the Lima Transfer Company, I didn't waste any time getting out there. I knew she'd had her furniture delivered under the name of Candice Austin, so I didn't have much doubt I'd pick up her trail again. But I was wrong.

The Lake Towers is a big white hotel, built in layers like a tremendous, frosted birthday cake, getting smaller at the top until finally there was nothing left but a big tower on it. It has a big, white, plaster lobby, with deep maroon carpeting and bright green chairs, with heavy plate-glass tables on little, black, iron legs.

I walked into the lobby and up to the desk clerk. I flashed my insurance adjuster's card and told him I was looking for a Miss Candice Austin who'd moved into the hotel in 1943, on the first of October. Without bothering to look up, he told me no one by that name was living there.

"Do you know all the guests in this joint by name?" I asked him.

"If they've been living here since 1943 I'd know them," he snapped.

I'd made him sore, but I'd been sure Krassy was still there and I was plenty disappointed.

"How long have you been here?" I asked him.

"Ever since the war was over in '45," he told me. I pulled out a picture of Krassy and showed it to him. "Do you ever remember seeing this gal?" I asked him.

"No," he said, "and believe me, if I'd seen her, I'd remember."

"I know she moved here in 1943," I told him. "Would you mind checking your records and verifying it for me?"

"Look, Mac," he said, "I don't have the time. Those files are seven years old. Christ! I wouldn't even know where to find them."

"I'd pay you," I told him.

"Naw," he said, "I wouldn't know where to begin."

"Is it okay if I ask around some of the boys here?"

"Sure, go ahead," he agreed, "but be careful the manager don't see you."

"How about me asking the manager myself?" I suggested.

"I wouldn't," he said. "He's a mean bastard. He wouldn't tell you anything, anyway. And if he saw you snooping around here, he'd throw you out."

I thought it over. Maybe the guy was right. Anyway, I could always ask around first, and if nothing happened, I could end up by talking to the manager. I went over to the elevators. There were six of them. I waited around for each one to hit the ground floor, then if there weren't any passengers for a few minutes, I'd show the elevator boy the photograph and ask if he'd ever heard of Candice Austin.

None of them had ever seen or heard of her. They were all young punks, anyhow, and none of them had been working at the hotel very long. Finally one of them said, "You might ask Syd; he's been around this place for years."

"Who's Syd?" I asked.

"He's the night clerk."

I gave the guy with the bright idea a buck and walked back to the desk. The day clerk I'd talked to was still on duty. I asked him what time Syd came on and he said at 8:30 P.M. It was shortly before dinnertime then, so I went out and had dinner in a cafeteria, in Evanston, and went to a show. When I got out, it was a little after nine, so I went back over to the Lake Towers again.

A round fat guy, somewhere in his middle fifties, was back of the desk. He had alert blue eyes, and wore a pair of front teeth well filled with gold. He was bald from the back of his collar straight up and over to his forehead. The hair on the sides of his head was thick, and he brushed it back. It gave a peculiar effect like the guy had parted his hair in the middle ... with a part six inches wide. He had on a snappy blue suit, and a little light-blue leather flower in his lapel. I asked him if Syd was in.

"I'm Syd," he told me. So I wound up the old insurance routine again, flashed my card, and did my act about the lost beneficiary. By this time, I could do it with both hands behind my back. Syd listened intently. I was glad, because I had him pegged as a nosy guy with an overgrown curiosity. When I was all through, I showed him the picture. He looked at it carefully and handed it back.

"Never saw her," he said finally. "Never heard of her, either."

My belly dropped clear down to the floor. "You were here in 1943 weren't you?" I asked.

"Sure I was here in 1943," he replied. "I've been here since '39."

We just stood and looked at each other. I couldn't think of anything to say. Then suddenly he thought of something. "What month did you say she moved in?"

"In October," I said.

"Wait a minute," he answered. "I was gone for a while in 1943; that summer I caught pneumonia, and when I got better I went to Arizona for the rest of the year. I lost forty-five pounds. She might have been here while I was gone."

"How long were you away?"

He checked his memory briefly. "I left Chicago in August, and didn't return until January of 1944. The hotel here was short of help, and wanted me back ... otherwise, I'd have stayed longer."

"It still doesn't make sense," I told him. "I know she moved in here the first of October with her furniture. Christ, in those days it was even tougher to get an apartment than it is now!"

"That's right...." he agreed.

"Well, she just wouldn't move in here for three months would she? Look," I continued, "could you check your old registrations for October of '43 and find out *if* she moved out again? Maybe that'll give me someplace to get started. I'll pay you for it."

"Sure," he said, "but you'll have to come back tomorrow. All those old records and transcripts are kept in the vault, and I won't have any time to go through them until late tonight. After 2:00 A.M. it is pretty dead around here, and I'll have plenty of time then."

I knew if I went home I wouldn't get any sleep. I'd stay awake all night wondering what Syd had found out about Krassy and then I'd have all day tomorrow to wait until he came back to work.

"That's great," I told him, "but if it's okay with you, I'd rather stick around and wait. It'll save me a trip back tomorrow night."

"It's all right with me," he said.

I thanked him, told him I'd be back, and left the hotel. The city of Evanston doesn't permit the sale of liquor and I had a hell of a long time to wait. I finally decided I'd go down to Howard Street. Howard Street is the dividing line between Chicago and Evanston. It's a wide-open little section and sells plenty of liquor and has shows and cheap night clubs. I caught an el to Howard and got off. I found me a bar and went in and parked up next to it. I ordered a couple of quick shots, then slowed up, reversed my field and started drinking beer. It was cheaper and I could kill time just as well. About 2:00 A.M. I slid off the stool and started back to Evanston.

Syd met me at the desk. "I was just going to look at the files now," he told me.

"Right," I said. I sat down in one of the bright green chairs, lit a cigarette and tried to get comfortable. The lobby was deserted. Once in a while some man would come through the lobby from the street, and twice couples came through, a little high and usually laughing. But they all had their own keys and didn't stop at the desk. In maybe half or three-quarters of an hour, Syd appeared carrying a small metal box with file cards in it. On the front of the box was a label which said, "June-December, 1943."

He sat the box on the desk and opened the drawer. Every so often there was a pink card which stuck out farther than the white ones. Each pink card carried a month typed on it. Under October, he pulled out the pink card ... and twisted it up on its end like a flag. Then he started sorting through the white cards back of it.

Right up near the front was a card: "Austin, Candice, Miss. Apt. 1901."

"She checked in all right," he told me.

"When did she check out?"

He looked at the card a little puzzled. "That's funny," he told me.

"What's funny?"

"Miss Austin didn't check out, but evidently she gave up her apartment in December, because Mrs. Dana Waterbury moved in December 24, 1943."

"Couldn't Miss Austin have shared the apartment with Mrs. Waterbury?"

He shook his head and showed me the card. It was ruled down the center. There was a check-in date written on one side of the line which said, "October 1, 1943." Then just below it was: "Mrs. Dana Waterbury, December 24, 1943."

"Why couldn't she?" I insisted.

"Because, it is a single apartment rented on a single-rate basis. In the second place, I remember Mrs. Waterbury ... she lived here quite a while ... three or four years. There was no one living in 1901 with her. She and her husband lived there until he went overseas."

"I thought you said it was a single-rate apartment?"

"It was," Syd said, "but during the war, the hotel didn't charge extra for service men on leave. Patriotism!" He laughed.

"Quite a gesture," I agreed. "You say you remember Mrs. Waterbury?"

"Sure."

"Did she look like that picture I showed you?"

"No," he said.

"When did Mrs. Waterbury leave?"

He looked at the card again. There was no check-out date on it. "She lived here long enough that it wasn't entered on this original card," he told me. "But as I remember it was in '46 or '47."

"Did Mrs. Waterbury leave a forwarding address?"

He shrugged. "If she did, we wouldn't have it now," he said, "it's been so long ago that all the mail stopped years ago."

"Who else around here might remember Miss Austin or Mrs. Waterbury?"

"I don't know," he said. "If the maid on that floor is still working here, she might remember. Or perhaps the housekeeper."

"How can I find out about the maid?"

"The housekeeper could tell you."

"What's her name?"

"The housekeeper? Mrs. Boos. She isn't here now, naturally, but she'll be on duty at eight o'clock in the morning."

"What time are you off work?"

"Eight o'clock."

"Would you mind introducing me to Mrs. Boos? It might help."

"Sure, I'll introduce you," he said. "You won't have any trouble getting her to talk; she's a regular old gossip."

I gave him ten bucks, which seemed all right with him. I told him I'd see him at eight in the morning and walked out.

I didn't try to go back to Chicago that night. I stayed in a small hotel, in Evanston, that soaked me plenty. In the morning I was back at the Lake Towers at eight o'clock. Syd was just coming off duty. He motioned me, and we rode an elevator to the third floor.

I followed him down the hall and around a couple turns. We landed up in a long, narrow room that had shelves built from the floor to the ceiling on all four sides ... leaving only enough space for the door on one side, and a window on the other. In the middle of the room was an old-fashioned, high, roll-topped desk. A gray-haired, middle-aged woman was sitting at the desk. She was wearing a gray shirt-blouse, and a black skirt. Syd introduced us.

"Mrs. Boos," he said, "this is Danny April, a friend of mine. He works for an insurance company, and he wants some information about former tenants in 1901. I knew if anyone could help him, you could." Syd smiled ingratiatingly, and I tried to echo it.

"Certainly, certainly," she replied. "What do you want to know?" At this point, Syd bowed out, told me good-by, and disappeared down the hall. I gave Mrs. Boos a quick run-down on my insurance story for Candice Austin.

"I wonder if you could tell me who the maid was that cleaned in 1901?" I asked her.

"I couldn't tell you," she replied, "it would be impossible. We rotate the maids on different floors constantly. There's no particular maid that is assigned definitely to a certain floor."

That was that. "You said you didn't remember Miss Austin?" I told her. She nodded. "Well, would you mind taking a good look at this picture and telling me if you've ever seen the girl?" I handed her the glossy print of Krassy. Mrs. Boos took it in her hands and stared at it intently. Then she sort of turned it a little to one side, and peered at it under a different light.

Finally she said, "Why, yes, I know her. But when I knew her she had black hair and looked a great deal older."

"Who? Miss Austin?" I asked.

"No," she said. "That's Mrs. Waterbury."

"Are you sure?"

"Positive!" She folded her hands and dared me to doubt her.

"When she moved in here," I said slowly, putting the thing together in my mind, "her name was Candice Austin. It's on the card downstairs at the desk. She must have gotten married while she was living here, huh?"

"Probably," agreed Mrs. Boos, "but this is such a big hotel that tenants can live here quite a while before I get to recognize them. I'm not in daily touch with them like the clerks and the rest of the downstairs staff. When I knew her she was already married. I had no way of knowing when or where she got married."

"Did you know her husband, Dana Waterbury?"

She shook her head. "No," she replied, "I never saw him. But he must've been killed in the war, because Mrs. Waterbury got married again and moved away."

"Oh, Christ!" I said to myself, "here we go again!" I took a deep drag on my cigarette, and kept talking. "Who'd she marry this time?"

"I don't know," said Mrs. Boos. "I remember reading something about it in the paper."

"Which paper? And when was this?"

"All I remember at the time there was a little announcement in the society section about her getting married. She was such a pretty woman," she added.

"You don't know the guy she married or where she moved?"

"I don't, Mr. April," she said. "It was long enough ago, that just barely remember it. That's all."

I ground out my cigarette on the sole of my shoe. There was no ashtray on Mrs. Boos's desk, so I dropped the butt in my pocket. "You say she looked older than this picture ... and had black hair. There's no chance you're making a mistake in identifying her?"

Mrs. Boos looked at me coldly. "I told you it was her," she stated distinctly, "and it is!"

I thanked her wearily and caught an el down to the Loop. I transferred back to my rooming house on a streetcar. Then I called Bud Glasgow at the office and told him I wasn't feeling so good and I wouldn't be in until afternoon. I felt plenty beat; I had a hangover off the beer I'd globbered the night before, plus damn little sleep, plus a hell of a disappointment and letdown.

Krassy was married. Right now she was married and living someplace with a husband. I felt the world had been wrapped up in a big slimy package and somebody had slapped me in the face with it. I took off my shoes and trousers, flopped down on my bed and drifted off into a restless sleep. Around noon, I woke up, washed my face and shaved. Then getting dressed, I went out and got some scrambled eggs and coffee, and by that time the world seemed a little brighter.

Not much, but a little.

I'd followed Krassy this far, and I might just as well play the string out. If I didn't ... I'd never forget her. All my life I'd keep remembering and wondering about her. And then another idea hit me. Maybe she wasn't married any longer! One husband had died; maybe the second one had too. Or maybe she was divorced. What the hell! Maybe she wasn't happy and someday I could talk her into a divorce. All sorts of crazy ideas ran around in my mind, chasing each other, getting all tangled up, tripping over one another, and then starting all over again. I laughed. But as long as I had something to hope for, I was happy again.

There was still one lead I could follow. Mrs. Boos had read the announcement of Krassy's marriage in the paper. She didn't know which paper ... or what year. I tried to tie the dates to make sense. The first desk clerk had been there since '46, and he didn't remember her. That might mean she'd been gone before he started work ... or shortly afterward. Of course, with her black hair, he might not have recognized her picture when she was blond. Hell! Syd hadn't recognized the blond picture either as the brunette Mrs. Waterbury. It took Mrs. Boos with a woman's eye for features and make-up to do that! Syd had promised to get me the check-out date of Mrs. Waterbury, but he wouldn't have it until the next day. I decided not to waste any time; I wanted to get going right away.

And then a thought came to mind. "Why had Krassy dyed that beautiful blond hair ... black?" But I shoved it aside. It wasn't important.

I started for the offices of the *Chicago Daily Record*. The library, or "morgue," is located on the second floor. Most newspaper libraries look alike. Usually they are a big, square room, with high, green metal files running all around the walls. In the middle of the room are a couple of long, plain tables covered with scissors, paste pots, and brushes. The librarian is nearly always an old newspaperman who is put out to pasture in his old age taking care of the files. Indexed and cross-indexed … back and forth … is damned near every name you've ever heard of. Anyone who's ever had their name in the newspaper, once, is usually filed there. The librarian keeps the files up to date by clipping current items out of the paper, and filing them in big, square manila envelopes.

That was also the *Daily Record* library.

I asked a nice old guy, in shirt sleeves and a vest, if he had anything on a Mrs. Dana Waterbury. In about ten minutes he shows up with an envelope. "Nothing on Mrs. Dana Waterbury but I got something on her husband … Captain Dana Waterbury. Want that?"

"Sure," I told him. I glanced over a couple of old newspaper clippings. He'd been quite a war hero, a combat pilot, and had been killed over Germany in May, 1944. There was a brief mention in the obit that he was survived by a wife.

I gave the file back to the librarian, and as a matter of routine, asked him to check on the names of Karen Allison and Candice Austin. He did. He had nothing on them. I thanked him and left.

Next I went over to the *Evening Express*. Same kind of library, same kind of librarian. Clipping on Capt. Dana Waterbury, nothing on Mrs. Dana Waterbury. Karen Allison? Nothing. Candice Austin? Nothing. By this time it was getting late, hut I figured I might squeeze in one more call at the *Daily Register*. The *Register* is a tabloid with a big night circulation in Chicago.

I hit pay dirt.

The librarian had one small clipping under Mrs. Dana Waterbury. In its blatant style the clipping announced:

LOCAL MILLIONAIRE BANKER WEDS
SOCIALITE HERO'S WIDOW

> This morning in a quiet service, attended only by close friends, Howard Monroe Powers, prominent Chicago banker, married Mrs. Candice Waterbury, widow of Captain Dana Waterbury of Philadelphia. They were married by Cook County Judge Winfield L. Visolotti.

There was a little more to it, not much. The story appeared in the issue of January 17, 1946. I asked the librarian for a file on Powers. He brought it and it was bulky as hell. From the number of clippings I knew Powers was a big shot. Among them was a duplicate of the one I'd read about Krassy's marriage. After reading some of his clippings, I discovered Powers was president of the Lake Michigan National Bank and Trust Company; chairman of the board of the Chicago, Midwestern and Pacific Railroad, and served as a director of insurance companies, universities, hospitals ... and so on.

It made me sick. It made my guts ache. What guy could buck competition like that? I was ready to give up. What the hell was the use? Then I discovered something.

In January, 1946, when Howard Monroe Powers married Krassy, he was sixty-five years old!

I added it up fast. Powers was now close to seventy. He was still alive, because I hadn't seen a death notice in the clippings. Krassy was twenty-seven or -eight.

Well, all right!

I still had hope.

CHAPTER FIVE
part 2 Krassy

Once again Krassy was moving. And once again, reminiscent of a past moving day, Krassy had a stop to make at a beauty parlor. Relaxing in the cab, she directed the driver from Oak Park, to a hairdresser in the Loop. "A new name," she told herself, "a new life ... and a new woman." The cab pulled out of the heavy stream of Michigan Boulevard, and glided smoothly to a stop before the flossy beauty salon. Krassy paid him off. He tipped his cap, and watched her cross the crowded sidewalk; he waited until she had disappeared within the doors before driving off.

In a small reception room, hung with soft, gray drapes, Krassy announced herself. "I'm Candice Austin," she said, "I have an appointment with Leon."

"Yes, Miss Austin," murmured the girl, "this way, please." Krassy followed her down a long, narrow hall, honeycombed with small cubicles ... each filled with a patient woman. Women sitting under driers, women in curlers, women holding heads over shampoo basins, women having hair combed, women having hair cut, women having hair touched up. Before one of these empty little spaces the receptionist stopped and turned to Krassy.

"Please be seated," she said. "Leon will see you immediately." Krassy entered the cubbyhole, removed her coat and hat, and sat down. In a few minutes, a slender, dapper man, wearing a white surgeon's smock buttoned completely up the neck, made his appearance.

"I would like to do something about my hair," Krassy told him.

"So?"

"I would like to make it black."

"Black?" asked Leon. He fingered the gilded silver hair, and gently rolled it between his fingers. "Most women would give a great deal to have hair like yours," he said softly.

"But *you* can do it all right?" insisted Krassy.

"Oh, yes ... I can do it easily," Leon replied. "If that is what you want."

"That is what I want ... to make it black. Raven black."

Leon shrugged and started to work.

Four hours later, Candice Austin registered in the Lake Towers Hotel. The room clerk waited in silence as the tall, black-haired woman, with the grave eyes and fragile, gentle face was assigned to apartment 1901. His eyes were impressed.

Krassy liked the Lake Towers; she liked the pretentious white building, the swinging glass doors, the rococo plaster mirrors and hanging chandeliers. She liked the uniformed doorman and bellboys and elevator men ... the obsequious service. Possibly for the first time in her life, she felt free to relax for a while ... free of the old fears in the temporary security of Collins' settlement.

Her apartment was small. It consisted of a living room, bedroom and bath, with a combination kitchen and dinette. Her furniture from Oak Park she rearranged many times. When she was finally satisfied, she viewed her new home with approval ... it was quiet and relaxed, with a casual dignity.

There was one more detail to attend to.

Krassy went to see a doctor. This particular man of medicine specialized in performing abortions. While maintaining an ethical practice, he performed his specialty on the chosen few having the right introductions and the right bank accounts. The success of this practice could be somewhat evaluated on the basis of a large and expensive home which he maintained, a three-car garage ... filled, an extravagant wife, and memberships in many exclusive clubs.

Attached to his waiting room were two general examination rooms, and a small, clinically clean operating room complete with table, sterilizing cabinet, and instruments. The doctor, a short, fat man with ruddy cheeks, thick black hair with a gray streak, and large horn-rimmed glasses, was vaguely interviewing Krassy. He had a small card which he pretended to be filling out.

"And how long have you been pregnant, Mrs...." he glanced down at the card and cleared his throat, "Mrs. Augman?"

"Two months," replied Krassy.

"And your husband?" He cocked his head, "I mean ... is your husband living with you?"

"He was," said Krassy, "but he's just gone into the service."

"Are you working?" the doctor asked.

"Oh, yes ..." said Krassy. "That's what worries me, doctor. I *must* continue to work ... and if I'm pregnant, I can't."

"Hmmmm," said the doctor clearing his throat again. "You have no family to help you?"

"Oh ... no," said Krassy. "And neither has my husband. They can't help me at all. Doctor, I must be able to keep on working. I ... we ... well, we haven't the money to support a baby, now."

The doctor gravely nodded his agreement. "You're sure you're only two months gone?" he asked.

"Oh, yes!" Krassy was definite.

"Well ... let me make an examination," he suggested and waved his hand generally toward the small operating room. Krassy arose, gathered her gloves and handbag firmly, and marched in.

Half an hour later, Krassy was resting on the small couch in the doctor's waiting room. The nurse asked her if she felt all right, and Krassy said she did.

"Go right home, now," the nurse told her. "And stay off your feet tonight and tomorrow. You'll be all right."

Krassy arose gingerly to her feet. She felt perfectly normal. She left the doctor's office, leaving behind the tiny fetus and four hundred dollars.

October in Evanston is a month of beauty. Krassy loved to walk the lake front streets, with the high arching trees turning from green to amber and vermilion and purple. Often she would wander the campus of the university filled with girls dressed in careless sweaters and skirts, and young men in uniforms wearing no insignia ... studying in desperate uneasiness, awaiting their service assignments.

But best of all, Krassy liked the lake. She liked the great stones piled and half buried along the beach which held off the wrath of the lake. The rocks, like mailed hands, protected the soft-skinned land against the gnawing of the waves. Under the clear, October skies, the water stretched away and across the horizon. Some days, the lake shimmered with a metallic sheen, and it would stir and seethe in mighty constraint, throwing small, deadly waves in a constant probing of the great stones and delicate sandy beach.

Occasionally, the day would be hazy, and the sky would fill with ghostly smoke, and then the lake would roar and shake its mighty fists in anger. Whitecaps would ride the waves with skillful ease, to throw themselves against the shore and break into spray that cast a million miniature rainbows. Krassy would sit and hug her knees and sometimes feel a restlessness build within her which throbbed to the restless tempo of the lake. Uneasily she would arouse herself, and walk back to her apartment ... vaguely dissatisfied.

In November, Krassy enrolled her services at the Servicemen's Canteen. Three nights a week she worked as hostess, serving sandwiches, coffee, and doughnuts ... and occasionally as a dancing partner. She listened to boys from Iowa, Colorado, and Arizona; to boys from Maine, New York, and Florida; to homesick boys and sophisticates. In a way the tragedy and comedy of GI brown and blue didn't touch her. From eight until twelve on Monday, Wednesday, and Friday she saw them come and go ... bodies without faces from cities, farms, and states which were only names. Krassy listened to their stories and their conversation without really hearing or caring. The Canteen was a sedative, a drug ... in a period of marking time. Something was going to happen. Krassy was sure of it! But what it was, she didn't know. She had time ... days or weeks or months. She was waiting.

She was careful, however, to avoid all the downtown Chicago shops and restaurants and clubs. Collins, and her life with him, was rapidly slipping into the past. Each week she became more detached from it, but she was careful to avoid any place where Collins might appear. Or where she might be recognized.

On the night of December 17, 1943, she met Dana Waterbury. Not at the Canteen, but at the Officers' Club, where she and several other hostesses from the Canteen had been invited as extra guests.

In her usual preoccupation, she was only half listening to the young officer with whom she was dancing. When the music stopped, she realized he had asked her a question.

"I'm sorry," she said, "but the music ... I didn't hear what you said?"

"I asked you," he replied distinctly, "what your name is?"

"It's Candice Austin," she said. "Why?"

"Because I think I'm going to marry you," he replied.

Krassy laughed. "Don't forget, Captain," she said, "I've heard that before ... in the Canteen."

"Possibly," he agreed, "but this time it's different. This time ... I mean it!"

"And what is your name?" she asked. "I always prefer to know a man's name before I marry him."

"Say! You're not already married?" he asked anxiously.

"No. But you haven't told me your name yet."

"It's Waterbury. I come from Philadelphia."

The music started again and couples began dancing. Waterbury looked down into Krassy's quiet, serene face. "Come on back to my table," he urged her. "Come on back, and let's have a drink ... and catch up on all our conversation." He guided her back to a small table, where two other officers were sitting. He made the introductions around the table and pulled out her chair. "You'll excuse us, please," he said to the others, "but Candice and I have several things to talk over." They laughed and stood up. "You'll excuse us, Waterbury," one of them replied, "if we do our drinking at the bar."

"You weren't very polite to your friends," Krassy said.

"I'm too busy to be polite right now," Waterbury said, "but I think they understand...." He signaled for a waiter, and continued. "Where do you live?"

She told him, and then asked, "How long are you going to be in Chicago?

"For a little while, at least," he said. "I'm here on a bond-selling tour. Those other chaps," he motioned toward the two men at the bar, "and myself were brought back from Europe ... especially for the big event." He laughed softly. "Perhaps the brass figured we should get a break before our number comes around again." He became sober, and nodded toward his friends. "Both those fellows have nearly doubled their missions."

"And you?"

"Yes," he said, "I have too."

Krassy swirled the drink around in her glass. "What did you do before the war?" she asked.

"Not much," said Waterbury. "I lived in Philadelphia. I went to Princeton and was graduated from there; I didn't study very hard. In the summers, my family moved up to Cape Cod, and most of the time I sailed. Have you ever been to the Cape in the summer?" he asked.

"Yes," said Krassy, "quite often."

"Did you like it?" he asked eagerly.

"I loved it," Krassy replied.

"Do you like sailing?"

"Oh, yes!"

"Where did you learn to sail. Here on the lake?"

"Have you ever been to Berkeley?" she asked cautiously.

"No," he said. "I've been to San Francisco many times, but I never got across the bay. Why?"

"Because Berkeley was my home ... when I was a little girl," she explained. "My father used to take me sailing there." She asked slowly, "Is your father still alive?"

"Very much so," replied Waterbury. "Right now he's in Washington. He's in the shipping business."

"Is that what you'll do after the war?" she asked.

"Probably," Waterbury agreed. "All my family have been doing it since

William Penn hired the family skiff," he smiled.

Krassy smiled with him. "And the rest of your family ... your mother? Do you have any brothers and sisters?"

"Yes. Mother is alive ... and I have one sister ... two years younger than myself. Hey! I seem to be answering all the questions!"

"Isn't that all right?" asked Krassy.

"Not at all!" he said. "I have several thousand to ask you. Such as why you're so beautiful ... and why haven't you been married before now? Are all the men in Chicago blind?"

"No," said Krassy, "they're not blind." She paused to take a cigarette from Waterbury, and waited until he lit it for her. "As a matter of fact," she continued, "I just moved to Chicago a few months ago."

"Where was your home?" asked Waterbury.

"Originally it was in Berkeley," she said. "Then both my parents were killed in an accident ... when I was quite young. Since then ... I've spent most of my time in school ... and just traveling around."

"No other relatives?"

"No," replied Krassy. "A few distant ones, but no close ones."

"That's rugged," said Waterbury sympathetically.

"Not too rugged," said Krassy bravely, "fortunately my parents left me enough money ... that I don't have to worry. But it is lonesome ... sometimes." She looked at her watch. "It's getting late," she added. "I should be leaving."

"I'll drive you home," Waterbury suggested. "We have a car at our disposal on the tour."

"I'd love it," said Krassy.

Waterbury went up to Krassy's apartment with her. She mixed him a drink, and seated him in Collins' favorite easy chair. Then she scrambled eggs and made coffee. They ate it off the coffee table in the living room. Waterbury stretched out his long legs, lit a cigarette, and jammed his hands in his pockets. "I like it here," he announced.

"That's nice," said Krassy.

"I wish I didn't have to leave," he said. His face was expressionless and his eyes steadily watched the ceiling.

"I wish you didn't, either," said Krassy. "But you must, you know."

"I may have so little time ... that I'd like to spend it all with you," he said.

Krassy shook her head. Waterbury arose from his chair and crossed over to the lounge; he seated himself beside her and put his arms around her. He kissed her, and Krassy returned his kiss with simulated passion.

"Don't make me leave. Not tonight!" His voice was urgent. Krassy gently disengaged his arms. Taking his face between her two hands, she looked directly in his eyes. "You want to make love to me, is that it?"

"Yes," Waterbury replied levelly.

"No," said Krassy. She stood behind the couch and held her arms behind her back. "I want to wait until I'm sure," she told him softly.

"I'm sure," he said. "Aren't you?"

"I don't know ... not really. But I'm going to wait until I am sure." No persuasion from Waterbury could change her mind. He returned to the club that night.

One week later, on December 24, Krassy married Dana Waterbury.

Waterbury, with his Air Corps connections, managed to secure priorities and seat reservations, and they flew to Philadelphia to spend Christmas with his family.

The Waterburys lived in an old, square, red brick house with a white-columned, rotunda porch, located in a quiet, dignified residential section by-passed by busier sections of the city. Massive green shutters hung at the windows, and the heavy, slate roof was neatly painted. The house sat well back from the street, and a narrow flagstone path wound its way to the door. The path was flanked on both sides by a hedge trimmed with military precision. Several great trees, now hung with snow, stood silently, and on guard, between the house and the street.

Dana Waterbury dropped his luggage on the porch and thundered the heavy brass knocker on the door. It was opened by an elderly maid, neatly dressed in a black uniform with a small white apron.

"Merry Christmas, Ruby!" he shouted.

"Why ... Merry Christmas, Dana! Mr. Waterbury, I mean," she cried happily. Then catching sight of Krassy, she smilingly stood aside.

"Candice, darling," Dana said, putting his arm around her and pulling her inside the door, "here we are. And this is Ruby. Ruby, this is my wife ... Mrs. Waterbury."

Ruby permitted her mouth to open in momentary surprise, quickly she recovered. "Merry Christmas, Mrs. Waterbury," she said. "And congratulations!" She turned to Dana in confusion. "I mean congratulations to you ... Mr. Dana."

Dana laughed. "Where is everyone? I want to show them a real Christmas present!" A tall, slender girl raced from an adjoining room. He turned in time to catch her as she flung herself in his arms.

"Dana! It's Dana!" she cried, wrapping her arms around his neck, hugging and kissing him enthusiastically.

"Wait a minute," he protested happily, "break it up. I have a brand-new wife here to show you...."

Krassy faced the tall girl, with shoulder-length hair. "Wife?" Chris asked. "Wife!" She turned to Dana in amazement, then smiled at Krassy. "Why, Dana ... you lucky man! Where did you ever find such a raving beauty!" She held out her hand to Krassy warmly. "Dana is such a dope sometimes ... I've always been afraid he'd marry a hag or something...." She looked at her brother fondly. "Anyway, I'm Chris ... welcome, congratulations, and Merry Christmas!"

Krassy smiled back at her. "Thanks," she said, "but I think I'm the lucky one." She hugged Dana's arm affectionately.

Dana put his arms about both girls and squeezed them. "It's okay ... and Roger ... as long as you both think I'm wonderful," he grinned. Mr. and Mrs. Waterbury, Dana's parents, descended the wide, turning staircase.

Chris catching sight of them called, "They're married ... isn't it wonderful?"

"Dana!" His mother stopped momentarily.

"Well, well, well...." Mr. Waterbury said softly.

Reaching the foot of the stairs, they hurried toward the couple. "Congratulations," said Mr. Waterbury cordially to his son, "and now do I get to kiss the bride?"

The Waterburys had a guest for Christmas dinner. A tall, white-haired man, with a tired face, deeply lined, he was an old friend and business associate of the elder Waterbury. A widower, spending Christmas in Philadelphia, his name was Howard Monroe Powers.

Seated at the big, white-linened table, in the spacious old dining room, Krassy accepted a plate filled with turkey, chestnut dressing, mashed potatoes and sweet potatoes, and cranberry sauce. Salads and side dishes surrounded her. "Where is Maria?" she asked herself. "My God! Whatever made me think of that?" Suddenly her hands were shaking and cold. She placed them in her lap and held them quiet. "No," she thought, "I won't think of her ... or anybody else. Now I'm right. This is where I belong." She picked up the heavy, sterling silver fork, with an indistinct crest worn smooth, and started eating. "Merry Christmas, to me ... from Krassy," she thought.

"How long are you going to be home, dear?" Dana's mother asked him.

"I could only wangle a forty-eight-hour leave," he replied.

"Are you returning to Chicago?" asked his father.

"Yes," said Dana.

"Then where?" asked Mrs. Waterbury.

"I don't know. As soon as this bond tour is completed, I'll probably get shipped back over."

"Where will you live, Candice?" asked Chris.

"I think I'll stay in Chicago ... at least for a while," replied Krassy. "I have a comfortable little apartment and know a few persons there ... now."

"Why don't you come and live with us?" asked the elder Waterbury.

"I'd love to ... later, perhaps," Krassy evaded.

"Don't worry, Charles," Powers pompously told the older Waterbury, "as long as she's in Chicago, I'll keep an eye on her." He turned to Krassy and continued: "As a matter of fact, if there's anything you ever want, while Dana's gone ... you just ask me."

Krassy lowered her eyes. "I'll remember," she promised.

"Uncle Howard means it," said Chris. "Why, he has so much money that it's a terrible shame!"

Powers laughed in amusement. "When you were little, you didn't think so. I remember the time your dad wouldn't give you a horse."

"Oh, yes!" Chris was delighted. "But you did. And it made father angry."

Charles Waterbury protested: "I thought you were too small to have a horse ... that's all."

"The moral of this is," Dana told Krassy, "if I'm gone and you should ever need a horse ... see Uncle Howard."

"She'll do no such thing," said Dana's mother, seriously. "Your father can buy all the horses anyone needs." And Krassy joined the laughter.

The next day, Krassy and Dana flew back to Chicago. The day they were married, Dana had moved his luggage into her apartment, so they settled comfortably at the Lake Towers. Occasionally, Dana would be away for two or three days at a time, attending bond rallies in Detroit, Cleveland, Indianapolis, St. Louis, Kansas City, Minneapolis, and Milwaukee. He would return to Chicago, after such a trip, tired and exhausted.

"This is a war of money and material," he told Krassy, once, holding up a drink and rattling it, listening to the tinkle of the ice. "Sometimes I feel like a damned fool being held up on display. 'Look,'" he mimicked, "'here's Captain Waterbury. Captain Waterbury has knocked down twenty Nazi planes ... Captain Waterbury is here, today, to ask you to buy more bonds ... MORE bonds!'" He leaned over in his chair and held his head in his hands, then straightened again. "The truth of the matter is that Captain Waterbury doesn't give a goddamn whether anyone ever buys a war bond. All Captain Waterbury is worrying about, these days, is when his orders will come sending him back to Europe ... to get his ass shot off!"

January slipped into February, and February into March. In March, Waterbury's orders arrived. "It looks like the tour is over," he told Krassy. The night before Dana left, he took Krassy to dinner at the Yar.

The once quiet, dignified restaurant was a hustling, voice-filled, clattering place. In a corner, at a small table, Dana ordered an elaborate meal, and a magnum of champagne. "We're not leaving here," he told Krassy, "until we kill that bottle ... and its nearest relative. When I walk out of here, I'm going to be very drunk and very happy. And you, too, my sweet."

The gypsy orchestra played, and Waterbury morosely filled and drained his glass ... time after time. When the food was finally served, he occasionally picked at it. Krassy was silent, answering only his direct questions.

Now that he was leaving, Krassy was sorry. Her sorrow was not a personal thing ... either for him or herself. She would miss him ... not that she was in love with him, for she had never deluded herself with the illusion ... but once again she would return to being lonely. He had given her the protection of his name, and clothed her in a new, and solid, respectability. She didn't try to look ahead ... after the war ... when she must pick up the threads of her life with him again.

Krassy had felt safe and secure with him. His assurance, and easy, good humor had been amusing; his love to her had been sincere and in it she had the satisfaction of stability. Behind him he would leave a loss of companionship.

They left the Yar and returned to her apartment. Dana was drunk ... and not happy. Silently he undressed, showered and slipped naked into bed. Krassy loitered in the bath. Eventually, she turned out the light and slipped into bed beside him. Waterbury pulled her to him, hungrily, and later he lay beside her, his head resting on her outstretched arm; his face partly pressed against the side of her breast.

Krassy found herself thinking of the other nights he had held her in his arms and made love to her. They had not been unpleasant, she thought. Yet never once had she been completely aroused by him, or swept up and away by his passion. She had found she could dissimulate ardor ... convincingly and realistically. In it, she found a certain physical satisfaction that in no way touched her emotions.

Now, she flexed her body in relaxation. "We haven't talked about so many things," he said suddenly. "Tonight I could spend telling you how much I love you, but instead of that ... there are some other things I have to say..."

"Perhaps some things are best left unsaid," replied Krassy.

"No," said Waterbury, "this concerns such everyday things as money. Yesterday, I went down to see Uncle Howard and his attorney. I want to tell you how things are ... just in case something should happen to me."

Krassy became very quiet.

"I've arranged to send you three hundred dollars a month," he continued, "from my overseas pay. I've changed my government insurance over to you ... and the money my grandmother left me."

"That isn't necessary," murmured Krassy. "I have plenty."

"It isn't a great deal," Dana continued. "When my grandmother died, she left Chris and me twenty thousand dollars each. That's all the money I have in my own name." He paused a moment. "Just in case ... anything did happen to me ... and you needed more, why Dad would take care of you. He has plenty, I guess."

Krassy didn't say anything. She stroked his head until he fell asleep.

In the morning, Dana Waterbury left. His absence made little difference in Krassy's life, although several events occurred as a result of her marrying him. First, in April she received a check for $300. Then in May, she received a second check, and later in the same month the news that Captain Dana Waterbury had been killed over Germany. As a result she collected $10,000 worth of government insurance, $20,000 from Dana's grandmother's estate, and a bonus. The bonus was a personal life insurance policy for $7,500 which Dana had forgotten to mention.

Howard Monroe Powers was of great help to Krassy in her collection activities. Powers' own high-priced attorney handled everything, with a minimum of effort, worry, and detail for Krassy.

As president of the Lake Michigan National Bank & Trust Company, Powers' office was a place of majesty and awe. Krassy enjoyed the respect and hushed reverence with which she was received and ushered into the presence of Powers. Usually he was seated at his tremendous desk, with leather fittings, and plate-glass letter holders. Directly behind him was a high, arched window of a single pane of glass, inset with a stained-glass shield. The shield was shining amber, with a crimson bar dividing it in half. Below the bar was a brown acorn; above the bar, a green oak tree. Curling around the shield was a ribbon with the motto: TRUST BUILDS OAKS FROM ACORNS. Krassy thought it very impressive, although the first time she read it, she thought it said, TRUSS BUILDS OAKS FROM ACORNS. She knew that couldn't be correct, so she read it a second time ... correctly.

Powers would rise from his seat and sweep gallantly around his desk to hold both of Krassy's hands. As her visits increased he increased, proportionately, the period of his hand-holding. One afternoon, he exclaimed, "Candice, my dear, you must have known I was thinking about you!"

"You were?" she asked.

"Yes," he said. "For months now you've been staying in ... not going anywhere. It isn't right. You're still young and have nearly all your life before you."

"I ... I don't think it's right to go out. Not yet, anyway," she said. She opened her purse, took out a small, dainty handkerchief and touched the sides of her eyes gently.

"Of course you're right ... in a way, that is, my dear," Powers hastened to reply. He patted her hand fondly. "But there are limits to everything. Perhaps it wouldn't be right to go ... well, drinking and cavorting around night clubs ... but who could find fault with your going to the opera?"

Krassy lifted her eyes questioningly.

"Yes," he said, "that would be perfectly all right. I have a season's box, you know ... and tonight is 'La Boheme.' I'll take you...." He paused for a moment before continuing with a forced little laugh. "After all I am old enough to be your father. Ha."

"And my grandfather, too," Krassy thought. However, she hurried to ask him, "You're sure it's all right? It isn't disrespectful to Dana?"

"Of course not, of course not!" Powers reassured her heartily. "And we'll even go further tonight. Suppose we plan to have dinner at my club this evening?"

"I think I'd like that," replied Krassy.

"It's settled then! I'll send a car around for you," Powers smiled and patted her hands again.

In Krassy's apartment was a small calendar in a tiny leather case. The drawings were done by an artist famous for his type of beautiful women with exaggeratedly long legs, tiny wasp waists, tremendous busts, and sensual eyes. Each month, Krassy carefully removed the last picture and deposited it in the drawer of her writing desk.

The calendar had belonged to Waterbury and, in his leaving, he had forgotten to pack it. In December, the last drawing was exposed and Krassy realized that Waterbury had been dead for over six months. With sudden impulse, Krassy opened the drawer of her desk and took out the old drawings. She picked up the small, leather calendar case, too, and carried pictures and case to the kitchen. She threw them away. She didn't feel badly about it; it wasn't an act of sadness. Rather, she felt a sudden swelling of relief. A part of her life had come to an end again, just as the calendar had come to the end of its printed time.

At first Krassy had received occasional letters from Chris and several letters from Dana's mother. She had written polite little notes in reply. Eventually the correspondence had trickled off, and now the only news she received of them was through Howard Powers.

Powers soon began to escort her constantly ... to plays, concerts, and opera. In the half-year since Dana's death, Powers' avuncular attitude had gradually changed.

With calculation Krassy had helped him change it. Powers was careful not to extend his interest obviously or beyond a point where it could be withdrawn without losing either his dignity or self-respect. He still patted her hands, and had progressed to the point of holding them in the theater. On rare occasions, he casually rested his arm over the seat in his car, permitting it to gently touch her shoulders. Krassy did nothing to stop his growing sense of possession. She took each opportunity to ask him about her clothes, and in return complimented him on his appearance, his new suits, his choice of plays and music.

She also permitted him to invest small sums of her money in stocks and bonds. Invariably they returned a profit to her. On one such occasion, she bought Powers a solid-gold cigarette lighter, and presented it to him. "You are the smartest man I've ever known," she told him and kissed him playfully. Powers seemed to return her kiss in the same spirit, but Krassy easily sensed the emotion he attempted to conceal.

"You are quite the nicest girl I've ever known," Powers replied gallantly. "Now I shall have to do something extra nice for you."

The year of 1944 flowed smoothly into 1945 and by that summer Powers was completely infatuated with Krassy. This was the situation Krassy had long been considering and had contributed her earnest efforts to promote. Just how far it would progress, and how it would ultimately end, was something that Krassy had not yet decided.

Powers was a well-preserved man in his late sixties. His wife had died some twenty years before ... and without bearing him children. Although he was a man of great personal wealth, he lived a lonely life, with few acquaintances, and only a handful of personal friends. On his wife's death, he had sold his great town house and, later, his farms in Lake Forest. Living alternately between his downtown club and his apartment on Lake Shore Drive, he spent little money on his personal life.

His one exception was the *Lorelei*, a beautiful fifty-six-foot schooner, with diesel auxiliary. During the war, it had been laid up, but to Krassy's delight, Powers refitted it, and completely manning it, planned a month's cruise to Mackinac Island and down the Great Lakes to Buffalo.

Krassy loved the long, sweeping lines of the *Lorelei*, and she would lie for hours aft, watching the creamy wake trailing behind in the blue waters of the lake. Or twisting on her back, she would shade her eyes with her arm and trace the towering masts above the mahogany deck and watch the spreading white acres of canvas against the sky. Sometimes Powers and the captain would let her take the wheel, and with her legs braced wide apart, she would hold the great, brass-bound wheel and feel the *Lorelei* like a live thing under her hands.

But at night, she would stretch restlessly in the berth of her small private cabin, and think to herself, "This can be mine … this ... and this ... and this," enumerating in her mind the fortune and influence of Howard Monroe Powers. Powers could give her the financial security she had always sought; protection against the filthy little house in the Yards, a golden barrier between her and cheap, imitation silk dresses in bargain basements, and lingerie bought from the crowded counters of five-and-ten-cent stores.

On some night, the creaking stays on deck would arouse her from sleep and hearing them, for a wild half instant, she would remember the sound of the bed in her father's house, and she would wait to hear the soft slap-

slap of Maria's feet on the floor.

She knew she could marry Powers, and she believed it was what she wanted. However, instinctively, she hesitated to take this final step. There was no other man in her life; carefully, deliberately she had withdrawn from any associations after Waterbury's death. His name had given her a respectability unhesitatingly accepted by Powers and his friends. Krassy was careful not to jeopardize this invaluable asset, and she kept it blameless and shining. It was her key to unlock Powers' millions ... if she could force herself to marry him.

There was another alternative, and Krassy debated it often. "I can have an affair with him," she thought, "but he's so stuffy and respectable it might cause trouble. One of these days his conscience would start bothering him, and that would be the end of it." If this was true, Krassy felt she would lose her most powerful weapon ... Powers' respect for her. She also considered the same type of pressure she had used against Collins; she might permit herself an affair with Powers and then confront him with her pregnancy. But although this had been successful in reaching a settlement with Collins, Krassy convinced herself it would not succeed with Powers. The situations, behind the two men, were entirely different. Collins had been married and at the financial mercy of his wife. Powers was free. And it was more than probable that if Powers fathered a child, at his age, he would demand the right to maintain contact with it; even to the point of adopting the child.

Krassy turned the subject over continually in her mind, and spent long hours considering it. Weighing her experience and instinct against the character of Powers, as she knew him, Krassy reached the reluctant conclusion that she must marry him. The thought of physical contact with him brought her a feeling of revulsion. "But he's nearly seventy," she thought, "he probably won't live very much longer. Maybe only a year or two. And besides, a man at that age oughtn't to be too hard to handle. He probably won't want to make love very often anyway."

In the bright sunlight of the deck, Krassy watched Powers standing stripped to the waist, wearing a pair of white duck trousers and white canvas sailing shoes with heavy rubber soles. She measured the slackness of his arms, and the sinking flatness of his chest. And although his skin was deeply tanned, he looked old. The loose, stringlike muscles of the flesh beneath his chin, the myriad tiny lines etching his eyes, forehead, and the corners of his mouth undeniably announced his age. Powers wore his age with distinction, it was true, holding his lean body erect. And with his silver-white hair, and quiet command, he demanded respect.

"But not love," Krassy thought, "nor even desire." The dry heat of his palms as he stroked her hands and arms brought an uncomfortable awareness to her. His occasional, fleeting kisses from pale lips were unpleasant. "But he is an old man," Krassy repeated, again and again. "I can stand it for a few years. And then? Then Mrs. Howard Monroe Powers with more money than she can ever spend! Whatever you want … yours! ... for the rest of your life."

Beating her way down from Mackinac, the *Lorelei* on her return trip brought Krassy within twenty-four hours of Chicago. The last night out, Krassy had dinner with Powers in his master's cabin. The steward cleared away the meal while Krassy and Powers sipped their after-dinner brandy. Suddenly Krassy emptied her brandy into the coffee cup and smiled up at Powers.

"I feel I should drink gallons and gallons of brandy tonight," she said. "I'm blue...."

"Why, my dear?" asked Powers.

"Oh ... this lovely trip ... the beautiful, beautiful Lorelei," she paused momentarily. "I wish it would go on forever," she added.

"Every trip must end sometime," Powers told her sententiously.

"Unless you're the Flying Dutchman," said Krassy.

"And you wouldn't like that...."

"No, of course not. I was just fooling. But honestly ... I've had a wonderful time, Howard. And," she hesitated and shyly dropped her eyes, "I'll miss not seeing you."

"But you'll see me," he protested.

"Oh, certainly ... but not every day ... not like this. Do you think it's forward of me to say that, Howard?"

"Not at all ... no! I'm very proud."

"Somehow I've come to depend entirely on you," she told him softly. "All the nicest things in my life are connected with you ... dinners, and plays ... and seeing people...."

"I hoped you'd say that sometime, Candice," Powers replied.

"Well ... it's the truth! I look forward to seeing you, Howard. I'm always happiest when I'm with you."

"Sometimes I've thought I took up too much of your time," Powers said slowly. "Perhaps you'd rather be ..." he swallowed, "... with younger men."

"Younger men!" Krassy scoffed. "I've had enough of younger men ... they're egotistical and crude and cruel, Howard. They're not like you … kind, gentle, and sympathetic."

Powers beamed his approval. "But I'm getting ... a little older," as an afterthought.

"I don't think you're old!" Krassy replied with candor. "I think you're the most interesting man I've ever known. You're handsome ... oh, yes, Howard, I've seen other women look at you...." Powers glanced hastily in the bull's-eye mirror on the cabin wall. "And you are so well, so distinguished...."

"You mean that, Candice?" asked Powers.

"I've never meant anything more ... ever!"

There was a long moment's pause. Powers studied the few drops of brandy in the bottom of his glass. Finally he said slowly, "Candice ... you've brought me happiness, too. Doing the things you liked has been fun. But because of Dana ... and his father ... I don't know what to say...."

"Forget Dana!" Krassy urged. "Forget the Waterburys. Dana is gone ... he'll never walk back into my life. I've nearly forgotten him already, Howard. You made me forget him!"

"Then," said Powers drawing a deep breath. "I'd like to go on making you forget him...."

"Why, Howard, what a lovely proposal!" laughed Krassy as Powers suddenly stopped.

Powers looked at her in surprise; then he replied firmly, "Yes, I guess it is." Krassy shoved back her chair from the table and slipped around to Powers' lap. Sitting on his knees, she wrapped her arms around his neck.

"Darling!" she whispered, and gently nuzzled his ear, "my dear, darling Howard...."

Powers kissed her fully on the lips. "When shall we be married?" he asked.

"Not right away," Krassy said hurriedly, "let's be engaged for a while first. It will be so wonderful being engaged to you. We'll have a wonderful time ... and then we'll get married. Just like saving the dessert for the last."

He laughed and hugged her tightly.

The next morning the *Lorelei* made Chicago. That same day, Powers bought Krassy an eight-carat diamond engagement ring. There was no formal announcement of their engagement.

But Powers insisted they must write the Waterburys. Krassy attempted to argue him out of the idea, but eventually wrote Chris at his insistence. Powers, himself, wrote a long, facetious letter to Charles Waterbury, concerning their engagement. Chris did not reply to Krassy, although Powers received a brief, four-line note from Charles offering conventionalized congratulations. After that, Krassy and Powers didn't mention the Waterburys again.

Krassy continued to see Powers each night for dinner, and accompanied him often to the opera that fall and winter. Occasionally she invited him to dinner at her apartment. Powers, seemingly was content to leave Krassy to her own activities, and he made no intrusions on her privacy.

The engagement brought no new, or overt, overtones into their relationship; Powers' air of possessiveness neither increased nor decreased. Eventually, Krassy's distaste of physical contact with him became dormant as he made no further demands on her. Powers wanted Krassy to marry him before Thanksgiving, but she postponed it to Christmas, and then again until after New Year's.

Finally Krassy married Howard Monroe Powers on January 17, 1946. They were married by County Judge Visolotti in his chambers. It was a quiet wedding attended by Krassy, Powers, the Judge, and two professional witnesses. Immediately after the ceremony, and before the papers became aware of the importance of the story, the couple left for a honeymoon in Mexico City.

The honeymoon was not without incident. Powers' possessiveness became immediately apparent. With a vigor and potency surprising to Krassy, he took her for his wife. His demands were intense and unyielding, and from their first night together Krassy fought desperately to hide her revulsion. Each night, with Powers asleep by her side, she struggled to control the trembling of her body, and the gagging hysteria in her throat. Holding her eyes closed, Krassy would force her mind to scan a black velvet curtain. "The curtain is black," she told herself, "and I am getting sleepy." She would repeat it over and over again. Sometimes it would be broad daylight before the black curtain dissolved before her eyes and she fell asleep.

By 1949, Krassy no longer used the black curtain to go to sleep.

Instead, she used a handful of phenobarbitals.

CHAPTER SIX

Danny and Krassy

Finding Powers' address was as easy as finding a bump on the end of your own nose. I just looked it up in the phone book and there it was ... a big, co-operative-owned apartment building on Lake Shore Drive. I went to look at the building, and I hung around across the street for a few minutes ... on the outside chance Krassy might come out and I'd get a chance to see her. After a couple minutes I left, as I didn't want to make myself conspicuous hanging around.

That night, in my room, I thought things over. "Danny, my boy," I told myself, "you've found her, but what the hell do you do now?"

I couldn't walk up to her and say, "Look, I know you. You don't know me ... you never even heard of me. But I've traced you all the way from the stockyards, kid, and I think you're terrific!" I had to use finesse.

Finally I got an idea. It wasn't too good, but it was the only thing I could think of. I got a small blue pocket notebook and a hand-clocker—one of those gadgets you hold in your hand and press a little button. It clocks up a bunch of numbers. I went back to Krassy's apartment house, and stood down by the corner. As each car would go by, I'd clock it off on the counter. Then every hour, I'd enter the time and the number of cars that went by. Once a kid came up and asked me what I was doing and I told him I was taking a traffic survey. No one else even bothered to ask me.

Around eleven-thirty, I saw a tall, black-haired woman come out of the apartment, and get into a cab. There was a cab stand right across the street from the apartment. Halfway down the street, where I was standing, I couldn't be sure if it was Krassy or not. After she left, I hung around for another hour.

The next day, at about the same time again, this same woman came out of the building. This time I was down closer to the corner and I could see her better. There was no doubt about it.

It was Krassy.

She looked thinner than I thought she would look, and her hat had a short veil which covered her eyes so I didn't really get too good a look. She got in a cab and drove off. I had a hunch, then, that she probably left the building around the same time every day. I didn't think it was smart to try to follow her in a cab from the stand across the street. It was possible that I'd get a cabby who might know her. So the next day, I picked up a cab downtown, and drove up Lake Shore Drive at eleven-thirty. The cabby turned around past the apartment building, and pulled over to the curb. We waited. In a few minutes, Krassy came out, walked across the street and got in a taxi. They started off toward the Loop and I told my jockey to follow them.

We tailed the cab down Michigan, and when it got over the bridge, it turned right to Wabash and started down under the el tracks. South of Monroe, it pulled up in front of an office building and Krassy got out. I gave my driver a bill and followed her into the lobby. She walked over to an elevator and got on it. The elevator was pretty well filled, but several other people were still trying to get on, so I managed to squeeze in, too. She never noticed me.

On the third floor, she got off and walked down to the end of the hall without turning around. At the very end was a heavy walnut door without a number or a name. She knocked at the door, waited a minute, and the door opened. She walked inside, and I was standing staring at the door.

There didn't seem to be much to do about it, so I went down to the opposite end of the corridor and lighted myself a smoke. I stood there and smoked it, and tried to figure what the deal was. The elevator stopped again, and two guys got off. They went through the same motions as Krassy, and disappeared behind the door. In a few minutes, another dame showed up, then another man, then two men, then two dames. They all went the same place as Krassy.

But by that time I had it figured. It's a bookie joint; a private club bookie layout. I didn't have a chance of crashing it, and I didn't want to. I was not ready to meet Krassy yet, and I didn't want her to know I was tailing her.

But one thing I did know, Krassy was playing the horses. Not that she couldn't afford it. With dough like old man Powers' you can play 'em, buy 'em, and sell 'em. About one o'clock the door opened and Krassy came back down the hall. I turned my back toward her as she got on the elevator. As soon as the door slammed shut, I beat it down the stairs and reached the lobby as Krassy was walking out the door to the sidewalk. She cut over to Michigan, then turned south and headed toward the Congress Hotel. She went through the hotel lobby to the restaurant. I hung around outside, and walked by the door once in a while. She sat at a table alone and drank three double martinis. After three double martinis, which is a hell of a jolt in the middle of the day, she ordered a light luncheon. She didn't act like she was expecting anyone ... and no one joined her.

She played around with the food on her plate, took a few bites, and then paid her check. When she left, she took a cab back to her apartment building. I called it a day and checked back to the office for a little work.

I tried to piece the thing together. I couldn't understand Krassy going down every day to play the horses when she could place bets over the phone. Unless, of course, old man Powers didn't want her to gamble. Being a banker, he might consider it bad form to have a wife shoveling dough away ... but then he could afford it. I eventually decided that Krassy was either bored or fed up, and was playing the horses because she didn't have anything else to do. The fact that she was drinking plenty martinis in the middle of the day made me pretty certain she was unhappy ... or sore at old man Powers.

But I still hadn't answered my big problem. How was I going to meet her? And what reason would she have to continue to see me afterward. I had plenty of time to try to figure something out, so I didn't try to rush it. It had to be right.

The next week, I stayed away from Krassy's building entirely. Then one morning, I couldn't stay away any longer, and I found myself walking toward it. A block away, I turned west off the Drive, and passed Astor Street. Halfway between Astor and North State, there's a big, old graystone house which has been cut up into small, expensive apartments. Back of the main house, by the alley, is a small coach house. Pulled up in the driveway, between the main house and coach house, was a long, blue station wagon trimmed in light wood. However, there was no doorway on the side of the coach house which faced the main building. There was a small recessed door which opened from the coach house into the alley, and another main door which opened from the side of the coach house facing the street.

A young guy, about my age, was loading the back end of the station wagon with luggage. The luggage was all expensive-looking with that deep, rich sheen which costs plenty. As I walked by, a cleaning truck drove up and stopped. The driver got out and walked up to this young guy carrying a couple of newly cleaned suits. The guy laid down some of his luggage and turned around and gave the driver hell. "Look," he said, "I told you to have those suits back here yesterday. Now I'm all packed and I'll be damned if I'm going to repack just for them!"

The driver said something which I didn't hear, then the young guy pointed toward the coach house and said, "All right! Take them inside and leave 'em." The driver stepped inside the door from the alley, and, in a minute out again without the suits.

"I'm sorry about those suits, Mr. Homer," he said, politely, "anyway, have a good trip."

"Sure," said Homer. He closed up the back end of the station wagon, locked it, and walked around to the front of the car.

"When will you be back?" asked the driver.

Homer checked the lock on the front and side doors of the coach house, and then climbed in his car. "Not until May ... or later," said Homer and stepped on the starter. "I'll call you when I get back," he added.

"Thanks," said the driver. "Have a good time."

Homer waved a hand at him and drove off. I walked on thinking to myself that some guys have it lucky. Here's this guy in the blue station wagon going to Florida, or Arizona, or California, or someplace for six months. However, I didn't think about it too much at the time, and it sort of slipped out of my mind. That night, though, it came back.

I propped myself up in bed, and shook a cigarette loose from the pack, and went back to wondering how I was going to meet Krassy. Suddenly the memory of Homer flashed back in my mind. Then the idea struck me.

I went back to Homer's coach house a couple times. There were never any signs of life around it. The front of it, which faced the back of the main building, was a completely blank wall. There were windows on both ends of the coach house ... the sides running parallel to the street ... but you couldn't see them from the main building. The main door, at the top of two short steps, opened from the sidewalk into the coach house. Next to the door was a mailbox and the name—Edward A. Homer. There was also the small, recessed door, which I'd seen before, that opened off the alley.

At the office, I sat down and addressed a couple of envelopes to myself

... writing very lightly in pencil. Inside the envelopes I stuffed some sheets of blank paper, sealed the flaps, and mailed them. The next morning the envelopes were delivered back to my office, postmarked and canceled. I erased my name and address with a gum eraser, and typed in Mr. Edward A. Homer with the address of the coach house. I figured Homer had left a change of address with the Post Office, and I needed some personal identification for what I had to do next.

Walking down Clark Street, I came to a dinky little hole-in-the-wall shop. Outside was a sign which said, KEYS MADE—50¢. I went in. A bleary-eyed old guy was sitting on a straight-backed chair, behind a counter about the size of a card table. On the wall back of him was a board with a number of nails sticking out of it. Hanging from the nails were a lot of blank keys.

"I want to get a key made," I told him.

"A duplicate?"

"No," I said. "I been out of town a couple days and I lost my keys. Now I can't get in my apartment. I want you to come up and make one."

"You got any identification?" he asked.

"Sure," I told him, and threw the letters I'd addressed to Homer on the counter, "Want more?" I started to fumble at my pocket like I was looking for my driver's license.

"Naw," said the old man, "that's okay." He picked a handful of blank keys off the wall, gathered several small hand tools, and stuffed them in his pocket. He locked the store behind him, and we grabbed a cab to the coach house, as I didn't want him to get a chance to ask questions. When we got there, he started to walk up to the front door.

"No! Not that door ... I left a chain on it. Better try the one on the side," I said and pointed toward the alley. I didn't want anyone to see him fooling with the front door. The old guy shrugged his shoulders and walked around the corner and down to the recessed door. I leaned up against the wall beside him and smoked ... keeping an eye cocked for cars going through the alley. But none came past.

While the old guy worked, he kept up a mumbling conversation about locks, and once he tried halfheartedly to sell me a new lock for the door. He finally found a blank key that fit. He rubbed it with a piece of carbon paper and put it back in the lock. Then he pulled it out and inspected it for a minute or two. Finally, he took a tool from his pocket and started gouging out nicks and cuts on the blank. Every few minutes he'd rub it with carbon paper, put the key in the lock and try it. Finally, the key turned in the lock and the door swung open.

"That's great," I told him and put my foot in the door. "How much do I owe you?"

"Three bucks," he said.

"Hell!" I said, picking the key out of the lock and putting it in my pocket, "your sign said fifty cents!"

"Fifty cents for the key," he explained, "and two fifty for making the call."

I paid him off, and as soon as he turned away, I stepped inside the door of Homer's coach house. The side door opened into a short, dark hall that led to the kitchen. The kitchen was gleaming in white enamel and chrome. At one end of it was a small dinette table painted a jet black, with four, light bleached wood chairs. Each chair had a Chinese red seat. A heavy, woven grass partition, like a corded rug with Chinese scenes, dropped from the ceiling and could be raised or lowered. When it was lowered, it completely separated the dinette section from the kitchen.

Opening off the kitchen was the living room. It was plenty big, covering the rest of the downstairs of the coach house. The floor was carpeted wall to wall in a deep, brilliant green. Modern furniture, upholstered in watermelon red, was grouped around the center of the room, and faced a tremendous fireplace. End tables and coffee tables were painted black. So was the fireplace, except it had gold designs on it. Above the fireplace was a huge plate-glass mirror, set flush against the wall and extending from the mantel to the ceiling. The walls of the room were deep, dusky gray. Groups of pictures, in narrow black frames, with big white mats hung on the walls. The windows, facing the street, contained Venetian blinds, and one big set of drapes hung from the ceiling to the floor. The drapes ran on a track like a stage curtain, and were completely drawn covering the entire end of the room and the three individual windows in it. The drapes were the same green as the carpeting.

Believe me, it was one hell of a fine room.

A small staircase ran from the living room upstairs to the second floor. Here, there was a bath with a plate-glass shower stall, a bedroom with an oversized bed, and another room. This extra room was about the same size as the bedroom and had been fixed up as a study. There was a carved desk, a small divan, two easy chairs, a big combination radio-phonograph, and a small television set. The walls were lined with bookcases and record cabinets.

I walked back downstairs and out to the kitchen. Hanging on the back of the kitchen door were the suits the cleaner had left nearly a week before. I switched on the light and it worked. Trying the tap in the sink, I found the water was working, too. But the telephone had been disconnected in the living room.

That afternoon, I called the telephone company, gave my name as Edward A. Homer, and told them I wanted the phone connected again.

"However, I want a private number now ... and I don't want it listed under Information," I said. The phone was reconnected the following day and I had my private number.

Then I was ready to meet Krassy.

Nobody can look too far ahead to plan things. I knew I couldn't introduce myself to her as Danny April, a small-time collection agent; also I was smart enough to know that I couldn't keep up a big front forever. But I figured that after she got to know me, maybe when the time came for me to tell her who I was, it wouldn't make too much difference.

Using Homer's apartment, I decided I had to use his name, too. I didn't dare take his name off the door, and I couldn't afford any slip-up. I tried on one of Homer's suits and it fit me pretty well; and I selected a tie from dozens hanging on the back of his bedroom door. When I was all dressed up, I walked over two blocks to Lake Shore Drive, turned left and walked another block north to the building where Krassy lived. A doorman, in a deep maroon military coat, opened the door for me.

"What floor is Mr. Powers' apartment?" I asked him.

"Twenty-third," he replied. "Is he expecting you?"

"Yes," I said. "Why?"

"Mr. Powers isn't home now," he told me.

"That's all right," I said, "I'll see Mrs. Powers instead." I walked by him and stepped quickly in the elevator, before he had a chance to ask my name and phone up to announce me. "Twenty-three," I told the elevator boy.

The elevator glided to a smooth stop, and I stepped off into a small, private foyer complete with a marble bench and a tiny fountain. A single, heavy door with a tremendous brass knocker opened off the foyer. I walked over and started to lift the knocker before I saw a small button set in the right side of the door. I rang it. In a few minutes, a butler opened the door. He had a heavy, white face with oversized bags under his eyes. His gray hair was parted on one side, and combed back along the sides of his head. He cocked an eye at me and wished me good day.

"I'd like to see Mrs. Powers," I told him.

"Is Mrs. Powers expecting you?" he asked.

"No," I said, "but I think she'd like to see me. Here, just a minute," I tore out a leaf of my notebook and scribbled on it, "One horse player to another." I folded it over a couple times and handed it to the butler. "Please give this to Mrs. Powers," I told him, "and tell her it's Mr. Edward A. Homer to see her."

He closed the door softly in my face, and left me standing in the foyer. I crossed over to the fountain and discovered there were live goldfish swimming around in it.

In a few minutes I heard the door open behind me, and a quiet, husky voice asked, "You wanted to see me?" I turned around.

It was Krassy.

For a minute my mind went blank, I couldn't say anything. She was as beautiful as I'd ever dreamed; she was the loveliest woman I'd seen in my life. But she looked older than I'd expected ... older and tired. Her face held a tiredness behind its serenity I can't explain. Maybe it was her eyes; at first you didn't realize how intense they were; they seemed to be looking, and trying *not* to see at the same time. Glistening black hair fell to her shoulders and framed her face with soft dignity. Looking up at me from under her delicate brows, she stood waiting for my answer. I'd forgotten her question when she asked me again.

"Yes," I said, "I wanted to see you. My name is ... Homer."

She nodded her head without speaking.

"Well ... I've seen you around once in a while," I said. "That is ... down at the club."

"Club?" she asked.

"Down at the bookie's."

"Oh."

"You see, it's like this, Mrs. Powers," I stumbled on. "I'm sort of in the business myself. I make a small book, too ... and well ... I just live around the corner, and I thought maybe it'd be more convenient to place your bets with me."

She just stood and looked at me; listening intently and sizing me up.

"You know ... not having to go downtown," I said, "and having other people see you...."

"What difference does it make if people see me?"

"Why, nothing ... I suppose," I said, "except maybe Mr. Powers doesn't approve of it ... or something."

"Possibly," she said and regarded me thoughtfully. It made me sort of uneasy. I couldn't tell what she was thinking; then it was as if she'd made up her mind about something and reached a decision. Suddenly she smiled and everything was okay again. "All right," she agreed, "I'll give you a try." She paused. "After all, I've always believed in helping the small ... businessman." She smiled, and her eyes lost that intense look, and she seemed to relax.

I pulled out my notebook and scribbled down my address and telephone number—Homer's, that is—and handed the slip to her. "You can either place your bets in person or phone 'em in," I told her.

I walked over to the elevator and rang for it. She turned and opened the big door to the apartment. I glanced back, and she had stopped in the doorway, and was looking at me. Then with a brief wave of her fingers, she closed it behind her.

Leaving the building, I was walking on layers of foam rubber and my legs had small steel springs that made me bounce in a way I'd never bounced before. I felt good ... I felt swell ... I felt terrific! I'd met Krassy and gotten away with it. She'd accepted my story and the way was open ... wide open ... to see her again. And to keep seeing her. She was as lovely as I'd imagined. She was one hell of a woman!

And then I started worrying, too. I had no way of knowing when she'd call me. I had to be at Homer's apartment to answer the phone. If she called a couple times, and there was no answer, she'd probably blow the whole thing off. That meant I had to stick around Homer's most of the day; at night it didn't matter. She'd never call at night, anyway.

The next day, I let myself in Homer's apartment at nine o'clock in the morning. I hung around until six that night without hearing from her. It was agony cooped up in that apartment waiting for the phone to ring ... but it never did. I stretched out on the lounge and tried to nap, but my mind was buzzing and I couldn't sleep. In the afternoon, I began to get hungry and there wasn't anything to eat in the place. I decided I'd have to put in a supply of food. That night, I returned to my room, depressed as hell.

The following day the phone rang around eleven o'clock in the morning. My heart jumped to my throat and I had trouble talking around it to answer the phone. But it was only the telephone company. They were checking the phone and wanted to know how I liked the service. I told them swell. Krassy didn't call that day, either.

By the next, I'd given up hope. I figured she'd just listened to my story, and brushed me off politely. Then the doorbell rang. I peeked out from behind the blinds, and she was standing by the front door. I hurried to open it, and she walked into the living room and glanced at it casually. "I thought I'd drop around to see how you were doing, Mr. Homer," she said.

"I'm glad you did," I told her.

"You don't seem to have much of a crowd here," she said.

"No. Most of my customers call me to place their bets. I got to be careful," I explained. "If a lot of people were seen coming and going from here, somebody would report it to the cops and I'd get closed up."

She nodded her head gravely. "Well, I won't bother you again," she assured me.

"I don't mean *you* ... Mrs. Powers," I said hurriedly. "I want you to come whenever you want to. I was just ... explaining ... why there isn't a crowd of people here. Look," I said to change the subject, "I was just going to have a drink ... can I get you one? Scotch, martini, brandy?" I'd discovered that the real Homer had laid in a good supply of liquor. He kept it in a big enamel cabinet under the kitchen sink.

"That would be nice. I'll have a martini ... very dry," she replied. I went out to the kitchen and mixed a shaker of them. When I returned, she'd taken off her fur coat, and was sitting idly in her chair. I gave her the drink. She tasted it. "Good," she told me. We sat and talked about horses, and she told me about her boat called the *Lorelei*. After her second martini, she opened her purse and handed me twenty dollars.

"Put it on Rocket Lady, in the sixth today at Santa Anita," she said. "To win." I jotted it down in my notebook. "What are the odds?" she asked.

That threw me. Then I started ad-libbing. "I'll call my partner," I told her, "he handles that end of it. I only work the front." I picked up the phone and dialed the number of a small bookie joint, located in the back end of a meat market just around the corner from my rooming house. A little guy by the name of Sam operates it for the syndicate. I used to see him around and, once in a while on Saturday nights, I'd run into him and we'd buy a few drinks. I hadn't talked to him in months, and I was sweating plenty. If he didn't recognize my voice, or wouldn't give me odds without me identifying myself, I was sunk.

"Hello, Sam?" I asked. "What're the odds on Rocket Lady, in the sixth at Santa Anita?"

"Who's this?" Sam asked suspiciously.

"Look 'em up then," I said, "I can't wait until *April!*"

"April?" He sounded confused. "What about April? ... Oh, sure! April! Danny April?"

"That's right," I said, sighing in relief.

"She pays six to two," he told me.

"Okay," I told him, "I'll call you back." I hung up the phone and turned to Krassy. "Six to two," I told her.

"All right," she said. She stood up and I helped her with her coat. Gathering up her purse and gloves she started for the front door.

"Look, Mrs. Powers," I said politely, "do you mind going out the side?" She stopped and turned around. "For your sake ... you know. That's why I have this arrangement. You can enter or leave by the side, and no one can see you from the street."

"No," she smiled, "I don't mind at all, Mr. Homer. As a matter of fact, I think it is a very good idea...."

As soon as she'd gone, I called Sam back and placed Krassy's bet.

"That's a lot of dough for you, ain't it, Danny?" he asked.

"Sure," I agreed, "but I got my own business now."

"You must be doing pretty good now, huh?" said Sam.

"Not bad," I told him. "Say, Sam, I'll get this dough to you before the race this afternoon. But I got one question to ask you. How good is my credit?"

"Well," said Sam slowly, "it's like this, Danny. When a guy don't need money, his credit is good. Far as I know, you always been a level guy. Why?"

"It's like this," I said. "I'm awful damned busy these days. Sometimes I don't get around to my office for a couple days, so what I want to know is if I place a bet on the phone, you'll cover it for me?"

"Sure ... within reason," said Sam.

"When I'm around I'll drop the dough off," I said. "But regardless I square my account with you the first of each month?"

"Look, Danny," said Sam, "you and I been friends. I don't like to see no guy, who's a friend of mine, get in trouble. Sure, I can give you credit if you want it, but Danny ... remember *I* don't do the collecting. The syndicate has guys ... *special* ... for that."

"Yeah, I know," I told him.

"Okay, just so you understand," he said.

After that my life began to assume a crazy sort of pattern. In the beginning, I didn't see Krassy every day. Sometimes she'd call me two or three days in a row and place her bet by phone; then she'd drop by in person, and stop for a drink, maybe a couple days in succession. However, the times of her phone call and the times of her visits were regular; they always fell between the hours of eleven in the morning and one in the afternoon. Partly because of the hours the tracks were open, and partly because of her own personal life, I guess. Mostly, she would place just one or two bets a day ... all of them to win. Her bets were anywhere from twenty to fifty bucks. I'd pass them on to Sam.

After I hadn't seen her for a few days, she'd appear in person and give me the money for the bets I'd covered on the phone for her. When she left, I'd hike over and give the dough to Sam. On her occasional wins, Sam would give me the dough, and I'd pay her off. She lost pretty regularly, and the amount would run from six hundred to maybe a thousand dollars a month. She didn't seem to mind.

There was one thing, though, that bothered me. Most horse players have it in their blood. They run a fever. But Krassy wasn't like that. She didn't seem to be particularly interested in either winning or losing. The amounts she lost, she could easily afford, I guess. But when she won, she didn't seem to get much of a kick out of it either. Another thing, most players spend a lot of time doping out weights, track conditions, jocks, and past performances. A real gambler knows each blade of grass inside the track any place the horses are running. But Krassy didn't. She picked a horse she liked for one reason or another ... and bet it to win.

Her phone calls became fewer, and her personal appearances more regular. I kept playing it straight. I never made a pass at her, or got out of line in anything I said. I always called her Mrs. Powers, although by this time she was calling me Eddie.

So I got in the habit of going to the office early, then getting up to Homer's apartment at eleven o'clock and staying there through one. After Krassy would leave, I'd go back downtown and work the rest of the day. My own business kept shaping up better and better, and I even hired another guy named Henry Spindel to help out on personal collections. Spindel and Bud Glasgow had no idea where I went when I'd leave for the coach house. I'd never mentioned it to them, and I'd never mentioned Krassy, either. I figured it was none of their business.

Eventually, Krassy stopped at the coach house every day, around noon. I'd always have a shaker of martinis mixed and we'd sit and talk. One day she mentioned something about music and I told her about the phonograph and room full of albums upstairs. She wanted to see what records I had, so we went up and she browsed through them. Finally, she pulled some out and I put the records on the machine. It was all longhair stuff, but she liked it. She sat curled up on the divan, sipping her martini and listening to the music. After a while, she said, "Eddie, you constantly amaze me."

"I do?" I asked.

"Yes," she said, "I'd never dream you liked this kind of music. Tell me about yourself."

"What's there to tell?" I said.

"Is Chicago your home?"

"No," I replied. "New York ... New York City. I was born and raised there." I figured I was safe in telling her that, because as far as I knew, she wasn't too familiar with New York. And I thought telling her I was from New York might impress her.

"Did you go to college?" she asked me.

I was beginning to like the idea of impressing her. I decided that Edward Homer, with this apartment, this kind of music, born in New York ... had to go to college! So I said, "Sure. But I only went two years ... to Columbia." Columbia was the only college I could think of around New York, and I knew a little bit about their football teams.

"Oh," she said. "But you don't speak like ... well, like a New Yorker."

"You mean my English is lousy?" I asked. "Check that off to evil companions. After all you don't need a degree to talk to horses."

She smiled again. "What about your family?"

"Oh, my folks still live in New York," I told her.

"What does your mother think about your gambling?"

"She doesn't know," I said, "she thinks I work for a broker."

Krassy watched the olive bobble around in her glass. Her face was thoughtful. In a little while she left.

Another afternoon, she appeared later than usual and downed a couple drinks quickly. She said, "Eddie, tell me, do you have a girl?"

"No," I told her.

"I should think you'd have a lot of them," she said. "You're a nice-looking fellow … with plenty of money."

"I always been pretty busy," I said.

"I never thought men were ever too busy to have girls."

"Not that so much," I told her, "but why play around and waste a lot of time and dough on a dame that doesn't mean anything?"

"Haven't you ever met a girl who did mean something?"

"Yes," I replied.

"Who was she? Tell me about her."

"If I did, you wouldn't like it, maybe," I said looking her squarely in the eyes.

She lowered her head slowly. "You might try it and find out," she replied softly. But all of a sudden my nerve left me; I was too scared, too afraid I'd say or do the wrong thing. I let it go by.

At Christmastime I had a few bucks in the bank. Not much, but the Clarence Moon Collection Agency had been making a little dough so I gave Glasgow and Spindel fifty bucks apiece, and took the three hundred and fifty bucks I had left. I went down to Jacobson's Loan Shop on North Clark Street and bought a little necklace of pearls ... a choker of real ones which had been left in pawn. The pearls weren't very big, and neither was the choker, but they were the real stuff. Then I got a black velvet box and put the pearls in it. I took it to a gift wrapping place, and they wrapped it in blue paper and pasted on silver stars. On my way back to the coach house, I stopped and bought a Christmas tree. One that was small enough to sit on the table, and a couple strings of electric lights.

I set it up in the living room and strung on the lights, and wrote a note which read: "Merry Christmas to Mrs. Powers." I put the card on top of the box of pearls and placed it under the tree. The next day when Krassy came over, she saw the tree on the table.

"What a lovely tree, Eddie!"

"You like it?"

"You know, I really believe you're a sentimentalist!" she walked over to the tree, and saw the package under it. She picked it up, then turned. "Is this for me?" she asked.

I told her it was.

"Let me open it now! I love presents! I can't wait to see what it is!" She turned the box over and over in her hands, as happy as a kid.

"Okay," I agreed.

Quickly she tore the wrappings from the box and opened it. Lifting the pearls in her hands, she walked to the mirror and clasped them around her neck. "They're lovely, Eddie!" she exclaimed, "Oh! I love them!" Then returning to the tree, she picked up the card and sort of motioned with it. "I want you to do me a favor," she told me.

"Anything you say," I said.

She held up the card. "Don't keep calling me 'Mrs. Powers,'" she said, "I want you to call me Candice."

"All right, Candice."

She crossed over to me, stood on her toes, and put her arms around my neck and kissed me. "That's for my lovely Christmas present," she said. Her eyes were close to mine, and I could see straight down into them ... like I was looking into real deep water, where the depth becomes so great that it seems to move and swell without the slightest ripple. I kissed her back. I kissed her hard for all the months I'd dreamed of her, and walked the streets trying to find her, and for all the love I had inside me ... for her.

Then she was crying and pushing me away. "Oh, Eddie," she cried, "Eddie ... Eddie ... Eddie...."

I took my arms from around her and stepped back. "Maybe I shouldn't have done that," I said.

"I wanted you to," she told me. "I've wanted you to do that since nearly the first day I met you."

"Then why are you crying?"

"I don't know ... just being silly, I suppose," she told me. "And I *am* married. What do you think of a married woman, Eddie, who lets another man kiss her like that?"

"If it's you and me ... I think it's great," I said.

"Eddie," she said softly, "before we go any further ... before we get too deeply involved with what we think and what we want, I want to tell you something."

"There's nothing you got to tell me," I said.

"Mix us up some more martinis," she said, "and let's go up to the study and play some music ... and talk."

"Okay." I went out and mixed up another shaker, and then we went upstairs. Krassy selected some Bach and put it on the phonograph. She leaned back on the divan and I sat down beside her, placing the shaker on the floor.

"Why do you think I married Howard Powers?" she asked me.

"I don't know," I said.

"It wasn't because I loved him," she said. "I've never loved Howard ... ever! Did you know I'd been married once before?"

I hesitated; then I decided I'd better say no. "No," I told her, "I didn't know."

"Well, I have been," she said. "I was married to a wonderful, fine man

... Dana Waterbury. He was killed in the war. I loved him, Eddie ... I adored the very sight of him. He was sweet, and good. Dana was the first lover I ever had, and he was my husband." Her voice caught in her throat, and tears filled her eyes. "When he was killed, Eddie, my world came to an end. There was nothing more to live for. There were no men ... there was no man, who could ever take his place. The idea of belonging to ... or loving ... another man was unthinkable!"

The way she said it hurt me like hell. "He was a very lucky guy." I finally managed to say.

"I was also a very lucky girl," she told me softly. "Howard was an old friend of the family's. Dana's family had known him for years ... he was 'Uncle Howard.' After Dana's death, Howard was good to me. He helped me over my loss ... my lonesomeness and despair. But Howard was an old man, old enough to be my own grandfather. He never talked about love to me ... Eddie. He just wanted to help and protect me. Finally he asked me to marry him, and I did."

"Why?" I asked. I poured out another drink.

"Because I *didn't* love him! Can you understand that, Eddie? I thought it would be like ... well, a father and daughter. Nothing ... nothing too intimate about it. We both could be happy, and have company ... and not be lonesome any more. I thought Howard was too old to fall in love."

"So?"

"So, at first it was like that. And then Howard started getting possessive and jealous. He started making love to me.... I couldn't stand it, Eddie. I hated it! I tried to make him leave me alone, but he demanded me ... as his wife. It's incest!"

She was shuddering and crying at the same time. I put my arms around her and held her close. I hated Powers so much my guts hurt.

"He wants to know where I go ... what I do. That's why I bet with you, Eddie ... just to put something over on him. It's just a tiny, little victory of my own, Eddie. And Howard detests drinking! I never drank before, but now I like it. Now I can go home, with my brain nice and fuzzy, and go to sleep for a while. And forget how unhappy I am!" Her eyes stared at the floor, hot, burning, and half crazy with hurt.

I took her chin in my hand and tilted her face toward me. And kissed her. "Why don't you leave the old bastard?" I asked.

"I'm going to, Eddie ... I really am. But I don't know where to go ... or what to do. I don't have any money of my own, and there's no place to go ... nor anyone to help me."

"I'll help you," I said.

"Eddie, do you know what you're saying? Howard has millions. He has power and connections! He could break you like ... a stick."

"To hell with him," I told her.
"Do you really love me?" she asked.
"Yes," I replied.
"Are you sure?"
"Sure, I'm sure! How about you?"
"Don't be silly, darling," she said. "I love you ... or I wouldn't be here. Which reminds me ..." she exclaimed sitting up, "I must go to buy you a Christmas present. A wonderful, gorgeous, gigantic present!"
"Wait a minute," I told her, pulling her back down beside me. "There's nothing you can buy with Powers' money that I'd like. Besides, I'd rather have you here for a few more minutes than anything else in the world!"
"You would? Oh, I love to hear you say that!" She slipped around on the lounge and put her arm around my neck; her lips were on mine ... suddenly demanding. I smoothed my hands down the side of her body and to her hips, and pulled her to me.
"Look," I whispered, "there's nothing I want except you."
She kissed me hungrily without answering.
"You know what I mean?"
"Yes," she was breathless.
I stood up from the lounge and took her hand. Without a word she followed me to the bedroom.

CHAPTER SEVEN
Danny and Krassy

The next few months dissolved in a rosy glow. I saw Krassy every day, except on Saturdays and Sundays. She explained that Powers was home on the weekends, and she couldn't slip away. I would mope around the coach house, eating my heart out, and loathing the thought that Krassy was with him. And always. I'd wonder what the answer was going to be. I wanted Krassy to run away from him ... to get a divorce ... to go with me somewhere ... anywhere! Yet I hadn't told her the truth about me; who I was ... just plain Danny April with a cheap, little collection agency. I'd become so tangled up in my own lies, that now I was afraid to tell her the truth. On the other hand, she was still playing the role of Candice Waterbury Powers, and somehow I had the feeling I must never let her know that I knew her real identity; that if I did, it would change our whole relationship.
I was still Eddie Homer, man about town, gambler, and bookmaker. Within the near future, the real Eddie Homer would return; the thought

of him walking in on Krassy and me gave me nightmares. Yet like a guy with a skinful of snow, I couldn't face realities; fact and fiction ... what were lies and what was truth ... were so mixed up in both Krassy's life and my own that I kept postponing making a decision. I couldn't bear to make a move that would keep me from seeing Krassy.

One afternoon Krassy appeared, her eyes bright within deep shadows, and I thought her face was swollen.

"Eddie, darling," she asked, "what are we going to do?"

"I've told you," I said. "Leave Powers and come away with me."

"We've gone all over that ... before. I'm afraid of him, Eddie ... for you as well as me."

I kissed her eyes, and held her to me. I could feel her body shaking.

"Don't worry about me," I told her, "we'll do whatever you want to."

"You know, Eddie, there is something ... oh, this will sound silly ... but it would make me very happy."

"What?"

"You could call me about dinnertime ... just to say hello. Dinner is the hardest time of all, my darling. I think of you, and our lovely afternoon together, and then I must sit down and face Howard...."

"But what about you getting a call? Wouldn't that make him sore?"

"I get a lot of calls ... from many different people. He'd never know. And if I couldn't answer, I'd just not take your call ... but you'd understand. And I'd know you were thinking about me...."

My heart sang, and I held her as tightly as I could. "Sure, baby," I said, "I'll call you. I'll call you every night. I'll say I'm John something-or-other ... what name shall I use?"

"Your own will be all right," she said. "Howard doesn't know who you are, if he should hear it ... and I'd love to hear it. Over and over, again."

"All right."

"And, remember, darling, if I can't answer it ... if Howard is too near ... you won't be angry?"

"I'll never be angry with you," I told her.

And so I called her each evening at six. I'd phone her apartment and the butler would answer. Usually he'd take my name and report back that Mrs. Powers was not at home. I'd hang up with a sick, bad taste in my mouth, hating the butler, hating Powers. Sometimes, though, Krassy would answer the phone herself, and we'd hold a short, whispered conversation and she'd tell me she loved me. Then I'd hang up and the world was a beautiful place for a lucky guy named Danny April.

In the afternoons, Krassy would come to the coach house, but she didn't bother to place bets very often any more. Mostly we'd sit around and drink martinis, and listen to the music, and make love. I moved the big automatic phonograph into the bedroom, and we'd lie on the Hollywood bed, with all the window drapes tightly drawn. The room would be cozy, and dark and warm. I'd prop myself up on an elbow and in the darkness I could faintly see the sweep of her body against the whiteness of the bedclothes. On the pillow, like a deeper shadow, her black hair spread like a mantilla around her head. Sometimes I'd place my fingers under her chin, and trace them lightly down her body, over her stomach and the roundness of her hips. She would be perfectly still, perfectly motionless like a carved ivory statue. Then she would catch her breath, and murmur softly to herself.

Once she said to me, "Darling, do you have much money?"

"No," I told her. "Not a lot ... not like Powers."

"I don't mean that," she smiled. "I mean do you have enough money to buy me presents?"

"Once in a while," I told her.

"No! I mean each day! Can't you buy a twenty-five-cent present for your mistress?"

"Don't say that!" I didn't like the sound of it.

She laughed aloud. "I think you're embarrassed, Eddie," she teased. "But I am your mistress, aren't I?"

"I'm nuts about you," I said.

"Then you must buy me a present. A new present each day! And you must never spend more than a quarter for it."

"What's the idea?" I asked.

"Just because I love to get presents," she explained. She leaned over and kissed me. "I've always liked presents ... and best I love to open them. So now I have you, I insist it is my right to have a present *every* day. Not a big present! And you can't spend over twenty-five cents for it. Remember!"

It amused me. I thought it was a very funny idea. "Sure," I told her, "I'll get you plenty of two-bit presents."

"You must wrap them nicely," she added warningly, "and be sure you put in nice cards." The game soon became a habit, a ritual. Each day, I'd buy her a little present from somewhere. A bunch of daisies or an egg beater. Sometimes, it would be a ball and jacks, a sack of marbles, a pocketbook edition of a novel, or a string of blue beads ... or any one of a thousand things on sale in the dime store. I'd wrap it up in gift wrappings, and put in a card appropriate to the gift.

With the blue beads, I wrote on the card: "Wear these sapphires at your lovely throat ... adoringly, Eddie." With the novel, I enclosed a card saying, "This proves my point ... see what'll happen if you don't leave Powers! Eddie." And so on, and so on. There were maybe twenty-five or thirty others. All of 'em were silly, and Krassy loved them. She'd pretend to hold her breath, and opening the package she'd exclaim on its wrapping. Then in surprise she'd laugh and hold up her present. "It's lovely, darling," she'd say joyfully and push the hair back from her face. "It's just what I need!" Then she'd kiss me, and read the note, and laugh some more.

It was a wonderful life all right. My life was revolving around Krassy. At night, I still slept in my old rooming house because I was afraid that lights would be seen in the coach house. In the morning, I'd get up and go down to the collection agency and work until ten-thirty. Then I'd go up to the coach house, around eleven, and wait for Krassy. She'd come over and stay with me until one-thirty or two. Then, after she went home, I'd go back downtown and work the rest of the day. At six, I'd call her from a downtown phone, then have dinner, and either go back to the office ... or I'd go home. Glasgow and Spindel were busy; the outfit was making money; I had Krassy; and I was damned happy.

And then there was the weekend that Krassy told me Powers was going out of town.

"Just think, darling," she told me excitedly, "we'll have a wonderful three days all to ourselves!"

"Where's he going?" I asked.

"To Washington," she said, and pushed it aside. "Business ... politics ... I don't know."

"What would you like to do?"

Her face lighted up with anticipation. "Let's do something wonderful ... something crazy, and lovely!" She stopped and thought. "I know! Let's go away someplace ... away from Chicago. Where no one knows us ... and we can be together."

Her excitement was gripping me, too. "That sounds great!"

"Howard is leaving late Friday night. So we won't plan to leave Friday. I'll let the servants go for the weekend, and you can pick me up about noon on Saturday."

"I don't have a car," I reminded her.

"That's all right," she said. "I have one ... we'll take it, and drive up to Wisconsin. Maybe we can find a little lodge with a big, stone fireplace, and pine trees ... and a lake...."

"Sure, baby," I agreed, "sure!"

"Pack an overnight bag with warm clothes. You pick me up about noon. Don't bother to ring the bell, because if I'm in the back ... I won't hear it. I'll leave the door unlocked, and you walk in. If I'm not around, I'll be back in my room packing."

"You make that apartment of yours sound like the Union Station," I said.

"It is," she said. "It is worse than Union Station ... it's cold and gloomy and stuffy. It's everything I hate! Just think, darling, I'll be away from it for three wonderful days!"

The next day was Friday, and Krassy came over as usual and we finished up our plans. I got some maps of Wisconsin and we looked them over and found a small winter lodge. That night, I couldn't sleep. Saturday morning, I got up early and shaved; I packed a small suitcase with a couple woolen shirts, a pair of heavy slacks, and some warm socks.

Promptly at noon, I stood in front of Krassy's building carrying my luggage. On thinking it over, I decided it would be better if I didn't go into the building with the suitcase. It might look funny or something. So I walked across the street to the cab stand, and made a deal with the last cabby in the lineup to keep an eye on it for me. I told him I'd be back in about ten minutes and gave him a buck.

As I walked in the building, the doorman stopped me. "Who did you want to see?" he asked.

"I want to see Mrs. Powers," I said.

"I'm sorry. Mrs. Powers isn't at home," he told me.

"I know she's home," I said, "and she's expecting me."

"Mrs. Powers isn't at home," he repeated. For a minute I was stopped, then I remembered that with Howard, and the servants gone, the doorman probably thought Krassy wasn't home either.

"Okay," I said, "so we won't argue. Just call up on your house phone and announce me."

"I'm sorry," he repeated flatly, "but Mrs. Powers isn't at home."

I started to get sore. At that point, I should have gone outside and telephoned her, and had her call the doorman and tell him off. But I was getting more burned by the second, so I shoved him to one side. He grabbed my arm.

"Take your hands off me," I said, "or I'll bust your goddamned face in!" He dropped his hands, quickly, and looked around. "Call Mrs. Powers and tell her I'm on my way up. The name is Homer." I got in the elevator where the operator had been watching with his mouth half open. "Any argument from you, Bud," I told him, "and you'll get it, too."

He didn't say a word. The doors slid shut, and we shot up to the twenty-third floor. I stepped out into the same private foyer. The elevator slammed its doors behind me and dropped down to the main lobby. I walked around the little fishpond, over to the door and started to ring the bell, then remembering Krassy's instructions I put my hand on the knob and turned it. The door swung open and I walked inside ... to find myself face to face with the butler.

"What are you doing here?" he asked.

I was confused ... caught off balance. I was still sore about the doorman, and I was surprised to find the butler in the apartment. Automatically I told him it was none of his business, but before I could say anything else I heard

Krassy's voice saying, "It's all right, Robbins. I'll handle this." Robbins gave a tight bow, and walked down the hallway and disappeared inside a door.

Krassy put her fingers to her lips, and motioned for me to follow her. She turned toward a high, arched doorway leading into a tremendous, high-ceiling living room. Three short steps dropped from the hall into the room. It was quite dark. Drapes were partly drawn over the two-story windows. On one side of the room was a huge fireplace ... big enough to barbecue a cow in.

Krassy was wearing a suit, with a small hat, and had on black gloves. She was carrying a large purse.

"What's the trouble, dear?" asked a man's voice. With a start, I realized a man was sitting, slumped deeply, in a chair before the fireplace. His back was toward us, and I could see only the top of his silver-white hair above the chair.

"Nothing, Howard," Krassy replied walking toward him. It was Howard Monroe Powers sitting there. He didn't turn around and Krassy walked up behind him ... still talking soothingly. My mind was frozen in surprise as I followed behind her.

"Was it that Homer fellow again?" he asked.

"Now, don't worry, Howard," Krassy said softly, "it's all taken care of...." She was behind him now, and she stretched out her hand and patted his head. Then removing her hand, she opened her purse and stepped back.

With one, smooth motion she produced a revolver, placed it at the back of his head and pulled the trigger.

There was a single shot.

And part of Powers' head seemed to fly across the room.

CHAPTER EIGHT

Danny and Krassy

Krassy whirled toward me and shoved the gun into my hands. I stood there, holding the gun, frozen to the spot. She turned quickly and ran toward the archway leading to the hall. Then I realized she was screaming.

"My God! My God! He's shot Howard!" she cried hysterically. The old gray-haired butler suddenly appeared in the archway and looked at me in horror. "Call the police!" she screamed to him. "He'll kill us all! He's mad ... crazy mad!"

The butler disappeared, and I stared at the quiet figure in the chair. The hair was the bright color of catsup now ... like a bottle had been emptied over the top, and was draining with slow inevitability down the upholstery.

Then I became conscious that several other people had entered the room. Down at the far end, standing in a little huddled group, were a maid, a cook in a white apron, and a chauffeur.

I knew I had to get out fast. My mind started to work again, as the first shock of surprise and horror began to wear off. Back of me, Krassy was still screaming. I knew the butler had phoned the cops and they'd arrive soon. I began running toward the group of servants. Somewhere, in their direction, was the kitchen ... a back door ... maybe service stairs. The maid and cook darted away shrieking in fright. The chauffeur stood his ground for only a moment, then he turned and ducked through a large door behind him. At a dead run, I followed at his heels through a big, formal dining room; he raced ahead of me through a tremendous butler's pantry and into the kitchen. He was struggling to open the back door when I caught up to him. Like a cornered animal, his eyes wild with terror, he turned on me and lunged. I swung my arm in a wide haymaker and hit him on the side of the head with the barrel of the gun. He dropped to the floor, in front of the door, his eyes rolled back, his mouth open. I had to drag him back from the door, and step over him, to wrench it open. Dimly, I heard a new sound ... a growing, screeching crescendo. The wail of police sirens.

I burst out into the back hall. For a second I hesitated, looking around, then I punched the button to the automatic service elevator. A red light went on, and indicated the elevator was coming up from the first floor.

Then I realized the sirens were still. The cops had arrived. By now they were probably in the building, and would be on their way up. I turned and ran back to the kitchen. Opening a drawer in an enameled table, I grabbed a silver knife, and a big metal meat cleaver. I rushed back to the hall, and the red light button showed the elevator had now reached the eighteenth floor. I turned and raced up the service stairs to the next floor above. The twenty-fourth. I heard the elevator stop below me at the twenty-third. With my ears at the sliding doors, I listened but could hear nobody in it.

I slipped the silver knife between the catch on the elevator doors, bending the knife nearly double levering it back. Then holding the narrow crack ajar, I slid the blade of the meat cleaver into the crack and jimmied the door all the way back. Holding the door open, I looked down directly on the top of the service elevator. It was about two feet below me. I held the door open, sat on the floor, and put the knife, cleaver, and gun in my pockets. Then releasing the door, I dropped down on the top of the elevator below me. Immediately the door clanged shut. It was dark in the elevator shaft, and it was cold. The wind roared up and down it like a wind tunnel. The top of the elevator was like a big wooden box, and I sat down on it, and wrapped my arms and legs around the heavy metal cable.

Suddenly the door, in the elevator below me, opened and it was filled with cops. "He didn't use this elevator," one of them said, "or it wouldn't be at this floor."

"The bastard probably used the service stairs!"

"Up or down?"

"How the hell do I know? I hope it was down. If it was, we'll get him when he tries to get out the back."

The elevator began to drop to the ground, me riding on top of it. That was around noon ... twelve-thirty, probably. I didn't think to look at the time. The rest of the afternoon, I rode the elevator up and down while they searched the building, the apartments, stairways, and even the little elevator shed housing the machinery on top of the roof.

By six o'clock that night, the cops were convinced I'd managed to escape from the building. From their conversations which I overheard, I learned that Powers' body had been removed, that Krassy had made her statements, and there was a dragnet out over the city for me. At dinnertime, the cops left, leaving a harness cop on the back exit, to prevent me from reentering the building ... in case I came back. He would be relieved at midnight.

By nine o'clock, the service elevator had practically stopped running. It was stationed at the first floor, and no one used it. I heard the cop pull up a chair and seat himself just within the back entrance of the building ... close to the elevator and somewhere to the right. After a while, I heard the rustling of paper, and knew he was settling down to read.

Reaching in my pocket, I pulled out a cigarette lighter. It was windy in the shaft and hard to keep the flame going. By its flickering light, I examined the top of the elevator and discovered a small, trap door which was used to make repairs, and which opened into the inside of the cage. The door pulled back on hinges, and I gently eased it open. It didn't squeak, and I pulled it all the way back, so it was lying flat on the roof of the elevator.

Stretching out on my stomach, I reached an arm inside the trap. I could touch the light bulb which was fastened to the ceiling of the cage. The bulb was hot, and it felt good to my fingers which were cramped and frozen. For a couple minutes, I warmed my hands until my fingers had feeling again. Then I loosened the bulb and plunged the inside of the elevator into darkness. Slowly I stood up on my feet, and raised and lowered them until circulation returned.

Once in a while the cop would clear his throat, or move around in his chair. I could hear him. I decided to risk smoking a cigarette. Not that the cop could see it, but maybe he could smell the smoke. My nerves were jumping and I needed one bad. So while my feet were coming back to life, I lit a cigarette and blew the smoke over my head ... hoping the draft would suck it up the shaft.

Finally, my feet were alive, I could feel with my hands, and my cigarette was finished. I moved directly to the edge of the trap door, and squatted down on my haunches. The inside of the elevator was pitch black compared to the lighter blackness of the shaft. Reaching in my pocket, I pulled out a handful of change. I selected a coin with my fingers, and dropped it through the trap door.

In the silence it rang like a bell.

I could sense the cop listening. Then I heard the rustle of his paper again. I dropped another coin through the trap. This time, I heard the chair squeak, and I knew the cop was standing up listening. His heavy, slow footsteps approached the elevator. Outside the door he was listening, I tensed myself, and dropped another coin. It felt big ... like a half-dollar ... and it chimed on the floor of the elevator.

The inside of the elevator flooded with light as the cop flung the door back and light poured in from the hall. He had pulled his gun, and he peered suspiciously inside. The darkness of the elevator stopped him for a minute. He stepped back, and let the door close. I could hear him walk back to his chair and pick it up. Then he returned, opened the door, and kept it propped open with the chair. He stood in the doorway and looked around the elevator. His eyes caught the flash of the half-dollar on the floor.

He stepped inside the elevator and bent over to pick it up. I could see his shoulders beneath me, under the trap door. I launched myself through the trap.

Feet first!

I landed on the cop square in the middle of his back, and it slammed him face down on the floor of the elevator. I rolled over to one side, freeing my right hand, and slugged him with the revolver. He went out fast.

I stepped into the hallway and made for the back exit, and in the light I realized I looked like hell. I was covered with grease and oil. Outside the building, I cut straight to the alley without being seen. Halfway down the alley, where it was good and dark, I paused by a pile of dirty snow, left over from a storm weeks ago, and tried to wash off my face and hands, and dried them on my handkerchief. I did the best I could, and felt I was a little cleaner; I put the handkerchief back in my pocket and headed toward North Avenue.

Run! Grab a cab! Swipe a car! Christ! I managed to keep a grip on my panic; a small remaining bit of reason told me I couldn't take a chance. A running man is suspicious; a cab driver has a memory; a stolen car can have an accident. So I walked. On North Avenue, I cut over to Clark Street, and started south toward my old rooming house. On Clark, I began to feel better. No one would give much attention to my dirty, battered look. Too many other people on that street look the same way.

I passed a small hamburger stand, and realized I was hungry. A guy and his girl were seated at the counter, and an old bum was gumming a cup of coffee. I went in and ordered a bowl of chili, a hamburger, and coffee. I made myself eat the food slow.

At the corner, I caught a streetcar and rode it down to Superior. There I got off, and cut over to my rooming house, stopping only to buy a couple papers.

No one was in the hall when I got home. I went up to my room, stripped off my clothes, and walked down the hall to the bath. I took a long one, but the water was cold.

So far everything was okay.

But as soon as I got in bed, I started to shiver. I shook like I had the D.T.'s. I couldn't stop it. Up to now, I'd been so damned scared I'd no time to think. Now it hit me! Like a club! I started to climb out of bed ... then realized I didn't have any place to go. I'd come home ... to the only place I knew. It was as good as any.

Back in bed, I started getting sick. I staggered to the bathroom and vomited. It didn't help any, I still felt sick. And then I began to think of Krassy! Why? Why had she done it? Why had she framed me? I rolled and tossed, and my body was hot, and my mouth was burning, I started sweating and the sheets became wet, and they wrapped all around me. Time passed in a funny, sticky, hot way, and then I remembered something else. I couldn't think very good any more, but I remembered I still had the gun which shot Powers. I had to get rid of it; had to.... Thoughts would jump complete in my mind ... then they would just sort of fade out. Where would I hide the gun? Blank. Cops would be watching trash dumps and sewers. Blank. I had to get rid of it fast. Blank. It kept up like that.

Somehow I got some clothes on and I walked over to Chicago Avenue. Out of nowhere, part of the night I'd been to Evanston and drank on Howard Street came back. I caught an el and got off on Howard. I walked north and toward the lake. Somewhere, in that direction, was a cemetery. I found it. The main gate was locked, so I walked around the high wall, until I found a place protected from the street. I was stumbling, and my arms didn't work too well, and I had a hell of a time hauling myself over the wall. It was dark, and there wasn't any moon, and maybe after twenty minutes I came to a grave which was still covered with fresh earth.

I got down on my hands and knees and started digging a small hole. I was careful to pull out each handful of dirt and place it beside me where I could find it. I clawed my fingers raw and bleeding, on the cold, half-frozen ground, digging a hole into which I could stretch my arm. I stuffed the revolver in the whole length of my arm, and then the knife and cleaver.

I filled the hole up with the same earth I'd removed, and was careful to do the neatest job I could with it. When I was through, I went around scooping up some handfuls of dirty snow and plastering them over the hole. When the snow melted, it would leave no trace of my digging.

I got back to my room all right. But I discovered I'd been up all night without socks or a shirt. And I hadn't worn an overcoat, either. I got back in bed.

That was the last thing I remember for two weeks.

Distinctly, that is. Time and day and night and things like that didn't exist. I had pneumonia. The next day, when I didn't show at the office, Glasgow came up to look for me. He had me taken to the hospital. All that time I don't know what happened. A couple times ... I think ... maybe I came out a little, because in the layers of my fuzziness a little idea kept skipping around. It wasn't an idea, exactly, it was more like, a memory which kept trying to tell me something.

Then when I started getting better, and could lie there in the hospital, and think a little bit, it hit me! The idea. I asked Glasgow to go to my room and bring me the newspapers I'd bought the night I escaped the cops.

The story of the killing was splashed all over the front pages complete with pictures of Powers and Krassy. Krassy was wearing the black suit and hat she'd had on in the apartment. The veil on the hat covered her eyes and the upper part of her face, and she held her head turned partly away. It wasn't a good picture, and you couldn't tell much about her looks, except you knew she must be a damned good-looking woman.

One headline read: GAMBLER KILLS MILLIONAIRE BANKER!

The other sheet, a tabloid said: GAMBLER PLAYBOY SHOOTS BANKER BEFORE PLEADING WIFE'S EYES!

Both of the stories followed pretty much the same pattern. One of them read:

> Edward Homer, notorious Chicago gambler, today forced his way into the home of Howard Monroe Powers, banker and philanthropist, and shot him to death before the eyes of his wife. Mrs. Powers, who had been molested by Homer's attentions, had left word that the gambler should not be admitted to the Powers' apartment. She was leaving to go downtown, when Homer threatened his way past the doorman, and broke into the apartment shortly after noon today. Forcing his way past Herbert Robbins, the Powers' butler, Homer went to the living room to confront the well-known banker.
>
> According to Mrs. Powers, who was present, but helpless, Homer approached Mr. Powers and said, "I've been waiting to

> give you this," then pulling a gun he shot the banker in the head as he attempted to rise from his chair.
>
> Mrs. Powers rushed from the room calling to the butler for help. Robbins immediately notified the police who hurried to the scene of the killing. Homer made his escape from the apartment, by the back entrance, after brutally attacking Arthur Buehler, the Powers' chauffeur, who heroically attempted to capture the killer.

There was more of the same with statements from the doorman who said he'd been given explicit instructions by Mrs. Powers to keep me out, but that I'd jammed a gun in his ribs and forced him to let me by. The elevator operator told how I'd threatened to slug him.

Robbins, the butler, maintained I had "either managed to pick the lock on the door, which was always bolted, or used a skeleton key" to get in. He told about meeting me face to face in the hallway, and my face "was a furious red with a very angry look." He also stated he'd seen me in the living room, holding the smoking gun still pointed at Powers.

Buehler, the chauffeur, gave a blow-by-blow description in which he and I fought in the kitchen, and I'd saved myself from certain capture only by shoving the gun against his head, then batting him with it.

The thing had sure shaped up. God what a beautiful frame! Krassy had pulled the old mousetrap play to perfection. I didn't have a chance! I told Glasgow that I wanted to catch up with everything that had happened since I'd been sick, and would he mind getting me back copies of the papers I'd missed. He got them all right.

The killing continued to be big news and there were lots of pictures of Powers ... old ones and mostly biographical; and there were pictures of Robbins, Buehler, the doorman, and even a so-called "composite sketch" of Homer drawn by a police artist from the descriptions given to him. It looked as much like me as an aardvark. Even my own mother wouldn't have recognized me from the drawing. But Krassy! Krassy was cagey! Her doctors refused to permit her to be photographed, and the only available picture was the one taken the day of the killing, the one with the black hat and veil, in which she looked like any one of a thousand other women, and not at all like Krassy Almauniski, Katherine Andrews, Karen Allison, Candice Austin, or Mrs. Dana Waterbury.

Her lack of pictures, however, didn't affect the continuing flow of details concerning the crime. Mrs. Powers told how she'd gone to my apartment once to ask me to stop molesting her. There were pictures of Homer's coach house, and a description of the "luxuriously furnished bookie rooms." The cops had fingerprinted the joint, and had found a number of prints which they couldn't identify.

Krassy also told how I'd attempted to shower her with expensive gifts ... which she'd promptly returned to me. As evidence, she showed the cops the notes that came with them "Wear these sapphires at your lovely throat ... adoringly, Eddie," ... and all the others, too.

And Robbins, innocently, backed her up on her story. He told how I called her every night around dinnertime and how "madame refused to speak to the fellow."

Mrs. Powers repeated her story over and over again. She had her witnesses ... plenty of them. Robbins, the maid, cook, chauffeur. She told about meeting me one day at the race track ... and how I'd forced my attentions on her. She'd never gone out with me ... never seen me alone, except when she had called at the coach house to plead with me to leave her alone. And at that meeting, so she stated, there were numerous other persons present who were making bets. These persons, however, never came forward to substantiate her story.

Then the cab driver, the one I'd left my suitcase with, decided he needed a little publicity, so he came forward with the suitcase, and told how I'd left it with him the day of the killing. The cops looked over the heavy clothing and decided I'd planned my getaway to Canada. They started looking in that direction.

That brought the situation pretty much up to date. The nurse walked in my room and said, "You'll be able to leave tomorrow, the doctor says, Mr. April."

And that was the answer. I was Danny April. I wasn't Eddie Homer! Hell! There was no such guy as the Eddie Homer the cops were looking for. Eventually, the cops would find the real Eddie Homer ... but it wasn't *me* ... it wasn't the same guy. I'd never been picked up by the cops, so I knew they couldn't match fingerprints back to Danny April. But there was something else! I *never* could ... *as long as I lived* ... afford to get picked up by the cops or fingerprinted for any other purpose. If I did, inevitably the prints would be matched.

And I was glad I'd loved Krassy the way I did. Because I had loved her so much, it had saved my life! I'd wanted her so badly, that I'd built up a person who was real to her. A person called Eddie Homer. She believed it ... and she was hanging a frame on the guy who'd loved her so much he had lived a complete lie himself.

Eddie Homer, the gambler, the bookie; Eddie Homer who lived in the coach house, and loved Bach, who was born in New York, and went to Columbia; Eddie Homer whose mistress she'd been ... didn't exist! He didn't exist anywhere in the world.

Except in her imagination.

The cops were going crazy trying to find him. He had no criminal record. He'd disappeared into thin air.

After I got out of the hospital, nothing new developed for a week. I went to the office each day; saw Glasgow and Spindel and read the papers. Then there was real news.

Eddie Homer had been found!

The real Edward A. Homer had been picked up, blue station wagon and all. He'd driven up to the coach house ... and straight into the arms of the cops.

But it wasn't the *right* Mr. Homer! Mrs. Powers couldn't identify him ... neither could the other witnesses. And Mr. Homer was mad as hell and threatened to sue everyone for libel. He proved conclusively, and with the aid of twenty reputable witnesses, that he'd been in Miami, Florida, the day ... the hour and the minute ... of the killing. He'd never met Mrs. Powers, and from his remarks, you got the impression he wasn't sorry, either. Then the old guy from the key shop stepped into the picture. He told about making a key for the coach house, but he couldn't identify the real Edward Homer as the guy he'd made the key for. All he could remember was he'd made a key for another guy. It was all pretty damn confusing.

But there was no doubt the original Edward A. Homer was innocent, and he proved he'd lived in the coach house for three years ... and had never run or operated a bookie joint. There or any place else.

It was a fine mess, all right! The cops were helpless. They kept trying to add up the situation, and finally decided that possibly Mrs. Powers, herself, might also be a little confused. But Mrs. Powers' undoubted sincerity concerning "an Eddie Homer" at this point had become an obsession and was unshakable. Her obvious sincerity, plus about thirty million dollars, plus the best legal counsel in the country, convinced the cops.

The inquest found that Howard Monroe Powers was willfully shot to death by an unknown person operating under an alias. Other aliases and true name unknown. It recommended that such person be found and turned over to the due process of law of the State of Illinois, County Cook.

But they never found him. Me, that is. And Mrs. Powers, unable to overcome her grief, has moved to France. The Riviera.

I'm just Danny April, owner of the Clarence Moon Collection Agency. And I get along pretty good. Except at night. Then I see the beautiful figure of a woman, on the bed beside me; her hair black as death and floating around her head like a mantilla. She doesn't have any face. It is smoky-like, and when I go to kiss it, it dissolves away and there's nothing there. Instead, I hear a faint, high scream of a siren wailing, and the doors break down and the cops are there. They're arresting me and they take me down to the station. They fingerprint me. Then a big cop looks up and laughs in my face and says, "Welcome, Danny April, we've been waiting for you." And they take all the change out of my pockets, and when they count it they call the electric company.

And they say, "We've got another customer for you." They drop the coins in a meter-box, and somewhere a dynamo starts whirring, and the lights start to flicker and a low moaning starts up in all the cell blocks. And then the cops say real polite: "Won't you please come in and be seated?"

The End

The Longest Second

Bill S. Ballinger

To Laura …

1

It can happen that the planets stand still and eternity holds its breath. A second becomes a lifetime, and it is the longest second in the world for you alone.

When I awakened, I stared straight above me at the ceiling—a large oblong shape painted a drab white. Someplace in the room a small hooded bulb threw a pale stingy light into the darkness. After a moment I could hear the moving of bodies, the rustling of clothes in the room, and I attempted to turn my head.

It was then I realized that my throat had been cut.

The pain ran down both sides of my neck, burrowing hotly within my chest. I gasped, choking for air.

The next day I regained consciousness again. A large glass jar of glucose hung above my bed, and drops of it flowed through a transparent plastic tube into my arm. The fluid poured life into my body; it didn't hurt. Soft rubber-soled footsteps approached my bed and a face, capped in nurse's white, peered down at me. Her face, long, thin, and preoccupied, broke into an impersonal smile when she saw that my eyes were open.

"Ah," she said; her hand appeared suddenly and her fingers touched my lips. "Don't try to speak. Just keep quiet, I'll be right back with the doctor." Her footsteps hushed away and I continued to lie there, feeling the throb of my pulse beating against the needle in my arm. From the corner of my eye, I sensed rather than saw the presence of a large floor screen. On the other side of the screen, I heard the giving of bed springs, the heavy turning of a body. Then silence.

Within a few minutes, the nurse returned, trailing a step behind a doctor. They stopped at the foot of my bed, and the doctor glanced over a chart which was attached there. He was a young man, with a pink-and-white skin and light brown hair cut short. He looked young.

Suddenly it struck me that I didn't know my own age. I didn't even know my own name.

The doctor lowered the chart and raised his eyes to look at me. "You're a very lucky man," he said, his voice serious. "You don't realize what a close call you've had."

Lifting my left arm, the one without the tube in it, I pointed to my throat. The doctor nodded. "Yes," he said, "your throat has been cut. Did you do it?"

I didn't know.

The doctor continued, "At present you're unable to talk. Frankly it's possible that you won't speak again." He watched me carefully. I felt no particular reaction. It was as if he were discussing someone else. He looked at me. I looked back at him.

It was the nurse who broke the silence. In an attempt to soften the blow, she said, "Well, we must hope for the best." Her voice sounded determinedly optimistic, as well as banal.

The doctor nodded. "In the meantime," he said, "you'll have to lie quietly. Don't try to speak, don't attempt to move your head. If you do, you may begin hemorrhaging. For the next few days we'll keep you under sedation. You'll spend most of your time sleeping." The nurse approached the side of my bed. Lifting my left arm, she swabbed it deftly with alcohol and then I felt the sudden bite of a hypodermic. The doctor and nurse disappeared behind the screen. After that I went to sleep again.

Perhaps it was the morphine which made it begin, but I found myself in a reoccurring nightmare. At first there wasn't much to it; it was only that the hospital room was no longer the same room. It was another room, darkly lit except for a light in the far corner. I kept waiting for something to appear from behind that spot of light. That was all. But the terror of waiting, the anxiety of suspense, the anticipation of fear were freezing. Never have I been so monstrously frightened.

As if this were a scene on a loop of film which kept going around over and over again, the nightmare continued. I waited, alone with my horror. Possibly I waited in this nightmare for three days, because it was three days later when I again recognized the doctor. Once more he was standing at the foot of my bed. When I focused my eyes on him, he inclined his head to look at me intently. "Well," he said, "you've had a long sleep ... seventy-two hours." I began to nod. "Don't do that!" he commanded sharply. "Keep your head as still as you can. I think most of the danger of hemorrhaging is over, but you must continue to be careful."

Tentatively, I raised my left hand and lifted a finger at him. He regarded me thoughtfully. I lowered the single finger, then raised two. I repeated this several times. Then he smiled and agreed. "That's a good idea ... excellent! Raise one finger for 'yes,' two fingers for 'no.' All right?"

I raised one finger. "We'll need some information for our records," he said, "so let's see if you can answer my questions yes or no. There was no identification on you when you were picked up by the ambulance. Do you have any identification?"

I raised two fingers: no. The doctor looked puzzled for a moment. "Are you listed in the phone book?" he asked.

Was I, or was I not, listed in the phone book? Not knowing my own name I couldn't say one way or the other. I couldn't answer. Desperately, I turned the palm of my hand upward in a noncommittal gesture.

Immediately the doctor grasped my meaning. "You mean you don't know who you are?"

Yes, I agreed, raising one finger.

"You've lost your memory?" he continued.

Yes.

"You've forgotten your name and address?"

Yes.

He ran his hand over the top of his short brown hair.

"Did you try to take your own life?" he asked me finally. Again I raised my hand, palm up, to indicate there was no answer.

Turning away from the bed, he absently pushed the sections of the floor screen together, shoving it to one side. "Tomorrow," he said, "you'll be well enough to see the police. Perhaps they'll be able to identify you."

He left the room, and for a few minutes I stared ahead of me, into space over the foot of the bed, thinking. Even then, I had no particular reaction to the situation. My wound caused me no great pain, only a combination of sensations. Burning was one; aching was another. These sensations were not actually pain, at least not in the literal sense, and were not too bad to bear. Possibly I was still under drugs.

Holding my hand before my face, I studied it. I could not remember having seen it before, and I examined it carefully and with curiosity. The hand was large, rather broad, and with strong fingers. The nails were trimmed and in good condition, showing they had received care. Turned over, the palm showed no calluses from laboring.

The back of my hand, under additional inspection, disclosed a shadowing of heavy hair; the skin was smooth and unwrinkled.

I hadn't used my hands to earn a living; this was the first fact I had been able to discover about myself. I dropped my hand on the bed. But my name. What was my name? Who was I? Then names began to run through my mind, coming from nowhere, without effort: Aly Khan, Duke of Windsor, Ernest Hemingway, Gary Cooper, Colonel Horstman, Adlai Stevenson, Goethe.

The flow stopped with a jolt. It was as if I had slammed down a floodgate. What had I been doing; what had I been thinking? These names which I recalled, which I remembered from somewhere, had come flooding back into my mind; but these were names which most people see and hear through newspapers, radio, television, motion pictures, and books during the course of their daily life. Did I really know them, or at least some of them? Or had I only heard about them?

In my excitement, I struggled to a sitting position. Immediately I choked, gasping for air, strangling, and I fell back against the pillow. From across the room I heard a voice say, "You better take it easy. You heard what the doc said."

After a few moments I could breathe again. Running my eyes past the foot of my bed, into the room beyond it, I searched for the voice. The end of a second bed came into view. I couldn't see who was in the other bed—only the two white pyramids the feet made beneath the sheet. The voice began again. It was a man's voice, high and unpleasant. "I heard the doc talking to you," he said, "and I gather you got to take it easy and not talk."

I said nothing, while the voice continued, "We're sort of roommates, us being in the same room." Into my mind flashed a fleeting picture of another room, a university room, with a heavily raftered ceiling and rough plastered walls. Another roommate far distant and past. But the scene fled immediately under the cascade of words in the room. "My name is Merkle, Edward Merkle. My friends call me Ed," the voice from the other bed went on; his voice droned as he told me about his sickness, about his operation. I closed my eyes while his words washed over me, smothering me under an avalanche of sound. Somewhere in a description of his job, I fell asleep, although there was something that I wanted to recall. But I couldn't recall it right then.

2

The Eighth Precinct station, in Manhattan, is located on Mercer between Third and Fourth Streets. It is a five-story building with a gray stone front; five steps lead up to the heavy, wooden, carved double-door. The upper halves of the door contain delicate ironwork, and are flanked by two metal lamps set against the façade of the building. At night these lamps glow with a greenish light.

The precinct runs from Houston Street, on the Bowery, across to Sixth Avenue (or the Avenue of the Americas), then uptown to Fourteenth Street. It is a cosmopolitan area including parts of the Bowery, manufacturing districts, New York University, sections of Greenwich Village, exclusive lower Fifth Avenue, shopping sections, Washington Square, a slice of Broadway, and innumerable side streets containing charming town houses, brownstones converted into boardinghouses, big modern apartments, walk-up flats, restaurants, cafés, bars, some night clubs, cheap hotels, expensive hotels, Sailor's Snug Harbor, Salvation Army posts, a constantly busy fire department, and many rich churches.

One hundred and eight uniformed police and sixteen detectives work out of the Eighth Precinct. As a rule, the Eighth is a fairly quiet and peaceful precinct, offering no particular problems to the men working in it. But, occasionally, when it does have a crime, it has a good one, or weird one, enough to satisfy anyone working on it.

It was approximately two A.M. when the call came through, and Precinct Detective David Burrows was assigned to it. He was on the midnight to eight A.M. shift. Mercer Street, which in the daylight has nothing to offer in the way of a view, early in the morning is dark, narrow, quite dirty, and is lined with melancholy buildings and warehouses.

Burrows drove, with two uniformed men, to the address reported and was nearly immediately joined by Detective Alvin Jensen, from Homicide East. From that moment on, the two detectives ... Burrows as the precinct detective, and Jensen from Homicide ... would cooperate, integrating their activities, and sharing the responsibilities.

Squad cars, three of them, were pulled up in the narrow tiny street, their headlights washing the night away from the front of the house with the body before it. The Squad cars were added to in number by the arrival of the police laboratory truck.

Burrows walked over to the body and looked down at it. Tentatively he touched the lifeless hand with the tip of his finger. He took a deep breath and said to Jensen, "This looks like a dandy."

3

Miss Pierson entered the room carrying a jar of glucose. "Time for another intravenous," she said. She hung the jar on a hook by the bed and attached a length of plastic tubing. Merkle watched her with interest. Anything in the room interested him; he refused to read, and spent his time talking to me. When the nurse placed the needle in my arm, Merkle said to me, "It was just a week ago today they brought you in."

"It was in the morning," the nurse corrected him, "about two o'clock in the morning."

"When they wheeled him in here, he was whiter than the sheet wrapped around him." Merkle paused, then added slyly, "'Course, that's not saying much, considering the laundry they got here."

Miss Pierson refused to be offended. "Perhaps you'd prefer to do your own laundry, Mr. Merkle."

Merkle shook his head. "Nope," he laughed. "But as far as he was concerned I sure figured he was a goner."

The nurse reached up to turn the small valve in the bottle, and the glucose began to run through the tube. She looked at me and said, "It was very fortunate for you that Doctor Stone was still in the operating room when you arrived." I asked her a question with my eyes, and she read it correctly. "Doctor Stone," she told me seriously, "is one of the finest throat surgeons in New York City. He'd just finished an emergency, a private case of his own, when you arrived. He agreed to do what he could." She checked the glucose to see that it flowed properly, then continued, "You can be thankful that Doctor Stone was here. Just sheer chance that he was too."

This was the first that I had heard of Doctor Stone. This man, a stranger, had saved my life; I didn't know whether to thank him or not. Perhaps I had a good reason for wanting to die, and didn't know it. Doctor Stone might have done me no favor after all.

Merkle, during his stay in the hospital, had picked up a number of medical terms which he enjoyed using whenever possible. He asked the nurse, "Was he in bad shock?"

Miss Pierson glanced at him. "Certainly he was in shock. The injury was bad enough, but the shock was worse."

"For a couple, three days," Merkle recalled, "everybody was running in and out of here with plasma and blood ..."

The nurse didn't reply. She walked out of the room.

"... and giving transfusions," Merkle concluded to no one in particular.

I could think clearly now, although I had no memory extending beyond the four walls of the hospital room. Three days of shock when I had first been received; another three days of sedation and drugs; then today. Seven days ... one week. For all practical purposes that was my complete life. Before that I hadn't existed. I was one week old now. My mind returned to the day before: my name? What was my name? I tried to recall what I had been thinking when I thought of the Duke of Windsor, Ernest Hemingway, Adlai Stevenson, but my thoughts were interrupted by the appearance of Doctor Minor.

Minor seriously studied my chart. Nodding gravely, he looked at me. "How are you feeling today? Good?" I signaled, yes. "I see you're enjoying a good lunch," he said, watching the glucose, and making an ancient hospital joke.

Merkle called from across the room. "Yeah, just chock full of goodness and real flavor!"

"Certainly," agreed the doctor, "it's glucier glucose." The doctor was satisfied with his display of wit. I didn't mind. I didn't care, as a matter of fact. Minor and Merkle, both, were trying to be friendly. Whether they were friendly didn't make any difference. If they wanted to make the effort, it was all right; frankly, I would have preferred they kept quiet.

Miss Pierson looked through the doorway and Minor signaled to her. She disappeared and in a few minutes a short, dark man walked in. He was wide in the shoulders, carried a slight paunch, and had a still, watchful face. He glanced at Minor inquiringly. "Okay, Doc?" he asked.

"I guess so," replied Minor, "but as I've told you, he can't speak. Don't try to force him or you'll have to leave."

The dark man nodded and turned his gaze on me. He regarded me impassively, standing a slight distance from the bed. For a moment he searched his pockets, and then removed a crumpled pack of cigarettes. He put one in his mouth, although he didn't light it. Finally, he said, "My name is Santini. I'm a detective from the Eighth Precinct. I got to ask you a few questions. The doc says you can signal me answers ... yes and no. Okay with me. Now, for the first question: do you know who you are?"

No.

"You don't remember anything?"

No.

"You don't remember who did it to you?"

No.

"You don't remember if you did it to yourself?"

No.

"You don't remember where you got that thousand bucks?"

No. I didn't know that I had possessed a thousand dollars. It explained several points, however ... why I should have a semiprivate room, why a specialist such as Doctor Stone agreed to do an emergency operation. Charity cases, especially police charity cases, don't receive that kind of treatment.

So I had a thousand dollars. Santini watched my face, attempting to read my expression. He read nothing which was exactly what I had to conceal.

Santini removed the unlit cigarette from his mouth, twisted the loose end of it together neatly so it had a small paper nipple, and replaced it in his mouth thoughtfully. "Well," he observed to no one in particular, "it's not often some guy is found in the street with his throat cut. Particularly if he is only wearing a pair of shoes and is otherwise as naked as the day he was born." Suddenly he stared at me. His eyes were very hard and very brown, set close together. They gave the impression of intense emotion ... curiosity, ruthlessness, and carefully repressed bitterness.

I stared back at him. I sensed his animosity which I could not understand. The detective represented a threat, a danger to me, and yet I did not know why this might be so. I couldn't see where my personal problem should make such a difference to him. After all I was the one who had been wounded; possibly I had even done it myself, and if I had, I couldn't see where it was any of his business. Finally he stared away from me and his eyes riveted on Minor. "You often find guys with their throats slit and a grand in their shoe, Doc?"

Minor regarded Santini with a fleeting expression of dislike. "Not often," he told the detective.

Santini shrugged. "'Not often,' the doc says. Me? I've never seen it even once before." He turned his attention back to me. "The shoes don't tell us much. We've tried to trace them ... nice expensive shoes, better than a cop wears. But not handmade. No, not handmade. Too many of 'em sold each year."

"What about fingerprints?" asked Minor. "And that old scar on his back?"

"Ah, yes, fingerprints and that old scar," replied Santini pretending to a sudden recollection, "well, I'll tell you. We checked with our own files and we don't have them. Then we checked with the FBI and they don't have them. Now we're checking with the Army, Navy, Air Force, and all the ships at sea. Maybe they got 'em, but we'll just have to wait a little while to find out." He turned his face to me and his eyes were hot on my face. "I think you're bluffing," he said softly, "and I don't think you've lost your memory. I got to take the doc's word that you can't talk, but I won't take it that you can't remember. You're covering up something."

"I don't think so," Doctor Minor corrected him. "It's very difficult to fake amnesia successfully."

"It is?" asked Santini sarcastically. "If you can't say anything, it's hard?" He shoved his hands in his pockets wearily. "Oh, hell! If a guy wants to knock himself off, I say okay. Let him do it just so long as he don't mess anybody else up. But if he doesn't pull it off, then I got to take time to run it down. Or take it the other way, somebody else gives him the knife and he knows it, why not say so? There's enough other things for me to do."

I could see Santini's point. It didn't necessarily interest me, and there was no way to discuss it with him.

"The woman, of course, says she never saw you before," Santini continued thoughtfully.

Woman? What woman? I wondered whom he meant? The detective again was watching me closely. I set my lips and noiselessly mouthed the word "who?"

"Who?" repeated Santini. "You mean the woman?"

Yes.

"The one who found you?"

Yes.

"Well," said Santini, "there's this woman by the name of Hill, Bianca Hill. Does her name mean anything to you?"

No.

"Nice, decent woman as far as we know. She found you bleeding all over her doorstep. She called the cops, then sat down and held her thumbs at your throat until the ambulance arrived."

First, I thought, it was Doctor Stone who sewed up the wound and saved my life ... for a cut of the thousand dollars, no doubt. Then, a woman named Hill sat on her doorstep and held my throat in her hands to prevent me from bleeding to death. Why?

Santini finally lit his cigarette. "I'm going now," he said. "I'll see you again. You won't be going anywhere for a while."

That afternoon, shortly after lunch, the hospital discharged Merkle. Before he left, he wrote out his home phone and address, and told me to be sure to call him sometime. It was quiet in the room after he had gone, and I didn't miss him. I lay in my bed, motionless, and permitted my mind to wander. There were many things I could remember, things which were in my mind, but which I couldn't connect up with anything. For instance, I knew I was in New York; I knew Fifth Avenue, the Empire State Building, Times Square, although I couldn't recall if I lived in New York or how I knew these other locations.

This chain of thought eventually led me to wondering about my name again.... Bing Crosby, Pablo Picasso, Charles Lindbergh, Colonel Horstman. Snap! Again my mind snapped shut. Slowly, very slowly, I went back over the names ... Crosby, an entertainer; Picasso, painter; Lindbergh, public figure; Horstman—? Who was Horstman? The name Colonel Horstman was familiar to me, as familiar as the others, but I couldn't identify him. Who was Colonel Horstman? I worked with the idea, approaching it both directly and indirectly, but I could carry the thought no further. I only knew that the name of Horstman was one I had known very well; but who he was I didn't know. It almost seemed as if he existed in another dimension, separated by time, space, memory ... and contact. Contact, in the sense of communication; that he could be reached only by another type of thinking, another mind, or another language.

The hospital didn't place a patient in my room immediately. That night I began to dream again. It was the old familiar dark room with the spot of light in the corner. I stood within the room waiting for someone to appear in the light. Cold sweat beaded my forehead while I waited. In my dream I waited all night ... all night for someone, or something, to appear. Whoever, whatever it was, didn't show up. But when I awakened in the morning, I knew that sometime it would appear.

4

With the cars, the lights, and the activity, the street had come alive ... at two in the morning. The uniformed police kept the curious at a careful distance. Gorman, from the Medical Examiner's office, was inspecting the body carefully but without changing its position. Gorman's activities had been shielded from the eyes of the curious crowd by a portable canvas screen.

A few feet from Gorman, Burrows and Jensen waited patiently for the doctor to conclude his preliminary examination. Final and complete posting could take place only at the laboratory.

Burrows said, "It doesn't look like a sex job, even if the body has been stripped."

"All except for the shoes," said Jensen. "Why take the trouble to remove the clothes and leave the shoes and socks?"

From behind them, in the house, a high, piercing wail screamed through the night. Burrows shivered at the sound. "Jesus," he said, "that gets me."

"Yeah," agreed Jensen, "that's the dame who found him. Gorman gave her a hypo, but it hasn't taken effect yet."

"We'll have to talk to her in the morning," Burrows replied.

"Sure. If we're lucky. By that time her own doctor will probably put us off for a week."

The wail trailed away lonesomely into the night.

Burrows picked up their conversation. "You think the shoes mean something? A symbol of some kind?"

"It could be. Remember the guy ... what's the name ... Clinton, who strangled three dames and always insisted on using a pair of smoke-gray nylon stockings?"

Burrows said slowly, "It could be that sort of thing but maybe it might be done to conceal the identity." He turned partly away, and cupping his hands lit a match. The flame burned yellow against the fullness of his face, etching and molding his features with shadows.

"It's pretty hard to conceal an identity these days," Jensen said in part agreement, "but it isn't impossible. Or possibly the idea is not to conceal who it is, but just to gain a little time by slowing up the identification."

Burrows dragged on the cigarette, the tip glowing red. "Or, I suppose, there's even another way to look at it. Maybe, being stripped is supposed to make for a quick identification, to mean something to somebody." He shrugged, half-humorously. "That's pretty damned farfetched, though."

Jensen neither agreed nor disagreed. He stepped around the screen and watched Gorman for an instant, then returned to join Burrows. "How's the doc getting along?" Burrows asked.

"He's still at it," Jensen replied.

5

Santini followed Doctor Minor into the room. "There's something about a hospital that always gets me," the detective said. "It isn't the smell, it's the feeling. You know, everybody waiting for something to happen. Waiting to get well, or go ahead and die."

"You get used to it," replied Minor. He looked at me, winked slowly, and turned back to Santini. "Take it easy with him again today," the doctor told him.

I thought about the wink. I didn't like the idea that Minor believed he was conferring any favors on me.

Santini said, "I'll take it easy, but before you go, Doc, give me a little run down on how his throat is."

Minor automatically reached for my wrist. Momentarily he seemed to sink within himself; whether he was counting my pulse or considering Santini's question, I couldn't decide. Then Minor dropped my hand, straightened his white jacket, and began to explain slowly. "The carotid arteries are on each side of the throat—on the far sides, that is—and are crossed by the jugular veins. The recurrent laryngeal nerve, one on both sides of the larynx, controls the vocal cords to the larynx. The larynx, as you probably know, is the voice box. Located below the larynx is the trachea ... the windpipe."

Santini was following the doctor's description carefully. He nodded his understanding. Minor continued, "The patient, here, received the main force of the blow across the trachea, nearly severing it, although it was still possible for him receive some air through his wound. He could not have continued indefinitely to breathe in such a manner, but he would not asphyxiate immediately. The force of the blow deteriorated at the sides of his neck, but not without severing one laryngeal nerve completely and badly damaging the other. His immediate danger was from loss of blood resulting from the wounds in the carotid arteries. Local application of aid where he was found prevented his bleeding to death quickly, and when he arrived at the hospital immediate surgery was indicated and completed."

"In other words," said Santini, "if the blow had cut him just a little deeper, he'd have died right away. As it is, he can't talk. Will he ever be able to?"

"Sometimes," Minor replied, "patients can recover the use, or partial use, of damaged vocal cords, and through practice learn the use of other muscles for compensation. But it is never what may be termed normal speech."

Santini began twisting the loose end of a cigarette, then put it in his mouth. "Maybe yes, maybe no, huh?" he remarked. Shrugging, he pulled a slip of paper from his pocket and glanced at it carefully. It seemed to me that he was pretending, and that whatever was written on the slip, he already knew very well. However, he continued to look at it, his brows wrinkled as he concentrated, and finally he said to me, almost indifferently, "Well, we know who you are."

I didn't say anything; I couldn't. It was Minor who asked, "Who?"

Santini went through the motions of reading from his report: "Name, Vic Pacific ... Victor, no-middle-name, Pacific. Age, thirty-six. Home, New York City, which is a lie." Santini looked at me for a contradiction. I didn't give it to him.

The doctor asked, "Where did you get the information?"

"The Army had his prints on file," Santini replied. "Funny thing though, the ID was slow coming through and it was a little jumbled. We can't find an address for him or, for that matter, much of anything else about him."

At the back of my mind, an alarm went off signaling danger, but I didn't know why.

"What information did the Army have?" Minor inquired. "Pacific claimed he was an orphan. The address he gave I checked on and find it is still occupied by some gas pipes off East River Drive."

"Was be in the war?"

"Sure. World War II. Good record. Tanks ... Six Hundred and Fourth. In Africa. Master sergeant. Wounded, that's where the scar in the back comes from. Hospitalized over there; discharged here." Santini deliberately folded his paper and returned it to his pocket. "No relatives," he continued, "and he wasn't married. No police record either. After his discharge he drew his terminal pay, and disappeared. Never applied for veteran benefits, medical attention, or anything else. He isn't heard of again, until more than twelve years later with his throat cut." He looked at me. It was a hard unpleasant look. "What the hell you been doing all this time?"

I held up the palm of my hand. I didn't know.

Santini asked the doctor when I would be able to leave the hospital, and Minor told him, "As soon as he's able to eat comfortably. Probably in a week or so. He's out of danger now, and is recovering his strength rapidly. His biggest problem is being able to eat and drink without pain. He'll come around."

Miss Pierson came into the room with another jar of glucose. She began to roll up my sleeve. Santini left, although Minor remained by the foot of my bed. He nodded in the direction Santini had gone. "Did Santini say anything which meant something to you?" he asked.

No.

"Perhaps it'll begin to come back to you slowly," the doctor continued. "Don't try to work at it too hard, or force yourself too fast. I think you'll find that little pieces of your past, here and there, will gradually return. One moment a certain key memory will return and everything else will fall into place." He turned and left.

At least I had a few things to work on. A few more things each day. Minor, however, didn't permit me to leave the hospital in a week. It was two weeks. During those two weeks I attempted desperately to recall the trouble I'd been in. Sometimes I could almost remember, it seemed, the night it happened. Mixed up in my memory was a dark room, a spot of light, and faces. Two faces in particular seemed to be present although I couldn't see them plainly, and other faces, a number of them, in the background. But then, at this point, I'd think, am I really remembering this, or is it only part of my nightmare which I now take for reality? My mind would veer off at a tangent and I'd say to myself, "No!" What really happened was in a car. I can just about recall the car racing and twisting through the street and ... Unfortunately, however, there was no reality to it and immediately I'd begin to think of something else—an alleyway, a short flight of metal stairs, a roaring elevated highway or bridge, a darkened office building. It made little difference what I recalled because there were no details connected with my unstable memories and, although for just a moment I might feel that I really was about to remember something important, my intelligence would contradict me. These memories were merely memories which anyone might have. They, might be from my past somewhere, but they didn't mean anything.

I felt that I couldn't trust anything I tried to remember. What Santini told me about being an orphan, for example. For some deep, basic reason, some instinct, told me it wasn't true. Obviously, I had also been lying about my address; it's impossible to live in a gas pipe. Why did I lie? I didn't know. I had to live somewhere. Where had I been living? Some forgotten touch of reason told me that recently I'd been living in New York. But where, and under what name, I didn't know either.

At night though it was even worse because when I was only half asleep it was difficult, impossible, to differentiate between insignificant events, casual facts, wild fancies, and dreams. How could I sort out what I might have read somewhere at some time; what someone might have described to me; what was my own personal history, or someone else's? I might have lived many places on the earth, or never stepped out of New York City. All the information in the world might belong to me, yet I didn't know what information was my own.

I tried to compile lists of names in my mind. I studied faces and photographs in the newspapers and magazines. I belabored my mind, searching and probing to remember one solid, specific detail. All that I could discover, seemingly, was that beyond the day I awakened in the hospital I had no past. My name was Victor Pacific; I was thirty-six years old, had been in World War II, claimed I was an orphan, and lived in a gas pipe.

The day I was released from the hospital, Doctor Minor and Miss Pierson saw me off. It was in the early afternoon, after lunch, and by this time I was eating farina, soup, soft puddings, and milk. The hospital had furnished me with a suit of used clothes and bought me some linen. In my pocket sixty-three dollars remained ... all that was left of the thousand which had been found on me. The surgeon and hospital had taken the rest. Minor shook hands with me. "If you don't feel right, come back to see me," he said. I nodded, and he hurried away.

Miss Pierson asked, "Where are you going?"

I shook my head. I had no idea.

She walked beside me to the main entrance and then said good-by. Outside, looking up to the sky, I saw the heavy, semi-smoky haze which seems to hang over the afternoon skies of Manhattan. It doesn't look like rain; it only appears that the air is heavy enough to shred with your fingers. I felt that I knew it well. Walking down the steps of the main entrance and reaching the sidewalk, I paused, attempting to decide what to do. It was obvious that I must find a place to stay for the night. Although I had no luggage, I did have sufficient money to pay for a room so there seemed no cause to be concerned. Cutting across the diagonally running street, on which the hospital was located, I reached Sixth Avenue. Turning south, I began to stroll slowly.

Passing a cigar store, I paused and stared at it wondering if I enjoyed smoking. I couldn't remember and it had never occurred to me before. In the hospital I hadn't missed tobacco. Walking into the tiny shop, I was assailed by the old familiar odor of tobacco, and pointing to a pack of cigarettes I purchased it. I lit one and permitted the smoke to trickle down my throat. It didn't cause me to cough, although I received no pleasure from it, and once again there was a fleeting illusion of a moment when something similar had given me enjoyment. I decided that once I had smoked, but had since forgotten the sensation. Stuffing the pack into my pocket, I threw away the cigarette and continued down the street.

Several blocks farther I passed a bisecting street with the name of Parnell Place. It was only two blocks long. The name was familiar to me, and when I searched my memory, I remembered that Santini in one of his conversations with me had mentioned it as the street which connected to Newton Mews where Bianca Hill lived. The Hill woman had found me on her doorstep.

Abruptly it occurred to me that I would like to see her. I did not feel grateful, in the least, to her for finding me, but I could pretend that I did, and have an opportunity to look at her. All that I could feel was a curiosity—a speculation concerning her not as a woman, but as the last link connecting me with my past.

Newton Mews was even shorter than Parnell Place—hardly a dozen feet wide, with very small, two-story, stone houses leaning heavily against each other. The street was paved with cobblestones, and a narrow sidewalk ran along each side of it in front of the houses. I walked slowly past reading the names on the mailboxes. One carried the name "Bianca Hill." The house, just wide enough to accommodate two windows, in addition to a door, had been painted a light gray. The windows supported yellow shutters, and the door was a Chinese black. The single stone step was flanked on either side by a delicate piece of ironwork painted white.

After pressing the doorbell, I waited for several minutes before I heard footsteps hurrying to the front of the house. The door swung open, and for a space of time the woman stared at me before recognition reached her. Then her face lighted up, and she grasped my hand. Impulsively she said, "Why, yes! You're the man who was hurt!"

I nodded. At this time I was forming the habit of carrying a small pad of paper and a pencil which I used to write messages. I wrote out my name and the single word "thanks."

"You can't talk?" she asked. I nodded. "What a pity! That's terrible! Well, come in, come in, and we'll have a drink. Can you drink?" Again I nodded.

She led the way into the house, past a tiny front living room with a carved marble mantel, into a considerably larger room which was both a kitchen and dining room. She seated me at a round baroque dining table and hurrying to the stove, removed a pot of coffee. "I was just stopping for my afternoon coffee-break," she said lightly, "and I'm delighted to have company. Perhaps I'll have a pony of brandy with it. How about you?"

I shook my head and wrote, "Just brandy, please." Coffee was too hot to drink as extreme heat still hurt my throat. However, I didn't feel the necessity to do the extra writing to explain this.

Placing two ponies on the table, a bottle of brandy, and filling a cup with coffee, she joined me. As she had walked before me into the dining room, I had noticed that she was a small woman—not over five feet two or three, with a nice figure compact in a pair of toreador slacks. Now, as she seated herself, I realized, with surprise, that she was still very young—somewhere in her middle twenties. Possibly it had been her name which had misled me to conceive of her as an older woman. Or perhaps it had been Santini's description of her as the "Hill woman" which had been responsible for my misconception.

Bianca Hill wore her hair straight back, and her hair was very black. At the back of her head was an elaborate silver ring through which her hair passed and it hung down well below her shoulders. Her eyes were dark, as dark nearly as her hair, and when she smiled, her teeth were very white. Her face was not beautiful, but it was striking ... and delicate, and in it I could read a ready sympathy and friendliness which someday would bring her unhappiness.

She lifted her cup to her lips, and her eyes smiled, curving upward almost into an Oriental cast. "Mr. Pacific," she said, "that's a lovely name. I'm glad you came to see me; I've wondered about you. Once I called the hospital, and they told me you were doing fine."

Nodding, I tasted the brandy. Her hands caught my eye. They were red, with burns over them. They were not pretty and I turned my eyes away.

"Tell me," she asked, "do you live in New York?"

I shook my head, then wrote out the fact that I had lost my memory completely. I had only my name, no family, no address.

She rose quickly from the table to refill her coffee cup. Then she asked slowly, "You have no place to go? None at all?"

No. I shook my head.

"Do you have any money?"

Reaching in my pocket, I removed the sixty-three dollars and placed it on the table. She understood, and I replaced the money in my pocket. Her eyes searched my face quietly, while she drank her coffee. Finally she said, "How perfectly awful! Is there anything at all you can do to earn a living? I mean ... do you remember any skill ... or job?"

I wrote "nothing."

"Is there a chance that you will get better ... remember someday?"

"Possibly."

The sudden whiteness of her smile animated her face, and her words began to tumble out eagerly. "I have an idea," she explained. "Perhaps it's a crazy one, and wouldn't work out very long. But I think it's terrible ... impossible ... for you to just wander out into the city! Not remembering anything, not having any help! What do you think?"

I didn't think. I shrugged, but it didn't lessen her enthusiasm.

"Everyone would say I'm foolish," she continued, "not knowing you, or anything. However, I believe a person should help others, don't you? Help each other ... mutually, that is. For a long time I've needed help here. Look! Look at these." She held out her two hands—red and disfigured. "I haven't been able to afford to pay enough to hire someone to help me." She hesitated for a moment, then continued more slowly, her voice a little embarrassed, "Perhaps you'd like to work for me?"

I scribbled, "Doing what?"

She laughed. "Oh, I make jewelry; silver, handmade jewelry. That would make me a silversmith, wouldn't it? At least partly a silversmith, because I work in copper too. I have my workroom here in the house—down in the basement. I sell everything I make through just two or three shops uptown on Fifth Avenue. My big problem is that I can't turn out many things because it takes so long." She laughed. "Consequently, I don't have much money."

My note to her explained I knew nothing about silver-working.

"Don't worry," she reassured me, "you can take care of the silver furnace, do the firing, the smelting, the pouring. I need help." She added, looking at her scars, "That's how I keep burning my hands all the time."

I nodded, but I couldn't understand why a woman wanted to be a silversmith anyway.

6

The lights bounced off the canvas screen, painting it a delicate silver in the blue-black night. But behind the screen, Gorman had tentatively completed his indelicate examination. He nodded, and two attendants walked leisurely away to the police ambulance to find the six-foot-long, covered, canvas box to remove the corpse. In the meantime, Jensen and Burrows joined the medical examiner, "What do you think?" asked Burrows.

"It's damned near impossible to make out very much under these circumstances," Gorman replied. "I'll know a lot more after I get through in the lab."

"Tell us what you can," Jensen urged.

"Well," said Gorman, slipping into his jacket, "he was in good physical condition. He might have been anywhere from thirty-five to forty-five years old. The features are so covered with blood, you can't tell; but the post on a few organs can narrow that down. He's six feet tall or slightly better, and probably weighs somewhere around a hundred and eighty pounds."

"Did you notice anything in particular?" asked Jensen.

"What do you mean?"

"Distinguishing marks or characteristics."

"Only the obvious under these conditions," Gorman said a little testily. "He has an old scar on his back. Looks like it might have been from a shell splinter."

"Anything else?" asked Burrows.

"Nothing now."

"How long has he been dead?" Jensen looked at the body which had been covered with a blanket.

Gorman glanced at his wrist watch. "He was dead at two o'clock, that much we know. Working back is hard ... the body stripped, left outdoors, I can't do anything but make a guess at this point."

"Go ahead, Doc, make it," said Jensen.

"And then have you guys swarm all over me if I change my mind later." Gorman was bitter. He'd had to revise his opinions before, and he resented being pushed into making decisions before having a basis for them.

"We won't hold you to it," Burrows said, easily.

"You're damned right you won't," replied Gorman, "because what I'm telling you now is only a guess. I'll help you if I can now and change my mind later if I have to." Both of the detectives nodded their agreement. "Okay," said Gorman, "so my guess is he was chopped off about midnight. It might have been as early as eleven, and maybe as late as one. I'll try to do better when I get back to the office."

7

"What do you think of this idea?" asked Bianca. "Upstairs there are only two bedrooms, and I have a friend living with me who pays rent, but downstairs in my workshop I have a big leather couch which used to belong to my father. And there's a shower down there too. You could sleep there, and have your meals here. I couldn't pay much in addition to that, but I'll give you what I can. A percentage of what I make?" She looked at me inquiringly.

I didn't know.

"You're free to leave whenever you like, but at least it'll give you a chance to look around and find something better." The sound of the front door opening reached us. Then I heard the light tapping of a woman's heels along the hallway past the living room. In the doorway of the kitchen appeared the figure of a tall, striking blonde. In her high heels she was nearly six feet tall, slender, with her hair combed back in a chignon—showing off the classical regularity of her features. When she saw me, she stopped. Stopped as suddenly as if frozen in her motion, and when she looked at me I realized her eyes were cold. She asked, "Where'd he come from?"

Bianca laughed. "Rosemary," she said, "may I present my new partner, employee, house guest, and the man who owes me his life, Mr. Victor Pacific."

Rosemary merely stared at me.

Bianca attempted to ease the situation. She said lightly, "You've heard of men who die for a woman? Well, Mr. Pacific didn't die for me, but he nearly died on my front steps." Quickly she placed another cup and saucer on the table. "Come on," she said to Rosemary, "join us. You look as if you've had a hard day."

The blonde slowly seated herself while regarding me hostilely. "Please tell me," she said, "what this is all about?" Bianca gave her the details. When she had finished, Rosemary turned to me and asked, "You mean you've completely lost your memory, and you can't speak a word?"

I nodded. I didn't really care if I stayed or not. I had passively accepted Bianca Hill's offer because it had seemed to make little difference where I stayed for a while. It was an easy solution as where to go and what to do, and I could leave at any time. But this new woman was one who worried me; I felt that she was probing, searching me for something. It might be curiosity, but it seemed to me stronger than that. She was beautiful enough, and undoubtedly could be quite charming if she cared to make the effort. It was obvious though, she neither liked nor trusted me.

Rosemary turned to Bianca. "You must be out of your mind or at least a little mad!"

Bianca smiled and said to me, "See. Remember, I told you everyone would think I'm crazy."

"But, dear," protested Rosemary, "this man, what has he done? If someone tried to kill him once, and didn't succeed, he may try it again. And this time you're in danger, and I am too."

Her objection amused me. I wrote her a note, "Perhaps I did it myself. I promise I won't do it again."

"I don't think it's very funny," Rosemary said. Her voice assumed an aggressive tone. "Bee, you know nothing about this man. You don't know who he is or what he's done! He may even be a criminal."

"If Victor were a criminal, the police would never have permitted him to leave the hospital," Bianca replied. It seemed to me a reasonable answer.

Rosemary continued her objections. "You just don't know!" Angrily she reached across the table and picking up the brandy bottle poured a large amount into her coffee. "He might be a criminal and the police just haven't caught up with him yet." She took several long sips of the coffee, and turned her attention back to me. Her eyes were as cold as before—which was very cold. "I tell you, Mr. Pacific, I frankly don't like the idea."

"Rosemary works very hard," Bianca explained apologetically, "and she's one of the busiest high fashion models in New York. Tonight she's tired. Don't mind her, tomorrow she'll be sorry."

"No, I won't!" Rosemary was obstinate.

"But I need help and he'll work hard," Bianca said. "Oh, Rosemary, where's your sense of ... fun ... adventure?"

"I don't have a sense of humor about some things." Abruptly Rosemary's tone softened. Affectionately she patted Bianca's hand. "All right, Bee," she said, "go ahead. Try it." Rosemary's cold blue eyes turned on me calculatingly, and she said very deliberately, "But no funny business, do you understand?"

Writing on my pad, I quoted, "'If you inquire what the people are like here, I must answer—the same as anywhere.'" I handed it to Rosemary.

She read it, raised her brows, and asked, "Where's this from?"

"Goethe" I wrote automatically. This surprised me, as I really had no idea where the quotation was from, and I had made no special effort to remember it. I crumpled the paper, put it in my pocket, and returned her stare, silently. She arose from the table and walked back into the hall. I could hear her footsteps ascending the stairs; somehow her steps sounded halting.

Bianca drew a deep breath. "Follow me, Vic," she said pleasantly, "and I'll show you around my factory." She opened a door to the kitchen and disclosed a short, steep flight of stairs leading to the basement. Her hand flicked the light switch, and she led the way down.

The basement ran the full length of the house, forming a single large room. In one corner, neatly partitioned off, was an oil furnace and water heater. The rest of the room held a series of long wooden benches, about hip high, with tall stools behind them. On the benches were racks holding neat rows of hand tools. Anchored firmly against one wall was a heavier bench which held a number of small anvils, the largest the size of my hand. It also held an automatic metal saw, a buffing wheel with a variety of attachments, and a metal container of acetylene gas with a torch.

Bianca pointed to a small brick furnace, approximately two and a half feet square, standing in the center of the room. "That's going to be your main job," she said. "It's the smelting furnace where I melt my silver and copper. See, that's the bellows down there." Her foot touched a flat, black board which projected from the furnace a few inches above the floor. "You operate that by foot, and it keeps the bellows going inside the furnace." She touched her back, and smiled, "The weary hours I've pumped that thing!"

Beside the furnace were several large paper bags marked "coke." I pointed to them questioningly.

"Yes, indeed," she agreed, "it burns coke. Usually we need a very hot fire ... extremely high ... around 1300 degrees F." Turning away, she walked to a corner of the room which contained an aged, black leather lounge. The piece of furniture was nearly flat, although one end was slightly elevated and curved under.

With my pad I asked her if I slept on it.

"Yes, and it's very comfortable. I've slept on it lots of times when I work at night. I'll get you some blankets and a pillow and you can keep them in that chest." She indicated a tool chest, about the size of a footlocker. "It has only a few tools in it, and I'll clean it out right away."

I shook my head.

"All right," she agreed, "you do it then." I nodded, and she smiled back at me. "Just one more thing. Over there is a bath and shower stall. It's all yours." She approached the foot of the stairs. "Lie down and get a little rest," she said. "I'll call you in about an hour for dinner."

She began to climb the stairs. About halfway up, she paused and looked down on me. "Who knows," she asked, "perhaps today marks the return of the guild system to the world?"

After she had disappeared up the stairs, I sat down on the leather lounge. I was very tired, and for a long time I merely sat. Finally I aroused sufficiently to light a cigarette. It still had no effect on me. Although my mind returned to Bianca Hill, it soon skipped over her to Rosemary. I thought, Rosemary? Rosemary what? I realized that I didn't know her last name. For some reason she distrusted or disliked me; and to a degree I was wary of her. I turned the thought of her aside, and stretched out on the couch. Bianca had not exaggerated. It was comfortable. My eyes stared at the ceiling; it had been painted a light green. Through the center of it ran a long fixture containing twin tubes of neon. There was plenty of evenly distributed light in the room which produced no glare. This was probably the most pleasant basement I'd ever lived in. Then I dropped off to sleep.

Bianca and I were sitting at the round dining-room table having dinner. With difficulty I managed to eat a little food and drank a glass of milk. Rosemary lounged leisurely into the room, drawing on a pair of white gloves. She was dressed in a smart black dress and wore a mink stole. "You look lovely," Bianca complimented her. "You're going out to dinner?"

"Yes," Rosemary replied, almost indifferently, "I'm supposed to meet some people at the Acton-Plaza." She looked at me and asked, "Do you know where that is?"

I'd heard the name but couldn't remember where it was located. "It's a hotel uptown on Fifth Avenue," Bianca said.

I nodded.

Rosemary said, "This man certainly sparkles with the conversation."

"That's cruel!" exclaimed Bianca.

Rosemary doubted it. However, she replied, "I'm sorry. I'm running along now and I won't be late." She left, and I heard the front door slam shut.

I wrote to Bianca asking Rosemary's last name. "Martin," she told me, "Rosemary Martin. She's beautiful, isn't she? It's a funny thing ... peculiar, I mean ... I've known Rosemary quite a while. We first met at a style show where she was modeling. I'd agreed to furnish some of my jewelry for the show, and when I delivered it, I met her. We liked each other immediately, and sort of kept in touch. Once in a while we'd meet for lunch. We were never close friends though.

"She had a lovely apartment uptown off of Fifth Avenue although I never visited her there. I think she was doing very well. And then one day she called me and said she was moving, and wondered whether she could move in with me. I not only was delighted to have her but the rent money helped, too."

"Why did she move?" I wrote out the question.

"She said she'd been spending too much money keeping up appearances living in the apartment, and so on. She just decided that for a while she'd like to try to save some money. Down here we live very inexpensively. Rosemary is very popular, and goes out nearly every night." Bianca smiled, and added, "To dinner. Saves food money, you know."

"Don't you go out?" I queried.

"Not often. Many times I work at night, and even if I don't by the end of the day I'm very tired. Usually I prefer to stay home ... read ... or just fool around."

I was sleeping soundly when the basement lights flashed on. I didn't know what time it was as I didn't have a watch. It must have been very early in the morning, possibly two or three o'clock. I watched Rosemary's legs appear on the cellar stairs, as she cautiously made her way down in her high heels. She stood at the foot of the steps, swaying slightly, and stared at me. She appeared to be drunk. I propped myself on one elbow and stared back. She was still dressed in her gown and stole.

"I don't know what your plans are, Vic," she told me, her voice flat and low, "but be careful. I don't want to get hurt. Do you understand?"

I shook my head, "No."

"Cut the act," she said. "Good night and sweet dreams." She returned upstairs.

That night I dreamed about the dark room with its spot of light again. All night, after Rosemary's visit, I stood waiting in my nightmare, bathed in a dripping fear, for whatever it was to appear.

8

The body had been removed. The lights flooding the small area had been turned off, and Gorman was preparing to leave. Jensen and Burrows, however, continued to hold him in conversation. Gorman fidgeted restlessly behind the wheel of the car from the Medical Examiner's office. He was anxious to return to the laboratory and begin his post-mortem examination.

"That was a real rough blow he took," Burrows said.

"It was nearly complete decapitation," the doctor replied.

"Yeah, right across the neck," Jensen agreed. "How do you figure it was done? With an ax?"

"No," replied Gorman, "it wasn't an ax. An ax isn't wide enough along the blade to make such a wound possible with a single stroke."

"As far was only one stroke?" asked Burrows.

"As far as I can tell right now."

"It must have been a hell of a knife," observed Jensen.

"I'm not sure it was a knife, either," said Gorman slowly. "At least not a knife in the sense you're using it. A single blow such as the one delivered would require an extremely long and heavy blade."

"Possibly a ... well, bayonet?" asked Jensen.

"Or machete," added Burrows.

"Something along that line," agreed Gorman. "I've got to get going now," he said turning the ignition in his car, and pressing the starter. "I'll get my report to you as soon as I can."

"When will that be?" asked Burrows.

"A preliminary report at least by noon," replied the doctor.

"Wait! Just one more question," urged Jensen. "Would you say that it took a lot of strength to deliver a blow like that one?"

"It would require an extremely strong man," replied Gorman. He threw the car in gear, pulled away from the curb, and headed down the street, his lights picking out the neat, old-fashioned houses in the night.

Jensen and Burrows stood alone together, each occupied with his own thoughts. A single patrol car remained in the street, waiting patiently to drive them to the precinct house. No predawn light trembled in the sky. It was the lonesome time, the most lonesome hours of the night.

Finally Burrows said, "I don't suppose it hurt much. It was a lousy way to go, but it was fast." He turned and began to make his way toward the patrol car.

Jensen followed him. The night air was chilly, and he shivered a little in the cold. Jensen, the same as Burrows, was a methodical man and he considered his partner's remark. Slowly he agreed. "Yeah, pretty fast. Not as fast as a gun maybe, but pretty fast just the same. Only trouble was, you might be able to see it coming."

9

Bianca said, "Of course it's possible to buy your silver already refined, rolled, and ready to use. It comes in sheets, like those over there, and in any gauge. But somehow I prefer to smelt and roll my own silver. Did you know that pure silver is not really pure?"

I shook my head and continued pumping the foot bellows to the small furnace.

"Well, it isn't. For each kilo of pure silver, seventy-five grams of copper has been added, otherwise it would be too soft." She opened the peephole door on the side of the furnace and peered in. Within the furnace, the crucible, a ceramic jar used for melting silver, glowed brightly. She nodded and closed the door. "Naturally," she continued, "I don't try to draw my own wire; that's an impossible job really. However, I do smelt my own heavy silver because then I can charge more money for it." Bianca walked over to a table and picked up a clipboard on which there was a sketch of a bracelet. The drawing was clean and crisply executed and showed a heavy, simple, silver band. Through the center of the bracelet was a single, light, wavy line which I, at first, thought to be a stylized thick-and-thin line.

"How do you like it?" she asked, handing me the drawing.

I wasn't especially interested one way or the other, but I didn't want to hurt her feelings by appearing indifferent. So I took the drawing and examined it. Immediately into my mind flashed the words *"Allah ma'ak."* Standing motionless with astonishment, being unable to understand my thoughts, I dropped my eyes to the drawing again, and the words repeated themselves, chainwise, *"Allah ma'ak, Allah ma'ak, Allah ma'ak."* The stylized line through the middle of the bracelet was a single line of Arabic writing with the phrase *"Allah ma'ak"* repeated over and over.

In the next moment, I knew the phrase meant "God be with you," and then the rest of the phrase popped into my memory, the rejoinder "*Allah yittawie omrak*—May God lengthen your days." Before I could think about it longer, Bianca said, "Take the tongs and lift the crucible out of the furnace." There was a pair of heavy tongs with insulated handles, and grasping them I lifted the ceramic jar, filled with molten silver, from the furnace. "Pour the silver into those trays," Bianca directed, "filling them just exactly to the top." The silver spread swiftly over the iron pans as I poured it. "We'll let it harden until it's ready for the rolling machine."

Putting aside the tongs, I again looked at the drawing. "Well, do you like it?" Bianca asked.

I nodded. Then I walked over to the bench and began writing. "Where did you get the idea for this center design?"

After reading my question, Bianca explained, "Rosemary had a bracelet ... Arabian; as a matter of fact she has some very lovely jewelry. I've never particularly liked Eastern design but this line of writing on it gave me an idea. I narrowed down the line, straightened it out, until it nearly forms a design itself. I think the result is rather interesting."

I didn't say anything. Walking into the shower room, I turned on the light. Building within me was a conviction that I was on the verge of discovering something important about myself. I'd had the feeling that I was thinking, writing, working in one world; this world was the present. Behind me, lost in my memory, was another world, another way of thinking, speaking, living. It seemed, if I could only for a moment pierce this veil of limbo surrounding me, that I would find the answer to myself.

Looking into the mirror, I examined my face. It appeared to be much the same as any other face. I wasn't dark, there were no special racial characteristics present, and there was nothing unusual in my appearance. Obviously, I didn't look as if I were Arabian, Moorish, Syrian, or of other Eastern descent. Why, then, I asked myself, should I be able to read Arabic? Turning away from the mirror I said, within my mind, "*ma'alesh*—no matter." After that I refused to think about it further.

The next day the front doorbell rang while we were at work, and Bianca asked me to climb the stairs to answer it. Opening the door, I saw Santini standing there. He pushed his hat toward the back of his head. Changing his mind, he took it off entirely and stepped inside. "This is nice and cozy," he said. "Who are you, the maid?"

Bowing slightly from the waist, I stood to one side and waited for him to say something else. "I wish I could make up my mind about you," he said. "I really wish to hell I could." We walked down the short hall to the kitchen, and then he inquired if Bianca Hill was around. I nodded, and pointed to the stairway leading to the basement. Santini went to the head of the steps and called down.

Within a few moments, Bianca appeared in the kitchen. "I'm sorry to bother you, Miss Hill," Santini said, although his voice was not apologetic, "but this is the first time we've all three been together since the night Mr. Pacific was ... indisposed."

"Yes," Bianca replied, "yes, I know."

Santini asked me, "Why did you head for this place just as soon as you got out of the hospital?"

Bianca hastened to save me the trouble of writing. "He told me he wanted to thank me," she explained to Santini.

"And he was so grateful he moved right in?"

Bianca flushed. "Not at all!" she replied indignantly. "He had no place to go and no job. So I hired him to help me."

Santini glanced at me for confirmation. I don't know why it was he seemed to dislike me so much. Not that I really cared whether he did or not. It was a matter of indifference to me. Instead of nodding my reply, I returned his stare. Finally he faced Bianca and asked, "Did you ever see this man before that night?" Bianca denied that she had ever seen me. "All right," said Santini, "what about Rosemary Martin?"

"She wasn't even here when it happened," replied Bianca.

"I didn't ask that," Santini continued doggedly. "Did she ever see him before that night?"

"Not that I know of. Furthermore, she didn't even want me to hire him, when she first saw him here."

"Smart girl," Santini remarked to himself.

I held up my hand, a pupil requesting permission to recite. Santini looked at me, and I began to scribble. "Question: Do you know how I got here that night? Walk? In car? How?"

After reading it, Santini said, "You must've been in a car. No one can walk around the streets nude, even in Greenwich Village, without someone seeing him."

"Did you find his clothes?" Bianca asked.

"No," replied Santini, "we never found them. He might have been knocked unconscious in a car, and his clothes cut off him."

"Why do you say his clothes were cut off?"

"Because he had his shoes on. It's hard to remove clothes over shoes, 'specially if a guy's unconscious, and shoes themselves are hard to take off. Pacific was stripped down to prevent a quick identification." Santini began walking to the front of the house. He continued, "But what I can't figure is why he was dumped out here."

"At that time of night," Bianca pointed out, "it's very quiet and dark here."

"There are plenty of other places which are quieter and darker," Santini told her. "After removing the clothes against identification, why not unload the body someplace where it'll take a few days to find it?"

"I don't know," Bianca said quietly.

"I don't either," Santini agreed, and he departed.

Suddenly I knew. Not that I remembered anything about it, but I knew the reason why I had been dumped from a car on Newton Mews. It was a warning to someone who would recognize me, but not have to identify me publicly. Who was that person? I didn't believe it was Bianca Hill. Bianca had found me by accident when she came home. Rosemary Martin? But what connection would I have with her?

Where had Rosemary been at that time? I scrawled the question to Bianca. "Rosemary," she told me, "was working out of town. She was in a big, three-day style show in Chicago." I couldn't imagine either of the two women being mixed up in it, so if it was not to be a warning to them it must be to someone else living in or near Newton Mews.

We went back down to the basement. Bianca picked up a chasing tool and began work on a pair of earrings. "You know, Vic," she said, "possibly you might be able to get some information from the Army, or the Veterans Administration in Washington."

I doubted it. Santini had, unquestionably, covered that thoroughly. Unless he was holding back information, he didn't know any more of my past than I did. I couldn't remember the men I'd served with; I could recall no Army friends; and it was not logical that my commanding officers would have known me well enough to offer any information after all these years. But what about Colonel Horstman? Perhaps I had known him well; possibly he might have been one of my superior officers. His name had been one of the first to come back to me at the hospital. My instinct urged me strongly that I had once had a close identification with the man. If I could locate him, he might help me.

Drawing my pad to me, I asked Bianca if the name Colonel Horstman was familiar to her. "No," she replied, shaking her head. At least, it eliminated him as a well-known public figure, although it did not disqualify the fact that I might have seen or heard his name publicly. However, I wrote to Bianca requesting her to call Santini and ask him to secure information from Washington concerning a possible Colonel Horstman whom I might have served under. She agreed to call him later, as she thought that Santini might not have had time to return to the station.

At dinner that evening Bianca and I were alone. Rosemary Martin was eating out. Each night she was always away for dinner, and I thought she was doing it to avoid me, although Bianca assured me this was not so. However, Rosemary seldom remained out late; usually she would return to the house around ten or ten-thirty. This, as far as I could determine, had nothing to do with morality, and was concerned only with the subject of sleep. She needed eight to ten hours of sleep each night to do her work.

Leaving the table, I headed toward the front door. Bianca asked if I were going out. I nodded that I was. "Do you want me to go with you?" she asked. I indicated that I didn't, and she looked at me rather strangely as I went out. Walking several blocks, I found a drugstore.

In the Manhattan telephone directory, I located a restaurant which specialized in Arabian cooking. The address was about midtown. I wrote it down on my pad of paper, and leaving the drugstore found a taxi, and I handed the driver the address. While he was driving me there, I felt the sensation ... an anticipation that I was on the verge of discovery. The nearly mystical feeling of having, at one time, existed in another time and place and person was stronger than ever.

The Garden of Plenty was located on a side street. The entrance was framed in neon tubing, and customers climbed a craggy set of stairs from the street to the second story of the building. The café was lit with a flat, gray light; the room was bare and undecorated except for tables and chairs, and a small cashier's desk. There was nothing on the walls, and no coverings on the floor. It was past nine o'clock, and at this time of night there were only half a dozen persons having dinner.

Several waiters were lounging in a group along a side of the deserted wall. One broke away and, approaching me, attempted to seat me in the center of the room. I moved along unhurriedly to another table near the loafing waiters. The waiter handed me the menu which was written in both Arabic and English. Scanning the Arabic side, I pointed to the items of coffee and melon. The waiter dropped his sullen air, and looked at me more closely. *"Mit ahlan wa sahlan,"* he said. He was welcoming me.

I wrote on the paper *"Moutta shakker,"* thanking him. He quickly returned with a small cup of thick Turkish coffee, very sweet, and a thin slice of Persian melon. Placing them before me, he retreated to rejoin his confreres.

Sipping my coffee, and toying with my melon, I listened to the waiters. The Arabic language with its repetitious phrases, and changing cadence from deep guttural to a high-pitched tremolo is deep, earthy, explosive sounding. I could understand very little of it—only a few words here and there in the conversation which seemed to be a series of complaints against the proprietor.

I realized that I had only a rudimentary knowledge of the language. At some time, I must have studied it and learned the more common words and phrases, and was able to understand it, in part, if it was spoken slowly and in the usual stereotyped forms of speech, but the colloquial tongue and rapid conversation were beyond me, I was not fluent in the language. The question came to my mind as to why I had wanted to study Arabic in the first place.

According to my Army record, I had served in Africa, spent some time in the desert, and been hospitalized. But so had thousands of other American troops. They hadn't learned Arabic, beyond a few words; I wondered why I had. Motioning to the waiter, I received my bill and left him a tip. He bowed and said, *"Hallet el-baraka."* With my paper I replied, *"El-baraka aleikum."* This age-old ritual I understood perfectly. At the door I paid the cashier and descended the stairs to the street.

I began walking west, across town, until I reached Sixth Avenue. The night felt good on my face, and I decided to walk back to the Village. It took me longer than I expected, and it was nearly eleven o'clock when I arrived at Bianca Hill's. As I prepared to ring the bell, a cab pulled up and Rosemary Martin got out. She paid the driver and approached the door. For a moment we stood there on the single step staring into each other's face. In the darkness her face seemed strangely smooth, dusted by the shadows and the moon into a mask. Only her mouth looked alive. It seemed black and twisted.

"What are you waiting for?" she asked.

I shook my head. I was waiting only because I had no key, and I did not wish to disturb Bianca unnecessarily.

Suddenly, angrily I thought, Rosemary unlocked the door and pushed her way into the house. I followed her. She went upstairs. I went down to the basement.

10

The MPR rolled up to the front entrance of the Eighth Precinct station. In the predawn darkness the metal lamps on each side of the door glowered greenly—alert against the evils of the city. Burrows hesitated momentarily before getting out, then said, "Well, I suppose I better get started on the reports." Paper work and routine were part of his life, but he never failed to resent them both.

"Okay," said Jensen. "I'll go on uptown and report in at Manhattan East. Then I'll get started on the ID."

"There's always the possibility that the guy's family will miss him and call in about it."

Perhaps it was the time, and the night. Jensen became stolidly philosophical. "I don't know," he said, "but did you ever notice that weird things like this never seem to happen to guys with families? Not that family men don't get in trouble, but they don't get in crazy kinds of trouble."

Burrows deliberately avoided Jensen's meaning. "Sure," he agreed. "If this guy was from out of town he might've been taken. It doesn't look like a mugging though. If he was from out of town, it might take longer to hear he was missing."

Jensen said, "We might never hear."

Burrows opened the door of the car and stepped out. "See you later." He slammed the door and stepped back as it pulled away. Lighting a cigarette, he entered the building. The desk sergeant looked up and greeted him as he came in. "Heard you got a good one," he said to Burrows. Burrows said yes, he had a good one, and climbed the flight of stairs to the second floor where the detectives' room was located.

Seating himself at a desk, he began to fill out the homicide report, marking in the upper right-hand corner "Preliminary and Tentative."

Name: Unknown
Sex: Male
Age: 35 to 45 years
Color: White
Hair: Light Brown
Eyes: Blue
Weight: 185 pounds
Height: Six feet +
Identifying marks: Scar on back

Address: Unknown
Next of family: Unknown
Address where body was discovered: 36 Newton Mews
Method of death: Knife
Time of death: 11 P.M. - 2 A.M.
Witnesses: None
Reported by: Bianca Hill
Address: 36 Newton Mews, New York City, N.Y.

Burrows looked at the heavy clock on the wall. It was a little after four A.M. He went off duty at eight in the morning. There was still four hours to go, and he had accomplished very little. He wasn't worried; he was a patient man, and he had learned one important fact: time was always on the side of the cops.

11

From Bianca I learned the names of the families living on Newton Mews. She had lived her entire life there and knew them all, having inherited the house from her mother. The neighboring families on each side were the Fairbanks and the Bains. Then there were the Cosgroves, Morisses, Janviers, Bryants, MacMurrays, and some half dozen others. They all had lived on Newton Mews for years and were quiet, respectable, and fairly well to do.

"I'm the financial black sheep of the street," Bianca told me. "After my mother died, I had practically no money. Just this house. One year, when my family was still alive, we lived in Mexico and I learned a little about silver-working ... just for fun. So I decided I'd try to see what I could do with it, as I've always loved to design things and make my own jewelry. It's been difficult to get established, and I've barely been able to make ends meet. My business though is getting better all the time, and I'm still optimistic."

From her description of the families on Newton Mews, I doubted that I had any contact with them before the night she found me. And yet I was convinced that my attack had been intended as a warning to someone living on the street.

Santini came over another day. He stayed only a very short time. "You think you remember the name of a Colonel Horstman?" he asked me.

I nodded.

"Miss Hill asked me to check for you. Washington said there was never a Colonel Horstman in the Six Hundred and Fourth with which you served."

I wrote asking him if he'd checked the records of any Colonel Horstman connected with the Army at all.

There was irritation in his eyes. "Of course I checked it," he told me. "No Colonel Horstman since the turn of the century. Then it was some old guy who was a major in the state militia during the Civil War."

Although this seemed to conclude Santini's interest in Colonel Horstman, it did not finish it for me. I knew that at some time I had known a Colonel Horstman.

Santini asked me, "When're you going to start trying to learn to talk?" I shrugged, as I didn't know. After he had gone, however, I thought it over. Doctor Minor had told me that there was a free speech clinic for laryngectomy patients—patients who had their vocal cords removed by operation because of cancer and other causes. The clinic was maintained by a number of hospitals; if I preferred I could work with a private teacher, but would have to pay for the lessons. As I didn't have the money, I decided to attend the free clinic. Bianca made the arrangements for me, and I began to attend twice each week.

The instructor at the clinic told me that a person speaks, ordinarily, through the combined use of his lungs, larynx, tongue, and lips. If the larynx has been taken out, or badly damaged, it's still possible that the lips, tongue, and lungs properly combined and coordinated can produce a certain type of speech. It doesn't sound natural, but it can be understood. Air is exploded through the mouth, and then the teeth, tongue, and lips form a distorted facsimile of sounds resembling words. These words are usually intelligible, but that depends also on how difficult the word is to pronounce. The clinic started me to make sounds which resembled the vowels—a, e, o, and u. At first, I could not even remotely imitate them.

Bianca didn't object to my oral exercises, and I continued to practice them while working. During this period of time, I had a strange feeling of passiveness. It was a time of waiting. Within me, however, was the belief that the mosaic of the passing days would eventually put together a small fragment of a pattern. I would then find other pieces, add them to the existing pattern, and at last find an answer to who I was, and what had happened to me.

It is not true to say that I was contented, but I was resigned to waiting.

My work was pleasant, and through Bianca I had developed a skill in soldering which removed the monotony of smelting and pouring. I arose each morning, had breakfast in the kitchen, worked during the day, practiced my speaking exercises, and went to bed at night. And nearly every night the old familiar nightmare would return to me.

The relationship between Bianca and me was changing; at least it was changing on her part. She casually began to inquire about my likes and preferences. This made me uncomfortable as I had no established preferences concerning food and other small things, and preferred to accept such as were offered. Occasionally she suggested that we attend the neighboring movie. I did not object to this, although I did not encourage it either, realizing to a degree that I was dependent on her generosity. As long as I stayed in her house, if gestures such as these caused the situation to be easier, I was agreeable.

Rosemary, on the other hand, became more irritable. She began to stay away from the house later into the night, and never again since the night she descended into the basement exchanged more than a few words with me. I never saw her alone; it was always in the presence of Bianca. But one evening, shortly after six-thirty, Bianca decided to make a hurried trip to the grocery. I offered to go for her, but she declined. As soon as she had left the house, Rosemary came down to the kitchen.

I was having a drink. "Did Bee go out?" Rosemary asked.

"Ow-t," I replied. By now I could manage a few distorted single-syllable words such as out, yes, no, and why. Each of the words had a singularly mechanical sound.

"Out?" she repeated it.

I nodded.

"Look, Vic," she said, "I've got to talk to you. I'm getting scared!"

"Me?" I asked in surprise.

"No! I'm not scared of you," she replied impatiently. "But you know who does frighten me!"

"No."

Nervously she lit a cigarette. "I guess you can't talk," she said. "I've seen your throat and it gives me the creeps. But you're not stupid. One thing I've always admired about you, you're very, very smart."

Rosemary did know something about me. She was the first thread leading into my past. I felt a surge of anticipation, and, in my haste to question her, I forgot that I could pronounce only a few words; for a moment I made meaningless sounds. "Listen," she said, interrupting me, "they know I'm here."

"Wh-y?"

"Because ... well, why do you suppose they dumped you out on my doorstep?"

She didn't bother to await a reply but continued rapidly. "By now they know you're not dead either. And I'm getting frightened ... petrified! With both of us together they've got their answer ... they'll grab us. I'm not waiting around any longer." The sound of the front door opening announced that Bianca was returning. Quickly Rosemary thrust a long, flat key in my hand. "Here it is," she whispered. "You keep it." Turning away from me, she added over her shoulder, "You know how to reach me."

Hastily she put the length of the room between us as Bianca entered. "Bee, darling," Rosemary said, "are you still doing errands this time of night?" Her voice was strained.

"I don't mind," Bianca replied.

"I'm running right back out," Rosemary said. "I'm not even going to bother to change." Rosemary looked directly at me, and said, "Good night." Her steps echoed down the hall, and in a moment the front door closed.

"How odd!" Bianca exclaimed. I didn't say anything.

Later that same evening the telephone rang. Bianca and I were sitting at the round table listening to records. The call was from Rosemary, and she talked to Bianca. I paid little attention to the conversation, but when Bianca returned her face was both hurt and puzzled. "Did you and Rosemary have a fight while I was gone?" she asked.

I told her no.

"On the phone just now she said that she was going away for a while. She isn't even coming back tonight to get her clothes."

I wrote on my pad, "She can't go very far in one dress."

"Rosemary said she had some other clothes in storage which she would get tomorrow." Abruptly her face became thoughtful, and she gazed levelly at me across the table. "Tell me honestly, Vic, is there anything between you and Rosemary?"

"No."

"I always thought that Rosemary felt uneasy about you. I couldn't understand it because I like you very much. It's occurred to me that you might have known each other."

Writing on my pad I told her, "I do not recall having ever seen Rosemary before I came to this house."

"If you had known her," Bianca was bemused, "why would Rosemary pretend not to know you?"

I didn't know why, but I remembered something else I wanted to ask Bianca. Via my pad, "The night I was nearly murdered are you sure Rosemary was in Chicago?"

"Oh, yes." Bianca assured me. "She called me from Chicago earlier that afternoon. She wanted me to airmail her some things she'd forgotten to pack. Her job came up in such a hurry that she had practically no warning of it."

"Why?"

"Well, actually she hadn't applied for the job. The day the fashion show was ready to leave for Chicago, one of the models became sick. At the last moment the fashion director called Rosemary to take her place. Rosemary had to rush like mad to get the plane."

"Oh." One event fell sharply into place. I had been meant as a warning to Rosemary. Unexpectedly she had not been present when my body had been delivered.

12

The desolate, bleak dawn edged slowly behind the buildings of the city, picking out a fire escape here, a chimney there. It seeped slowly into skylights and windows, edging doorways, silhouetting poles. Burrows sipped his coffee. He decided that it tasted foul because of the cardboard container. For a moment he considered the possibility of throwing it away; then he changed his mind and decided to drink it because it was hot. The phone on his desk rang loudly, and he reached out his hand to pick it up. "Burrows, Eighth Precinct," he said.

It was Jensen. "I just got a call from Gorman," Jensen said, "and he found something. When they got the stiff to the lab, Gorman removed the socks and shoes for further examination. In one shoe he found a thousand-dollar bill."

Burrows digested both his mouthful of coffee and this information. "Was the bill concealed in the sole of the shoe?" he asked.

"Not sewed into the sole, or anything like that," Jensen replied. "It was just laying inside the shoe with the foot and sock resting on it."

"Is the bill a phony?"

"It looks plenty good," Jensen replied. "I asked Gorman the same thing. It isn't listed in the Counterfeit Detector."

"Ask him to send it over," Burrows said.

"I already have," Jensen replied.

"A grand bill is a hard thing to get cashed. You just can't walk into a store or a hotel and get change for it. Mostly you got to get it cashed at a bank."

"Sure," agreed Jensen, "and even then you have to identify yourself. If a guy's got a thousand bucks in one bill, it means he knows someplace he can get it changed. That also means that somebody knows him."

"I'll get the information out to the banks first thing this morning. Maybe they've got a record of it." Burrows took another swallow of coffee. "Gorman have anything else on the shoes?"

"Not yet. They'll give 'em the usual dirt and lint test. Probably won't find anything though, if the guy was walking around the streets here."

"Gorman push up his time on the report yet?"

"No. He still says around noon."

"Okay," Burrows agreed heavily. He and Jensen hung up, and he began to work back through the reports from the Correspondence Bureau. In these reports would be listed all recent fugitives, criminals, and missing persons. The reports are bound in heavy black covers, and all detectives are expected to memorize their contents. But the amount of information is too great. Burrows was looking for someone who might resemble his corpse.

13

I handed a slip of paper to the locksmith, together with the key Rosemary had given me. He read my question, "What kind of a key is this?"

The locksmith took a casual glance at the key. It was two and a quarter inches long, but less than a sixteenth of an inch thick. There were no grooves on its sides; although the lower edge of the key had the usual notches cut from the metal. On one side, stamped into it, were the initials KCLSK. The locksmith said, "This is a key to a safe deposit box." He pointed to the initials, "It was made by the Kingston Company, Lock Safe Key." Looking up at me, he asked, "Where'd you get it?"

I wrote to him that I had found it. Then I asked if there was any way to identify the box, so I could return it to the owner. "Not that I know of," he replied, "unless you want to advertise in the paper, and even then I doubt that a person can identify one key like this from another unless he tries it in his own lock. You might ask at a bank about it, though. Maybe they'd have some ideas."

One bank was probably as good as another, and after I left the locksmith's shop, I walked uptown on Sixth Avenue. On the corner of Sixth and Fourteenth Street, I entered the first bank I found—The Merchants and Chemists Exchange—and located a vice-president seated behind a desk, at the rear of the main lobby. It took some time to explain to him that I had found the key, and to ask if there was any way to locate the owner to return it. He looked at the key, examining it, and said, "There're a number of lock and safe companies who furnish keys and boxes to banks for their safe deposit departments. Also there're a number of companies, which are not banks, who rent safe deposit boxes out to customers. As a rule, it costs about twenty dollars if a depositor loses his keys and the lock has to be removed and new keys made. Ordinarily, however, a box holder is given two keys when he rents a box, and as soon as he loses a key he has another made from the remaining one for only two dollars. It would hardly seem worthwhile for you to spend much effort in trying to return the key."

I was trapped badly. I thought it over, considering every angle. Rosemary obviously knew where the box was located and to whom it belonged. But where was Rosemary? Several days had passed and Bianca had not heard from her. Even if I should locate Rosemary again, there was no way I could make her tell me unless she wanted to do so. Quite calmly the scene flashed into my mind that I was beating it out of her with my fists. It didn't surprise me; I suppose everyone envisions such signs of violence occasionally. In reality, if I killed her, I would still not know the secret of the box.

I decided that I must continue to attempt to locate the owner of the box through my own efforts. Later, if Rosemary should give me any information, that would be all right too. Pulling away the muffler, which I wore as an ascot, from around my throat, I pointed to the scar. It was still very red and ugly. After he had taken a good look, the banker looked down at his desk. I put the pad to work again.

Giving him my name, I told him that I had no family and had been in a bad automobile accident; witness the scar, and that I could not speak. As a result of the accident, I had lost my memory. This deposit key was my own, but I did not remember where it was located. "It was probably in the same bank where you did your personal or business banking," he told me. "Do you remember that at all?"

I shook my head. On his desk was a small sign which read: C. K. Swan. I wrote, "Mr. Swan, do you have any suggestions?"

Swan thought about it for a few moments. "Well," he said, "first you might try to find out through the banks if one of them has you for a depositor. If you locate an account of your own, you'll probably find you have a safe deposit box in the same bank. If that doesn't work, there's a small publication in New York called the *New Amsterdam Safe Box News* which circulates through most of the deposit departments of the various banks and box companies. I'll give you the paper's address, and you might get them to run an ad for you requesting information."

"Yes," I agreed.

Picking up his phone, Swan called the bank's vault department. "Mr. Kraft," he said, "this is Swan. Can you give me the address of the *New Amsterdam Safe Box News*? Yes, if you please. I'll hold the phone." Cradling the receiver to his ear, Swan reached for his personalized memo pad. The pad was printed with:

...from the desk of
C. K. SWAN, vice-president
Merchants & Chemists Exchange Bank

As the voice of Kraft spoke in his ear, Swan began to scribble on the pad, but his pen was dry. Hastily, he tore off the sheet and reaching for another, wrote the address of the paper with a pencil. Handing the slip to me, he said, "Why is it, whenever you want to use a pen it's dry?"

I didn't know. However, I nodded politely and wrote on my own pad, "Thanks very much." Swan arose from his desk. "Good luck," he said. "If I can help you, let me know." We shook hands, and I walked out of the bank.

That evening, very laboriously, I described to Bianca the fact that I had a thousand dollars in my shoe when I had reached the hospital. I went on to explain that evidently I had possessed some money before I had been attacked, and that it was possible I had maintained either a savings account or a checking account at a bank. Unfortunately, of course, if this was true, I couldn't remember it.

"Don't you think that Santini has checked this?" Bianca asked.

I explained that I thought he had undoubtedly gone through the motions of it, but that it was dubious if all the banks had been covered and, as the situation was not a very important one to the police, no particular pressure existed for them to explore it further. Bianca agreed with this reasoning. She suggested that she call the banks, herself, to discover if I had an account any place, as it was obvious that I could not call them myself.

In Manhattan there are between four and five hundred banks, including their branches, listed in the classified telephone directory. Bianca began at the top of the list, but very quickly it became obvious that she would have little success. All of the banks refused to give her any information over the phone. After a number of failures, one bank indicated that such information was given to established businesses for credit references.

I had been sitting at the table while she called. Placing the phone back on its cradle, she approached me and rested her hands on my shoulders. "Vic," her voice was sympathetic, "you mustn't get discouraged. Perhaps we'll think of something else." Her fingers picked at my shirt. I looked up into her face; quickly she turned her face away.

It was at that time I remembered Merkle. When he had left the hospital, Merkle had given me his address, so I decided that I'd call on him. That night I took the slip of paper with his address and set off. Merkle lived in a small, reconverted two-room apartment located in a basement of an old brownstone house.

The door to his apartment was beneath a stoop of stone stairs to the first floor, and was protected by a heavy wrought-iron grille. Rust had gnawed the edges of the iron, and it was pocked with leprous orange spots. After I had rung the bell, Merkle opened the door and peered out into the night. Recognizing me, he asked me in. The living room was furnished with cast-off furniture including an overstuffed couch, cane chairs, and a rough mat rug, although it contained an obviously new television set with a very large screen. Plates with remains of crusts, toast, daubs of jelly, half-eaten sandwiches, and drying desserts littered the end tables, seats of the chairs, and tops of the furniture.

"Well, well, well," exclaimed Merkle, his face contorted into a too friendly smile, "my old roommate! How're you? All right?"

" 'Ess," I told him.

"Huh?"

" 'Ess," I repeated, nodding my head.

"Oh, you mean yes! So you've gotten your voice back."

It seemed too much trouble to go through the effort of putting up with such a clown. But, on the other hand, I might be able to use him. Sitting down, I began writing. My original paper pad and pencil had been exchanged for a small permanent pad which was covered with a heavy sheet of transparent plastic. I wrote on the plastic with a wooden stylus, and when I was finished, by lifting the plastic sheet away from its dark background, the writing disappeared, and the pad was ready for use again. It eliminated all the discarded scraps of paper, and the problem of carrying pencils and pens. I attempted to explain to Merkle that I wanted to trace a possible account through the banks. At once, Merkle brought up the subject of the police. "Won't they do it for you?" he asked.

I gave him the same explanation I had given Bianca, although there was another reason which I had not explained to either. If I had an account, I didn't know where the money had come from, and I was not sure that I would care to have the police probing it. Certainly not until I knew more about it myself. However, I said nothing of this to Merkle. He accepted my explanation, as had Bianca, and he sat for a while deep in thought.

Like so many lonely persons, Merkle was anxious to be friendly and to be of help. I was ready to accept his help, but I did not care to have his friendship. Finally he said, "I think I told you that I work for Sampson, Smith and Tobler. It's a big wholesale hardware supply house. They get a lot of orders from a bunch of little stores all over the state, and they've got a sort of system, worked out. They have these double cards ... post cards ... printed up, stamped, and everything. All you have to do is address them. There's a place to check on the second card which is torn off and returned in the mail. So why don't I swipe a supply of them from the mail room? You can address them to the banks, fill in your name as the guy to be reported on, and then see what happens."

It sounded all right except that the cards would be returned to Sampson, Smith and Tobler. I pointed this out to Merkle. He waved away my objection. "So what?" he asked, and grinned. "I'm head clerk in the mail room and I get the mail first. Any cards coming with your name on 'em, I'll just tear up and throw away—unless it says 'Yes' or has something about you. What could be neater?"

I agreed that nothing could be neater and told Merkle that I'd return the following evening to pick up the cards.

It was not late when I reached Bianca's house. She was waiting for me, and when I entered the kitchen I found her seated at the round table, deep in thought, a glass of brandy in her hand. She arose, somewhat unsteadily, and I realized that she had drunk too much. This surprised me as she usually drank very little. Hesitating for a moment, she approached and then threw her arms around me. Immediately she buried her face in my shoulder, and I could feel the shaking of her body. I stood there motionless, wondering about the cause of her distress.

She released her arms and stepped back. "There was a phone call for you while you were out," she told me.

"Yes-s?"

"But no one except Rosemary or Santini knows you're here."

That was true so far as I knew.

"It was a man's voice. He spoke with a foreign accent. When I said you were out, he wanted me to give you a message."

"What?"

"He said just to tell you one word—that you'd understand. I can't pronounce it the way he did, so I wrote it down." She walked to the table and removed a sheet of paper. On it was written in English the single word "*Attl.*" I stared at it. Abruptly Bianca turned away, wrapping her arms around her breasts as if to keep warm. "Vic," she said softly, "Vic, I'm frightened."

Attl, in Arabic, means "kill."

I was frightened too.

14

Burrows was on the lobster shift, twelve midnight to eight A.M. in the morning. Because of his new assignment, he decided to wait until later in the morning ... all day if necessary ... until information began to come in. He had heard nothing more from Jensen and deduced from his silence that the bureau of identification had failed to come up with anything. It was still too early, at eight o'clock, for information to arrive from Washington.

But it was not too early for Burrows to report to Lieutenant Scott, in charge of the detectives at the Eighth Precinct. Scott arrived promptly at eight o'clock. He had been at the Eighth only a little over a month, and had been transferred there from the Seventeenth where he had served five years. Under the revitalized departmental rotation system, Scott had been moved to a new precinct.

Burrows handed Scott a copy of his report, and quickly filled in, verbally, the developments between two and eight A.M. Scott, who shouldered many responsibilities, thought to himself, "What the hell. This case, at least, isn't going to be a hot one, and it's still brand new." However, he said to Burrows, "Has everyone here had a chance to look at the stiff?"

"No," Burrows replied, "just Jensen and me and a couple of the uniformed men. Gorman has the body down at the lab."

"When Gorman's through, we'll try to get them moving on it. Better get some pictures and put 'em up on the board."

Burrows agreed. It was difficult to get the detectives in the precinct to go to the morgue to view the body. Reporting in three shifts, at different hours of the day, and having their own assignments to cover, few of them found time to make such an effort, unless it was a spectacular case. They far preferred to make their examination and identification from photographs whenever possible. "The prints from the photographic department should be here anytime," Burrows said.

Scott nodded his approval. "You know," he continued to Burrows, "that bit about the shoes and the grand bill might mean a lot of things. Back in the thirties, it used to be the custom to find a squealer in the street with a penny in his mouth. For a while, a crooked gambler would have an ace of spades in his pocket. Sometimes hoods like to get fancy ... dramatic."

"This doesn't look exactly like a mob killing," Burrows said. "It might be, of course, but usually they prefer to use a gun."

Scott was inclined to agree with this reasoning, at least to a degree. "Not a mob, not a syndicate exactly," he said slowly. "But the job looks pretty well organized. It doesn't look like some guy did it all by himself. The knock-off and the details were handled pretty well."

15

"Vic," Bianca repeated, "I'm frightened. Who was that man who called you?"

I shrugged. I didn't know. However, my calmness was returning.

"Why don't you sleep upstairs tonight in Rosemary's room?" she asked.

"She's gone and I'd feel more safe."

With my pad I attempted to allay her fears although I agreed to change my quarters from the basement to the top floor. I had been waiting for an opportunity to inspect Rosemary's room since the night she had left; however, I had not wanted to be surprised by Bianca, so I had done nothing.

"I think I'll go upstairs now and go to bed," Bianca said. "When everything's clear, I'll call you."

I nodded, and sitting down at the table began to read the paper. Some fifteen minutes later Bianca called down to me. This was the first time I had been above the street level of the house. A narrow stair ran to the second floor and opened on one side into a very small hall. A second side had a bath; the two remaining walls of the hall, opposite each other, contained doors leading to bedrooms. Bianca's door was closed.

Switching on the light in Rosemary's room, I looked around me. The room was small with two narrow windows overlooking the back of the house. It was attractively furnished with a four-poster bed, a marble-topped antique chiffonier, and several Victorian chairs. A long strip of mirror, with an elaborate gilded frame, stretched from the floor to the ceiling on one side of the room. Everywhere there was evidence of a woman's former occupancy ... cosmetic bottles and boxes on the chiffonier, a delicate odor of scent permeating the room, an ivory and silver hairbrush, comb, and hand mirror, a pair of slippers peeping neatly from behind the corner of a chair.

Undressing quickly, I turned out the light and stretched out on the bed. At the sound of the giving of the springs, Bianca called, "Are you in bed, Vic?" I knocked loudly against the side of the bed with my fist. "Good night," she said. Deliberately I made myself go to sleep for a while.

I awakened from my regular nightmare with the dark room and the spot of light. The fine perspiration of fear bathed my body, but this was no different than usual. According to the small bedside clock, it was three in the morning. Cautiously I raised myself from the bed, moving my body very slowly, so the sound of my arising might not be announced by the springs. In my bare feet I crossed the hall, and through the door I could hear Bianca's deep and regular breathing.

Returning to Rosemary's room, I closed the door completely, and turned on the light. Systematically I began to search her room. When I opened the top drawer of her chiffonier, a scent of sandalwood filled my nostrils. For a moment I had a feeling of nostalgia ... a lonesome memory of having smelled it before in some forgotten moment of delight. The fleeting impression disappeared as suddenly as it had come, and I was left alone. According to Nietzsche, blessed are the forgetful: for they get the better even of their blunders.

One after another, I searched the drawers, finding nothing but stacks of scented lingerie, stockings, and clothing. In the first closet I searched the pockets of her dresses and suits, her coats and jackets; the toes of her shoes ... all standing in a neat, feminine line.

This took some time as it was necessary to move quietly and carefully to avoid awakening Bianca across the hall. Unsuccessful, sitting on the side of the bed, I permitted my eyes to explore the room. Directly above the bed was an oil painting, an original with a large white frame. Arising, I removed the picture, turning it over to examine its back; there was nothing concealed there, and the picture was returned to its original position. Carefully I inspected the chairs with their cushions and backs; next I went over the bed, inch by inch, testing the posts for concealed holes. The only object remaining in the room which I had not scrutinized was the large mirror. It was extremely heavy, and I could not imagine Rosemary having the strength to take it down and rehang it by herself. I walked over to it, and stood looking at it.

Finally I ran my finger along the edges on the underside of the glass. There was a folded piece of paper attached to the back with Scotch tape. Returning to the chair, I unfolded the note. It read:

> Dear Vic:
>
> Knowing you, I have no doubt that you will find this after I leave. I'm writing only in case I don't have a chance to see you alone tomorrow.
>
> You must have good reason for your pretense of amnesia and have planned accordingly. I don't know what your plans are, but I've gone along with them. And I've taken enough chances for you that I still expect my cut, as you promised.
>
> I'm sure I saw Amar yesterday and I'm getting scared. You can contact me under the old name at the same place.
>
> R.

I reread the note, but it still meant nothing to me. I knew no Amar who had frightened her. At some time I had promised her a cut ... an interest ... in something which I could not remember. She had another name which I was expected to know, and she would be staying at a place with which I was supposed to be familiar. The note confused me, and it filled me with a sense of helplessness. I was stifled with the silence surrounding me, caught up in wrappings of the unknown, trapped by my own ignorance of past danger.

With the morning I remembered that Bianca had once mentioned Rosemary Martin's former apartment. Bianca gave me the address, located just off Fifth Avenue, and late that afternoon I went up to see if Rosemary was there. The apartment was situated in the east Sixties, and the building although small was pretentious. There was no doorman and the lobby opened directly off the street. The lobby was paneled and had an inlaid marble floor, and it contained six brightly polished mailboxes. I examined the names on the boxes, carefully, although there was no Rosemary Martin. The other names were meaningless ... Roache, Townshend, Curtis, Levy, Wainwright, and O'Brien. However, I jotted them down on a slip of paper. As I was preparing to leave, the inside door of the lobby, which was locked, opened and a dignified-appearing man, in his late fifties, came out. He looked at me, nodded pleasantly, and opening the street door went outside.

After a moment or so, I followed him. He sauntered down the street and on the corner of Fifth hailed a cab. I did not recognize him although it had seemed to me that his greeting had been more than the casual one of a stranger. I caught the bus down Fifth Avenue, and getting off walked over to the IRT and took the subway to Merkle's neighborhood.

By the time I arrived, Merkle had returned home from work. "I've got the cards," he said letting me into his apartment. It had not been cleaned since my previous visit. He gave me a cardboard box which held the double post cards, all of which had been pre-stamped. I thanked him for them. "How about staying and having dinner with me?" he asked. I didn't care to stay, but I felt obligated and, besides, he appeared so pathetically anxious for company that I agreed. "We won't eat here," he hastened to explain as soon as I had accepted, "but there's a good place right around the corner."

We went to the restaurant he had in mind. It was a dreary one, and the food was very bad. I made the best of the situation although I could not eat much of the meal. When we parted, Merkle reassured me that I had no worries concerning the cards. He would be sure to let me know if I received replies of any value from the banks.

As I turned down Parnell Place, walking the short distance to Newton Mews, I had a feeling that I was being followed. This sensation was immediately followed by a sudden flash of memory which duplicated the identical sensation of being watched. For an instant of time I was returned to the cab of a truck. Around me was a limitless horizon of sand which swelled to the height of hills and small mountains. Throwing the truck into gear, I raced the motor; the truck lurched forward, and behind me there was a tremendous explosion. A piece of metal bit into my back. Then the memory snapped off as abruptly as it had arrived. That was all I remembered.

But I had the same sensation now, as I had in my partly forgotten memory. Turning quickly, I looked down the street. It was dark and I could see no one. This did not surprise me because in order to see anyone I would have to inspect carefully the rows of dark doorways which gaped in the houses. This I did not wish to do. Instead I continued on my way, remembering that Rosemary had seen someone named Amar. My own attackers had known that Rosemary was living in Newton Mews and had delivered me there as a warning. As she had pointed out also, they undoubtedly knew that I was still alive. And this was confirmed by the telephone call which Bianca had taken. So, quite obviously, I was being watched, and someone was watching me now.

There were several plans which I could consider. The first was to shake off my follower and attempt to disappear; there were several drawbacks to this idea. To tell the truth, I had very little money and no prospects for getting more soon. I was comfortable where I was. Also if Rosemary Martin attempted to get in touch with me after I had disappeared, she would have no way of finding me. By remaining at Bianca Hill's, Amar, or whoever was interested in my actions, knowing where I was, would have the opportunity to disclose himself ... or his intentions.

The second plan was to permit the situation to remain the way it was for a while. This I decided to do.

Stopping suddenly, I again turned in the street, reversing my direction, and walked toward Sixth Avenue. After several blocks, I came to a hardware store which was still open at nine o'clock in the evening. Entering, I moved down an aisle between two long counters and stopped before a display of steel carving knives. The proprietor waited attentively while I selected a blade ... thin and narrow, about nine inches long, with a straight, bone handle. I pointed to it and indicated that I wished to examine it. The blade was of excellent Swedish steel. Attached to the handle was a small gummed sticker with the price, and I paid the man behind the counter from my diminishing roll of bills. I did not want to have the knife wrapped, and I slipped it in my pocket while he watched. He didn't say a word.

When I returned to Bianca she asked me if I had eaten dinner. I told her yes. "When you didn't return, I began to get worried," she said. I pointed out that it would have been difficult for me to phone her. She agreed that was true, and shortly afterward went upstairs. I waited for a long time until the sound of her movements had ceased completely. Then, quietly, I went down to the basement.

Placing the knife on my finger, I moved the blade forward and back until I found the balancing-point in it. The handle was much too heavy, and with a chasing tool I hollowed a hole in the bone until I had secured the balance I wanted. Then cross-boring at a point just above the blade, where it entered the handle, I made two small holes. These I filled with silver, using the holes to anchor the metal, until the blade, at that point, only slightly outweighed the handle.

Keeping my mind entirely blank, I followed the pattern of a forgotten skill. Instinctively I held the point of the blade lightly between the thumb and index finger of my right hand, the handle falling straight down and away. Whirling sharply, I swung my arm in an overarm throw, releasing the knife which arched cleanly through the air and made one complete turn before burying itself in the wooden stairs. I regarded this with no surprise; I had known it would happen so. However, I didn't know *why* I knew it.

Prying the knife from the wood, I turned off the lights and made my way upstairs. With the knife on the table by the side of my bed I went to sleep. This night when the nightmare returned it had altered slightly. There was the same long dark room with the spot of light in it. I was still waiting for someone to appear in the light, but while I was waiting I kept trying to reach the knife which was in my jacket and to call to someone. It seemed that my fingers could not quite reach the knife, and the words on my lips were strange ones.

The next day I addressed the cards from the list of bank names in the telephone directory and mailed them out. When I went down to the basement, Bianca said, "I thought I heard you down here in the shop last night."

"Yes."

She waited for me to make some explanation, I suppose, but I did not feel like making one. After a moment she continued, "Is there anything I can do to help you?" I told her no, there wasn't.

When she went upstairs for lunch, I walked over to the power bench, and snapped on the grindstone. Turning the knife on the stone, I honed it to a needle point with razor sharpness on both edges. A shower of sparks ... red, with elongated points like stars ... danced along its blade while the steel snarled against the stone. It was beautiful.

When I lifted the knife in my hand, it felt right ... light, balanced, eager to jump. I placed a piece of cork over the point, and wrapped the blade in heavy brown paper; it would carry safely in my pocket until I should have an opportunity to make a sheath. Frankly I did not know why the knife gave me such satisfaction and security; a revolver would have been a greater and better protection. To be honest I did not know where to buy one, or how to secure it, as the sale of firearms in New York is illegal without a permit. However, I did not worry about this, because I didn't want a revolver; with the knife I was content.

Later I queried Bianca again concerning Rosemary Martin. This was a slow process, although Bianca had become expert in interpreting my nods and the few words which I could pronounce to supplement my writing. I wanted to know the places where Rosemary liked to go, places where she might possibly attend again at some time or other. "Well," Bianca told me, "lots of girls have favorite places where they go on dates ... the Stork, '21,' Copa, and so on, but Rosemary never liked night clubs very well. At least I don't think she did." She paused and glanced quickly down. After a moment she lifted her eyes. "Why are you so interested in Rosemary?" she asked. "First you wanted the address of her old apartment. Now you're trying to find out where she might be having fun."

I wrote on the pad, "I feel bad about her leaving. I don't think she's angry with me, but I'd like to find her to apologize in case she is."

"Oh, don't worry," said Bianca. "If she's angry, she'll get over it. Why don't you forget it?"

"No." I continued with my questioning. "Rosemary," she told me rather reluctantly, "liked smart places for dinner ... the Chateaubriand, Maude Chez Elle, and the best restaurants. After dinner she would sit around for a while talking and have a liqueur and coffee, and then come home early. She wasn't interested in floor shows and comedians."

"What was that hotel she seemed to go to a great many times?" I wrote.

"You mean the Acton-Plaza. It was one of her favorite places. It's rather old-fashioned, you know, in the sense of ... well, good service and tradition. Rosemary even liked to go there for tea on Sunday."

That was the name which I had been trying to recall. I decided that I would try to pick up the trail of Rosemary Martin at the Acton-Plaza.

16

At ten o'clock in the morning, Burrows was beginning to get a little tired. By this time, usually he was home and asleep. The city around him had hit its stride, trucks waddled through the narrow streets of lower Manhattan, buses and taxis raced the main avenues, and the men in the Eighth Precinct, occupied by their duties, came and went in an even-flowing stream. Burrows had been out to breakfast at a small diner located near the station. When he returned, he settled down to wait until he heard from Jensen. While he was waiting, he worked on the endless reports which seemed to drown his working hours—a case of vandals breaking a shop window, a burglary in an apartment with the theft of a portable typewriter and radio, a pedestrian injured by a motorcycle, a reported incident of a Peeping Tom, an alky found dead near the Bowery.

The phone rang by his side, and Burrows picked it up. It was Jensen calling from Centre Street. "We got an ID on the stiff," Jensen told Burrows. "It just came in from Washington."

"The FBI?"

"Yeah, but it came from the Army files."

"Who was he?"

"A guy named Pacific, Victor Pacific."

"Pacific?" repeated Burrows. "That name sounds familiar."

"Yeah," laughed Jensen, "I thought so too. But I guess I was thinking of the Pacific Ocean."

"Sure," agreed Burrows, "everybody's heard of the Pacific. But what I guess I meant was it sounds peculiar ... like a phony. Who the hell would ever have a name like Pacific any more than they'd have a name like Atlantic or the Red Sea?"

"Well, this guy had it. He had it through the Army."

"You get anything else on him?"

"Nothing but his old address," Jensen replied. "All the information on his old record will be coming through in a few minutes."

"Where'd he live?"

"On Thirty-third right out in the middle of the East River."

"I don't get you," Burrows said.

"He was listed with an address Six-sixty something East. Are you familiar with that neighborhood?"

"A little," replied Burrows cautiously.

"That address just doesn't exist. If it did, it would either be in the middle of Con Edison utilities or in the East River. All it means is that this guy Pacific was using a phony address."

"If the name is false and the address a phony, this guy must have had something to hide. It's funny we don't have a record on him."

"Maybe Pacific was a small-time torpedo just starting out when the war broke. He might not've been picked up yet. And after the war he went straight. The FBI didn't have anything on him for a record."

17

Most of the cards for me ... Victor Pacific ... had been returned from the banks; at least all of them that would be returned. They had arrived over a period of two weeks; about half of the banks didn't bother to return them, and I interpreted this to mean that they had no record of me as a depositor. The other cards, which were returned, were all negative. Merkle seemed as disappointed in the result as if he had been gathering information for himself. I told him that it didn't matter, and for no reason whatsoever continued to see him occasionally.

One day, while I was using my key to Bianca's house, I remembered a

Lock-Aid. This memory, from the past, slipped into my mind, and with it the knowledge that the possession of one was illegal even for the police; although the FBI do have them. It is impossible to buy one, but as clearly as I knew how to dress myself, I knew how to make one.

A Lock-Aid is an ingenious, spring-driven device which plunges a needle between the tumblers of a lock, forcing it open. The contrivance is remarkably simple and operates with a trigger, although it requires a great amount of practice to use one successfully. Skillfully handled, a man can open nearly any locked or double-locked door.

I made up a list of the supplies I needed to make one, and the next time I saw Merkle I gave it to him. He could get what I wanted from the hardware supply house. "Sure," he agreed, "I can get this stuff for you. Nothing to it. But what do you want it for?" The supplies, in themselves, meant nothing and were ordinary pieces of hardware. As I did not wish to tell him their purpose, I shrugged off his question. He looked as if his feelings had been injured, although he finally said, "Well, okay. This junk won't cost you nothing anyway. I'll lift it out of stock." I was indifferent to his generosity; Merkle appeared to have the inclination of a jay for petty thievery and seemed to enjoy it.

In the meantime, I had fixed a pattern to watch the Acton-Plaza twice a day ... at noon, and then in the evening at dinner. The hotel, a great old structure, was honeycombed with entrances and small lobbies. Its towering elegance was cluttered with fountains, benches, plants, shrubs, and twisting, carpeted corridors. On the main floor there were six dining rooms and restaurants.

It was impossible for me to watch all the entrances at the same time. I felt a curious resignation concerning the hotel, and was convinced that, eventually, Rosemary Martin would appear. Returning day after day, I merely waited in one or another of the lobbies, and after a reasonable length had passed, I would leave.

Once I had Bianca call the hotel to inquire if Rosemary Martin was registered there. She wasn't. Bianca, however, had appeared disturbed by my request, so after that I had Merkle call at intervals of several days. "Who is she," Merkle asked me, "a girl friend?"

I indicated that she was. This was something that Merkle could understand. "When'd you meet her?" I didn't reply. "Since your accident?" I nodded. "She must have plenty of dough to be staying up there," he said. "Has she got a friend?"

I told him no, she didn't have a friend. I didn't attempt to explain beyond this; I didn't want to insult Merkle, however, because I believed I might need his services again. Indeed, I needed them again very soon.

Writing out an advertisement asking for information concerning a safe deposit box in my name, I gave the ad to Merkle to run in the *New Amsterdam Safe Box News*. On his lunch hour, Merkle faithfully made the trip to the office where he left the ad and paid for it with the money I gave him. Inasmuch as the publication appeared only once a month, there were a number of days to wait before the next issue with the advertisement.

Bianca and I continued to work each day on her jewelry. I began to enjoy a pleasure from working with the molten metal, the cold black silver, and the delicate tools. From time to time, when I had an opportunity to be alone in the shop, I would remove the Lock-Aid and work on it. Eventually, when I had it completed, I wrapped it in a newspaper and hid it beneath the heavy leather couch. Then, at convenient intervals, I would take it out and attempt to open the locked doors in the basement. It took me many hours of practice before I regained the skill necessary to operate it.

Bianca no longer continued to wear her shirts and slacks while working in the shop. Little by little she changed over to wearing sweaters and skirts which made her appear a great deal more of a woman—and less of an artist. At first I was ill at ease when confronted by her change in appearance; it was not impersonal. The relationship between us was not impersonal either, and the circumstances disturbed me. I wanted no ties of sentiment, no obligations of emotion, but I found myself being bound, against my own wishes, by this woman, who seemed to desire it. She was attractive, affectionate, amusing, and had offered me her help when I needed it. And to face this fact of help honestly, I still needed it. In accepting her help, however, I did not wish to assume any personal obligations with it. Consequently, I worked as hard and as efficiently at my job as it was possible for me to do, to help erase emotional indebtedness, although I realized that soon I would have to move from Bianca's home.

That time had not yet arrived, but it would come ... depending on Amar. It was true that I did not remember him, and would not have recognized this implacable man, but he was responsible for having me threatened and followed, and the day would arrive when I should want to escape his surveillance. On that day I would disappear.

My time and patience were eventually repaid when I picked up Rosemary Martin's trail in the Victorian Court of the Acton-Plaza Hotel. The Court is a highly ornamented, many mirrored, muchly marbled, bepalmed tea rendezvous in the hotel. As I approached it along one corridor which runs parallel to the Court, Rosemary was leaving from a door which is opposite a bank of elevators. I hurried forward, but was unable to call or reach her before she had stepped into one of the lifts. Angrily I stood before the old-fashioned indicator above the closed door, and watched in frustration the hand on the dial as it stopped at the third, ninth, and fifteenth floors. Rosemary Martin had gotten off the elevator on one of those three stops.

When the elevator had returned to the main lobby, I studied the face of the operator carefully, so I would recognize him again. It was hopeless, at that moment, to question him about Rosemary through the time-consuming use of my pad as his elevator was constantly in use, and he could not take the time necessary for my laborious questioning.

As Rosemary Martin had not been wearing a coat, I felt sure that she was living in the hotel. A delay until I had secured a photograph of her would not be too important, and with her picture my questioning of the elevator operator would be greatly simplified. When I returned to the house, I asked Bianca if she had a photo of Rosemary. She told me that she did not have one. I explained to her what had happened at the hotel, and why I wanted one. "You might get one from her model agency," Bianca suggested. "She always worked through Gaynor."

In the morning Bianca called Gaynor. The agency had not heard from Rosemary for some time; she had not been in touch with it, and had accepted no jobs through its efforts. There were pictures in the agency's files, which it used for professional purposes, and Bianca received permission to borrow one of Rosemary Martin. "I'll stop by to pick it up," Bianca said on the phone, "or possibly I'll have it picked up by someone else if that's all right." The agency said that it was.

At Gaynor's there was a large reception room filled with chairs, seats, and padded benches occupied by men, women, and children in all stages of beauty, distinction, and age; they were waiting for interviews, picking up messages, and going out on modeling assignments. Rosemary Martin's picture, in a large Manila envelope, was waiting at the information desk; in the photograph she looked elegantly expensive, and appeared sensually aloof. To me, it seemed a true interpretation.

I returned to the Acton-Plaza. Before contacting the elevator operator, I wrote on my pad, "Does this guest of the hotel live on the 3, 9, or 15 floor?" When the elevator descended, I waited until it had emptied of passengers, and then approaching the operator, I handed him a five-dollar bill. He stuffed it in his pocket, and then I gave him the photograph of the woman and the question I had prepared. Glancing first at the picture, then reading my question, he nodded and said, "Yes, the ninth."

Quickly I wrote, "Do you know her room number?" He told me no, he didn't know it. An elderly couple entered the elevator, followed by several other persons. They all appeared impatient to be taken to their floors. There was time for only one more question. I wrote and handed him the pad, "Do you know her name?"

"Nope," he replied, returning the pad to me, and shutting the elevator door in my face. Taking the photograph, I walked back to the main lobby where the registration desk was located. I showed the picture to the clerk, and inquired if a woman answering to this description was registered on the ninth floor. After reading my inquiry, the clerk replied that he didn't know and asked me for her name. As I didn't know what name she was using, I couldn't tell him that; we were at an impasse.

However, I returned to the elevators and took one to the ninth floor. After I had stepped off it, I stood for a moment attempting to impress the plan of the floor in my mind. Unfortunately, there was no floor desk, or clerk, where I could ask for information. Seemingly the plan of the ninth floor was similar to a gigantic grid. A main corridor ran along each of the four sides of the floor; two smaller corridors ran horizontally, and two others vertically, within this main rectangle. Banks of elevators opened on three of the four main corridors, and it was impossible to select a central position from which to watch all the elevators or all the halls. Rosemary Martin could reach the ninth floor from any one of three places in the lobby, and could get off on one of three different corridors on arriving. Obviously I could not spend any length of time in the halls without arousing suspicion, nor could I question the different chambermaids without one of them reporting my questions to the management. I decided that I should not linger on the floor, so I went down to the lobby and left the hotel.

That evening I visited Merkle and he told me that he had called the *New Amsterdam Safe Box News* and they had a reply for me. My advertisement had struck some information. He seemed to be extremely pleased, and he drew his lips back over his stained brown teeth in a wide smile. "I'll go over there tomorrow and get it for you. The office isn't far from my job, and I'll pick up the reply on my lunch hour." It was decent enough of him to offer to do it because it was still difficult for me to go to strange places and talk to new people even for the most simple reasons. My ability to speak only a few simple words and the laborious writing of questions combined to make me an object of curiosity. For my efforts brought looks of surprise, then sympathy which I did not want, and I avoided these embarrassments whenever possible. When circumstances were unavoidable ... such as in the case of the elevator operator ... I would do it, but whenever I could, I preferred that Bianca or Merkle do the talking. I thanked Merkle for his offer, and arranged to see him the next evening and get the letter from him.

After dinner, on the following night, when I arrived at his apartment, the heavy grilled door beneath the steps was ajar. Ringing his bell, I pushed open the door and walked into his rooms. Merkle was seated in his shabby chair with a gaping wound in his head above the temple. A battered clock, on a cluttered table, pointed to a little past nine o'clock. Merkle usually arrived home around six-thirty, as I knew from the times I had met him for dinner, which indicated that he had been dead for a maximum of two and a half hours. The blood on the back of the chair, his shoulders, and on the rug was dry.

His shirt collar was disarranged roughly, and his stringy tie had been pulled very tight—although not enough to have strangled him. It looked to me as if he had been grasped by the throat, with a very powerful hand, pushed down into the chair and then given a tremendous blow on the side of the head. For an instant, I seemed to recall such a hand, and my fingers trembled as I reached inside my coat to touch my knife. It was there. The impersonal coolness of the steel reassured me, and I returned to my examination.

The wound had been caused by a heavy object, most probably metal. Fingerprints cannot be left on a body or its clothing, and I had no hesitation searching Merkle's pocket to find the letter from the *New Amsterdam Safe Box News*. But it was not there. When I explored the littered apartment though, I was more careful, and worked with the thickness of my handkerchief wrapped over the fingers of my right hand.

The appalling filth and disorder of Merkle's rooms were both an asset and hindrance in my search. There were very few places where Merkle might file or hide anything, yet he had only to lay an envelope down and it would disappear into the general confusion. However, my search did not turn it up. Before leaving the apartment, I switched off the lights and, with my handkerchief, wiped the doorknob and iron grille, and closed them behind me.

To face my feelings honestly, I could feel little sorrow for Merkle. The life he had led, and the future which he could expect, were not worth the living. Merely to cling to life in order to be able to breathe, to eat for the purpose only that one's organs may continue to function, is not enough. Perhaps Merkle was happier; at least, he would not be as unhappy.

Nor did I feel that I should assume the responsibility for his death. Merkle had thrust his friendship upon me which I had not particularly desired, although I had accepted it, and he had run for me this last deadly errand which I had not requested. The truth was that I had accepted it as a matter of convenience, and I did not believe that Merkle had been betrayed by either life or death. He had been human, weak, a bore, and a fool and—as every other man must do—had died. He had died, however, from a blow to the head instead of perhaps pneumonia or an infected kidney.

As I walked away, I slipped my knife from out of its sheath, and carried it, with the hilt cupped in my hand, the blade up the sleeve of my coat. It was possible, I thought, that Merkle's body might not be discovered for some time, possibly even days. But I also wondered if the letter of reply had been found by his murderer. Merkle might have been killed accidentally before the letter was found, or fatally struck in an attempt to force him to produce it. Whether the killer had it now, I could not be sure. The knife in my sleeve seemed to come to life; it burned against my wrist. Before me stretched the streets of Manhattan, clothed in the blue-brown night, and I said to myself, "Amar, sometime soon we must meet."

18

Jensen said, "I thought maybe it was better if I came down and we could bat this stuff around." He was sitting by Burrows' desk, and he looked rather tired. Jensen lit a cigarette, then placed it in an ashtray without smoking.

Burrows had several pages of notes which Jensen had phoned to him earlier. They concerned the Army record of Victor Pacific. Burrows looked at the notes in his hand, and then at the preliminary report he had filled out. "Well," he said to Jensen, "fingerprints don't lie."

"I know what you're thinking," Jensen said, "but don't forget that was a long time ago. Maybe other things don't stay the same for fifteen years or so, but fingerprints don't change."

"Gorman said the stiff was six feet or better; that means maybe six one or two. According to this Army information, he was five eleven."

"That was only Gorman's first guess. It's hard to measure a body lying down flat. Maybe Gorman was wrong."

"By maybe three inches?" asked Burrows. "I don't think so!"

"That's a lot," agreed Jensen, "but suppose Gorman was out by one or two inches. Say the stiff is six feet. The Army report says five eleven. In those days everybody made mistakes including the Army doctors."

"At induction centers there was a shortage of doctors, and the ones they had were damned busy," Burrows agreed reluctantly.

"Sure. Most of them had to use enlisted personnel to help out ... medical assistants. I remember when I went in some sergeant stood me up against a wall with a scale on it. He took a look at where my hair reached—and that's how tall I was." This was not exactly the truth, but Jensen at the moment believed that it was.

"Well," said Burrows, "I wish Gorman would get his report finished and up here."

"Don't take Gorman's remarks that he made too seriously. He told us, himself, that he was just taking a guess at the time. Remember? He said he could always change his mind."

"I'd feel better if Gorman said the stiff was really only six feet tall. I'd feel a lot better. I can see the difference between some overworked med assistant slapping a guy through a line and saying he was five eleven, and a doc later on says he was six feet. A report just can't be that wrong—five eleven and maybe six two."

"Unless he was a growing boy," said Jensen. He tried to make a joke of it. He continued seriously, "I've read of guys who've taken stretching exercises at gyms, using some kind of harness, which added an inch or two to their height."

"You don't mean it though," said Burrows.

"'Course I don't mean it," agreed Jensen. "I just said it, because it came to my mind, but it's downright foolish."

19

I debated, with myself, concerning the next step forced on me by the murder of Merkle. He had picked up a reply to my ad in the *New Amsterdam Safe Box News*. Undoubtedly the reply had arrived in a sealed envelope through the mail, and there was a possibility, although a remote one, that the envelope had carried a return address which the magazine might have kept as a record. With the discovery of Merkle's death, the police would attempt to trace his actions during the last day of his life and possibly discover his trip to the publication. On the one hand, I did not want to be connected with Merkle's death in any way, but on the other, if there was a remote chance of finding the source of the reply, I did not wish to miss it. Another month would pass before the ad could be run again, and it might not be answered a second time.

With some hesitation, I decided that I would call at the *New Amsterdam Safe Box News*, and accept the consequences as a calculated risk. The office was on the sixth floor of a shabby building filled with mercantile jobbers. In an outlying office, which served as a reception room, a middle-aged typist pounded a heavy machine and answered the single phone. In the second office was the editor and sole member of the editorial staff. He was a man named Holcombe, with balding head fringed in sandy hair. His desk was crammed into a narrow space surrounded by green metal filing cabinets, and the top of it was littered with clippings, paste pot, scissors, and blank dummy pages of the magazine.

After I had explained to him that I had come to pick up any replies to my ad, Holcombe called to the typist, "Any replies to ad P-61?"

Deliberately she sorted through a thin stack of envelopes and shook her head. "No," she replied, "nothing." She returned to her typewriter, then paused and raised her head. "Say," she observed, half to herself half to Holcombe, "I think there was one." In another moment, she bobbed her head positively. "Yes, there was one. It was picked up yesterday."

Holcombe turned to me. "Did you get it?"

"No," I told him. Then on my pad I explained that probably it had been picked up for me by a friend.

"He'll give it to you then," Holcombe assured me.

I nodded, then added, "I may not see him for a few days. Would you have a record of it?"

"You mean a return address?"

That was what I meant. "Sorry," said Holcombe. "After all we're a highly specialized publication. We carry very few ads, and there's never any problem concerning the replies."

Deciding that it was better not to arouse curiosity or comment, I dropped the subject and left the office.

The next day I read in the papers that Merkle's body had been discovered. The story was brief and appeared on the inside fourth page; it said that Merkle had been absent from work, and when his office called him had not answered his phone. As he was known to be a bachelor, it was feared he might be ill, and a fellow employee had stopped by to see him. The police theorized that Merkle had been killed as a result of a burglary attempt. His apartment indicated that it had been searched but whether anything of value had been stolen was not known.

The police, I knew, would carry through their investigation as far as they could, and then drop it. Merkle was unimportant; he was nobody. The authorities could not waste too much time on this unspectacular little man.

It became increasingly important, however, for me to talk to Rosemary Martin. With Merkle's death, I desired to remain even more inconspicuous than in the past, and I did not want to be held or questioned by the hotel for loitering on its premises. I believed that Rosemary Martin was staying very close to her own room, and I would need help to locate her. Therefore, I selected the name of a detective agency at random; it was located on Fifth Avenue just above Forty-second Street; this was a good address and it gave me confidence that the agency was efficient. I went up to see it.

On the office door was the name "Bell, Investigators," and the offices looked prosperous. A young woman at a switchboard doubled as a receptionist, and she introduced me to a Mr. Delton. I do not know whatever happened to Mr. Bell. I never met him, but Delton seemed to be in charge. He was a short compact man with heavy features and a full, thick upper lip. We went into his private office and I showed him the picture of Rosemary Martin. Then, slowly, I pieced together my story for him; it was not all of the story, but it was enough for him to know. When I had finished I put my pad to one side, and he summed it up briskly.

"You say this young lady is a friend of yours and is staying at the Acton-Plaza, is that right?" I nodded. "You believe she is living in a room on the ninth floor, and is registered under a name other than her own?"

"Yes."

"You want us to find what room she is in?"

"Yes."

"That shouldn't be too much of a problem," Delton told me, his voice efficient. "I assume, though, this is not a matrimonial case. You assure me on that?"

"Yes."

"We don't handle matrimonial investigations," he continued, "for financial reasons. Such investigations involve a great amount of time ... day, night, appearances in court to give testimony, and so on. It isn't possible to make a profit from them. We stick to legal investigations—furnish plant and bank security, messengers and guards ... that type of work. I don't want to get involved in anything complicated. Do you understand?"

I indicated that I did.

"Okay. I think we can locate this woman for you very easily, if she is still at the hotel. If it takes half a day it will cost you fifty dollars; if we spend a full day, the fee is one hundred."

Between what little money I had left, and what Bianca had been able to pay me, all that I could afford was the fifty dollars. I decided to gamble it through. Delton appeared capable, and with any luck might quickly locate Rosemary Martin. I nodded my approval to his terms.

"Please sign here," Delton said energetically, indicating a short half-form on which he had written, "Miss Rosemary Martin staying at Acton-Plaza. Locate room where living and assumed name." I signed it, using the name Kenneth Sloan. "Thank you, Mr. Sloan," said Delton. "Now do you care to give me a check?"

Naturally I did not care to do so. Instead I placed five ten-dollar bills on his desk. "I'll call you as soon as I have anything," he told me. I shook my head, and again returned to my pad. I wrote that I would get back in touch with him. We parted with that understanding.

There were no follow-up stories in the papers regarding Merkle. I began to feel more easy, although in reality there was little for me to worry about. It was doubtful if the police could find a motive for the murder of Merkle. It had been an act of expediency, possibly even of accident. Merkle had no past which might have involved him with murder. If the police should trace him to the *New Amsterdam Safe Box News*, they would question me. But even then, if I denied all connection with Merkle, other than a superficial acquaintanceship struck during our stay in the hospital, there was nothing that could be proved against me. It was not fear of the police which kept me out of the investigation; rather it was a desire to remain without surveillance or restraint to pursue my own affairs.

I told Bianca about my visit to Bell, Investigators and that evening asked her to call Delton. There was an answering service on the agency's line at that time of night, and the operator offered to have Delton call back. I didn't want him to know my number, so I shook my head and Bianca left a message that Mr. Sloan would call in the morning.

She called again the next day, and Delton told her that Rosemary Martin had been located; she was occupying room 944 in the Acton-Plaza, and was registered under the name Nell C. O'Hanstrom from St. Louis. After relaying this information to me, Bianca remarked thoughtfully, "What a peculiar name to use. Who ever heard of such a name as O'Hanstrom?" The name meant nothing to me; yet Rosemary Martin had expected me to recognize it, to remember it.

"I can't imagine why Rosemary should want to hide," Bianca continued. Taking a deep breath, she asked suddenly, "Vic, what was there between you two?"

I shook my head.

"You mean you don't know? Or do you prefer not to talk about it?"

Both.

Bianca grasped my hand. I could feel the heat of her palms, the warmth of her skin as she pressed it, and the gesture made me uneasy. I attempted to draw away, but she clung, to it saying, "There's something wrong, something awful going on. I don't know what it is—it's all around us. I can feel it waiting to ..." Abruptly she turned, then stepped away. More composedly she added, "Forget Rosemary, forget everything except that you're starting a new life. I have a little money saved ... not much ... and I'll lend it to you. Go away. Stay away from New York for a while. Then come back when you've completely regained your health."

I attempted to tell her that I couldn't leave.

"Why?" she asked. "Is it because you love me?"

I told her no—that I didn't love her. That I didn't love anyone. This was true and I believed that I should tell her the truth.

"I'm sorry," she said, after a moment of silence. Her voice was very low. "I shouldn't have asked you that. But you see, I love you." She turned her head; there was moistness around her eyes. "You don't love me. You don't love anyone," she glanced around the kitchen as if seeing it for the first time. And it seemed to me that she was addressing her remarks to it. "I'm not a doctor or a psychiatrist or anything, but I am a woman and I know just one thing. You've never loved anyone or anything in your whole life!"

There was nothing to say. I wanted to tell her that I was grateful for her help, that I appreciated her kindness, but she continued before I had an opportunity to order my thoughts. "It's very funny," she said, "because the time you came here from the hospital, I felt very sorry for you. I really believed you needed help." Half a thread of laughter caught in her throat. "There was no one to help you, no place for you to go. I remember, you were terribly thin and looked so sick." She shook her head, as if clearing it of the memory. "A man who is sick and thin and needs help is just sheer, downright irresistible to a woman who's sentimental. Then, having you around, being with you ..." She shrugged, leaving the sentence unfinished.

I felt embarrassed, and a little angry, that Bianca had caused this scene. I had grown fond of her, and she had been of great help to me. By forcing a rather commonplace sentiment into our situation, she had made the position untenable and I must prepare new plans. I wrote on my pad that it would be a good idea if I found another place to live. Eventually, of course, I would have moved anyway, but to move at this time was inconvenient.

She agreed. "I suppose so," she said slowly, "because now I know that you don't really need help, at least, not my help. I don't think you needed it ever. Within you there is an unbreakable will which protects you, a hardness which shields you from everything ... and everybody ... except yourself. Whatever it is that is driving you, whatever you're looking for—you'll find it without my help."

At that moment I felt that a door to another world stood before me, and by taking a single step through it, I would understand. Understand myself, the past, the present, the future. On my tongue were words and ideas which I could express and which would be understood. It was as if my brain had been thinking at a distance, translating other words and ideas for me, but not thinking as my own brain would perform. The words which I wanted to shout were not English or French or Arabic or words of an international language but words and phrases which to me were clear and clean, and as sharp as crystal, cutting as a razor's edge, compact. The instant of attainment was gone, and I was back in the room with Bianca, and all that remained was the memory of a quotation from Schopenhauer: Intellect is invisible to the man who has none.

It was agreed that I would move on the week end, which was still three days away, but events forced me to leave before that. I waited until seven o'clock that evening before going to the hotel to find Rosemary Martin. I believed that seven o'clock would be a logical time to find her in her room, at which hour she would probably be dressing for dinner. However, when I knocked at her door, there was no reply. As there was the possibility that she might be in the room and had refused to open the door, I stood silent before it for a long time. Although I listened intently, I could hear no rustle of movement within the room.

Returning to the main lobby, I remained uneasily by the bank of elevators which rose nearest to the location of room 944, hoping that I might see Rosemary Martin. This was by far the longest period of time that I had remained around the hotel, so after additional minutes passed I decided to return to the ninth floor and wait for her in her room. The corridor was vacant and shielding the Lock-Aid with my body, I released the spring, shooting the needle between the tumblers of the lock. On the third attempt, the lock opened, and I entered the room, closing the door behind me. The chamber was dark; in a moment my hand flicked the switch by the side of the door and the lights jumped on.

The bedroom was oblong with two windows at the far end of the room opposite the door. A large double bed made up, but with the spread mussed as from someone lying on it, was placed on one side of the room. Across from the bed stood a chest of drawers, and next to it a dressing table with winged mirrors. A chaise longue was placed before the windows, and a reading lamp on a small table rested beside it. A door, slightly ajar, opened into the bath in which the lights were out.

Still wearing my coat, I sat on the side of the bed and lit a cigarette. In a short time, I needed an ashtray and looked around for one. There were two—one each on the chest of drawers and the dressing table. Both of them were clean and unused, and unless Rosemary Martin had been out of the room all day, this fact seemed strange. She smoked and there should be evidence of ashes. On the other hand, I told myself, she might have cleaned them herself, before going out.

As I was now standing by the chest of drawers, I opened them. They contained neat stacks of lingerie, stockings, nightgowns, and other usual items. In the bottom drawer were three handbags.

The bags had been emptied of their contents, or the contents had been transferred to the one currently being carried. They all contained scraps of old sales receipts, match folders, bobby pins, and one held a badly creased post card. It was a very cheap, highly colored scene of the New York skyline such as is sold in nearly every drugstore in the city. There was no address and no postmark on the back of it, and it obviously had not been sent through the mail. Written on it, however, were the words "Ten o'clock Tuesday morning." I was returning the card to the bag, when I paused and stared at it a second time. There was something very familiar about the writing, and quite suddenly I realized why this was so. The sentence was in my own handwriting. I put the card in my pocket.

The dressing table disclosed nothing except a complete line of cosmetics. In the clothes closet, I again found something of importance. Another purse of Rosemary Martin's was there; this one was evidently the one she was carrying. It held a compact, room key, billfold containing nearly six hundred dollars, comb, mirror, a cigarette case, lighter, and a number of receipts. Dumping the contents on the bed, I examined them carefully. Tucked into the billfold was a corner from a newspaper clipping which read:

... early college rowing races on Lake Quinsigamond near Worcester, Mass., and on Saratoga Lake, N. Y., but the Intercollegiate Rowing Association in 1895 settled on the Hudson at Pough....

That was all the clipping had contained, except that the date "1895" had been underlined in pencil. Rosemary Martin, to the best of my memory, had never mentioned collegiate rowing; I could not understand why she should carry a clipping concerning the sport in her billfold. However, I slipped the clipping into my pocket and returned the articles to her purse, placing it back in the closet.

As I left the closet, I heard the sound of scraping from the bathroom. Immediately the sound ceased, resumed after a moment, then lapsed into complete silence. Caution urged me to leave the bedroom, then I decided that whoever was in the bath had seen me and recognized me anyway. My knife found itself in my hand, and I approached the partly opened door warily. The sound resumed, and I thrust the door open.

Rosemary Martin was hanging by her neck in the shower stall.

The body rotated slowly, and the heel of one mule scraped gently against the side of the stall. I turned on the light and in the glare of the white tiles I was reminded of a morgue. As she turned on the end of a leather belt, I could see that she had been dead for some time and her features were bloated and distorted with the disfigurations of strangulation.

Her neck had not been broken. This point, combined with another, troubled me. She had not tied her hands, and it is very difficult for a person to strangle herself to death deliberately. After losing consciousness, self-preservation causes a person to fight the rope, to tear free. I was sure that these points would not be overlooked by the police either.

I thought to myself, why did this have to happen now? I felt no particular sorrow that Rosemary Martin was dead. Whatever our relationship might have been in the past, I was sure that it had been one of convenience and selfishness for us both. I had lost precious time and information through her death; and the suspicion of her murder would bring the police to my door.

Returning to the bedroom, I examined the mussed bed, and it seemed to me a certainty that she had been strangled there, and then removed to the other room. In the closet I found a pair of walking shoes, and I removed the laces and knotted them together. With this heavy cord, I tied her hands loosely behind her back, using a knot on one wrist and a slip knot on the other—such as a person tying it herself would be compelled to do.

My concern, an anxious one, was to escape from the hotel without being seen by anyone who might later tell the police. I carefully wiped away my fingerprints from both rooms with the aid of a bath towel. At the closet, I opened the purse again and removed five hundred dollars from it. I needed the money now, and I was convinced that Rosemary Martin needed it no longer. Deliberately, I took the time, forcing myself to check carefully that I had left nothing behind me. With the post card and clipping in my pocket, the dead cigarette flushed down the drain, I looked out into the corridor. A couple was approaching down the hall, and I closed the door, waiting patiently for them to pass. After a few more minutes, there was no one in sight. Hurrying to a fire stairway, I descended to the sixth floor, where I returned to the main corridor and rang for the elevator.

Once I was on the street, without incident, I took a deep breath of the evening air.

20

"The eyes check," said Burrows. "Blue."

"Sure," agreed Jensen, "and the weight isn't bad either."

"One sixty in 1942," Burrows glanced at his note, "and Gorman says one eighty-five now."

"That's not too much difference after all these years. How many guys you know weigh the same as they did in the war? Twenty-five pounds isn't too much if a guy's taking it easy and living it up a little."

"The stiff didn't look fat though," Burrows remarked. "If he weighed one hundred and sixty pounds then, wouldn't one eighty-five look a little heavy ... like he'd gone a little to fat?"

"I don't know," Jensen said honestly. "I agree the stiff didn't look fat ... just good and husky. I'd say that if Pacific had been a real skinny guy ... one twenty-five, one thirty, something like that, he might've looked like a tub at a hundred and eighty-five pounds. But in 1942, Pacific was just twenty-two years old. The war, regular meals, and the heavy work filled him out."

"I guess you're right. It did to a lot of men. Pacific might put on twenty-five pounds and not look fat." Burrows got up from his desk and walked over to the window. He looked out for a moment then returned to Jensen and sat down again. "If Pacific was twenty-two when he got drafted, that would make him around thirty-seven, thirty-eight now."

"Yes. Gorman said the stiff was anywhere from thirty-five to forty-five years old."

"That would put Pacific right in the middle of Gorman's guess."

"Sure," agreed Jensen. "What's wrong with that?"

"Nothing," Burrows replied slowly, "but it's that old spread again. Everything is spread."

"The eyes are blue, the fingerprints check. There's no guess or spread about them."

"Damnit!" Burrows exploded impatiently, "I wish Gorman would get his report finished and tie this up. You can say what you want to about it, but five eleven and six one or two is a hell of a spread; thirty-seven and forty-five is another spread; one hundred sixty and one hundred eighty-five pounds is just more of the same thing. I feel like I'm talking about two different guys entirely."

"Except for the Army," Jensen replied patiently.

"Sure. Except for the Army."

"Time changes everything," explained Jensen. "Look at the Army record. It says Pacific's hair was brown, not dark brown, or anything else, just brown. On your own report you described it as light brown. If I'd been making out that report, I'd have said sort of sandy with gray in it. We're all talking about the same guy, but everybody talks a little bit differently from everybody else. It doesn't mean anything. Once he had brownish hair, now it's got a little gray in it."

21

I moved from Bianca's that same night. Rosemary Martin was dead, and because she was dead it was logical that I leave the house at once. Rosemary Martin, Merkle, Santini, Doctor Minor ... all the persons who had crossed my life since the day I had regained consciousness in the hospital meant nothing to me. But when the time came to say good-by, I was not so convinced regarding my sentiment toward Bianca Hill for there was a generosity of spirit within her which I recognized to be unusual. The rest of the world, and the people in it, existed only to prove my own reality. They were shadows which passed me each day, in a world made of present fragments and fleeing hours. I knew only that each man is a product of the whole of humanity; the seed which is passed down from ten thousand grandfathers; his present, his virtues and vices, are the product of his past.

I had no present, because I had no past.

It was impossible for me to explain this to Bianca. Bianca read my explanation silently. It was only about Rosemary though I did tell her I felt I owed her that—and I knew that when Rosemary's body was found the police would question Bianca, and Bianca knew I had been looking for Rosemary. When I told her that I was leaving, she began to cry. Her face shadowed, and she no longer held back her tears.

"Vic, Vic," she spoke softly, "what will you do? Where will you go? Whoever tried to kill you before will certainly try again!"

I pointed out that my unknown assailants could have killed me many times over, but had not. They wanted me alive—at least for a while.

Then she said, "Rosemary, poor Rosemary ..." I touched her shoulder, a gesture of sympathy which I thought might help her, and she stopped her crying after a moment, and said with determination, "I don't believe that she killed herself!" I had to agree with this, although I did not tell her so. She repeated, "Vic, I just don't believe it!" Then I saw her eyes begin to cloud with doubt as she looked at me, and I knew that she was thinking that I might have killed Rosemary Martin. I said nothing, and permitted her to wrestle with her doubts. Then her fear passed, and she attempted to regain her composure. "Rosemary knew something that you've forgotten. She knew you from the past."

I nodded. Bianca's observation had been obvious. I left her, and went upstairs to pack my few belongings in a suitcase which I had to borrow from her. As I prepared to leave, she said, "But why go now? You can't escape them. You'll be as safe here as you will anywhere."

With my pad, I attempted to make plain that Rosemary Martin would be identified, and very soon the police would be checking with Bianca regarding the time the two women lived together. I did not want to see the authorities again, to be hampered by them or their questionings. When they inquired concerning me, Bianca was to say that I had moved away, and she did not know where I had gone. This would be true because I had no idea where I would stay.

After she had agreed to this, I made one last request. I asked her not to tell the police that I had known Rosemary Martin in my past, nor that I had called on her at the hotel. I did not ask her to lie about this, because Bianca was a very poor liar. I merely told her not to volunteer the information. The police, I knew, would attempt to locate me, but it might take them time to do so without this added motive.

With my suitcase, I walked to the door. As I stepped over the threshold, Bianca called to me. "Vic! If you need help always call me!"

"Yes," I told her. For an instant something about her touched my heart.

On Eighth Avenue, near Fourth Street, is a Spanish hotel named the Castillo. I didn't know it was there until I passed it, carrying the suitcase. It was a shabby place with a linoleum-covered lobby containing a few chairs and scattered tables. Along one end was a long counter which advertised that it was also a travel agency to Puerto Rico, Cuba, and South America. I decided it was a racket hotel which specialized in flying native labor back and forth—and fleecing them. If I was correct in my surmise, then everyone in the hotel minded his own business, and it would be a good place for me to stay. I went in.

An emaciated room clerk, with jaundice-tinted skin, and plastered hair, spoke English. I registered under the name of Harold Rocks. The name made no difference, especially as I paid for my room a week in advance. The room was what I had expected, but I didn't care.

Before going to bed, I took out the post card and clipping which I had found in Rosemary Martin's possession, stuffed my pocketbook with the five hundred dollars inside the pillow case, and left my knife on the floor beside the bed. Then I went to sleep. About two in the morning, however, I awakened.

During my sleep, one answer had arrived. I had found the key to the name Rosemary Martin was using at the Acton-Plaza ... Nell C. O'Hanstrom. It was the kind of name no one could possibly have, or if having, use. And yet there was a certain lucidness, a vaguely defined sense about it which made an off-balance logic. Subconsciously I had worked it out, or at least very nearly so, and all that remained to do was to write it on my pad. I put it down:

Colonel Horstman
Nell C. O'Hanstrom

If I accepted the premise that the apostrophe in O'Hanstrom represented a second letter "o," then the name "Nell C. O'Hanstrom" was a simple anagram for the name "Colonel Horstman."

This was enlightening, although I still did not know who Colonel Horstman was. Was it possible, I asked myself, that Rosemary Martin had been Colonel Horstman? This was ridiculous; not by the most absurd stretching of my imagination could I believe it. The name did not belong to her. This I knew instinctively, not even if Rosemary Martin had been a colonel in any of the women's services during the war. And even this most slender of possibilities was completely eliminated by the fact that she had been too young to even consider serving at that time.

I sat in the night, smoking cigarette after cigarette. It is in the predawn hours that facts sometimes become stripped and naked under scrutiny and examination. It is possible for them to become distorted too—blown up to a new importance, inflated with despair and emotion. The connotation of the name Horstman to me was not an unpleasant one; I felt that at some time I had known him well; that he had been my friend. I was anxious to find him again, to see him, to secure his help. I decided that Rosemary Martin had used his name, in an anagram, because she had obviously expected me to recognize it; it was a name filled with meaning and good intent for me, and I was expected to know it.

After reaching this decision, I returned to bed. My nightmare began with my sleep. The same long dark room, the same spot of light at the end. Outside the radius of light, there was movement and preparation in the darkness ... a quickening of the black shadows, but no materialization. When I awakened, my knife was in my hand, my body was covered with sweat, and daylight was pouring through the dirty window of my bedroom.

I had breakfast at a bar and grill in the neighborhood. As I drank the muddy coffee, I examined the post card again with its cheap, gaudy, lithographed scene of the New York City skyline. While I sat on a stool, carefully looking over the colored card, the full light of the day reflected from the imitation marble top of the counter and struck the post card, and I observed something which I had not noticed before. Near the top of one of the buildings, a tiny hole had been punched with a pin or needle. It might well have remained invisible except for the roving ray of light. There was no question that the hole was there, and had been punched there deliberately.

The reason for its presence seemed clear. It indicated the building where I was supposed to meet Rosemary on some Tuesday, in the past, at ten o'clock in the morning. Unfortunately, however, I failed to recognize the building. At one time both Rosemary Martin and I must have known the address well, and an indication had been sufficient for her to determine my intention. But now to me it was only a small colored area on the card, rearing slightly over other similarly colored areas. There were neither towers nor ornamentation such as the Empire State or Chrysler buildings to set it apart. From the card, it appeared to be located north and slightly to the west of the Empire State structure, although the relative distance was impossible to determine accurately. Taking the card, I went down to the public library, but the maps of the city offered me no help as I didn't know the name of the building or its location.

I rode the subway back downtown and got off at Fourteenth Street. There was no particular reason for doing this except that I had become tired of riding. I was anxious to escape its confines and the rushing roar of its dark journey, and decided to walk the rest of the distance to my room. On Twelfth Street, between University Place and Fifth Avenue, I passed an ancient, six-story building, the front of which was a patina of smoke, dirt, and soot. Outside the doorway was a sign "Expert metal worker wanted-6th Flr."

The building was occupied by various manufacturing companies, one on each floor. A decrepit elevator wobbled in its shaft, from side to side, cautiously inching its way to the top where I left it. The sixth floor was occupied by the Warner Stained Glass Company, a cavernous area the overall size of the building—dark and blanketed with a layer of gritty dust. At the front by the windows several six-foot-high partitions had been installed to separate three desks. The rest of the floor was littered with heavy wooden tables, and tremendous shelves to store glass.

A man who identified himself as the shop foreman approached me and asked what I wanted. I wrote that I wanted a job. He told me his name was Haines and he inquired concerning my experience—especially in stained glass work. I told him that I had no experience in that particular field, but that I had been a silversmith, and might qualify as a metal worker. He regarded my pad which I had been using to answer his questions, and he asked me if I was a veteran. I told him yes. This impressed him favorably as he was a veteran too, and evidently he decided that I had been wounded. This was true enough, but not in the sense he thought, and I didn't disillusion him. Haines motioned me to follow him toward the rear of the shop. On the way, he said, "We keep only four regular employees: an artist who does the life-size cartoons of the designs, two glass workers ... call 'em cutters ... and a metal worker. I do a little bit of everything."

He stopped by a large bench which held a number of strips of U-shaped lead. The foreman selected an irregular piece of blue-colored glass and handed it to me. "Let's see you completely solder around the four sides with lead," he told me. On the bench was an iron which was hot enough to use. I had no difficulty in doing the job—which was relatively coarse work compared to my experience soldering jewelry for Bianca Hill. Haines inspected it, and said, "It looks pretty good. There's a little knack in shouldering the glass more solidly in the lead, but you can pick that up pretty quick."

I indicated that I could. When he asked me for more personal information, I told him my name was Rocks and I lived at the Castillo Hotel. Evidently he had never heard of the Castillo, which was all right with me too. We shook hands and agreed that I would start work the next day. The job satisfied me for several reasons; although I had the five hundred dollars which I had taken from Rosemary Martin, I had no way of knowing how long the money would have to last. I might need it for emergency reasons, and the job at Warner's would permit me to keep it in reserve. Also, if I should be traced by the police, the fact that I was working would be in my favor; I would have visible means of support. It paid a good salary, far more than Bianca Hill could pay, and was an excellent excuse for me to have left her house.

The evening papers indicated the importance of an efficient publicity department. At least for the Acton-Plaza. Rosemary Martin's body had been found at the hotel; she had been correctly identified although she had registered under an assumed name. She had not been working recently, according to her agency, and it was believed that she was despondent. The police thought she had committed suicide. That was all. Brief, short, proper; no suppression of news, the freedom of the press upheld, and the advertising department of the Acton-Plaza not embarrassed.

I did not know and could only speculate how much information the police were going to dig up or how much they already knew. However, I was quite sure that I knew the reason Rosemary Martin had been murdered. After I thought the situation through, this was the way the facts appeared to me: Amar, or the group with which he was working, had located the safe deposit box. He had received this information in the letter forwarded to me through the *New Amsterdam Safe Box News* the night that Merkle was killed. Knowing the location of the box, he had to secure the key. It was inevitable that I had been searched thoroughly the night I had been taken for a ride, so Amar was sure that I did not have it. He reasoned, then, that the key was in the possession of Rosemary Martin, and now that he was in a position to use it, he went to get it. It took him a while to locate her at the Acton-Plaza, and when he did it was too late. I had the key. Furthermore, I thought, Rosemary Martin had been calculatingly murdered. While Merkle's death might have been accidental, her death had been deliberate. Even if Amar had been convinced that she no longer held the key, he had a reason to believe that I couldn't use it if Rosemary Martin was dead. So, she was dead.

Amar could be expected to call on me in the near future. In the meantime, I attempted to merge into the colorless background of the Castillo by spending my days at the Warner Glass Company and staying close to my room in the evenings. My job interested me, and I was content to work—marking time until I could gather more facts and turn them into actions. Haines had explained that the methods used in creating stained glass windows vary in only the slightest details from the way they were made in the thirteenth, fourteenth, and fifteenth centuries. The tools are better; that is about the only difference.

In the shop there was an order for an extremely large and elaborate glass window to be made for a new library on Long Island. This window would require a long time to complete. In the beginning an artist conceives the design for a window and executes it in a colored miniature. From this miniature the glass artist draws cartoons to life size, and the cartoon in turn is rendered on pieces of heavy brown paper; this paper is, in truth, a pattern which is cut into exact shapes to fit the design of the window. Glass is cut by means of this paper pattern, assembled, and soldered with strips of solid lead.

I had constructed the outer, arched frame of metal for the window, and no one would examine it or be working with it again until the final assembly of all the pieces. Consequently, I soldered the safety deposit key, which Rosemary Martin had given me, into one end of the frame. It was safe there; no one would find it; and should it be necessary, I could remove it at any time.

Several nights later, I called Bianca on the phone. It was difficult to make myself understood without the use of my pad. I repeated several times, "See you?"

"You wish to see me?" she asked finally.

"Yes."

"Why don't you come over here?"

After a slight pause, she said, "I don't think the house is being watched by the police."

"No."

"Shall I meet you then?"

"Yes."

"Where? Oh, let me think." She finally named a small restaurant a few blocks from her house and I agreed to meet her there.

I was waiting in the back of the café, in a small booth, when she appeared. She appeared tired, and looked worried, although she smiled when she saw me. "How are you?" she asked. I told her that I was fine.

"The police came to see me," she said. "They got my address from Rosemary's old modeling agency. They asked me nearly a million questions."

"Me?" I asked.

"Yes, about you, too. I told them that you had worked for me for a while, then became tired of the job and left. I didn't know where you had gone."

"Thanks," I said.

Bianca sat listlessly, a cigarette in her hand. Occasionally she smoothed the wrinkles in the tablecloth, a nervous gesture leveling the little mountains and valleys. Finally she said, "The police asked me if I had ever met a man named Howard Wainwright. When I told them that I hadn't, they asked me next if Rosemary had ever mentioned his name. She never had."

I looked at her inquiringly. "Wain-wright?" I attempted to ask.

"Yes," she replied. "Wainwright. It seems that he was some kind of wealthy broker, or he did something like that, down near Wall Street. Rosemary was supposed to be seeing a great deal of him."

In the back of my mind the name repeated again and again ... Wainwright, Wainwright, Wainwright.

She continued, "Well, the police went to see Wainwright and discovered that his office was closed. He'd disappeared; no one knew where he was or where he is now."

I knew this information about Wainwright was important. I wanted to know more. As yet, I was unable to place his name, but I recognized it. It was unfortunate that I was unable to go back to see Delton, but I did not care to push my luck too far. Delton, I hoped, would keep quiet regarding his activity in locating Rosemary Martin at the Acton-Plaza. He did not know my name, naturally, but I could be easily identified because of my voice. I didn't believe that Delton would volunteer information to the police, and there was a reasonable possibility that, unless they should come across his trail, he might know nothing of the murder having occurred. The papers had carried it inconspicuously enough to have escaped his notice.

Wainwright, I decided, would have to be investigated through other channels.

Bianca opened her purse and peered into a tiny mirror. Without glancing up, she asked, "How do ... do you have enough money to live on?"

I assured her that I had enough.

She snapped shut her purse and arose to her feet. Although I followed her to the front of the café, I permitted her to leave by herself, as a precaution in case she was followed by the police. "Call me again, Vic," she said. "Call me anytime."

I told her yes, that I would call her.

After Bianca Hill had gone, I smoked another cigarette. I continued to turn the matter over in my mind: I had my throat cut; Rosemary Martin was murdered; a broker named Wainwright had disappeared. This was not coincidence—there had to be a connection. In my head I heard the word *"Jahsh,"* the Arabic word for donkey. It was my own sense telling me that I was an ass. Of course there was a connection ... Pacific, Martin, Wainwright! Merkle had been insignificant and unimportant, a pawn caught out of position. But Wainwright ... and suddenly I remembered the name ... had been important. I had better find out more about him!

22

Jensen looked at his wrist watch. It was nearly twelve noon. He yawned. "Christ, I'm sleepy!" he said.

"We should hear from Gorman pretty soon," Burrows replied.

"You know," said Jensen, "it was a funny thing how the war did a lot of good for a bunch of those young hoods. After they came back, they'd had it. Today they're nice peaceful citizens."

"Maybe. But you can't say that about Pacific. Anybody who ends up getting his throat slit can hardly be called a nice peaceful citizen."

"Yeah, but maybe it wasn't his fault. Although I doubt it. A guy can be killed in a stick-up or a mugging ... accidental-like, and it isn't his fault."

"But this wasn't a stick-up or mugging," Burrows objected.

"I know it." Jensen was becoming irritable through fatigue. "What I was going to say was that Pacific might've started out as a young punk. The war ... the discipline ... sort of straightened him out—at least for a while. Ten, fifteen years. Then he got back into the old routine again."

"He had a good Army record," Burrows said.

"Sure. Six Hundred and Fourth Tanks ... a damned good outfit. A rugged one, too. Pacific bucked all the way up to sergeant in a good company."

"I see he originally asked for service in the Rangers."

Jensen laughed. "Remember those days?" he asked. "You were a good mechanic, say, and you asked for service in a truck depot ... someplace, or something, you knew something about. And what did you get?"

"A job taking shorthand in Alaska," replied Burrows. "But what I'm beginning to believe was this guy Pacific was a tough character right from the beginning. The Rangers ... the Scouts ... were just about the toughest. Like the English Commandos."

"Judo, hand-to-hand combat, sure. But a lot of young guys thought they'd like it. Anyway, what Pacific got wasn't a creampuff. The tanks in Africa were plain misery." Jensen removed a number of papers clipped together, unfolded them, and glanced at the detailed report. "It says that he got his in a little place called Al-Slaoui. His tank got trapped and was blasted out direct by artillery. The rest of his crew was killed. He got it bad in the back, and was reported dead. There was a short retreat but twenty-four hours later there was a general advance and Pacific showed up at the field hospital after the line had been straightened out again. He was hospitalized in England, and then given a medical discharge and returned to the United States."

"He was lucky," said Burrows.

"Sure he was lucky," agreed Jensen. "A lot of those guys never came back. But then his luck ran out. After all this time he finally got it." Jensen for a moment became a philosopher, "And so, it just proves—everybody gets it in the end anyway. You can't live forever."

"No, but I'd like to try," said Burrows.

23

I asked Haines, "Okay?" and handed him a note in which I had requested permission to take an extra hour on my lunchtime. "Sure," Haines agreed. I walked over to the subway at Union Square and caught a train to Forty-second Street. The other side of Broadway I located the address of

Panoramic Photography, Inc.

Within the office there was the indefinable smell of drying negatives, developing fluids, and chemicals which always seem to be associated with photographers ... even a street photographer. A morose man, with a lantern jaw, sat patiently while I wrote out my request. "Do you have any pictures of the New York skyline?" he repeated my question aloud as he read it. "Hell," he said, "does the ocean have salt?" His name was Donlan, and his company specialized in aerial photography for maps and survey work, including oil pipe lines, canals, and other commercial projects.

Placing the colored post card on his desk, I pointed to the minute pink building in the skyline, then wrote that it was important to me to identify that building. Donlan inspected the card with unconcealed distaste. "This thing was highly retouched from a cheap shot to begin with," he said. "The lithographers have probably been using the same plates for ten years." He inspected the card again, this time very carefully, and finally established the identity of several buildings. "Let me see what we've got in the way of shots of this particular area," he said, walking into the next room. He rummaged through a number of large, wooden filing cases and returned to his desk with a thick pile of photographs. Sitting down, he thumbed through the pictures, occasionally tossing one aside. When he had completed this task, he gathered the half-dozen selected shots and began to examine them again. "Here's the Empire State Building," he said, "which is easy enough to recognize. The building you're trying to identify is uptown in relation to the Empire State and to the left which would make it to the west." He returned to a study of the pictures, and after a long silence said, "I think, maybe, the building you're interested in is either the Amco or the National Federated. It could be either one depending on the angle and altitude the original shot was taken. They are nearly directly behind each other and separated by a distance of two blocks. The Empire State Building is on the corner of Thirty-fourth Street and Fifth Avenue. The Amco is on Thirty-sixth near Sixth Avenue and National Federated is behind it on Thirty-eighth." Leaning back in his chair, he concluded, "At least that's my guess and it doesn't cost you anything."

I thanked him and left the office of Panoramic Photography, Inc. As it wasn't far to walk, I went down to Thirty-eighth and looked at the National Federated Building. If the building was pink, it was that color only in the feverous mind of the lithographer. It was the same as any other building. In the lobby a directory of the building contained a long list of names of the companies located in it. I read the list carefully, but failed to recognize any name or find a company which held any significance for me. A little later, two blocks away, I again studied the directory of the Amco Building, another tall, gray skyscraper with floor upon floor of identical windows. When I left the lobby of the Amco Building, however, I had something to think about. Among its most conspicuous tenants, and located on the ground floor, was the First International Export Bank.

When I returned to work, Haines asked me if I had taken care of my business, and I told him yes, that I had. During the afternoon, as I worked with my metal and glass, I first began to have an understanding of myself. It was the glass which began to make me understand. Two types of glass are used, traditionally, in making stained glass windows. There is the true stained glass which is called "pot-metal" glass, and it is one color only—red or blue or green or purple or any other color—all the way through.

The other kind of glass is called "flashed-glass" and is a combination of two colors, although one color must always be white. Each color of glass is an individual sheet, and the two sheets are fused, melted, and glazed together such as red and white; green and white, blue and white, and so on. By the use of acid, the over color, which is always the colored sheet, never the white, may be etched away in areas where desired. The white sheet, thus exposed, may be re-etched and stained, but only to one color. That color invariably is yellow or gold.

In such a manner, a piece of blue flashed-glass may be blue in one place, white in another, and gold in a third.

Since I had talked to Bianca, it had become increasingly obvious to me that I needed help to find out more about Wainwright. I had remembered that his name had been one of those listed in the apartment building where Rosemary Martin had lived formerly. An attorney, I decided, might be the best source of help. When Warner's closed that night, I returned to Union Square and wandered down Broadway in the direction of lower Manhattan. The buildings in this area are all old, run-down, and contain few prosperous tenants. In the lobby of one, near Ninth Street, I discovered the names of a number of attorneys. I jotted down their office numbers and then began calling on them. The first three offices I visited were closed for the night, but the fourth was open, and a short, pudgy lawyer named Bozell was ruffling papers at a battered desk.

He stared at my throat constantly, which made me uncomfortable, and when it was possible for me to speak a word, he seemed startled that I should do so. Finally I stopped trying to talk at all, and relied entirely on my pad. In this manner, I explained to him that I wanted to get as much information as possible concerning Howard Wainwright, his brokerage business, and any other available personal information. Bozell agreed to do this. When I asked him the cost, he named a price which I considered far in excess to what I could pay. As I had no desire for an argument, and because of my voice could not have debated with him anyway, I shook my head and prepared to leave. Bozell grasped me by the arm, and suggested that he might have overestimated the amount of work I wanted him to do. I made it clear to him that he understood perfectly what I wanted. He then proposed that I name a price, which I did. I offered him fifty dollars; he countered with one hundred, and we agreed on eighty. It was understood that I would return to his office, the following evening, at the same time.

The newspapers, that night, carried little additional information concerning Rosemary Martin. Buried deeply in the body of the publications, each story was much the same. She had not been working recently as a model; she had been living under a fictitious name; and there was a hint, a vague one, of a possibility of an unhappy love affair which caused her to take her own life. As far as I was concerned, I was content to let the story stand that way; perhaps the police would accept it too.

By now, having become an accepted resident of the Hotel Castillo, I had little difficulty securing any illicit comforts that I might require. There had been developing within me a pressure, a building of desire, a nameless craving for something which I must have known at one time, and which I subconsciously was anxious to acquire again. It was not liquor. Although I drank brandy and, on occasion, whisky I received no particular pleasure from them. I did not enjoy their taste, and the effect of intoxication seemed to me more in the nature of a sickness, a reeling in the head, than enjoyment. I had no desire for women either. This did not indicate a lack of virility, or a slackening of masculinity, within myself, but only that I had no emotional needs. Residing within my body was a vacuum, a total lacking of all desire, and within my brain was the inability to join the world around me. But, in searching my mind, and discarding the needs of liquor and women, I remembered hashish.

I realized that I wanted to smoke it, and that a forgotten memory of my past had been urging me nearly beyond endurance. At the Castillo, I slipped the room clerk a twenty-dollar bill and urged him to get me some. After carefully putting the bill in his pocket, he said, "I can't get it for you. They don't peddle it around here." His black, greasy hair gleamed under the hanging light. I felt a terrible rage begin to rise, and I leaned across the desk to stare at him. He read my anger in my face, and hastened to explain, "I can get you some sticks of marijuana though." As marijuana is the Western cousin of the Eastern hashish, I agreed and went up to my room to wait for the cigarettes to be delivered.

Eventually there was a knock at the door, and when I opened it a very thin girl smiled at me. "You wanted some sticks?" she asked. I nodded. Stepping into the room, and opening her large, black purse she removed half a dozen tightly rolled cigarettes. I could see the large blue veins on her slender wrists; her face was emaciated which gave her features a sharpness not displeasing, but she had used a powder far too light for the olive tones of her skin. As she handed the cigarettes to me, her eyes covered me without interest, and she smiled mechanically. "Would you like me to stay around awhile?" she asked. I told her no, that I didn't want her to remain. It was obvious that the desk clerk had sent her along to earn himself an additional commission.

The girl shrugged indifferently. "Okay," she said, "maybe you'd like to get with it later. If you do, call me yourself. My name is Margarite." She gave me her number and left.

Stretching out on the bed, I lit one of the cigarettes, dragging the smoke deep into my lungs, holding it there until it had been filtered by my blood. And it came to me that in the past, I had done this many times. As the drug began to take effect, I felt my indifference vanish; I turned on my side and as from a distance watched the insulation of apathy stripped from me layer by layer. I felt a sadness that this was so, as it seemed to me better to feel nothing, to lose nothing, than to feel emotions again intently.

Imperceptibly my mind began to tighten, drawn taut by a garrote of the thin gray smoke. I thought of Amar, and sat up in my bed, swinging my feet to the floor. Clearly, lucidly, with a refreshing cool hatred stinging my senses, I sat through the night.

In the morning I went to Warner's, but my mind was not on my work, and I attended my job desultorily until I could return to see Bozell. In his office he motioned me to a chair. "I have a few facts for you," he told me importantly, while scratching the back of his neck. "They were rather difficult to gather." He snapped the middle fingernail of his left hand, with the thumb nail of his right. "I had to give the impression that I was representing a creditor with possible action against Wainwright and his company," he continued.

I didn't say anything. I sat on the chair and waited.

Bozell said, "As you know, his name is Howard K. Wainwright, and he was head of his own company ... a very small one incidentally. He was not a member of the Board of Exchange, and only occasionally worked through brokers who were. Wainwright claimed to be only an investment consultant. No one seems to know who his clients were or anything about them. And so far no client has come forward to press a claim against him since his disappearance."

Writing out a question, I requested more details about Wainwright's office.

"It's a small one, as I told you, but located on Wall Street. Sometimes he used a typing and answering service although he had a girl, a foreign one, working for him. She was the only staff he had."

I asked her name.

"Sara ... something or other," Bozell replied.

I knew the answer to the next question, but I wanted it affirmed.

"Wainwright lived on Sixty-third Street off Fifth Avenue," Bozell answered. He gave me the address, and it was the same building where Rosemary Martin had once lived.

"I also discovered that the authorities were looking for Wainwright to question him regarding the death of some woman he had once known."

Had they located him yet?

"No. Not yet."

How long had he been gone?

"No one seems to know exactly. Three or four months at least, possibly even longer. His disappearance wasn't reported; no one seemed to care."

What about his apartment and his office?

"Both of his leases have been in effect for a number of years, and his rent is paid by an annual check. The landlords would have no complaint."

I let Bozell know that I'd contact him if there was any additional information I needed. As it was still very early in the evening, I decided to return to my hotel. There I had another smoke and attempted to evaluate the situation. Wainwright had disappeared about the time I had been assaulted; it was probable that he had been killed. He and Rosemary Martin had lived in the same apartment building which was certainly more than a coincidence. It seemed to me a matter of importance that I should look around Wainwright's apartment, although the danger of such action was evident. Undoubtedly the police had already searched his premises, and it was probable that they might still have it under guard.

However, the more I considered this possibility, the less probable it became. The police force is always undermanned, and with Wainwright absent for a number of months, it did not seem reasonable to assume that the police would make more than an occasional check-up on his apartment. Certainly they would not maintain a twenty-four hour watch as a matter of routine, so I decided that I would wait until very late and then visit Wainwright's place.

At two o'clock in the morning, Sixty-third Street seemed to be deserted. The lobby of the apartment building, with the brightly polished mailboxes, was lighted by a discreet fixture, and from its glow I discerned that Wainwright's apartment was number 3-A. Again carefully checking the other names, I could discover nothing which might be connected with Rosemary Martin or O'Hanstrom. It seemed logical to suppose that after Rosemary Martin had moved from the building, her apartment had been rented by someone else.

Located next to the self-service elevator, which stood waiting with doors open, in the lobby was a small stairway. I decided that I would walk up which would give me an opportunity to survey the hall before approaching Wainwright's apartment. When I reached the third floor, I opened the stair door slightly and could see that the hall was deserted. There were only two apartments on the floor-3-A in the front, and 3-B in the rear.

Using my Lock-Aid, I easily opened Wainwright's door. Pulling on a pair of gloves, I turned the knob and walked into his apartment, closing the door behind me. There I stood for a moment with my back to the wall, listening; but I could detect no signs of life around me. Across the room, light filtered into the apartment through the windows which faced the street. Closing the venetian blinds, I drew the heavy drapes across the windows and plunged the room into complete darkness. I struck a match and turned on a table lamp. Placing the lamp on the floor, I piled several pillows on top of it to dim the glow to a feeble light. With these precautions, the light could not be detected from the street.

The apartment consisted of a large living room, a bedroom, with a smaller dressing room, a dining room, kitchen, and directly adjoining the kitchen was a maid's room with a bath. This room, however, had been furnished and equipped as a small office and contained a desk, typewriter, and other equipment. As soon as I opened a file, I realized that someone had searched the place before me. All correspondence had been removed.

The desk disclosed little more. One drawer contained a stack of unused stationery with the imprint "Howard Wainwright, Investment Counselor." There was nothing to draw my attention to it, and I nearly passed by it, but before closing the drawer, I lifted the paper and riffled it with my finger. From someplace in the middle of the stack, a memo page dropped out and planed to the floor. I put the stationery back in the desk and picked up the piece of paper. On it had been typed the notation:

Mecca. Al-Suweika. Sept. 2241
Oct. 4333
Nov. 8781

Placing the paper in my pocket, I finished searching the desk, but there was nothing more to be found. As for the rest of the room, it too had been thoroughly cleaned out.

The bedroom closet disclosed a number of men's suits hanging neatly in a row, together with top coats, shoes, and other apparel. The pockets contained a few match folders, paid receipts months old, and that was all. A second large closet was completely empty.

It was in the dresser that I again came across the trail of Rosemary Martin. I had searched through a tall chest of drawers which held Wainwright's linens and had found nothing unusual. Next, turning to a large period dresser, I opened each of its four drawers end found them empty except for one thing. The scent of sandalwood!

The memory of the night when I had searched Rosemary Martin's room at Bianca's house returned; the same odor of sandalwood had clung to her dresser. Habits are difficult to break, and Rosemary Martin had followed her regular custom of scenting her dresser with this particular scent. The meaning of the empty closet and the empty dresser became clear. At one time she had been living here in Wainwright's apartment.

Although I had no way of exactly determining the time, it seemed probable that she had occupied this apartment when Bianca first knew her, and then had moved down to Greenwich Village. And yet, after all the months, why had the scent of sandalwood remained? Why had it not disappeared, or why had Wainwright not put his possessions in the dresser?

I was reminded of what Bianca had said. When Rosemary Martin had moved to the hotel, she had told Bianca that she had some clothes in storage. Undoubtedly she had been referring to the clothes she had left here in Wainwright's apartment. She must have possessed a key, and had returned to pick them up. According to both the police and Bozell, Wainwright had been gone for months. Did Rosemary Martin know where he had gone? That question I could not answer.

But I was still thinking about it when I stepped into the darkened living room. Immediately I felt the snout of a revolver in my back, and a voice said, "Sir, the waiting was not in vain."

24

The phone rang. Burrows looked at the clock. It was twenty past twelve. "That's probably Gorman," he said, speaking to Jensen. When he picked up the phone, it was Gorman, the Medical Examiner.

"I just got through with the posting," Gorman said, "and I can give you my findings now over the phone. I'll send the official report to you later."

"Okay," agreed Burrows. He drew a pad of paper forward on his desk to make notes.

"Well," Gorman began, "I wasn't too far off on most of my original guesses. The body weighs a hundred and eighty-seven pounds, is six feet and one-half inch. Originally light brown hair, now somewhat grayed, and was in good physical condition for whatever his age was."

"What do you mean by that?" asked Burrows.

"I can't really nail his age down by an examination, you know that. I can put it within certain probable limits. When he was alive he probably looked and acted younger than he was."

"Meaning what?"

"From his appearance he could have been around forty, a few years either way. But the body organs ... arteries and so on ... might indicate he was older."

"Maybe he just drank it up too much," said Burrows.

"Possibly. Anyway, he was nearly decapitated from the blow of a large, heavy blade."

"How large and how heavy?"

"Practically a sword. As a matter of fact, you could call it a sword. An examination of the shoes and socks showed no foreign matter; no dust, sand, cement, or anything like that which would not ordinarily be found in New York."

"That means he was living here?"

"Not necessarily. But at least he hadn't worn those shoes out of New York recently. The shoes are well worn, although in good condition, so he'd been wearing them for some time."

"What was the time of death?"

"Between twelve midnight and one o'clock. Finely drawn, that is. I can't be too positive on it. Fifteen minutes to half an hour each way might still be too close."

"What about the scar?"

"Undoubtedly an old wound. Characteristic ... star shape and so forth. I've seen a lot of them from the war."

After Gorman had hung up, Burrows relayed the information to Jensen. "The doc did pretty well the first time around," Jensen remarked.

"Sure," said Burrows, "but ..."

25

For a moment I stood motionless. Behind me the voice continued, "I am a patient man, and patience is repaid ... *khlas.*"

Khlas ... the end. The revolver remained firmly planted in my back, and I extended my arms to the side, holding them away from my body. I could feel a hand pat my coat and trousers for concealed weapons, and then cautiously dip into my pockets and throw their contents on the floor. "The key, if you please," the voice told me after it was obvious I had no key in my possession.

The revolver moved slightly from my body, and it was then that my reflex took over. Instinctively I stepped back, jamming quickly and hard against the barrel of the revolver, turning it to one side. Without effort my knife jumped into my hand from the sleeve of my jacket, and I thrust over my shoulder without turning. The blade bit into the arm behind me even as the revolver was falling to the floor.

I pivoted and held the point of the knife against the man's stomach. He grasped his wounded shoulder with a hand, and I motioned him to turn around. Reluctantly he complied with my command. When his back was to me, I scooped the gun from the floor and held it in my hand. In the dim light of the room it was difficult to see my adversary and I circled him completely; he was short, very slender, a man of middle age with intense black eyes and heavy dark hair. Although he was dressed in American-tailored clothes, he did not wear them well, and I believed that he might be Amar. For a moment, I was undecided about slipping my knife into him quietly and holding his mouth, but I discarded the idea and, instead, hit him over the ear with the revolver. He dropped to the floor and lay without moving. From his pockets I removed all the papers and objects he was carrying, as well as his billfold. Leaving him unconscious on the floor, I gathered up my own possessions and left the apartment.

I was in a hurry to get back to the Castillo to pack up my belongings and leave. Since I'd taken his money Amar would be unable to follow me without a delay. That delay would permit me to lose myself again somewhere in the city. At the hotel the room clerk was reading a paper behind his desk and didn't look up when I carried my suitcase through the lobby. Hailing another cab, I rode uptown and stopped the taxi when we passed a desolate-looking hotel on lower Broadway. It was called the Arena and would do as well as any other.

In my new room, which was only a slight improvement over the Castillo, I spread out the contents of the man's pockets which I had taken from Wainwright's apartment. There was a short letter addressed to Amar Al-Kariff reporting the sailing of a vessel some two weeks before to a port in Africa and it was typewritten and in English. The letterhead was the "Tajir Transportation Company" with offices in Damascus, Mecca, and Cairo. Inasmuch as the letter was not in an envelope there was no way to determine from where it had been mailed. Also I recognized the word Tajir which, in Arabic, means "wholesale-import-export merchants."

A fountain pen, mechanical pencil, and cigarette holder I took apart to examine, but there was nothing in them. In the billfold was Amar's driver's license which listed his address as a YMCA, an amusing piece of fiction. There were also half a dozen neatly printed personal business cards with his name and the Tajir Transportation Company—listing a business address in the extreme lower West side in the steamship and dock area. In addition to the cards and license, I found a ring holding five keys, and ninety-one dollars.

I put the money in my pocket, tore up the letter and cards, and threw the billfold and key ring into an air shaft.

The morning brought me a new problem to consider: should I return to my job at the stained glass window company? I wanted to get the key from the window where it had been soldered, but it might be advisable to wait until I needed it. If Amar Al-Kariff had followed me from the Castillo to my work at Warner's, he certainly would be waiting at my job to pick me up again. On the other hand, he might have been watching for me only at Wainwright's, or looking for someone else there, although this seemed open to doubt, as he had called me at Bianca's on the phone, hoping to force me into action. I believed he had come upon my trail originally through trailing Rosemary Martin, and undoubtedly had lost me again when I moved to the Castillo. Under these circumstances, I decided, I should return to Warner's and regain possession of the key immediately.

Reporting to work as usual, and removing the key at the first opportunity, I wrote a note to Haines explaining that I felt sick. He told me to go home, which I did, although I did not return to my new hotel until after riding uptown on the IRT, then circuitously by foot going through Macy's and leaving by an emergency fire exit. On the street, I found a cab and rode to the Arena; it was not probable that I had been followed.

After returning to the hotel, I took out the memo slip which I had received from Swan at his bank, with the heading:

> ... from the desk of
> C. K. SWAN, vice-president
> Merchants & Chemists Exchange Bank

On it Swan had jotted, in pencil, the address of the *New Amsterdam Safe Box News*. I erased carefully his writing and with a pen wrote: "This will introduce Mr. Victor Pacific, one of our depositors who recently has been ill. Any information you can give him will be appreciated."

I signed it C. K. Swan with a flourish.

At the Amco Building, as I entered the First International Export Bank, Bianca was waiting for me inside the door. We returned to the lobby where I laboriously explained to her what I wanted her to do as it had been impossible for me to even attempt it over the phone when I had called her to arrange our meeting. When I told her my plan, she agreed to help although her eyes held a number of questions. Re-entering the bank, we went to the desk of Mr. Jackson, one of the vice-presidents. I handed him the memo from Swan which he read; then he told us courteously he would do what he could.

Bianca smiled and said, "I'm Mr. Pacific's nurse. It's very difficult for him to speak, so with your permission I'll speak for him."

"Certainly, certainly," Jackson agreed.

"Mr. Pacific, before his illness, was in the importing business. However, because of his accident, he has suffered a partial loss of memory and cannot remember all the details of it."

Jackson asked, "Can't his company help him?"

"No," explained Bianca, "he had a small, personal business and because he was away for so long, his secretary had to find another position, and she can't be located."

"Certainly he must have kept records?"

Bianca, with the dexterity of any woman acting, gently shook her head, smiled slightly, and pretending to hide the gesture from me, tapped her forehead slightly. "It's possible Mr. Pacific put his files away suddenly just before his sickness."

"Oh." Jackson shifted his eyes to me, then quickly looked back at Bianca. "Well," he said, "I'll help you if I can. What do you want to know?"

"Only if Mr. Pacific had an account with this bank."

"I can find that out easily," Jackson replied. As he reached for the phone on his desk, Bianca Hill added smoothly, "Of course, while he was ill, he insisted on using a number of names. One of his favorites was O'Hanstrom."

Jackson requested the information from the bookkeeping department. He held the phone for a few moments before turning back to Bianca Hill. "There's an account here in the name of Nell C. O'Hanstrom," he told her. "Nothing for Pacific."

I printed on my pad, "How about Tajir Transportation Company, and a man named Horstman?" and handed it to Bianca. She repeated the question to Jackson. He shrugged, and again spoke into his phone. After a short wait, he nodded and hung up the receiver. "Yes and no," he said. "There is an account for the Tajir Transportation Company, but there is no record of a Horstman." Leaning back in his chair, he terminated further questions, as he told Bianca firmly, "In both instances these accounts seem to have no connection with Mr. Pacific. One is a *Miss* O'Hanstrom and the other, the Tajir Company, is an international corporation."

Bianca thanked him politely and rose to her feet. But I wasn't satisfied. I scribbled another request. Reading it, she turned to Jackson and asked, "Is there any objection to our asking some questions in your safe deposit department?"

"Not at all," Jackson assured her.

Downstairs, in the basement of the bank, we were passed through a door with shining metal bars, and into a reception room which contained a tremendous, round, time-operating door. There I huddled myself deep into my muffler, keeping my face averted as much as possible. Bianca made a quick explanation and referred to Jackson as her authority to ask questions. The officer in charge of the vault accepted her story and, quickly searching through an alphabetical listing of names, reported that Nell C. O'Hanstrom had a safe deposit box, but there was none for Horstman, Pacific, or the Tajir Transportation Company.

Bianca Hill asked the man a question, a good one, which had escaped me. "Did Miss O'Hanstrom authorize anyone else to have access to her deposit box?" Turning to me, she explained, "I used to be deputized for my mother when she had one."

After a moment's examination of the files, we were told that a Mr. Wainwright, Howard K., had been deputized to gain admittance at any time, and he had been issued a key. This information tied back to what I had decided previously. Rosemary Martin was directly connected with Wainwright in her personal life and in business.

Another question remained, however. What was in the safe deposit box? It was possible that Wainwright or Rosemary Martin had been through it before her death. But, inasmuch as I had Rosemary Martin's key in my pocket, I decided that she could not have been near it. She had been too frightened to keep the key and had given it to me. Undoubtedly Wainwright had the second key so that left just the two of us.

On the street, Bianca asked, "Where are you living now, Vic?"

I shook my head. Taking me by the arm, she said, "You're right. It's better that I don't know. Is there anything else I can do for you?"

Since we had left the bank, I had been considering the possibility of getting into the safe deposit box. Stopping in a doorway, I again depended on my pad to explain to Bianca that it was too dangerous for her to see me again, but that she could help me a final time if she had any samples of Rosemary Martin's handwriting.

After reflecting a moment, she replied that she might have a few notes or cards that Rosemary Martin had left behind. I asked her to send them to me in care of general delivery, the third zone. She promised to do so immediately.

Although I now knew that Rosemary Martin and Wainwright had held a joint safe deposit box, I was equally sure that somewhere in New York I had held one of my own. There was the reply from the *New Amsterdam Safe Box News* to support this conviction as the request for information had been in the name of Pacific. And suddenly I knew, equally as well, that Amar had not been able to find that reply in Merkle's apartment. Merkle had been clubbed too hard, accidentally before he had an opportunity to tell him, and a search at the apartment had not revealed it. Perhaps Merkle had left the letter behind him at the hardware company after work. If this premise was true, then Amar, the night we met in Wainwright's apartment, had been asking for Rosemary Martin's key, the duplicate of Wainwright's, and not for the key belonging to me, Victor Pacific.

There was time, I decided, to trace my own safe deposit box later. Perhaps by finding the answer to Rosemary Martin and Wainwright, I would find my own answer, too. Certainly there had to be a direct connection between the three of us.

Much depended on me getting into the O'Hanstrom box in the bank, but I was not sure that I could do it.

There was quite a wait at the hospital before I could see Doctor Minor. Finally he walked down the hall and shook hands with me. "How are you doing?" he asked. I told him, "Fine" in my talk-around voice. Minor seemed as pleased as if I had been a trained parrot. "Keep it up," he said. "Someday we'll have you singing in the Met."

I doubted it. However, I laughed politely, then penned the question which I had come to ask him. He read my note and looked thoughtful. Finally he said, "Yes, you did look different the night you were brought in. You had a small, closely trimmed military mustache. It's a rule of the hospital not to permit mustaches except when patients can care for them, and obviously you couldn't. But more important, you had lost so much blood that it covered your face and hair. Consequently, we had to clip the hair from your forehead and temples."

After further discussion, I realized that my appearance had been altered, somewhat, through the shaving of my mustache, the closer cropping of my hair, which I had continued to follow since leaving the hospital, and my own loss of weight. Although, to be accurate, I was again gaining pounds and broadening.

Bianca kept her word, and acting promptly mailed a letter to the post office which I picked up the next day. She had enclosed two short notes Rosemary Martin had written her; one asked Bianca not to wait up for her as she would be late, and the other had been in connection with a birthday gift. Fortunately, there were enough lines and words for me to piece out the spelling of the name Nell C. O'Hanstrom. Wherever possible, I compared the letters and selected the most naturally written ones. I then had photostatic copies made, and cutting out the individual letters pasted them next to each other to form the two names and the initial. I had a capital "N" and "H," but no "C" and no "O."

After many false starts, and a great amount of effort, I finally wrote and approved a specimen of the name, the letters linked together as they might have been written by Rosemary Martin. I did not use the middle initial "C" as I had nothing to follow in the capital use of this letter, and decided that I would be safe to gamble on dropping it. The letter and capital "O" I could not drop and this caused me difficulty; eventually I selected a simple script with a slight ascender near the top.

Because Bianca had been to the bank with me, and might be remembered, it was not advisable that I should return with her. Yet I needed help. I trusted no one else, and knew no one unless it was Margarite, the girl who had brought me the marijuana at the Castillo. I did not trust her, although I felt that her temporary loyalty could be purchased. And, because of her own personal activities, she would hesitate to turn to the police. Finally, of course, and most conclusively there was no one else I could ask. She had given me her phone number, and I arranged with a bellboy at the Arena to call her and have her come to my room at the hotel.

26

At one o'clock in the afternoon, Jensen had decided to go home to get some sleep. After leaving Burrows, he checked back in his office at Homicide Manhattan East, located on East Thirty-fifth Street. There, however, a message was awaiting him from the Bureau of Identification. After completing a call to Centre Street, in reply to the message, he returned to the Eighth Precinct to see Burrows again.

When Jensen walked into his office, Burrows said, "I thought you were calling it a day."

"So did I," Jensen replied. His eyes were red rimmed from lack of sleep. "Something new turned up and I thought I'd better pass it on to you ..."

"I was just leaving too," Burrows groaned. "What is it?"

"I got a message from Turner in the fingerprint bureau to call him. So I did. He'd just reported on duty at noon, and running through last night's reports thought the name Pacific rang a bell."

"So," asked Burrows, "they goofed up on it?"

"No. It wasn't their fault. They didn't have any prints on record. What happened was this. Turner remembered picking up an ID through Washington a long time back. He remembered the name, that's all, and be decided to check it against the files. He did, and the name is there on the master file, but the print card is gone."

"Gone?" Burrows was surprised.

"Sure. Gone!"

"Why'd it be gone?"

"Don't ask me. I don't know."

"But," Burrows objected, "no one can buy his card out of those files. Pacific, even if he'd been a big shot, couldn't have gotten it."

"Maybe Pacific isn't Pacific at all."

"It's got to be Pacific. Look, everything changes in this world except one thing ... fingerprints."

"Yeah, but why'd the card be gone?"

Burrows shook his head. "J. Edgar Hoover couldn't put on enough pressure to lift that card," he said.

"I know that. Anyway," said Jensen, "Turner checked on the duplicate file and it's the same guy all right."

"Victor Pacific?"

"Yeah. Victor Pacific."

"I got an idea," said Burrows. "Stick around a few minutes. Let me check up on something else. I got an idea. I want to see."

27

When Margarite knocked on my door, I opened it. She walked into the room carrying the same large handbag she had carried the last time. "You wanted to see me?" she asked.

She lounged indolently across the room and seated herself on one of the hard wooden chairs. I looked her over carefully. Margarite's skin was olive in color; her features were good and were in no way grotesque. In a sullen, knowing way she might be called attractive. But there was no question regarding her appearance; she looked like a chippy ... clothes too tight, too gaudy, heavy make-up, a brazen, half-defiant air. I felt discouraged; she looked nothing like Rosemary Martin had looked, and I was filled with doubts regarding my ability to carry through my plan. Yet I had no alternative, and could only hope that Rosemary Martin might not be remembered at the bank where hundreds of customers appear daily.

At first Margarite was wary when I explained to her ... laboriously ... that I wanted her to learn to forge a signature, and she must learn to sign it quickly and easily in public.

"No, thanks," she told me bluntly, "I got enough troubles without looking for more."

I described to her the safe deposit box and told her that it had belonged to my wife who had since deserted me, that it contained some important papers which I needed badly, and there was no other way to get them.

"Where's your old lady now?" Margarite asked me.

I told her that I didn't know where she was.

"In New York?"

"No, not in New York."

"How much is it worth to you?"

I told Margarite that it was worth a hundred dollars. She considered this new piece of information thoughtfully. "All I got to do is go down to the bank with you and sign a card with the name Nell O'Hanstrom? That right?"

"That was correct." I also instructed her that if anyone asked her, she was to say that her middle initial was "C."

"And there's no chance jamming up against the cops?"

"No chance."

Although at last she agreed reluctantly, once she had given her word, she entered into the scheme heartily. I handed her the piece of paper on which I had carefully copied the compiled signature of Nell O'Hanstrom, and she promised to practice it and return to see me the next day.

After she had gone, I went through the items which I had collected from Rosemary's past. The significance of the newspaper clipping, concerning the early collegiate rowing races, eluded me. The date 1895 was important evidently, and the numerals could be a reminder of many things—a street address, a telephone number without the exchange, or it could be the number to the deposit box. As I considered the different sides to the problem, I reached the conclusion that it was a round-about, too elaborate a concealment for anything as simple as an address or telephone number, but for a safe deposit box, it might be an excellent reminder. It would be necessary for Margarite to give the bank attendant the number of the safe box; she could use 1-8-9-5, and if it was wrong, she could then pretend that she had forgotten. The bluff might work.

The next day when Margarite returned I handed her a sheet of paper and instructed her to write. She wrote rapidly the signature of Nell O'Hanstrom. Picking it up, I compared it with the one I had pieced together. It wasn't too good, but it wasn't poor either.

"How'd I do?" Margarite asked.

I shook my head, and wrote, "You must do better."

"All right," she agreed sharply, petulant because I hadn't praised her. "I'll try. When do you want to go to the bank? Today?"

"Tomorrow."

"Okay, I'll practice some more." Before she left, I carefully explained to her how I wanted her to dress. "Sure," she told me, "I got a coat. It's sort of old, but it's plain and made out of cashmere." That was the one I wanted her to wear.

When we appeared at the bank, Margarite came as close to looking like a lady as she might ever do. Before leaving the hotel, I had insisted that she remove most of her make-up, leaving only her lipstick. She wore a plain casual coat and medium pumps; her hair was groomed, glistening beneath a small hat. We had rehearsed, step by step, the procedure to be followed at the bank. Margarite assured me that she understood her part perfectly, and I believed that she possessed the self-confidence to carry it through.

As we walked down the winding narrow stairs of the bank to the lower level, I slipped her the key to the safe deposit box. Outside the grilled door, I pressed the electric bell and we were buzzed inside. For this trip, I had purchased a pair of glasses, with plain lenses, and a new hat which I wore solidly on my head. I hoped that no one would recognize me from my previous visit with Bianca. No one did. The attendant who had met Bianca Hill was occupied with other clients of the bank, and to the one who checked with us Margarite said firmly, "I want to get into box 1-8-9-5."

The attendant gave her a card and a ball point pen. "Please sign here," he said.

Casually Margarite scrawled the signature of Nell O'Hanstrom, and handed the card, together with the key, to the attendant. Holding the card, he stepped to a file case and checked the signature. For a second he hesitated, and I could feel myself tense. Then he asked Margarite, "What is your middle initial?"

"C," she replied, "as in Charlotte."

"Thank you." He motioned us to follow him within the heavy round door, and stooping slightly inserted first his master key, then the key handed him by Margarite. He opened an oblong-shaped metal door and removed a steel box. "Come this way," he told us.

We followed him into a corridor which had a number of private rooms opening off it. Each room contained a desk, chair, light, and writing equipment. The attendant placed the box on the desk and, leaving the room, closed the door behind him. I could hear it lock.

"Here we are," said Margarite.

"Yes." I handed her a hundred dollars, and motioned for her to stand in the far corner of the room, facing the wall. When she had done this, I opened the box while shielding it with my body.

Inside was a stack of ten-thousand-dollar U. S. government bills ... ten of them, a hundred thousand dollars. In a large Manila envelope were a series of bankers' acceptances varying in amounts from fifty thousand to a hundred thousand dollars. They were made out to Howard Wainwright and were good for credit in any bank in the United States, or around the world. These acceptances were issued by several banks, for a total of nine hundred thousand dollars. As issued, they would not show up in the books of any bank as an account. Traditionally they are used by importers and exporters.

We left the room and Margarite returned the box and key to the attendant. He relocked the box, and gave back the key. Without another word, we left the bank. "Well, honey," she asked me, "did you get what you wanted?"

I didn't know. I now had a million dollars which had belonged to Wainwright, and which might not do me any good. A ten-thousand-dollar bill is not considered currency, and it is not easy to cash. To cash such a bill, the person must be known and identified at a bank. Bills of such size are used primarily for the transfer of funds by large corporations, exchange of credit in the stock market, and other commercial purposes.

"It must have been awful important," Margarite continued. "You seemed to be taking a lot of papers." I didn't attempt to reply, but kept on walking a little faster, and she hurried to keep step with me. Panting from the exertion, she said, "If it was really so important, a hundred dollars isn't much money. Maybe you could give me a little more." Her voice carried a professional whine.

We were passing a subway entrance, and I stopped suddenly. Drawing her to one side, so we were partly concealed by the covered doorway, I reached in my pocket and withdrew a twenty-dollar bill. Holding the bill in my hand so she could see it, I slipped the knife into my other hand, the blade protected by the sleeve of my coat.

Margarite looked at the bill, then slowly she turned her eyes to see the hilt nestled in my palm. I stood that way until she raised her gaze and looked me in the face. Trembling she drew the coat closely around her. There was no need to say anything; the message was quite clear; she understood. Taking the twenty dollars, she ran down the steps of the subway and disappeared.

Back at the Arena Hotel, I regarded my face in the mirror. Since my last visit to see Minor at the hospital, I had decided to regrow my mustache. Only three days had elapsed; not enough time to do more than shadow my lip. Carefully I shaved around the line of growing hair, then darkened it with a wax pencil. The mustache seemed to leap, nearly full grown, into being. I observed it carefully, attempting to determine the amount of change it produced in my appearance. A mustache will not disguise a person if his features are well known; it will, however, change the impression of his face.

The phone rang, which surprised me, as no one except Margarite knew where I was staying. I picked up the receiver and said, "Yes?"

"Hello, Pacific?" It was Santini's voice. "I'm down in the lobby, and I'm here to see you. I'll be up, don't try to run!"

I had no intention of running and hung up the phone. Within a few minutes, I heard the elevator door slam, and his footsteps approached my door. I opened it. "Well," said Santini, "it's real nice seeing you again, Pacific." His voice, however, was not friendly, and the meaning behind his words was twisted. He came into the room and sat on the bed without removing his hat or coat. It seemed that he was perched there, like a bird of prey, and he moved his head slowly from side to side as he looked around. "Nice place you got here," he said. "Mind if I look around?"

"Yes."

He appeared surprised. "You mean you mind if I look around?"

"Yes." On my pad I wrote rapidly, "Do you have a warrant?"

Santini read it, and he drew his lips into a circle of surprise. "I need a warrant to look around a little? A warrant between two old friends?" He watched me very closely.

I wrote, "That's exactly what I mean!"

Santini rose deliberately to his feet; I stood facing him. We were less than two feet apart, staring at each other. Santini's hands were by his side: I had no fear of the man; before he could reach his gun, my knife would be in him. After a pause, he shrugged and reseated himself on the bed. "All right," he said, steadily, his voice without emotion, "I can always come back if I got to. I didn't come here to take you in—which I could. I just came for a nice quiet talk."

I nodded, but I remained standing within arm's reach of him.

"You get around, Pacific," Santini continued conversationally. "I keep getting ideas that you're not a nice guy. For instance, things happen to people who you know. Not good things either. You know what I mean?"

"No."

"Take a little, inoffensive, worked-out guy who shares a hospital room with you. Somebody knocks off the side of his head. You didn't do it, did you, Pacific?"

I didn't do it, shaking my head firmly.

"Of course I wouldn't suspect that you did. Although I kind of feel you would've done it, if you'd wanted to. Cops get crazy ideas about people." He took a drag after lighting his cigarette, and watched me. "Why don't you sit down?" he asked.

I remained standing, waiting for him to continue. There was more to come. Santini was working his way through the preliminaries until he reached his subject of importance.

"Cops are lucky guys, let's say. They all work together which helps them plenty. A dirty rat of a ... a mug, a wise guy, doesn't have anybody else to work with except other rats. Sometimes it takes the cops awhile to put everything together, but usually they get it done." He awaited a reply from me. There was none. Santini drew a deep sigh. Although his eyes pretended pain, they watched me coldly. "Now, let's take that beautiful dame who lived down at the Hill woman's when you were working there. Did you know she was strangled, and after she was dead, somebody hung her up in a shower stall by her neck?"

"Pa-pers," I told him.

He nodded. "Yeah," he agreed, "there was a little something about it in the papers." Pushing his hat to the back of his head, he scratched his scalp. "I guess somebody didn't like that Martin dame much. Did you like her, Pacific?"

"Yes."

"There were no fingerprints in her room, so we don't know who went up there to twist her neck. But a funny thing happened. You know what? We discovered this Martin woman had a boy friend, a real john, a rich guy named Wainwright. She lived with him for a long time. Look, let's even be fair about it—maybe they were married. We don't know, and maybe nobody knows. But this Wainwright is missing, has been gone for months. We go up to take a look around Wainwright's apartment, and do you know what we find?"

I shook my head.

"This time we find plenty of fingerprints. We find fingerprints of the Martin woman, the laundryman, the grocery boy, a cleaning woman ... practically everybody in the neighborhood, and besides that we find fingerprints of a guy named Victor Pacific." Santini leaned forward and searched my face. "Maybe you were a friend of Wainwright's too, huh?"

On my pad I wrote, "I don't know that I ever met Wainwright."

Santini nodded. "Good for you. Keep it up. Doc Minor is fooled by your act, I'm not." He arose from the bed and walked to the door. "Don't bother to try to take a powder on me, Pacific. I can always find you again." He stepped out into the hall and was gone.

I waited a long time in my room. Then finally I called the desk. "Bellboy," I requested. When the bellboy arrived, I wrote on my pad that I wanted him to go to the drugstore and buy me a plastic bag and a roll of waterproof tape. When he returned, I took the materials and locked my door.

In the bag I placed all the bills, except one, which I had taken from the safe deposit box, as well as the key, gun, and papers from Rosemary Martin and Amar. The plastic bag was waterproof, and I sealed it carefully with tape. Outside my window was a pair of rusty hooks set about two feet in the building wall on each side of the window ledge. These hooks, during some forgotten day at the Arena Hotel, had been used for the safety belts of window cleaners. I hung the bag, tying it securely, on one of the hooks, then closed the window. No one would see it hanging high and colorless against the wall, in the back of the building where my room was located. Santini could return to search my room while I was away, but would not find the bag outside it.

Santini in his conversation with me had etched away one layer from the flashed-glass coloration of my past life. I did not believe that, as yet, he realized the importance of what he had discovered. But I realized it.

28

When Burrows returned to his desk, Jensen looked up expectantly. Burrows sat down, his face thoughtful. "Well?" asked Jensen.

"We've got Pacific on the master file, but there's no personal file, and nothing in the records."

"I'll be damned!"

"Let's go in and report it to Scott." They walked across the detectives' room to Scott's private office, which was partitioned from the main area by a metal section with glass windows. Scott was busy on the phone and waved the two men to chairs. After hanging up, he turned to them. "Lieutenant," said Burrows, "on this homicide I reported to you earlier, we have an identification of the body. It's for a Victor Pacific, resident of New York City, address unknown."

"He wasn't a bum, not with a thousand dollars on him," said Scott, "but why the address unknown? Did he have a record?"

"The address unknown is a result of a phony Pacific gave to the Army when he was drafted. Evidently he's been living either in a different city or here under an assumed name, but what Jensen and I wanted to report was about the record." Burrows turned to Jensen. "You tell Lieutenant Scott what you found out."

Jensen cleared his throat. "Well, Turner in the fingerprint office was late coming through because he wasn't on duty at the time. But when he heard the name Pacific, he thought it sounded familiar, and he found the name listed on the master, but the card was gone. That's why the ID had to come from Washington. Of course, there was another card in the duplicates when Turner checked, but no one would have caught it the first time."

Scott looked thoughtful. "It was taken out, but why?"

"Sir," Burrows said, "after Jensen told me, I got a hunch and looked in our own master file for the Eighth. We also have the name Pacific. But there's no personal file and no records on him. That's why we missed here, too."

Scott fretfully lit a cigarette. The details of hundreds of faces, thousands of names, scores of thousands of crimes had passed through his mind in twenty-five years. Pacific, he thought, Victor Pacific. I should know it, does it sound familiar? Or am I kidding myself and just think so? Where did I know it? Not as a killer ... he wasn't a murderer. A thief ... no, not a thief. But there's a tag I can't forget, or have I forgotten it? If his name was on the Eighth's master file, that means he was picked up in connection with this precinct. I've only been here a little over a month, it must have been before my time. What's the matter! Let's drop it and chew Burrows out about it. Let Burrows and Jensen, the bright boy from Homicide, worry about it.

Scott said to Burrows, "All right, stay with it. Find out what happened. If any stuff has been brought out of our files, I will personally throw the cop into the middle of Siberia myself!"

29

The building on Wall Street was tall and very narrow. The lobby, with a cigar counter just inside the door, stretched along one side of the building—a marbled alley—to the elevators, two of them. On the directory board I located Wainwright's office; it was on the eleventh floor. When an elevator arrived, I stepped into it and waited for what I expected to take place. The operator, an elderly washed-out little man, greeted me, "Mr. Wainwright! I see you're back."

"Yess." My throat was unusually stiff and I pronounced my few words with more difficulty than usual. In the enclosure of the elevator, my voice sounded extraordinarily guttural and harsh. "Yess," I repeated.

The old man seemed to take no notice of the quality of my speech. "You've been away quite a while. Have a good trip?"

"No. Sick," I told him.

On the eleventh floor, I found the office at the rear of the building. I had no key, but I did have my Lock-Aid and I did not hesitate to use it. After stepping inside, I had no recollection of ever having seen the office, but as Howard Wainwright I must have spent a lot of time here in the past. Looking around curiously, I saw there were only two rooms—a secretary-reception room and a large private office. The furniture was good with a feeling both of money and restraint ... a good combination for an investment counselor.

It did not take long for me to discover that all the important books and ledgers had been removed, as well as the business correspondence files, and I sat down behind my desk, attempting to recapture some feeling from the past, some memory. I wondered if Horstman had ever come to this office. Perhaps he had visited me many times and that was why I remembered his name. The idea became a conviction, although not a memory, and I wondered how I could get in touch with him.

On one side of the room stood a tall mahogany bookcase, and my eyes glanced over the titles ... commercial law, money and banking, business reference books, until I reached a matched four-volume set entitled *Rommel's War in the Desert* by General G. K. Henry. Leaving my chair, I walked to the bookshelf and removed the four books. Leafing through them, I found a completely detailed history of Rommel's entire series of campaigns, together with topographical maps compiled with great detail. General Henry, I read, was head of the U.S. Army War College and this was an official Army report of the campaigns.

There was nothing secret about the books as they were on public sale, but the presence of them in my office could only be accounted for by my interest in them. It was true that I had served in some of the campaigns myself; this might explain why I had the books.

After a few more minutes spent in looking around the office, I left it, closing but not locking the door behind me. When the elevator reached the street level, the same operator detained me as I prepared to step out. "Just a minute, Mr. Wainwright," he said. "I happened to think of something. There's been an awful lot of people around looking for you. Your secretary asked me to give you this whenever you came back." He reached a thin hand up to the mirror in the elevator and removed a plain white envelope which he handed to me.

"Thanks." I handed him a bill.

On the street, I tore open the envelope and withdrew a sheet of paper. On it had been written the message, "If you get this, please call me at once. J." After the initial was a telephone number.

I didn't know J., I had no recollection of her. The elevator operator had said she had been my secretary; I wanted to see her. Returning from the lower end of Manhattan back to Fourteenth Street, I made another trip to Bozell's office. He was in. Patiently I wrote out the information I wanted him to relay over the phone. Then he dialed the number.

"Hello," Bozell asked, "is this Mr. Wainwright's secretary?" There was a pause, and then he said, "No, no, I'm quite sure this is the correct number. Mr. Wainwright received your message from the elevator operator in the office building." My former secretary seemed worried about the call.

Motioning Bozell to hold the receiver so I could share it, I listened to her conversation. It was a soft pleasant voice, slightly accented, and I heard her say, "If Mr. Wainwright is there, let me speak to him."

"I'm Mr. Wainwright's attorney," Bozell replied, "and he can't speak to you. He's been in a bad accident, and it's nearly impossible for him to talk."

"How do I know this isn't a trick?" she asked.

"Trick?" Bozell seemed puzzled. "I'm an attorney," he repeated. "My name is Bozell, Frank M. Bozell, and I'm listed in the telephone book. Look me up, and call me back at the number listed. That way you'll know." J. evidently agreed to this, because Bozell replaced the receiver on its cradle.

Quickly I wrote on my pad concise directions and handed them to the attorney to read. The phone rang, and it was J. calling back. Bozell relayed my instructions to her. "Mr. Wainwright will meet you at any time and place you suggest. He'll wait for you on the street, and you can drive past in a taxi and see him for yourself. Then, if you are convinced, you can stop and talk to him."

The girl approved this suggestion, and agreed to my waiting on the corner of Fifty-seventh and Fifth Avenue at five o'clock that afternoon. I was to be standing by the curb in front of Tiffany's.

At that time of day, there is heavy traffic flowing along both Fifty-seventh Street and Fifth Avenue, and taxis travel in long lines. It would be difficult to stop or follow anyone in another cab, and J. realized it. I was thinking about this, as I waited according to our agreement, and about ten minutes past five, I felt a light hand touch my arm. Turning, I looked down into the face of a slender, swarthy-skinned girl, with great brown eyes and hair bleached to silver gilt. "Mr. Wainwright," she said softly, her words sibilant, "it is you after all." I nodded.

She glanced around anxiously and said, "You must be in trouble. You have been followed, no?"

I didn't know; Santini might have a man on me, but I didn't think that Amar had picked me up again. However, there was nothing to be gained by standing on the corner, so we walked down Fifty-seventh Street until we came to a large antique gallery. Entering it, we pretended to examine a cabinet filled with *objets d'art*.

With my pad, I explained to her that I had been in an accident and had suffered a complete loss of memory, that I didn't remember anything at all, not even her name. "Oh!" she exclaimed. She regarded me for a moment, then said, "My name is Juahara."

I urged her to tell me everything that she could ... not to bother about sequence ... just whatever came to her mind. This she did with little prompting. She had come to work one morning, and I had not appeared. After calling my apartment and receiving no answer, she began to be concerned. Because there was very little to be done around the office, she had not discovered until the afternoon that the check and bank books, ledgers, and other confidential business papers had been removed. At first she had intended to call the police, but then she had decided that I would not have wanted that.

"Why?" I asked.

She looked away from me. "Because of your business," she said finally. "The police and then the government too much might discover."

"What?"

"Truth, truth. Among my people is the proverb, 'With only one eye, you are king among the blind.'" She continued with her story. That night when she left the office and returned to her one-room apartment, two men had been awaiting her—Amar and a great black man named Ghazi. "They asked me many questions to which I could give no answer," she said and held out her right hand. I looked at her healed, scarred fingernails where they had been mashed and torn. "They threatened to kill me if I reported their visit," she added, "and I knew their promise they would keep. So I ran away and hide."

Why had she risked getting back in touch with me?

"Because," she explained simply, "I need money. I want to go away. Far away. My hair, its color I change; I hide; I wait for you. I hope if I find you again, you will give me money."

One of the clerks in the store had begun to hover around us, making it difficult to continue the conversation. Outside, the five o'clock traffic rush had subsided and it was now possible to find a taxi. We took one back to the Arena Hotel. There in my room, I continued to probe into the Arabian girl's story.

What was she doing in the United States?

"At the first, I came to study as a student. When I am finish, I do not wish to return to my own country. To live here, I like. I take a job for you."

What did she do for me? What was her job?

"Mostly I translate and write letters for you ... to Syria, and Lebanon, Iraq, Egypt, and Saudi Arabia."

What were the letters about?

"About provisions—oils, animals, wines," she explained. "Always quantities of such things to Mecca, to Al-Suweika market in Mecca," her voice trailed away.

What was wrong with that?

"Nothing wrong with that. Merchandise goes on dhows ... always on *bum* or *baghala* through Red Sea. Many times whole cargo lost because of British gunboats." She turned her eyes away. "Gunboats never sink dhows, but merchandise lost anyway."

That meant something was being smuggled. What? Drugs?

"No drugs," Juahara replied. "I swear by God I do not *really* know. It is not of my business."

I thought hard. Under the desert sands what was buried? What was buried that was so valuable, so precious that it would be worth smuggling? Not gold, because there was no gold there. Oil? Why smuggle it? However, I decided to ask Juahara, and she shook her head. "No oil," she told me, rising to her feet. "Now I go."

I wanted to detain her. What about the provisions—the oils, wines, and animals?

Juahara looked at me strangely. "In this country, there are many strange things: fruits which are made of glass, vegetables of wax, could not animals be made of metal?" She clutched her hands desperately, almost defiantly, and said, "Wainwright, *Khawaja*, many things I do not know, so I cannot tell!" She glanced down at her mutilated fingers, and continued, her voice pleading, "I have been afraid to work for a long time. I have so very little money. Perhaps your generosity will give me enough to go away?"

I told her I would give her the money, and then asked where I had done my usual banking. She named a bank near the office on Wall Street. I asked her to return to the hotel around noon the next day for her funds. I wasn't positive that I could cash one of the ten-thousand-dollar bills the same day, and I did not want to lower my nearly exhausted cash fund.

She agreed to return.

The bank presented no problem when I cashed the bill. It was the National Security & Trust, and as Howard Wainwright, I had maintained my company account there. It was still there with a modest balance. Cashing it in, I deposited eight thousand in the account, took one thousand dollars in a single bill, and the balance in twenties and fifties. While I was at the bank, I made inquiries concerning the possibility of a safe deposit box in the name of Pacific, Wainwright, and O'Hanstrom. There was no box under any of the three names.

Juahara returned promptly at noon, the following day, and I gave her five hundred dollars. It was not through generosity, as she was prepared to believe, but I was anxious to have her out of the way. She could be dangerous in the hands of Santini, if he found her; I had run the risk of having her seen in my hotel, because I did not believe that Santini or any other detective following me would recognize her on sight. Now it was desirable that she disappear forever.

After accepting the money, Juahara thanked me and prepared to leave. I attempted to let her know that I was sorry for the trouble her job had caused her, and I asked her again if there was anything more she could tell me.

Her eyes, dark and black, regarded me impassively beneath her pitifully streaked hair. Behind her eyes, I thought I detected a fleeting moment of sympathy and then it was gone. She shook her head. "It is strange," she spoke slowly, as if recalling thoughts she had long considered, "that around some men violence is carried like a cloak. It is the breath of their life, it is the music of their soul. They are indestructible, except to be destroyed by their own hands. After you had disappeared, I did not believe that you were dead, even after Amar and Ghazi, the Sudanese, to me swore that you were. The reason I did not betray you was not because you were my friend—for you were not my friend—but because, if I had betrayed you, I would have been killed. If, to those men, I had given information, so soon as my lips stopped their speaking, I would have died. As long as I denied them what they asked, there was a chance through God's grace that I might live."

What was the information they wanted?

"Where you kept your bank accounts, did you hold boxes of hidden safety?"

That was all?

"Not all. They asked of other things, of a woman named Rosemary Martin. And of keys, did you have keys hidden within the office. But always they would ask again of banks where you kept money."

Had a man named Colonel Horstman ever called on me at my office?

Juahara was becoming impatient; perhaps recalling her torture had made her uneasy, and she was anxious to escape. She pulled her coat around her, and walked to the door. She stood there a moment, her hand on the knob before opening it. Finally she said, "Him I never met. Sometimes a letter would come addressed to you as Mr. Wainwright. When I opened it, another sealed envelope was held within. On this envelope would be the name Hans Horstman. This I to you would give unopened, and you would put it away, and tell me you would deliver it to the man." She took a deep breath. "Perhaps, this man can help you."

Had she ever heard from Horstman? Had he ever called on the phone?

"I know not. If he called, he did not say that was his name."

She turned the knob on the door, pulling it gently. "Good-by, Wainwright, *Khawaja*," she said politely using the term of respect. "Perhaps someday your troubles will be over. However, I say to you, if you do not sleep at night, that often I have remembered, when I was a small girl, I hear what happens at the market of Al-Suweika in Mecca." She bowed her head very slightly, and then the door closed behind her.

It was very quiet in the room after Juahara had gone. The dirty tan walls seemed to be listening. There was a tenseness, an air of expectation, the waiting for another voice—the voice of Colonel Horstman. An illumination filled my mind, and in a moment it seemed I would hear his voice, remember it as he had spoken to me, and then the feeling dimmed and died away. The moment was gone. After a while, I left the room and went back to Wall Street, and once again to the office of Howard Wainwright.

This time I searched the office very carefully looking for a lead ... a clue ... a hint ... anything to lead me to Horstman. I had nearly completed my search, without success, when the door opened and Santini walked in. "If you'll tell me what you're looking for," he said, "I'll help you look for it."

At the bookcase, I removed the four volumes of *Rommel's War in the Desert* and carried them over to the desk, placing them on top of it. Santini picked one volume up, and leafed through it carelessly, then replaced it, “Reminds you of old times, huh, Pacific?”

I shrugged.

Santini sat down in a leather chair and lit a cigarette. “I promised to look you up again,” he said.

I wrote on my pad, “‘One must have a good memory to be able to keep the promises one makes.’” It was a quotation from Nietzsche.

After reading it, Santini said casually, “I wondered how long it would take you to remember conveniently you were Wainwright.”

It had been Santini, himself, who had tipped me off that I was Wainwright. The day he told me about Wainwright’s apartment being covered with my fingerprints. The night I had broken into the place, and been intercepted by Amar, I had been careful to wear gloves. I couldn’t have left prints, unless I had been there before. However, I did not feel it necessary to explain this to Santini, so I said nothing.

“I still can’t figure out your racket,” Santini continued. “So far I haven’t been able to dig up anything illegal about this joint. It wasn’t a bucket shop or anything like that.” He removed his cigarette and regarded the end of it, consideringly. “Of course I could always dig up a technicality under the state law about operating a business under an assumed name.” He replaced the cigarette in his mouth, and reaching inside his coat pocket withdrew a large heavy envelope. “I got all the dope on you here,” he said, running his thumb along the edge of the envelope. “You interest me, Pacific-Wainwright, and I’ve sort of been working along on you. My own time and expense. But I got an idea I’m not going to have to nail you with a technicality.”

I watched Santini carefully. Behind his mask of casualness there was a new threat, a new assurance which I had never sensed before. This time I did not believe that he was probing for information. He seemed to be waiting now for something, but what it was I didn’t know. He stared back at me, his eyes flat and cold, no longer hot and angry as I remembered from the first time I saw them at the hospital.

“Luck, Pacific,” Santini continued, “is only for crapshooters. In a man’s life, he doesn’t have luck—he has other things. He has the mistakes other people make, sometimes he can take advantage of a whole series of errors by people he’s never seen. Maybe it’s the time and the place and the human element of inefficiency which is on his side. These things work for a while, and he thinks he’s lucky but not forever.” He stood and carefully snubbed out his cigarette in a heavy bronze ashtray on my desk. Indifferently he touched the four stacked books. “Pleasant reading,” he said quietly. He walked out without looking back.

Carrying the books under my arm, I left the office a few minutes later and took a cab up Broadway to see Bozell. He was in and I asked him if he knew anyone who had contacts in Africa, Saudi Arabia in particular. Bozell knew another attorney who had handled a legal case for Maxwell Claussen, a former foreign correspondent for the New York *Daily Register.* Could Bozell, through his friend the attorney, call Claussen and arrange for me to meet him. Bozell told me that he would try. I gave him my address at the Arena Hotel, and paid him another small fee.

"I'll call you as soon as I can arrange something," Bozell told me.

30

"Well," said Jensen, hanging up the phone, "I just got some news about that grand bill. It was one of a series from the Federal Reserve Bank of New York."

"Where was it delivered?"

"A hundred thousand dollars in thousand-dollar bills to the National Security & Trust Company right here in the city."

"When?"

"Months ago."

"Evidently they don't do much business in thousand-dollar bills," said Burrows.

"Who does? The National Security & Trust reports that they issued the bill, but as they are past the serial number now, they don't know who picked it up."

"Was it Pacific?"

"They have no account for Pacific, and they can't identify him."

"Was it passed as one of a series?"

"The bank can't tell, but there's a good possibility that it was. Grand bills don't just float around. Usually they're part of three or five or ten thousand dollars for big cash transactions."

Burrows looked thoughtful. His eyes, red rimmed from lack of sleep, stared past Jensen, out the window on Mercer Street. He turned Jensen's information over in his mind, and said slowly, "There's another possibility, a good one that it was just a single bill. Suppose Pacific wants to beat it out of town, and he's got a little money, a grand or so. He doesn't want to carry all of it around in a roll, so he converts it into a single thousand-dollar bill."

"That's all right, except for one thing."

"What?"

"Why doesn't he tuck it away in his pocket or a billfold, any place but the sole of his shoe. A guy walking around on a bill like that would destroy it in a day or two."

Burrows agreed. "Yes, that's right." After a pause, he continued, "You might figure then, that he didn't intend to carry it around in his shoe very long... just temporary, for a few hours. So, what was the reason for hiding it in his shoe, then?"

"Because," replied Jensen, "he was planning to meet somebody. He had a date set up to meet somebody he was afraid of; somebody who might frisk him. Pacific wanted that bill for emergency reasons, but he didn't want it found on him and maybe taken away."

"That adds up," Burrows said.

"It adds up. But we still don't know if Pacific got that bill himself from the National Security & Trust, or whether he got it from someone else."

"It doesn't make too much difference one way or another. He had it."

31

That afternoon and evening I remained in my room at the Arena reading the books by General Henry. In the long technical descriptions of Rommel's successes in desert warfare, I could find no hint to help me. But as his tide of success slowed, eventually stalled, and the Afrika Korps began its retreat, I began to follow the report with more and more interest. I studied the detailed maps carefully, marking with an increasing excitement the routes of defeat and disaster.

Late that night, I had another smoke, stretched out on my bed and went to sleep. Sometime, early in the morning, the old familiar nightmare began again. It returned with the room, the spot of light, the faces forming in the darkness. And the waiting ... the long wait. But now it seemed that the faces were beginning to approach the light and I could nearly identify them while I was waiting to hear a voice. The voice, I knew, would sweep away the veil of terror, would make the truth clear. The scene hung suspended in time, revolving slowly in space ... a mobile turning, twisting.

When I awakened, I could not return to my sleep. I left my bed and drew a chair close to the window and looked out into the night where there was no dawn, and the buildings stood row on row like sentinels around a world into which I could not enter, and from which I could not escape.

With the first light which weakly infiltrated the cracks and crevices of the streets, I threw myself on my bed and fell once more into a restless sleep. I was awakened later in the morning by my phone. It was Bozell calling to tell me that he had talked to Maxwell Claussen and arranged for me to meet the correspondent at the International Press Club. "I explained to him about your difficulty talking, so he understands. He'll meet you at the door going into the bar at noon."

The International Press Club is located in a reconverted townhouse on East Thirty-sixth Street, and I met Claussen, a wiry man with thick gray hair, at twelve o'clock. Bozell had evidently described my appearance as Claussen came up to me and introduced himself when I appeared. We moved into the bar, and sat down at a small table. After ordering drinks, he said to me, "I understand you're interested in Saudi Arabia."

I told him yes, I was, and I wrote out a question on my pad.

After reading it, Claussen said, "In Saudi Arabia about 15 per cent of the population are slaves. Slaves in the true sense of the word, owned body and soul by their masters. About ten thousand slaves a month are run through the Red Sea past the British gunboats. The runners drop the slaves in Arabia near the Asudi Desert. The main route to Mecca, which is the chief slave market, is through Yemen."

In reply to my next question, he explained, "The British can't stop the running because before their ships can overhaul the slave boats, the slaves are tossed overboard in irons and drowned."

"Why?" I asked.

"Why?" Claussen appeared unable to determine my exact meaning. "Why, what?"

I tried very hard. "Why slaves now?"

"Oh!" he replied, "I think I understand what you mean. Well, Saudi Arabia in particular, and a few of the other minor Arab states, have made millions through their oil money. The countries are all underdeveloped and they need slaves to build the new construction, as well as to work on the coffee and sugar plantations. They need slaves of both sexes. The biggest market is in Mecca and is called AlSuweika. The largest slave market for women is in Jidda."

My next question was more involved, so I wrote it.

Claussen said, "Certainly all this is well known. It's on an international scale too. A report on this situation was made to the United Nations, but it was shelved, too hot to handle because of the international oil situation. So, no official action was ever taken."

"Thanks," I told him. We finished our drinks, and I left. I decided to move into Wainwright's apartment. The room at the Arena was inconvenient and depressing. I had sufficient funds, and there was no reason, except for Amar, to remain out of sight. Santini had found me, and I knew that Amar would find me, eventually, too.

All of Wainwright's clothes were in his apartment, or most of them were there ... sufficient, certainly, for my needs. I removed the plastic bag with the money and certificates from outside the window, and packed it, together with my clothes, in the suitcase. Checking out of the hotel, I took a cab to Third Avenue where I stopped at the Midtown Moving and Storage Company. I arranged to put the suitcase in storage, using the name of P. Victor, and paid the rental for a year in advance. I could get to the suitcase any day that I desired, and it was easier to conceal the storage check than the money and the bankers' acceptances. My cab had waited for me, and from the storage company I continued directly to Wainwright's place.

For two days I lived quietly, not leaving the apartment except for meals. My time I spent waiting, waiting for Amar. There was no reason to try to run away. Although I had a fortune in Wainwright's bankers' acceptances, I could not cash them in another city, or country, without good identification. They were made out to Wainwright, and only here in New York could I prove that identity.

I believed, however, that Horstman might help me. But I had no way to contact him except through Amar. If I had judged Horstman wrong, I might have to eliminate both him and Amar later, but at least I would have a better idea of my situation after talking to him.

My plight was desperate, but not entirely hopeless, from what I could determine. I believed that I now understood part of the past story. Undoubtedly I had been acting as banker and investor for the Eastern syndicate represented by the Tajir Transportation Company. The profits from this company, or at least part of them, were smuggled into the United States for reinvestment as a protection against political changes in the East. Tajir, according to the hint from Juahara, dealt in the slave traffic. But on what was based the company's original capital?

I thought I knew. Under the sands of the desert, Rommel in his retreat had cached guns, ammunition, half trucks, and remnants of his arsenal. This was the basis for the slave trading. Moslem peoples all over North Africa needed arms for their insurrections, and were willing to trade slaves for guns. The guns cost the traders nothing, and the slaves could be sold for a profit. Someone, at one time closely connected with Rommel, knew where the arms caches were. That man had organized a vast and lucrative business built on that knowledge. He had many lieutenants in strategic spots around the world; I had been one of them; Horstman, undoubtedly, had been another.

Part of their funds had been channeled through me, and I had been robbing them. I felt no guilt about it. Gun running and slavery are not respectable occupations; my employers were murderers, slavers, and thieves. I, too, was a thief robbing other thieves. I was sorry only that I had not been more clever.

I had needed the help of Rosemary Martin to set up false accounts; she had agreed and had accepted a percentage for her share. My death, rather my attempted death, had been meant to frighten her, or goad her, into trying to secure the money for herself so it could be recovered from her later.

Rosemary Martin had been unable to convert the bankers' acceptances into cash, and she had frozen into inaction. Amar and the syndicate had waited, but the wait was too long. By that time I had recovered and Rosemary Martin had returned the key to me.

This theory of past events I worked out slowly, in the solitude of the apartment, over a period of several days. It seemed to me that the syndicate and I had reached a stalemate. I had the money, but I could be killed before I had a chance to use it. If I were killed, it could not be recovered. As long as most of it might be recovered there was no reason why the syndicate and I couldn't reach a compromise.

Amar appeared the third evening. I had been waiting and when his knock sounded on my door, I expected him. He stood quietly, his hand in his pocket holding a revolver, and he asked politely if he could come in.

I stood to one side and he edged past me, watchful and alert. In the living room he crossed to the far side, and seated himself in a chair. "You were expecting me, of course," he said, no question in his voice.

"Yes."

"Otherwise you would not have returned to live here." He regarded me uneasily. "You are sure of yourself."

I shrugged and lit a cigarette, waiting for Amar to deliver his message from someone higher up. Finally he relaxed in his chair, although one hand remained in his pocket. He said, "You have caused much concern. *El Saiyid* made a trip especially to see you in person." His eyes watched me, flat spots of danger. Then he added, "An honor not often conferred."

I thought, *El Saiyid* ... in Arabic the principal tribal shaykh. I was not sure if Amar meant the title literally or whether, perhaps, in slang he meant the "boss." I said nothing, waiting for Amar to continue.

"He has arranged a meeting for tomorrow night. Eleven o'clock at the office."

"Where?"

Amar regarded me impatiently."Tajir," he replied.

"No! Here."

He shook his head. "Orders are explicit. Eleven o'clock at the location of Tajir."

I had no intention of meeting *El Saiyid*, Amar, and the syndicate in their office or in the dock area. I was anxious to have the meeting too, but it must be held in my apartment. "No!" I told Amar flatly. "Here!"

Amar smiled. It was not a pleasant smile, although it held much of satisfaction in it. "It was anticipated," he said, "that you might not approve of the place of meeting. So we have arranged an inducement that you will not decline. Miss Bianca Hill will be waiting for you. By then she will be greatly comforted to have you appear. No?"

"Bi-anca?"

"Yes. She will be held until tomorrow night. If you appear as requested she will not be harmed." He arose from the chair and moved toward the door. "In case you doubt El Saiyid's generosity, Miss Hill will be in front of the office. When you appear, she will be released." He slipped through the door and was gone.

Immediately I went to the phone and dialed Bianca's number. The phone rang for a long time. No one answered.

It was certain that Amar was telling the truth about holding her. But to invite disaster because of her was to be a fool. I told myself that it was too bad, but there existed a possibility that after questioning her she would be released, because she did not have information of any kind dangerous to the syndicate. I decided that I would not permit myself to be forced to meet their terms; my concern was to bring *El Saiyid* to my apartment and, on my own ground, I would be safe. Here I could negotiate.

After I went to bed, I did not go to sleep immediately. I turned my plans over in my mind, examining them carefully. But thoughts of Bianca Hill interposed, disturbing me. These memories were unnecessary and, I felt, were sentimental. They could hold no importance in deciding my own actions. There were only two points to consider: my own safety, which I believed I could resolve; and retaining as much of the money as I could through bargaining. The rest was inconsequential.

There were pleasant memories of her which I tried to forget, but they would not go away. She was in a danger in which she had no choosing, for which she was paying because of the loyalty of her own nature. I pushed the covers from the bed and stretched on the sheets, knotting the pillow hard beneath my head. Sleep was a long time arriving.

32

Santini held the photograph in his hand and said to Burrows, "I got some stuff on this guy if you want it." Santini, who was on the four P.M. to midnight shift, had arrived for work and had seen the picture on the bulletin board.

"Sure I want it," Burrows replied. "When the picture was put up we were waiting for an ID. We have it now; it's for Victor Pacific."

Santini shook his head. "This guy isn't Victor Pacific!"

"Huh?"

"Who is he then?" asked Jensen. "The ID said Victor Pacific."

"I can tell you positively that this stiff isn't Victor Pacific."

Burrows took the photograph from Santini's hand and studied it carefully. Jensen hunched his straight chair closer to the desk, lit a cigarette, and placed his elbows in a comfortable position. Finally Burrows said to Santini, "Suppose you give us what you do know about it."

"I don't know who Victor Pacific really is, but he was one guy. This guy is somebody else." He pointed to the photograph. "I got an idea who he is and what he was. That part won't take very long to give you. He was a no-good, slippery operator. As far as I can find out, he never did a decent thing for anybody in his whole damned life. He had the heart ... the morals of a crocodile."

Jensen said, "He sounds like a nice guy."

Burrows regarded Santini thoughtfully. "It's a funny thing. I had a hunch about this right from the beginning." He turned to Jensen and asked for affirmation, "Didn't I?"

"Yeah," Jensen agreed sourly.

"I had a feeling that something was screwy. Tell me though, there didn't happen to be *two* Victor Pacifies, did there?" Burrows asked Santini. "Even with a name like that, there might possibly be two of the same out of a couple of billion chances."

"No," said Santini, "it's not like that at all. There was only one guy named Pacific who entered into the case at any time. Once, though, I considered the possibility there might've been two guys too."

Jensen deliberately removed his elbows from the desk, reached over, and picked up the photograph of the corpse. He made one last attempt to put the situation back into perspective, then gave it up. He said to Santini, "Well, maybe you better give us everything you got. I still can't believe this stiff isn't Victor Pacific."

"Okay," agreed Santini. "Here's how it is."

33

I arrived near Markham Street about a quarter to eleven and walked the last block toward it, approaching slowly. Within my shoe, I could feel the concealed bill I had tucked there in case of an emergency working against my foot. The office of the Tajir Transportation Company was located in a squat, dirty, red-brick building. It was three stories high, backed against the east side of the street facing the docks across from it. Overhead, the humming tires of the cars racing on the West Side Highway sounded like swarms of angry bees in the night. By the docks, the streets are paved with stone blocks, and occasional trucks rumbled heavily in the semidarkness of the poorly lighted streets.

For a number of minutes, I stood concealed by one of the pillars of the overhead highway, blending into its shadow, while I watched the car parked before the Tajir building. In the distance, a clock struck eleven and I stepped away from the safety of the structural pillar and walked cautiously toward the auto. As I drew near, Amar left the doorway of the building and stood beside the car. He watched me approach, his face hidden in the shadow beneath his hat. "You are prompt," he said.

"Bi-anca?" I asked.

He didn't reply. His hand moved to the door of the automobile and when he opened it, two men stepped out. Reaching behind them, they guided the blindfolded woman. "Bianca?" I repeated.

"Vic!" she said. "Oh, Vic!" I touched her shoulder. "May I take off this blindfold now?" she asked.

"No!" I told her, taking her arm and moving slowly down the street. If she removed her blindfold, if she could identify the building, or the men, her life would be in danger. Amar and his two men fell in silently behind me.

"Vic," Bianca asked, holding my hand as she stumbled in the darkness, "are you all right?"

"Yes," I told her.

"What is happening? Are you in trouble?"

"No."

Her breath caught in a sigh, half tears, half laughter. "I'm glad ... so relieved! I've never been so frightened in my life. I was worried about you."

"Bi-anca," I whispered in reassurance as we turned the corner. The cab was still waiting where I had left it. Opening the door, I helped Bianca Hill into the taxi, and removed her blindfold. The three men stood apart, faint silhouettes in the night. "Home," I told her.

Bianca nodded. In the textured darkness of the cab, I could see her eyes wide with fear. "I'll go home," she said. "Will you come over later?"

"Yes," I told her. She leaned forward and kissed me. Then I closed the door of the cab, and it drove away.

Amar stirred. He stepped quietly to my side, the two men behind him. We turned, retracing our steps to the Tajir building. The rhythm of our strides met, fused, and became one sound along the deserted street. Indefinite, hazy points of light ... aureate yellow spots on the tiger of the night ... gathered in shallow pools on the sidewalk, and hung suspended in the air. After moments of silence, Amar said softly, "I do not understand it. There are many things in this life, which it is not given to understand. That woman is worth five million dollars to you?"

We walked on, his words only half heard in my ears. I was filled with a composure, a resignation, and an acceptance of peace which I had never known before. In the world out of which I came, there must have been few things which money could not buy—including women and security and power. And all these things, which were desirable in themselves, I had exchanged for the safety of a woman I didn't love. I realized that Bianca Hill represented a world to which I was a stranger. She had touched me deeply with her giving, and had offered me an opportunity to rejoin men in a life that had never previously existed. I had accepted the gifts she offered, taken them, used them without pleasure because I had not known their worth. Her love and compassion had enabled me, for the first time, to see into another world as she saw and believed. It was a world of men and women, and not phantoms; a world of deep sleep and pleasant dreams, not nightmares; where words have meaning, and a man need not live alone in the desolate spaces of his own spirit.

Beside me, Amar spoke again. I did not look at him although I could sense that he shook his head in wonderment. "Five million dollars!" he said. And it was then that the full implication of his meaning burst over me washing me in fear. I had a million dollars in Wainwright's name. Somewhere, then, I had four million dollars more ... Tajir's money converted first to Wainwright, and then reconverted to Pacific. I had concealed it carefully ... too carefully! ... behind names and words and places.

We turned into the building. Inside it was dark, and the dampness of the waterfront wrapped a shroud of cold sweat around the metal stairway as we climbed to the second floor. The hair on my head began to crawl, and a dryness clung to my tongue, my mouth, my lips, my throat, making it impossible to swallow. Because now it is too late. I can't make a deal on Wainwright's money alone. This is big, too big. It's important enough for the top man to come all the way from Africa. Five million dollars lost. I have one million, but where are the other four?

There is one chance, and one chance only ... Horstman! If Horstman is at the meeting there's hope. We have much between us. I know it. I've always known it. Horstman is a friend of mine! A man I can trust! If he's there, Horstman may be able to make the council see that I *don't* remember where the money is concealed. If I'm executed I can never remember it! I'll return all of Wainwright's holdings without argument.

But Horstman, be there, be there!

Here's the door. It's strange that in a moment like this my eyes should take the trouble to see so clearly—the grain of the wood, the dust on the lettering. What does it matter except it is a moment or two of life? Now Amar is opening it politely, too politely, and when I step through it, I'll be leaving the land of the living.

This is no dream, it is the moment of the nightmare from which I will never again awaken. There in the shadows of the room is the desk. And above it, the bulb. It hangs from a cord and throws its helpless light against the darkness. The darkness is gathering together, to materialize, to rustle black within black, to expectorate the forms of the council.

There he is, big, black as Satan, with his white porcelain eyes. Ghazi. In his hand, the short scimitar. It flashes, but this is not yet the instant.

First, the pronouncement. Step forward, *El Saiyid*. I had forgotten you were tall, and growing old. Your face is lined by the gullies of the bitter years, and all your power cannot wipe away time's dust from your cheeks. Where now are the tens of thousands of lives you have stolen and wrecked and killed? You have sold man's spirit by the pound, and twisted human dignity into furry shapes.

You bow, *El Saiyid*. Your mocking bow is not lost, and at last you speak. You speak in German, and I remember now, it is our native tongue. We were brothers in blood, you and I, and I will return my blood for yours. It will run from our lips for a long time.

El Saiyid!

Down my sleeve it slides, into my hand it leaps, through the air it sings. This is the longest second of my life.

34

Santini said, "The first time I saw him he was in a hospital with his throat cut, that was about a year ago. He got well. Now he's in the morgue with his throat cut again, but this time it's for keeps."

"You've got all the facts now?" asked Burrows.

"Yes. What took me so long was getting the Army to relay the information from Berlin. He got it before I could grab him. He got it worse that way; all I could've done was get him deported probably. He outsmarted himself, that's all."

"You've been on this a long time," said Burrows, "What didn't you like about it?"

"Well, you see I kept asking myself why would this so-called Victor Pacific disappear completely after he got back from the war. He could've drawn a small pension for his disability if he'd wanted to; he had insurance, bonuses, and all that over the years which he never took advantage of."

"He didn't need it," observed Jensen.

"That's right, but a guy can't live fifteen years without leaving a trace anywhere either. So Pacific had to have one of two motives."

"Either he'd been in trouble, or he wasn't Pacific," said Burrows.

"That's the way I figured it," replied Santini. "There was no record of Pacific anywhere, so I decided that something had happened. The fingerprints, from his Army record, threw me off. But when I thought about it, I decided that if Pacific had been wounded, he might've been killed, too. So maybe this guy shows up with Pacific's dog tag, identification, and papers; he's put in a hospital, and then he's shipped back to the United States."

"Sure," said Jensen, "but he'd be fingerprinted again in the hospital and the prints sent to Washington."

"In those days," said Santini, "with three million sets of prints going through the Army, when this guy's identification prints are taken in the field and forwarded to Washington for his record, they're swamped with the others. The prints are put on his record okay, but they aren't checked back against his induction prints." Santini walked to his desk and removed a heavy folder from it. "I took this stuff out of the files to work on it whenever I had a chance. It took me a while to wise up to what had happened."

"What'd the Army say?" asked Burrows.

"They checked the prints at my request and admitted right away that they'd goofed up. Mathematically speaking, they had to make a mistake once in a while, the human element was too strong. They just used the new set of ID prints instead of the original because they thought they were both the same," said Santini. "Then when the two sets weren't the same, the Army checked the German files and found them."

"Who was this guy?" asked Burrows.

"He had three names. Pacific and Wainwright were two of them. He was once a lieutenant colonel in Rommel's outfit," said Santini. "His real name was Hans Horstman."

The End

Bill S. Ballinger Bibliography (1912-1980)

Barr Breed series:

The Body in the Bed (Harper, 1948)
The Body Beautiful (Harper, 1949)

Joaquin Hawks series:

The Spy in the Jungle (New American Library, 1965)
The Chinese Mask (New American Library, 1965)
The Spy in Bangok (New American Library, 1965)
The Spy at Angor Wat (New American Library, 1966)
The Spy in the Java Sea (New American Library, 1966)

Non series novels:

Portrait in Smoke (Harper, 1950)
The Darkening Door (Harper, 1952)
Rafferty (Harper, 1953)
The Tooth and the Nail (Harper, 1955)
The Black Black Hearse (St. Martin's Press, 1955; as by Frederic Freyer)
The Longest Second (Harper, 1957)
The Wife of the Red-Haired Man (Harper, 1957)
Beacon in the Night (Harper, 1958)
Formula For Murder (New American Library, 1958)
The Doom Maker (Dutton, 1959; as by B.X. Sanborn)
The Fourth Forever (Harper, 1963)
Not I Said the Vixen (Fawcett, 1965)
The Heir Hunters (Harper, 1966)
The Source of Fear (New American Library, 1968)
The 49 Days of Death (Pyramid, 1969)
Heist Me Higher (New American Library, 1969)
The Lopsided Man (Pyramid, 1969)
The Corsican (Dodd Mead, 1974)
The Law (Warner, 1975; novelization)
The Ultimate Warrior (Warner, 1975; novelization)

Non fiction:

The Lost City of Stone (1978)
The California Story (1979)

Made in the USA
Lexington, KY
15 September 2018